Acclaim

Jessica Sorensen

"Sorensen's portrayal of...relati [...] love, as well as the longing to escape one's past, raises her above her new adult peers."

—*RT Book Reviews* on *The Secret of Ella and Micha*

"Romantic, suspenseful and well written—this is a story you won't want to put down."

—*RT Book Reviews* on *The Coincidence of Callie & Kayden*

THE SECRET OF ELLA AND MICHA

"A fantastic story...very addictive...This book will hook you in and you will feel hot, steamy, and on the edge of your seat.

—Dark-Readers.com

"A beautiful love story...complicated yet gorgeous characters...I am excited to read more of her books."

—SerendipityReviews.co.uk

"Fantastic...a great read...I couldn't put this book down...I was sad when it came to an end." —TheBookScoop.com

"A really great love story. There is something epic about it...If you haven't jumped on this New Adult bandwagon, then you need to get with the program. I can see every bit of why this story has swept the nation." —TheSweetBookShelf.com

"Absolutely loved it...This story broke my heart...I can't wait to get my hands on the next installment."

—Maryinhb.blogspot.com

"Wonderful...delightful...a powerful story of love...will make your heart swoon." —BookswithBite.net

The Temptation of Lila and Ethan

The Temptation of Lila and Ethan

JESSICA SORENSEN

FOREVER

NEW YORK   BOSTON

Forever
Hachette Book Group
237 Park Avenue
New York, NY 10017

www.HachetteBookGroup.com

Printed in the United States of America

RRD-C

First Edition: May 2014

10 9 8 7 6 5 4 3 2 1

Forever is an imprint of Grand Central Publishing.

The Forever name and logo are trademarks of Hachette Book Group, Inc.

The Hachette Speakers Bureau provides a wide range of authors for speaking events. To find out more, go to www.hachettespeakersbureau.com or call (866) 376-6591.

The publisher is not responsible for websites (or their content) that are not owned by the publisher.

Library of Congress Cataloging-in-Publication Data

Sorensen, Jessica.
    The temptation of Lila and Ethan / Jessica Sorensen. — First edition.
      pages cm
    ISBN 978-1-4555-7489-6 (pbk.) — ISBN 978-1-4555-7490-2 (ebook) —
ISBN 978-1-4789-2552-1   1. Young adults—Fiction.   2. Interpersonal
relations—Fiction.   I. Title.
    PS3619.O743T46 2014
    813'.6—dc23
                                                                    2013035425

Acknowledgments

A huge thanks to my agent, Erica Silverman, and my editor, Amy Pierpont. I'm forever grateful for all your help and input.

To my family, thank you for supporting me and my dream. You guys are wonderful.

And to everyone who reads this book, an endless amount of thank-yous.

The Temptation of Lila and Ethan

Prologue

Lila

Beauty. Vanity. Perfection. Three words my mother adores. They mean more to her than her husband, her daughters, and life. Without these attributes, she thinks she'd be better off dead. Without me having these attributes, she would disown me. Be flawless. Shine bright. Never, ever do anything less than excel. These are her rules and the vanity that makes up my life. And my father isn't any better. In fact, I think he might be worse, because even with beauty, perfection, and flawlessness, I'm still never good enough.

The constant need to be perfect continuously overwhelms me and makes me feel like I'm going to be crushed from the pressure. Sometimes I swear my house can shrink and expand, that the walls can close in and then retreat. When I'm alone in my house, the space feels overly immense with too many rooms, too many walls. But when I'm in it with my parents it seems like I can't get enough space, almost as if I can't breathe, even if we're on opposite sides of the house.

Maybe it's because I'm always doing something wrong and they're always reminding me of my unforgiveable mistakes. Either I'm not doing enough to appease them or I'm not doing things well enough. There are always rules to follow. Sit up straight. Don't slouch. Don't talk unless you're spoken to. Don't screw up. Be perfect. Look pretty. We have expectations and standards to live up to. We must be perfect on the outside, despite what's on the inside. I get so exhausted by *the rules*. I'm fourteen years old and all I want to do is have fun for once in my life and not wear sweater sets, slacks, and designer dresses, not worry about my hair being shimmering and sleek, my skin flawless. If I could, I would cut off my hair and dye it some wild color, like fiery red, or streak it with black. I would wear heavy eyeliner and dark red lipstick. I would do anything as long is it was really me. At the moment, I'm not sure who that is, though. I only know the me my mother created.

I'm getting tired of it. I don't want to worry about what everyone thinks of my family. I don't want to have to sit at a dinner table that is big enough to seat twenty when there are only three of us. I don't want to be forced to eat food that looks like it still needs to be cooked. I don't want to endure one more dinner where I'm told every single thing I've done wrong. I want them to just let me be myself and maybe, perhaps tell me that they love me. I don't want to feel like I'm always screwing up. I want to feel loved. I really do.

"Lila Summers," my mom says, her tone clipped as she snaps her finger at me. "Don't slouch at the table. You'll get bad posture and it will mess up your height, or worse, you'll get a hump on your back. Imagine how hideous you'd look then."

Blowing out a breath, I straighten my shoulders, lifting my chest up, and continue to push the food around on my plate with my silverware. "Yes, *mother*."

She shoots me a dirty look, displeased with my disrespectful tone. She just had her regular Botox treatment and her face looks frozen in place; nothing moves, wrinkles, or reveals any kind of emotion whatsoever. Then again, that's how my mother is with or without Botox treatments. To show feeling is to show weakness, something my father and mother despise, along with failure, underachievement, and embarrassment to the family name, something I frequently cause.

"But doesn't it seem just a little bit silly," I say, knowing I'm treading on thin ice. My father hates when we question the rules, but sometimes I can't keep my mouth shut, because I keep it shut too often. "To not be able to slouch just a little since we're the only ones here."

"Maybe we should start having her eat at her own table," my father says, taking a bite of his asparagus. "You know how I feel about distractions while I'm eating." He's always in a pissy mood, but he's extra pissy today. He had to join my mother at a mandatory meeting at my school with the principal because I got caught ditching yesterday. It wasn't really a big deal. I just missed gym, but they got called in and that in and of itself caused an embarrassment to my father, which he repeatedly reminded me of in the car ride home.

"She never does anything right," he'd said to my mother as we drove home. "I'm so sick and tired of the drama. Either she needs to straighten up or she needs to go."

He'd said it like I was a dog or something equally as easy to discard.

My mother continues to glare at me from across the table, warning me to keep my mouth shut, that my father is not in the mood for any arguing—like he ever is. She has blue eyes and blonde hair identical to mine, but her hair has started to gray so she dyes it once every couple of weeks so her roots won't show. She gets manicures, won't wear anything else besides name-brand designers, and has a shoe closet that's as big as a lot of people's houses. She likes her expensive wine and of course her medication. I hope to God I don't grow up to be her, but if my mom has her way, I'll be married off to some well-known family's son, despite the fact that we won't be in love. *Love is stupid. Love won't get you happiness*, she always says. It's how my mother and father met, which is probably why they sit on opposite ends of the dining table and never make eye contact. Sometimes I wonder how I was ever created, since I've never even seen them kiss.

My father's phone chimes from inside his shirt pocket and he slips it out, checking the screen. He hesitates, and then silences it before returning it to his pocket.

"Who was that?" my mother asks, even though she already knows. We all do. Even the maids.

"Business," he mutters and stuffs his mouth with asparagus.

Business is his twenty-four-year-old mistress, who my mother knows about but won't ever say anything to my father about. I overheard her talking to her mother about it and they'd both agreed that it was a sacrifice of her luxurious life. My mother acted like it was no big deal, but I could hear the hurt in her tone then like I can spot agitation in her eyes now. I think it makes her feel like she's losing her beauty and youth, since she's getting older, grayer, and the wrinkles are starting to show.

"Well, will you please tell business not to call at the dinner table?" She stabs her fork into her chicken. "And Lila, I will not warn you again. Sit up straight or you will go to your room without dinner. You're going to end up with a hump on your back and then no one will ever want you."

"I really think we should reconsider sending her to that boarding school in New York that you sent Abby to," my father says without looking at me. He straightens his tie and takes a bite of food. "Actually, I think we should. I don't want to have to worry about raising her anymore. It's too much drama and I don't have the patience for it."

"Now Douglas, I don't think we need to send her that far away," my mother says, letting the mistress call go like it's as easy as popping one of the pills she takes every morning.

It's almost the same conversation they have every single night. My dad says, "Hey, let's send her away" to which my mother replies, "Now, Douglas."

"She's been getting into too much trouble." My father

grimaces, cutting his chicken. "Skipping school to go shopping and hanging out with people who aren't up to our standards. She has average grades at best and zero accomplishments besides looking pretty. I ran into Fort Allman the other day and his son just got accepted to Yale." He stuffs a bite full of chicken into his mouth and chews it completely before speaking. "What do we have to show for ourselves, Julie? Two daughters, one who's been to rehab two times and the other who's probably going to end up pregnant before the end of her freshman year of high school. She needs some sort of direction."

"I'm not going to get pregnant," I argue, feeling myself shrink, my shoulders hunching in. "I don't even have a boyfriend yet. Not a serious one anyway."

"She's too much of a flirt." He talks over me with disdain in his voice, like he's ashamed of who I am. "She's turning out to be just like Abby and I don't want another one of those in our house. I want something I can be proud of and boarding school may be able to turn her around, if it isn't too late already."

It feels like I'm running out of breathing space, the walls closing in, ready to crush me to pieces. My shoulders bend inward even more until I'm pretty much curled up in a ball.

"She will turn into someone you'll be proud of—I'll make sure of that. I promise," she says in a timid voice, rearranging her vegetables on the porcelain plate. "She just needs a little bit more discipline."

"And if she doesn't?" he asks. "Then what?"

She doesn't answer, cutting her chicken into thin slices, and I can hear the knife scraping the plate.

My father looks at me and his brown eyes are cold, his jaw firm, and his expression stoic. "At her age I already knew what college I was going to go to, where I'd work, and I even helped my father out at his office three times a week. What has she accomplished? Looking pretty? Wearing nice clothes? Becoming you, Julie? I don't see how that will be beneficial to her future. Unless she can find someone to marry her, which at this point, I can assure you no one will." He says it with such arrogance and self-worth. "She needs to start focusing less on boys and clothes and more on school and work. She needs to stop being such a God damn screwup, and until she does I don't want her in this house."

I tell myself to breathe, that the walls aren't really closing in and that I'm not going to get crumpled into pieces. That the feelings stabbing inside me are just feelings and one day I won't feel so worthless—one day I'll feel loved. That my father is just being himself, the same way his father was with him (I know because I've seen it). My sister, Abby, assures me there's an entire world out there, past parents, money, expectations, and vanity. One that you can be yourself in—be free to be whoever you want, whatever that might be. She says she's free now and it's the most breathtakingly wonderful experience ever, despite her less-than-perfect living conditions and life choices.

"Douglas, I really think—" my mother starts, but my father cuts her off, holding up his hand to silence her.

"You assured me when we decided to have kids that I wouldn't have to deal with them," my father says, his tone chilled like ice. "You said that *you* would take care of them and that I would only have to focus on my job. But now I'm here, with daughter number two and she's giving me just as much of a headache as daughter number one. This is not what I signed up for."

For some reason, I picture my father on his wedding day scribbling his John Hancock on a contract that says he won't have to deal with his kids if my mother chooses to have them.

"I'll do better," I dare say. "I promise, I'll try."

"You'll *try*." My father lets out a low, derisive laugh as he drops the fork onto his plate. "Julie, she needs to go to boarding school. It'll be good for her." He doesn't speak to me. He rarely does, like I'm not good enough for him to speak to.

"Fine, we'll send her," my mother says abruptly, with her chin tipped low. "I'll set it up first thing on Monday."

"What!" I know better than to raise my voice at the dinner table, but this has to count as an exception. I shove my plate forward as I place my hands on the table. "You can't do that! I'm not going anywhere!"

My dad overlaps his hands on the table and finally speaks

to me. "I will do whatever the hell I want. You are my daughter, you carry my last name, and therefore you will act how I want you to and go wherever I send you. And if I say go to boarding school, then you will go."

It feels like there's no room left between the walls and the table and myself. I'm going to get smashed between them if I don't get out of there. I push my chair back from the table. I know better than to act like this, but I can't seem to stop myself. "What about my friends? School? My life here? I can't just leave that all behind."

"Your friends aren't suitable for you," my mother says. "They've got you missing school and getting into trouble."

"They have not," I protest. "I've barely done anything and what I have done is normal for a teenager."

"Sit down," my father demands. "You will not get up until you've finished your dinner."

Shaking my head, I step back from the table. "This is such bullshit!" I've had only a few outbursts like this and every one resulted in my being punished by a very long lecture about how insignificant I am to this family.

He scowls at my mother. "Take care of your daughter."

She quickly stands up, placing her hands on top of the white linen tablecloth. "Lila—"

I hurry out of the dining room, heading for the stairs, but at the last second, I turn for the foyer, taking long strides, eager to get the hell away from this place, just like my sister Abby did. I want to run away from them. Disappear. She used to do it all the time until one day they sent her away and she never came back to the house again.

I hear my mom yell and her high heels click across the marble floor as she chases after me. "Lila Summers, don't you dare leave this house!"

I throw open the front door and the warmth and sunshine surround me. The house alarm also goes off, but I don't turn back to turn it off. I sprint down the brick-paved driveway and press the code for the gate to open. I can hear my mother shouting, but I run through the gate and down the sidewalk, seeking freedom. I want to get away from *them* and *their* rules. I can't go to boarding school. I have a life here. I have friends who care about me, and without Steph, Janie, and Cindy, I'll have no one. I'll be alone.

The idea is frightening and the fear sends an adrenaline rush through my body. My legs and arms move quickly, carrying me down the block. I don't stop running until I reach the bus stop a couple of miles down the road where the neighborhood changes from massive, eccentric mansions to ordinary, less appealing suburbs. I've ridden the bus only once, but I think I can handle it, and right now I have no other option. I don't have my phone on me so I can either wander around, go home, or take the bus to my sister's place and stay there for a little while. Reaching into the pocket of my pants, I take out a twenty dollar bill. Then I sit down on the bench and wait for the bus that goes downtown to the main street in the city.

It takes a while for the bus to arrive and I'm kind of

surprised that my mother doesn't show up by the time I'm boarding, although the idea of her endeavoring to come to this area seems implausible. I try to pretend that it's not a big deal, even though it is. I'm glad she didn't show up so I don't have to hear her lectures. But if I admit the truth to myself, the painful, ugly truth, I wish she had shown up because it'd mean that maybe she cared about me enough to look for me.

The bus ride takes forever and the seat I end up in has a funny smell to it, like unwashed socks mixed with a very overwhelming floral scent. It's crowded, too, and some of the people look really sketchy. Like the guy across from me who keeps licking his lips as he stares at me. He has his shoelaces unlaced, there are holes in his jeans, and he looks only a few years older than me. He's not ugly but the scars and slightly bumpy skin would make my mother instantly deem him unworthy of the finer things in life. Only the beautiful deserve to be rich. (I actually heard her say this once to my grandmother during one of their drunken heart-to-hearts.)

"You got any cash on ya?" he asks, sliding to the edge of his seat, rubbing his unshaven jawline.

I shake my head and turn my knees toward the wall. "No."

"You sure?" He eyes the pockets of my pants while he keeps licking his lips.

"Yes, I'm sure." I scoot toward the window, while he continues to stare at me like a creeper.

"You are fucking fine. You know that?" he asks and for a second I feel flattered, but in an uncomfortable way. "Are you lost or something?" he wonders and when I don't answer, he puts his hand on my knee. "If you want, I can help you find your way back home."

"Don't touch me," I utter quietly, my pulse accelerating as he glides his hand up my leg.

"Why, sweetheart?" he asks, his hand reaching my thigh. "It's okay, you know that."

I don't move right away. It takes me a minute to sort through the confusion in my head, because my head and my body are saying two different things. It's not like a guy hasn't touched me before, but for some reason this guy's hand on my thigh makes me feel special. Human contact, skin to skin. I hate that I feel starved of it and there's a slight bit of enjoyment his touch brings, which makes me feel ashamed and dirty, yet at the same time wanted. And I rarely feel wanted.

Working up the courage, I fling his hand off my leg. He starts laughing at me, but doesn't say anything else, and finally he gets off the bus, making a remark about me going with him so he can show me a "real good time."

I unstiffen a little once he's gone and try to stay focused on the outside as the bus passes street after street, the sun dipping lower on the horizon until it vanishes altogether. My reflection stares back at me through the window nearly the entire ride: my deep-set blue eyes, shoulder-length blonde hair, and my fair complexion that's so smooth everyone thinks I wear makeup but I don't. Beauty. I get told I have it all the time and people seem envious of it, yet it never gets me what I want. Love. Affection. To feel whole inside instead of so empty.

It's dark by the time I reach my destination and the air has gotten chilly. The neighborhood my sister lives in doesn't help either. It's in the rundown section and there are a lot of people roaming up and down the sidewalks littered with garbage. There's a man passed out on the bench at the bus stop, along with a group of guys standing in a circle shouting in front of a vacant building with boarded-up windows. One of the guys notices me when I step off the bus and he nudges the guy to the side of him, saying something in a low voice. They both look at me and I don't like the expressions on their faces or the fact that they're three times my size.

I veer to my right, even though my sister's place is to the left, just to avoid walking by them. I keep my head tucked down, wanting to hide what I look like, because, like I've experienced before, my looks can cause trouble.

"Hey, where you goin', baby?" one of them shouts out, his eyes following me. "Come back here and play."

I take off and don't slow down until I've rounded two of the corners on the block, practically making a U-turn. Finally, I reach a quieter area of the sidewalk, which borders a chain-link fence around a junkyard. I continue walking with my head tucked down, walking swiftly, until I reach my sister's apartment a few blocks down.

I remember when I first visited her, how shocked I'd been.

She'd just been kicked out of the boarding school for drug possession and my dad wouldn't let her move back home or give her any help financially. She'd left home a loudmouth who liked to speak her mind, and rebelled every once in a while, but nothing major. When she returned, she was subdued, addicted to drugs, and barely acted like the sister I remembered. This was the only place she could afford and I'll admit it's disgusting. Most of the windows on the outside of the three-story brick building are either broken or boarded up and there are people sleeping on the stairway. My mother calls it a crack house where trashy, unwanted people live, and she tells me she'll never, ever visit my sister. I manage to make it to Abby's floor without any confrontation from the people sleeping on the stairs or the woman shouting obscene things to a man who lives across the hall from her. It takes five knocks to get my sister to answer the door and as soon as I see her, I can tell she's blissfully high.

"Hey, Lila," she says dazedly as she blinks her blue eyes. "To what do I owe the honor of your being here?" She's wearing an overly large gray sweatshirt and cutoffs, something my mom would disown her for wearing, although I guess my mother already kind of has so it doesn't really matter.

"Hey." I wave idiotically, feeling uneasy.

She opens the door wider so I can step inside. "I bet it was Dad, right?" she jokes disdainfully as she shuts the door behind me. "He must have sent you here to check up on me and make sure that his dear daughter is doing okay and isn't dead in a ditch somewhere."

"I just needed some place to go to clear my head," I tell her, drawing a deep breath as I turn in a circle, taking in her living room that's the size of the foyer in my house. The air smells smoky and kind of like garbage and there are all these eccentric glass vases everywhere and a lot of alcohol bottles. "Mom and Dad don't know I'm here," I say, facing her. I think about giving her a hug, because I really need one right now, but she looks so fragile, like if I hug her too tight, she might crumble.

She looks so much different from the last time I saw her and it's been only six months. Her blonde hair looks greasy and thin and her pores are huge and she has a few sores on her skin that look like pimples she's been picking at. Her lips are really dry and she has a couple of cold sores. She's lost a lot of weight, which isn't good since she was already too skinny to begin with.

She blinks her eyes at me and then motions to a tattered plaid sofa that fills up the narrow living room. "You can have a seat if you want," she says, flopping down in the sofa herself.

I brush some crumbs off the cushion and take a seat. There's this weird-looking lightbulb on the coffee table, sketched with colorful art, and I reach for it. "What is this? Art?"

"Don't touch that," she snaps, slapping my hand away. "That's not art, Lila."

"Oh, sorry." I'm starting to regret coming here, since she seems unhappy to see me and is completely out of it. "Maybe I should go." I start to rise to my feet, but she grabs my arm and pulls me back down.

"No, don't go." She sighs. "It's just that…" She scratches her head and then picks at her face. "I don't know why you're here, especially since Mom made it pretty clear that the family was going to disown me."

"I would never disown you," I tell her, remembering how we once used to have a good relationship, before boarding school came along and then her drug addiction. "I just…it's just that…Dad's sending me off to boarding school," I blurt out. "The same one that you went to."

She stays quiet for quite a while, staring at the lightbulb on the coffee table. "Why? What happened?"

I pull a guilty face. "I got caught ditching school."

She shakes her head and hatred flashes across her face. "Dad is such a fucking asshole. It's like you can never screw up. Not once, even if it's something small. And if you do…if you do, then you no longer exist to him."

I don't disagree with her. In fact, I've felt pretty nonexistent for most of my life. "What should I do?"

She shrugs. "There's not much you can do…not until you're eighteen and can get the fuck away from our parents."

I slouch in the sofa, staring at the colorful poster on the wall that has a picture of a guitar on it. "How bad is it?"

She picks up a lighter from the coffee table and reaches for the lightbulb. "How bad is what?"

"Boarding school?" I ask, watching her with curiosity. *What is she doing? Who is this person sitting beside me? I barely even recognize her.*

She puts the lightbulb up to her mouth. "Not any worse than being at home." She flicks the lighter and starts moving the flame along the glass. I have no idea what she's doing, but it feels like I should look away. So I do.

"So I can handle it?" I stare at the dark hallway that leads to a door covered with strings of beads. "I mean, going there. It won't be that bad, right?"

She snorts a laugh and then it's echoed by a cough. "That all depends on how great you think our home life is."

"It not that bad," I say, but the lie is thick in my throat.

She snorts another laugh. "Oh, Lila, don't kid yourself. Our home life is a bunch of shit based on lies for the public eye. To everyone, we seem like the perfect family, but on the inside—behind closed doors—we live in a hollow shell of a home. No hugs. No kisses. No affection. An unemotional zombie mother who's obsessed with her beauty and money. An absent father who hates us and prides himself on telling us that all the time, letting us know how much we annoy him just because we exist." She coughs again, louder, until she hacks something up and then spits it out onto the floor. "It's like he wants us to be as miserable as his father made him."

I finally glance back at her and she's setting the lightbulb down on the table and I notice the air is a little musty. "What is that?" I ask, pointing at it.

"Let's hope you never find out. Let's keep hoping you live some kind of rainbows and sunshine life instead of this."

"But I thought you said things were better out here. That you felt freer."

"I do feel freer." She yawns, her eyelids growing heavy. "But I don't want this version of free for you."

"But if you don't like it then why do you do it?"

"Because it makes me happy and all the dark things in the world not so dark." She drops the lighter on the table, considers something, and then draws her knee onto the couch as she turns to face me. "You want some sisterly advice?"

"Umm…" I glance around at the apartment that I'm fairly certain is littered with drug paraphernalia. "I guess."

"*Live* your life, Lila, the way that *you* want to, not how Dad wants you to or anyone else." She reaches for the lighter on the table again, her eyelids growing heavier and she begins to ramble, looking dazed and barely coherent. "And if you end up at the boarding school keep clear of the trouble-making guys, the rough-looking, wild, and dangerous ones. They can make you feel really alive and loved and like life can actually mean something. But all they fucking do is use you. And they'll only bring you down with them. They don't really love you, Lila. They don't. Love doesn't even exist, despite how much you want it to."

I wonder why she's telling me this. "Um...okay."

She never explains further and that is the end of our conversation. She gets up and starts cleaning the house like a robot dosed up on sugar and caffeine. I sit there and watch her, wondering how she got to this point in her life, so ugly and broken—so messed up. Was it because of a guy? One she loved? Is that why she said that thing about love?

A week later I go off to boarding school with her words of wisdom a shadow in my mind, there but barely. The problem is she forgot to warn me about the guys who seem perfect on the outside, the ones who are charming, seemingly unflawed, and make you feel loved for the very first time. She forgot to tell me about the illusion of love and the darkness that comes with it. That eventually when the illusion is gone, the walls close in on you, crush you, and all you're left with is feeling more unloved and worthless than you did before.

Ethan

I'm sitting at the kitchen table, surrounded by garbage, alcohol bottles, and cigarette butts in probably the shittiest house in the neighborhood, which is saying a lot because there are a lot of shitty houses in this town. It's dark outside and the guy who owns the place decided to go 1960s hippy style and decorate his entire house with lava lamps. He's also got a black light so the house has this haunting glow and everyone's teeth look stupidly white.

A year ago I was an average guy, going to school, and getting decent grades. Now I'm an almost seventeen-year-old high school dropout who's sitting in some druggies' house, unsure of how the hell I got here. It feels like I'm abruptly plummeting off a cliff, hanging out with a bunch of people who I barely recognize and who don't seem to care about anything but getting high and talking about how hard their lives are.

At first the fall was kind of fun and easy, especially turning off my thoughts, because they drive me fucking nuts. But then things descended toward rock bottom and I can feel myself about to splatter against them. I don't want to be in this deep. Not just because I hate needles. I mean, I can stand them to an extent, as long as they're going in someone else's body, not mine. This should be enough to keep me out of situations like these, yet here I am watching some guy shoot up right in front of me, for no other reason than I'm kind of curious and can't seem to find a good enough reason to get up and leave. Plus, there's London, my one weakness in this world, despite how much I want to deny it. London is the one person who I'll make dumb choices for, even when I know they're dumb choices. She's the reason I broke my no-girlfriend rule.

The owner of the house flicks the needle with his fingers and then aims the tip at his forearm. He opens and closes his hand a few times, pumping his fist, then makes a final fist before he plunges the needle into his forearm, sliding it under his skin, deep into his vein. I wince as his muscles tighten, and then he pulls it out and drops the needle onto the table in front of him next to a spoon. He flops back in the kitchen chair and lets out a moan that seriously creeps me out.

"And that's how you get high, fuckers," he says, as his eyes roll into the back of his head. "This seriously feels…" He drifts off, his head flopping to the side.

I'm trying to figure out why I'm still here. I know why I *came* here. Because of London. I first met her almost a year ago. She'd been really drunk at this party I was at and needed a ride home. Somehow that ended up becoming my job. At first I was pissed and made a point to be an ass the entire drive home. But then she started crying to the point where I thought she was going to pass out, so I pulled the truck over and she immediately took off into the field to the side of us.

"You have got to be kidding me," I'd muttered, shoving the truck into park. I've never done well with crying and for a moment I considered just letting London run and get lost in the dark. After seriously contemplating how big of a douche I was being, I couldn't just leave her there. Cursing under my breath, I got out of the truck, chased her down, and found her crying in the middle of the field.

"Look, I don't know what the problem is, but I really need to get you home," I said, stopping in front of her, working to keep my cool. It was getting late, the sky already gray and I wanted to have time to go back to the party. "So could you please do me a favor and get in the truck?"

She shook her head, hugging her knees closer to her. "Just leave me here."

"Oh, trust me, I'm seriously considering it."

"Good." She buried her face against her knees. "I don't want to..." She trailed off, wiping her eyes.

I stood there in the middle of the dry grass, trying to figure out what the hell to do—if I should ask questions or keep my mouth shut. I was about to leave her when she started to sob, like these gasping, hyperventilating sobs. I suddenly had a flashback to when I was around eight and my dad went through this phase where he would beat the shit out of me every time he was coming down from his pain medications and I used to curl up in a ball and sob. It really wasn't a big deal or anything and it only lasted, like, a year, but still, it sucked at the time.

Even though I had no idea why London was crying, I felt a little sympathy for her because there was obviously something going on. "Look, are you okay?" I crouched down in front of her. "Do you want me to take you somewhere else besides home?"

Her tears silenced and when she peeked up at me, she had a cynical look on her face, which surprised the shit out of me. "Like where? Your place? So you can fuck me?"

"No." I stood up and took a step back because the girl was seriously intense. "I was just trying to help. That's all. But if you're going to be a bitch about it then I'll let you sit here and cry."

Her eyes stayed on me as she rose to her feet and her sadness gradually shifted to inquisitiveness as her gaze strayed up and down my body. "You're an asshole."

"Thanks," I muttered, not giving a shit. It wasn't the first time I'd been called this. In fact, I'd been called a lot worse.

"If you really want to help me," she said, grabbing hold of my hand, "then stop talking."

Before I could respond, she dragged me back to my truck on the side of the road. I thought she was going to pour her heart and soul out to me or something, but instead we climbed into the truck and she took a joint out of her bra. We smoked it and when we were done, she asked me if I wanted to fuck her. As much as I loved sex, there was something about her— sadness in her eyes maybe—that made me hesitate for the first time since I'd started having sex. Sure, London had a rebellious, skanky kind of look to her, in her tight leather skirt and cleavage-baring top, but she also looked like she was hurting inside. It felt like she was searching for a way to get rid of the sadness and at the moment it seemed to be sex.

"Maybe I should just take you home," I'd said, putting the joint out in the ashtray of my truck.

"Why?" she questioned in a feisty tone, raising her eyebrows. "Are you afraid of me or something?"

I shook my head and rolled my eyes. "Don't be fucking ridiculous."

She eyed me up and down. "Are you a virgin or something?"

I snorted a laugh. "I haven't been a virgin for two years, sweetheart."

She smiled condescendingly. "Then what's the problem?"

"I have no idea," I lied.

She kept biting her lip and her eyes were all swollen from crying and there was mascara running down her cheeks. I hardly knew her, but I wanted to take that sad look off her face, which is something I didn't want to be thinking. *No strings attached. No relationship.* Those were my rules.

"Then have sex with me." She'd scooted across the bench seat and pressed her lips against mine roughly, biting my bottom lip. I thought about pulling away, but I was too turned on and ended up thinking with my cock and kissing her back.

We had sex in the backseat of my truck. Rough, sweaty, passion-filled sex that blew my mind at the time. I mean, I'd had sex before, but this was different and all that overthinking and wanting to be alone momentarily dissolved into desire for something more in life, not that I could figure out what.

After that I kind of became addicted to her and her erratic, impulsive, wild behavior. She introduced me to a world of weed and we'd spend hours having sex, never really talking, making our relationship easy and perfect, never complicated.

And now, six months later, I'm sitting in a heroin addict's house because she asked me to be here. It's not my scene. I mean, I get high and everything with weed and I've tried cocaine a few times, but heroin is a whole other ballgame, one I'm not sure I want to play.

London extends her arm across the table. She's got short black hair, streaked with purple, and her eyebrow is pierced, along with the spot just above her lip, next to a gnarly scar that runs from the side of her nose to her lip. I've asked her a ton of times how she got it, but she refuses to tell me. She refuses to tell me a lot of things.

"Ethan?" London looks in my direction with a hopeful expression on her face. "I can't shoot myself up. Will you please, pretty please help me?"

I pull a wary face and shake my head. "Sorry, I don't know how."

"I know you don't, baby, but I can tell you how to do it. It'll be fine, trust me." Her eyes plead with me to help her as she runs her free hand through my hair, trying to warm me up. "Please, I really need this."

She always really needs something and I usually let her, because she's not mine to own, but this . . . this might be a little too much.

"Since when are you into this stuff?" I ask her, glancing around at the people lying around on the living room floor. "I've been with you for the last six months and I've never seen you do anything but weed and coke."

"Well, I guess you don't know me that well, then," she snaps, jerking her hand away from my hair. "And you haven't been with me. I just let you follow me around."

I'm getting aggravated. I crack my knuckles against the table and then pop my neck. "Well, I'm not helping you with this." She pouts out her lip, but I don't feel bad for her.

"That's not going to work on me," I tell her. "Not with this."

"I'll help ya, baby." This guy who's her age—I think his

name is Drake or Draven or some weird vampire-sounding name—comes walking into the kitchen. He's a complete ass-hole and disregards me, looking at London like she belongs to him or some shit. "You got a needle?"

She shakes her head and tucks her hair behind her ear, brushing it away from her shoulder and I can see her tattoo on her shoulder: *broken*. I asked her what it meant once and she said it was because she was broken. I asked her why she thought that and she shook her head and told me she didn't want to talk about it. That she just wanted to fuck. She says that a lot.

"Just the one right here." London flicks the used needle that's on the table and my face twists with revulsion.

He plops down in the seat next to her and picks up the used needle that belongs to the guy passed out on the table. Then he picks up a spoon and a lighter.

"You know that's not sanitary, right?" I ask London, tug-ging down the sleeves of my plaid shirt. "Or smart?"

"Since when have I ever claimed to be smart?" She arches her eyebrow at me, daring me to tell her otherwise.

"Never, but it doesn't mean you have to act like an idiot." I glance at Draven or Drake or whoever he is. "When you're obviously not."

"Well, Drake's going to do it for me," she states, with a challenge in her eyes because she knows it's a sensitive subject. I hate looking weak and right now I'm letting some guy take control over my girl.

I glance at the needle in the guy's hand as he extracts some liquid from the spoon. I want to punch him in the face. I want to yell at him. I want to yell at London, not just for doing it now but because I'm starting to wonder if she's done this in the past, shot up with dirty needles. Shit, what if she gave something to me. But I don't yell at her because then I'd be a replica of my father always yelling at my mom. Honestly, what I really want to do is run out of this damn house because I don't want to be here.

"Can't we just go?" I say. "There's gotta be something else you want to do. We can go hang out with Jessabelle and Big D."

"Those two are amateurs," she retorts and I can tell by her firm tone that she's not going to back down because once London makes up her mind, there's no changing it.

"Who brought the whiner to this place?" the guy interrupts, targeting a glare at me. He nods his chin toward the front door. "If you're not big enough to handle it then get the fuck out."

The guy is twice my size—thick neck, tall, hefty—and I'm not one for picking fights anyway. "Just come with me," I say to London. "I can take you home or I can take you back to my place."

"To do what? Talk? Make out? Fuck?" She shakes her head. "That's not what I want right now, Ethan. What I want—what I need—is this." She directs her attention back to the needle and pumps her fist a few times. "God, I need this so bad."

Something's obviously bothering her and it seems like for once I need to get to the bottom of it before she does something drastic even for her. "London, please just come with me and tell me—"

"Shut the fuck up, Ethan!" she cries, slamming her other hand down on the table. Some guy in the living room busts up laughing and the guy high in the chair tips over and falls to the floor, hitting the ground hard. No one seems to care. "I don't need a fucking hero. Or some pathetic little high schooler trying to save me. What I need is to be with someone who will give me what I want and allow me to live my life how I want."

Grinding my teeth, I shove up from the chair. "Fine. Do whatever the fuck you want then. Find someone else. See if I give a shit." I do give a shit, though. Really badly. I want London, more than I've wanted anyone else. I've always secretly wished I could just leave all my stuff behind, hitchhike across the country, and write about what I see and feel and how much I hate being around people and the world and the constant chattering. It always feels like there's the rest of the world and then me. But now there's London and me. I think I might be in love with her even though she's kind of messed up in the head and I really don't know much about her. But I'm the same way. I rarely share who I am and confuse the hell out of people when I do. Deep down, I think we could be beautiful together, living in our own little messed-up world, where we would talk about being outsiders and living life to the fullest. But not like this. Not with fucking heroin in our systems.

London's emotions mix in her expression as I head for the door. She looks enraged, irritated, and hurt, but I keep putting one foot in front of the other. As I leave the kitchen, I get this small urge to turn back around and try one more time to convince her not to do it, but when I glance back over my shoulder, the guy's already plunging the needle into her forearm. Shaking my head and internally cringing, I storm out of the house, knowing she'll call me either later tonight or in the morning to pick her up, like she always does. That's the thing with London. She always comes back to me no matter what and I'll probably always take her back, because in this lonely world, she's the only person who gets what it's like to feel out of place. She promised me that no matter what happened, she'd always come back to me and she always has. So when she doesn't call me by the next morning, I instantly know that something has to be wrong. And for the very first and last time, she doesn't come back to me.

Chapter One

Lila

I'm having a where-the-hell-am-I moment. My arms are flailing, my pulse fitfully racing as I struggle to get my bearings. I open my eyes, but I can't place a single thing about the room I'm in, other than I'm naked in a bed, sweaty, and super gross. My head feels like it's stuck in a fishbowl as I try to recollect where I left my pills, but I can't even remember where I am. There are photos on the walls, none of anyone I recognize, though. The closet is open and it looks like there's some kind of football uniform in there. *Did I sleep with a football player? No, that doesn't sound familiar.* My gaze slides to the opened condom wrapper on the nightstand and I feel relief wash through me. I'm on birth control and everything, but that only protects from pregnancy. *God, I really need to stop doing this.*

I've become accustomed to these kinds of situations, waking up in unfamiliar places with a headache, panic, and consistent, recognizable shame inside me that I know belongs there, just as much as the air in my lungs and the blood in my heart. I don't deserve to feel anything better after the decisions and choices that I've made. I know what I am on the inside now and I don't fight it anymore. It's both liberating and heartbreaking because this is how I have to be—who I am—and it's sad. But I can smile on the outside, show the world how happy I am, since that's what's important, even if I'm dying on the inside.

The routine is very simple and I know it like I know the back of my hand. I open my eyes, take in my surroundings, try to remember something, and then when all else fails, get the hell out of there. I slowly sit up, trying not to wake the guy lying in the bed next to me. He's got dark brown hair and a pretty sturdy body, but his back is turned to me and my memories are hazy, so I can't place what he looks like from the front. Maybe that's for the best, though. Whatever I was looking for with him—love, happiness, a blissful moment of connection—obviously never happened. And I'm at a point in my life where I doubt if it ever will.

Holding my breath, I climb out of bed and slip my dress on, covering myself up, along with the scar winding around my waist, reminding me of why I'm here. I attempt to get the back row of buttons done up, but my fingers are numb, like I was doing something weird with them last night, which could be a possibility. I do have tendency to get a little extreme when I'm that drunk. The fingernails sometimes come out, and back in boarding school I got deemed the slutty biter/screamer. Although, sometimes I wonder if I do it out of pleasure or from the fear that seems to surface when I have sex. And that confusion is *his* fault. I'll always hate him for that, even if I thought I loved him and would have done anything for him at the time. But how could I really, when I was way too young to feel love? Even now, I still haven't felt it and I'm twenty years old.

Leaving my dress unbuttoned, I collect my shoes and tiptoe toward the door. I notice a wad of cash on the nightstand beside the bed and a ring that looks like a football championship ring or something. There's also a stale sandwich on the dresser and several empty beer glasses.

"Ew, I must have really been drunk," I mutter, cringing at the food and then double cringing when I catch my untidy appearance in the mirror on the wall.

Making a repulsed face, I slip out of the room, thinking I'll be out in the hallway of one of the dorm buildings on campus. But I'm in a large, open living room with columns around the walls and picture windows everywhere, letting light easily flow in. The floor is marble and there's a large white rug spread out. It has to be a condo or something, with how fancy it is, not a dorm.

There are a couple of guys and a girl sitting on a leather couch in the middle of the room, watching a flat-screen television mounted on the wall just beside where I stepped out. I can't remember anything other than shots, a chic club, a sleek black Mercedes, someone's hands and lips on me, wishing I could black out, and then I must have gotten what I wanted because after that I remember nothing.

The guys simultaneously look up at me and I notice they're older, like maybe twenty-four or twenty-five, which makes me feel too young to be here, yet older guys seem to be my thing, at least when I'm drunk.

"Hey." One of them nods his scruffy chin at me. "You look a little lost."

"Yep, I'm totally lost." I force a smile, even though I'm frowning on the inside, and I hold my head high as I do the walk of shame. They start laughing at me and I find myself wishing I were someone sassier, like Ella, my best friend and old roommate. But I'm not. Sure, I can be sassy when the time calls for it, but right now I feel icky, gross, and disgusted with myself because I just woke up, my makeup's worn off, my hair's a mess, and my clothes smell like alcohol. Plus I'm crashing. Badly. And I don't have anything on me to help balance my mood.

I rush across the room and throw open the door. As I step out of the condo, I hear one of them laugh and say something about me being easy and slutty, but I close the door and shut out their voices. I walk down the hall and trot down the stairs to the bottom, where I push the door open and step outside into the sunlight and the lukewarm November air. Being outside makes me feel a little better, except I still can't recognize where I am. It's a condo complex—that much I get.

"Crap," I mutter, pressing my fingers to the brim of my nose. I have a splitting headache and my hair smells like beer and my pores feel sticky. I hike across the lawn toward the corner of the street so I can read the street sign, knowing it could be worse. I could be in one of the lower-class areas of Las Vegas, but this looks like it's a nice area, located near some cul-de-sacs and upper-class homes. When I reach the corner of the street, I shield my eyes with my hand and squint up at the street sign. Damn it, I'm way too far away from my apartment to walk. I can either take the bus, which I haven't been a fan of since I was fourteen, or I can call someone. The only person I really know around here anymore—the only one who I trust seeing me like this—is Ethan Gregory. He's the one and only bad boy I've ever had in my life and the one and only guy who's never wanted to sleep with me, which makes him seem less bad to me, but to all the other girls he sleeps with, not so much.

I first met him two summers ago when I went with my best friend Ella back to her hometown. He was the best friend to the guy Ella was in love with, Micha—although she wouldn't admit it at the time. While those two were working out their problems, I spent a lot of time with Ethan and we hit it off. There was this strange connection between us, like we understood each other, even though we were from totally separate worlds: rich and poor. Even when I went back to school in the fall, we still talked on the phone. And then he moved here and we've been hanging out pretty much ever since.

Cursing under my breath, I find my phone that luckily is still in the side pocket of my dress, and then I punch in Ethan's number.

He answers after three rings and his voice is laced with amusement. "Well, hello, lovely Lila. What'd you do this time?"

I ignore the ripple through my body that his voice always causes. After knowing him for a year, I've pretty much become an expert at discounting the emotions he always brings out inside me, which is a good thing for many different reasons. For one thing we live in two separate worlds: I like nice things and Ethan is very unmaterialistic. He calls me spoiled a lot and I call him a weirdo because I don't get half the things that he does, like refusing to buy nicer clothes when he has the money for them. He's so sexy and if he'd wear jeans without holes in them and new shoes and shirts he'd look so much better.

Plus, even though I hate to admit it, my mother's words always echo in my head: *If you can't find a man to take care of you then you'll end up living in a crack house, just like your sister. Find a wealthy man, Lila, and hang on to him no matter what sacrifices you make.* Despite the absurdity of it, I can't seem to get the mental picture out of my head of me curled up in a ball on a ratty old couch, dressed in rags, smoking crack from a pipe, and it scares me.

"I didn't do anything...I don't think anyway. I just need a ride," I say in a whiny voice because I'm tired and filthy and disgusting.

"Again?" he replies, pretending to be annoyed but I've gotten to know him well enough to know he really isn't. He just likes people to think he is because he likes to seem tough and a badass. But I know he's not. He's actually really sweet and talks and listens to me and gives me candy canes. I still have a drawer full of the ones he gave me, unable to eat them or throw them away because then it feels like I'm losing a nice moment in my life with a guy and those kinds of moments are very rare, if nonexistent.

"Are you there?" he says, interrupting my thoughts.

"Yes, I need a ride *again*." I sink down on the curb, attempting not to think of candy canes and red lacy bras. That was a one-time thing. We both agreed that there would be no hooking up. Although, I agreed to it only because he seemed so eager to make it clear it would never happen again. "So will you or won't you come pick me up?"

"God, you're snippy today," he remarks with humor in his tone. "And I don't think I want to deal with it today. I'm too fucking tired from the woman I screwed last night. She really wore me out. Plus, I have to be to work later today."

"Don't be an ass." I scowl, even though he can't see me. "Please quit messing around and just come get me. Pretty please."

He pauses and then sighs, defeated. "I'll come get you though, but only if you say it."

"I'm not going to say it, Ethan. Not today." I prop my elbow on my knee and rest my chin against my hand. He wants me to tell him that I'll be his sex slave, something he made me promise to say the last time he picked me up. He doesn't really want me to be one, though. He just thinks he's funny.

"That was the deal," he reminds me. "If I ever had to come pick you up again."

"But I made the deal when I wasn't this cranky," I say and grimace. "When it seemed like a good idea."

"Fine." He surrenders way too easily and it makes me smile just a little. "But next time I'm making you...In fact, I might even actually make you be my sex slave the next time you call me," he says and I sigh heavily. "I'll head out in a few."

"Thank you," I tell him, stretching my legs out onto the road. "And I'm sorry for being so pissy. I'm just hung-over."

"You didn't go out with that douche from the club, did you?" he asks and I can hear him moving around. "Because I told you the guy seemed sketchy. Although all the guys you've hooked up with seem a little bit sketchy, if you ask me—rich, preppy douche bags."

"They're not douche bags. They're just different from what you're used to." I yawn, extending my arms above my head. "And no, I didn't go home with the guy from the club... I don't think anyway. I can't even remember who I went home with." I cringe as I try to put the pieces together, but I can't even seem to find one full piece.

"Lila..." he starts, but then decides against it, probably because he sleeps around just as much as I do. "Where are you exactly?"

I breathe a sigh of relief, grateful he's not giving me anymore crap for my sexual mishap. I'm hung-over and having withdrawals and I can feel myself verging on a meltdown, something that can never happen, let alone in the open. "I'm on the corner of Vegas Drive and Rainbow."

"Where exactly? In like a store or a house or something?"

"No, I'm sitting on the curb."

He's quiet for a moment. This isn't the first time he's had to pick me up under these kinds of circumstances and it probably won't be the last. It's kind of our thing; we share our stories and never judge each other, despite how bad and ugly the stories are. He knows things about me that no one does, like how my father treats me, and I know things about him, too, like how his dad used to beat his mother and how he despises him for it. "I'll be there in, like, fifteen to twenty minutes. Don't go wandering off anywhere."

"Where would I go?" I pull my knees up and lower my forehead onto them. "It's too damn hot outside to even breathe."

"And try not to get into any trouble," he adds, disregarding my comment.

"Fine." I roll my eyes and then squeeze them shut, inhaling the sweltering air. "And, Ethan…"

He pauses. "Yeah."

"Thank you again," I say softly because I really do feel bad for making him do these things for me. He's always so nice about it, too.

Another pause and then he gives an overexaggerated sigh. "Whatever. You're welcome."

We hang up and I feel slightly better. He's always there for me, even when he doesn't want to be. He's the only person I really talk to anymore and I worry what will happen if he decides to leave me.

I lie down on the sidewalk and twist my platinum ring

around on my finger as I stare up at the melting blue sky and the blinding sunlight. For a moment I don't care about how filthy the ground is or the fact that my dress is undone and my eyes are starting to sting. In fact, for a split second I know I belong there and nowhere better. But as I press my cheek against the scalding concrete, I remember that I was taught not to lie on the filthy ground. I sit up straight and trace the ugly circular scars on each ankle, the mark of my biggest imperfection both inside and out.

The sun bears down on me as I attempt to remember some details of the previous night. But as usual, I'm drawing a blank. If I keep it up, then I wonder if one day my head will just be as empty as my heart. But on the bright side—my mother's bright side—at least I'll still have my beauty and that's all that really matters.

Ethan

You know that point where you're about to wake up, but you can't quite seem to get your fucking eyelids to open so you get kind of stuck between being awake and asleep? Well, that's pretty much where I've been for the last four years. I feel stuck. Trapped in the same place, unable to move. In a life I'm not sure I want, yet I can't seem to figure out how to change it. I've felt differently only once and the person who brought the sunnier side out of me is no longer in my life. Although, sometimes Lila gets me close to breaking out of the daze, but in a different way, one based more on anger and sexual frustration than an actual deep emotion.

I even tried to escape the trapped feeling of my life once. I packed my shit and hit the road with no real destination other than to escape the trapped feelings that had been festering inside me for years. It wasn't bad being alone on the road with no worries about where I was going, but what I learned quickly was that you can't escape life, no matter how much you want to.

I wake up to "Hey Ho" by the Lumineers. It's the ringtone Lila picked out for herself, even though I told her it wasn't my kind of music. She insisted that it was the perfect song choice for her, and I meant to change it but I forgot and now I just don't care. In fact, it's kind of growing on me, like her.

I run my hand over my face, rubbing the drowsiness away, and then reach for my phone on the nightstand beside my bed. I answer it and give Lila a hard time because it seems like it's becoming a tradition. She calls me when she needs help, usually with a guy-related issue, and either I listen to her complain about it or go bail her out from whatever situation she's in.

It's the third time she's called me this month and it's only halfway into November. She told me once, over way too many shots of tequila—which always makes her dark alter ego come out—that she'd been like this since she was fourteen, never giving me an exact reason. Honestly, she seems to be going on a rapid downhill decline since Ella left, even taking a semester off of school, but I think that might have to do with money more than anything. But I'm worried she's lonely or something. A lot of people can't handle being alone, and I think Lila might be one of those people.

I remember the first time we had a real talk, back in Star Grove, where we first met. Our best friends had a thing for each other and we kind of met through them. During the first real time we spent together, we drank a bottle of Bacardi while my dad repainted her car that someone had spray-painted, talking about life, our weird views on casual, meaningless sex, and how at one point in our lives our parents treated us like shit, although Lila's still do.

I'd been flirting with her the entire night, because that's what I do and then Lila tried to get me to screw her. I'd declined since we were both trashed out of our minds and I have rules about having sex and being wasted. I have to be sober enough that I can remember the sex—and the girl. Plus, I don't think of Lila like that. Well, I try not to anyway. I have had a few slip-ups, where I crossed the no-touching rule I made, but I always make sure to play it off as casually as I can, reminding myself that I have rules about relationships for a reason, to keep me out of relationships because I don't want to end up like my mother and father. My father is always yelling at my mother and I'm always worried I'll turn out like them— or him really. Getting emotionally involved with someone leads to an unhealthy, disastrous relationship, where someone will get broken. Take my mother and father. She got pregnant while they were dating, they got married, and twenty-five years later they're still married and hate each other, although they'll never admit it. Instead, my father yells and tells her how stupid and shitty she is all the time and my mother pretends that everything's okay. That it's normal for people to talk to each other like that.

The only exception I ever made was with London, and after what happened with her I promised I'd never make an exception again because I never want to feel that much loss and guilt over losing someone again. But I really struggle with following the rules when it comes to Lila. I even had to add a no-touching rule that exclusively applied to her after I gave her candy canes last Christmas, about a year ago, when I tried to put my hands and tongue in places they didn't belong.

Sometimes it is hard to keep my hands off her, though, and I slip up. The girl is fucking gorgeous, in a model, Hollywood, way-too-perfect actress kind of way. She's got flawless skin, perfect curves, her body proportioned just right. But she's kind of high maintenance. The first time I took her to a pub, she refused to eat the food because she thought eating pub food was too gross and kind of beneath her high food standards, but she's slowly progressing and I've even got her to eat ribs with her hands once, which was hilarious to watch.

After I get off the phone with Lila, I put away the bracelet London gave me and my journal, filled with pages of haunting memories and thoughts. I took both of them out of my dresser during a bout of depression last night, trying to find something that doesn't really exist anymore, because I chose to walk away from it. Or maybe it never really did exist, yet I continue to hold on to it and allow it to haunt me, never talking to anyone about it because the idea of talking about London aloud seems impossible and almost like I'd finally be letting go of her and I'm not ready for that.

I get up and get dressed in jeans and a red T-shirt, then grab a five from my stash of money hidden in a box underneath my dresser. I work part time in construction and since my apartment is dirt cheap and I don't really need anything else besides food, gas for my truck, and occasionally new clothes, I pretty much save everything I make. Tucking the five in my back pocket, I head out the door. I make a quick stop at the nearest Starbucks and use the five to splurge on getting Lila an iced latte because I know she loves them and it might help her with her hang-over. It's early in the afternoon, but still warm. That's Vegas for you, though. Even the fall seems like summer in most areas.

When I finally reach the corner of Vegas Drive and Rainbow, I park the truck where Lila's lying down on the sidewalk with her legs stretched out into the road.

I hop out of the truck and shut the door. "What the fuck are you doing?" I ask, rounding the front of the truck with the iced latte in my hand. "Trying to get run over or something? Jesus, Lila."

She angles her head back and peers up at me. Her blue eyes are bloodshot, her mascara is smeared, and her blonde hair is all tangled. Usually she's so put together, even when I pick her up the morning after, and it's a little bit shocking to see her like this. Still, she's beautiful as hell, but I'll never admit that to anyone out loud.

"Is that for me?" Lila eyes the coffee, licking her lips.

I hand it to her and she guzzles it down, then pulls a face. "Did you have them put nonfat milk in this?"

I shake my head. Sometimes she can be so high maintenance. "No, I forgot your specific instructions, your highness, but you're welcome for getting it for you."

She glares at me. "Thank you," she says with an attitude and then starts sipping on the drink again and I struggle not to ask questions about the condition she's in, because I want to know what the hell happened to her and how she ended up here, looking like she does. "Don't say anything," she mutters, then gradually straightens her legs. She gets to her feet and brushes the sand off the backs of her legs. "I've had a rough morning as it is."

"You mean a rough afternoon," I correct her and then step back from the curb with my hands up in front of me when she targets me with a death glare. "Fine. Jesus, I'll keep my mouth shut."

"Good." She walks toward the truck door, drinking from the straw and swaying her hips. I notice the back of her dress is unbuttoned all the way, so her smooth skin is exposed to the sunlight. God, if I didn't have my rules I'd seriously bend her over and have her take it from behind.

I check her out for a little bit longer and then back up toward the driver's side. "Why's your dress undone?"

She shrugs, swinging her shoes in her hand. "I couldn't get my fingers to work this morning."

My lips threaten to turn upward into a full on smirk. "Why? Were they preoccupied too much last night or something?" I joke, and suddenly way too many images of her flood my head, her fingers sliding up her inner thigh and then slowly entering herself.

She jerks the door open, narrowing her eyes at me, and I add, "What? You're the one who brought it up. If you don't want me to tease you, then don't set up the punch line."

Shaking her head, she presses her lips together and hops into the truck. She'll be pissed off at me for, like, the next ten minutes, but then she'll get over it. She always does.

After I get in the truck, I pull out onto the road and turn up the stereo. We barely speak the entire drive and when I pull into the parking lot of her apartment, I figure she'll bail and then call me in a few days when she needs me to rescue her again.

But when she opens the door, she says, "So are you coming in or what?"

"I guess, if you really want me to." It's not like I have anywhere else to be. Micha, my best friend and old roommate, is gone and I don't work on the weekends anymore. "But I'm not sleeping with you no matter how much you beg."

"I never beg," she says and then her face contorts with confusion as she frowns down at the ground. "At least from what I can remember I don't."

I climb out of the truck and meet her around the front, aiming the keys over my shoulder to lock up the truck. We make our way across the parking lot beneath the heat of the sun and I pull my sunglasses down off my head to cover my eyes. I remain slightly behind her, checking out her ass and her lower back peeking out of her still-opened dress. Finally, I have to rip my gaze away and step up beside her, otherwise I'll end up unable to keep my hands to myself.

"You need to stop blacking out when you get drunk," I say, nudging her playfully with my shoulder. "Drunk is okay, but getting so shit-faced you have no idea what you're doing is really fucking bad, Lila. Even I'm not that bad."

"You're not bad at all." She attempts to smooth her hair down with her hand, but it only makes it stick up more. "You just pretend like you are. But deep down, you're a really nice guy who likes to write in a journal."

"Hey, I told you that in confidence." I scowl at her as we make our way up the steps to her second-story apartment. "You were never supposed to utter that aloud."

She pats her pockets for the keys. "Well, then you never should have told me because I kind of have a big mouth." Her arms fall to her sides and her eyes scan around her feet and then down the steps behind her. "Crap, I think I lost my keys."

"Okay…so go ask your landlord to unlock it for you. It's not that complicated," I say, shaking my head at her.

"I can't ask him."

"Why not?" I lean on the railing, squinting against the sunlight as I assess her.

She lowers her chin, allowing her hair to fall in her face, like she doesn't want me to see her expression. "Because...if I do...then he'll ask me for rent."

"Why?" I ask. "Are you behind on it or something?"

She peers up at me through her eyelashes. "I may or may not have paid the last couple of months," she discloses, her forehead furrowing.

"Why? You're not broke." I hate to say it, but it's kind of obvious by the fancy clothes she's always wearing. Hell, she's got a platinum ring on her finger, for God's sake.

"But I am," she insists, crossing her arms over her chest. "My dad canceled all my credit cards a while ago and I have only, like, eight hundred bucks left."

"Then pay your rent with it." I gape at her. "Or pawn that ring on your finger."

Shaking her head, she covers the ring on her hand, looking almost panicked. "No way. This was a gift from someone I used to know."

"So you'd rather live on the streets than get rid of your gift?" I cock my eyebrow at her. "*Really?*"

"Yes, really," she says simply, her arms falling to her sides.

I tighten my jaw, growing frustrated. "God damn it. You do this all the time, you know that. You need to start being more responsible..." My eyes widen. Holy fucking Jesus, I sound just like my father. Shit. He's always lecturing my mom about her flaws. This is the reason why I don't let myself get into relationships and I'm not in one with Lila, so why am I acting like this?

She laughs scathingly and jabs her finger against my chest. "Oh, and like you are. You get drunk and sleep around and work in construction."

"Hey, I never claim to be responsible." I lean in, lowering my voice, trying to shake off the feeling that I'm acting just like my dad. *No, this is different. You're trying to help her, not control her.* "But I do work and pay my rent."

She huffs, stomping her foot and crossing her arms. It's not the first time I've witnessed her temper tantrums when I don't give in to her, but it still gets on my nerves as bad as the first time I saw her do it. "Ethan, will you please just help me out?"

"How the fuck am I supposed to help you out?" I ask. "Pay your rent so you can get let in? Because I'm not doing that." But a voice inside my head laughs at me, telling me I'm full of shit. That I would pay it for her if she asks, that I'd do anything for her if she flat out asked me to.

She sticks out her bottom lip and makes me soften just a little. "You can pick the lock," she suggests, and when I start to frown, she grips the bottom of my shirt and clutches on to it. "Please, please, please. I'll owe you big time."

"You already owe me big time, for being a pain in the ass and calling me all the time to come pick you up from random guys' houses," I tell her, dragging my hand across my face. "And I don't want you to owe me. I just want you to get a job or something so you won't get kicked out of your apartment."

"Okay, I'll work on getting some cash." She bats her damn eyelashes at me intentionally—I can tell because there's a smirk forming at her lips.

Sighing, I stick out my hand. "Give me one of those pins in your hair."

She releases my shirt, plucks a pin out of her hair, and hands it to me. Grunting and pretending I'm more annoyed than I really am, I bend down in front of the door and quickly pick the lock. When I shove the door open, she jumps up and down, clapping her hands.

"Thank you! Thank you! Thank you!" She throws her arms around my neck and embraces me tightly.

"Don't thank me," I tell her, uneasy and kind of turned on, something I always feel whenever she hugs me. *Lila is off limits. She's a friend. Just a friend. It'll never work out. Relationships never work out. Look at the one that you had.* "Just pay your damn rent and quit losing your keys."

"Yes, boss." She rushes into the house eagerly, leaving the door open behind her, and hurries toward the hallway. "I'm going to take a quick shower."

"What the hell am I supposed to do?" I ask, standing in the entryway of her two-bedroom apartment, which is much nicer than mine: painted walls, a crack-free floor, and the carpet isn't loose. "Sit around here and wait for you? Is that what you want me to do?"

"Don't pretend like you're totally not enjoying the idea." She pauses at the corner of the hall and grins. "Besides, you could just come join me."

I roll my eyes, suppressing a smile. "I've already told you a thousand times that you can't handle me, baby." I bite down on my tongue on the *baby* slipup. I don't use endearing terms with women. Ever. My dad used to use them on my mom when he was trying to kiss up to her after he beat her and she'd always let him butter her up. It made me hate affectionate terms and affection in general.

She turns around and puts her hands on her hips, arching her eyebrows. "And vice versa."

"Oh, I don't doubt it," I say, because I picture Lila as being extremely bossy and orderly in bed and I like women who get caught up in the moment, who love to do things without thinking about them first and who can completely and utterly let go of everything going on in the world. Who don't care if they have money or material things. I like women who are like London. The problem is, she seems to be the only one of her kind and she no longer exists.

Lila laughs and I roll my eyes again, feigning annoyance. Then I chuckle when she sticks out her tongue and I have to bite on my own because the movement draws all my attention to her mouth. Despite the no-touching rule I made, I still can't help but picture the many things I'd like her to do with her mouth that would require a lot of touching.

Once she vanishes down the hall, I get comfortable on the sofa and start channel surfing, but I can find only three channels and I wonder if she hasn't paid her satellite bill either.

"Damn it, Lila," I mutter and then take my phone out of my pocket. I think about just calling Micha and asking him to ask Ella, Lila's best friend, to call Lila because she's obviously gotten in over her head, but then it just seems weird and makes me seem like I'm scared of Ella, so I call her myself.

She answers after two rings and I can tell from her tone of voice that she's trying to figure out why I'm calling her. "Ethan?" she asks warily. "Is something wrong?"

"No," I say. "Or maybe... I don't know... it all kind of depends."

"Depends on what?"

"On whether you've talked to Lila lately or not."

"I haven't heard from her in, like, a week," she says. "I texted her the other day, asking her how she was, and she said she was fine."

"Well, I think she was lying to you." I slump back in the sofa and something pokes me in the back. "Maybe you should call her." I reach around behind my back and pull out an empty prescription bottle. The label's ripped off so I can't tell what it was for. I wouldn't think anything of it, but I used to keep my drugs in something similar and it gets me wondering. *No, there's no way Lila would be doing drugs. She's way too fucking preppy.* I twist off the cap, glance inside, and then take a sniff. It doesn't smell like anything I'm familiar with. Shaking my head, I put the lid on and toss it onto the table in front of me.

"I've actually really needed to call her," Ella replies. "Because I've been meaning to tell her...something..."

"You're being weird," I point out, kicking my feet up on the table.

"Yeah, I know," she admits. "But I'm being like that for a reason."

"Well, if you have a reason then I guess we're okay," I joke sarcastically with a heavy sigh. Ella and I have always had this issue with each other, due to the fact that it always felt like she was interfering in Micha's and my friendship. We're not as bad as we used to be, but our clashing personalities will always sort of hinder us from being good friends. "Look, can you just call her and talk to her?"

"Is she there now?"

"Yeah, but she's in the shower."

"And where are you?" There's insinuation in her tone.

"Sitting on the couch." I click the television off with the remote. "Where else would I be?"

"I don't know." She pauses and I know whatever she's about to say is going to irritate me. "In the shower with her or watching her take one."

"Well, I'm not," I say dryly, more offended than I probably should be. "Look, just call her, okay? I'm going to go."

"Fine," she mutters. "God, you're in a bad mood."

I'm not sure who hangs up first, but we probably do it at the same time. I'm about to put my phone away when I get a text. I'm guessing it's Micha, because I figure Ella went and told him that I was being a jerk, but I'm surprised to find that it's from London's mom, Rae. I haven't talked to her in more than seven or eight months, around the time I decided to give a go at living my lonely wanderer dream, living my life to the fullest, mainly because Rae had called me and reminded me of everything that happened, the stuff I've tried to forget—the life I tried to forget, yet I always feel imprisoned by it. But when I hit the road, there was the whole Micha and Ella drama. Micha was boozing it up, going completely fucking crazy because he thought Ella cheated on him. I remember when I got the call from Lila telling me what was up.

"You need to go to New York, now," she'd said.

"Um, no thanks," I'd replied. "I'm trying to escape people, not go to a city packed with way too many of them."

"I don't care what you want," she said, sounding like a spoiled brat, which she did a lot. Then she proceeded to tell me how Ella had told her, after multiple shots, that she'd only told Micha she'd cheated on him because she thought it was the only way he'd let her go. That he was too good for her and her insanity and deserved someone better.

As much as I agreed that Ella was insane, I didn't think the two of them should split up. They have the kind of love that most people, including myself, will never understand or experience. I don't think I even had it with London.

So I'd agreed to go to a city I hated, to help fix the problem and try to make things right between the two of them even though it wasn't my responsibility. Why do I always try to fix things? I have no fucking clue, other than it drives me crazy when other people are acting crazy when clearly they have it really good.

I slide my finger over my cell phone screen and read the text over.

Rae: I know we haven't talked in a while, but I wanted to check up on you and see how you were doing.

That's not the real reason why she's texting and I know it. She wants the same thing she wanted from me seven or eight months ago.

Me: I'm fine.

Rae: Have you thought anymore about taking a trip to Virginia?

Me: Not sure I can.

Rae: Why not? You know it'd be good for both of you.

Me: No, it wouldn't.

Rae: Please, I really need your help…London's getting worse.

And there it is. The real reason she's texting me. She wants hope. She needs to know that she's doing everything right. And she wants me to give her the resolution. But I can't because giving her false hope—going there and seeing London—means finally letting go. And I'm not sure I'm ready for that yet, whether I can allow myself to let go and fully accept reality. That what's done is done and I have to let go and move on.

> **Me:** You know it's not going to do any good. It didn't the last time I tried and from what you told me seven months ago, everything's still the same with her as it was after the accident.
>
> **Rae:** But I want to change that. If you'd just come visit her, you might be able to change it. You were so close to her when it happened.

No, I can't. No one can. You know this—everyone does—and I don't want to see what I lost. My finger hovers of the button as I deliberate what to type back to her.

"Oh my God, I feel so much better," Lila says, tousling her wet hair with her fingers as she walks out of the hallway wearing only a towel. My jaw nearly hits the floor. It's a really, *really* fucking short towel, one that gives me a view of her thighs and if she turned around, I could probably see the bottom of her ass.

"Is that a hand towel?" I ask, half joking, half serious.

"No," she replies simply. She seems more relaxed and laid-back than when I picked her up. "Just a normal towel."

I try not to stare as she sinks down on the sofa beside me. She doesn't even bother trying to keep the towel closed and I get a glimpse of her thighs, which I've touched once so I know how soft her skin is. Just seeing them, I have to ball my hands into fists so that I'll keep them to myself.

"I really needed to get last night off of me," she says, shaking her hair out. It falls against her bare shoulders, sending beads of water trickling down her skin. "I felt so gross."

"Is that why you were being so bitchy?" I stuff my phone into the pocket of my jeans. I need some time to think and process what she's asking me to do and if I can finally do it, not to give her hope but to say my good-bye.

She shrugs, examining her fingernails. "I guess so," she says nonchalantly, putting her hand on her lap. "Hey, do you want to go out tonight or something?" Lila smiles cheerfully at me as she relaxes back into the sofa, with her hair swept to the side. "Drinks are on me for being a pain in the butt."

"I don't think I can," I say evasively. "Did you get a phone call from Ella by chance?"

Lila shakes her head and twirls a strand of her damp hair around her finger. "No, but I left my phone in my room, so maybe I missed a call."

"You should call her." I pat her bare leg, slipping up again on one of my rules that I set with her: no inappropriate touching.

I'm about to quickly pull away when she shudders under my touch and my muscles ravel as my palm presses against her warm, slightly damp skin. We both freeze and I swear to fucking God I can hear both of our hearts pounding insanely. This isn't the first time that an awkward, intense moment has happened between us and I'm starting to think it won't be the last. I know I should pull back, because it's going to go somewhere beyond the friend zone if I don't, but her breathing accelerates, her chest rapidly rising and falling, her breasts heaving up and down with her deep, ravenous breaths. My cock goes hard and the idea of touching her is so tempting. Suddenly, like my damn hand has a mind of its own, it's slipping up her leg. Her skin is as soft as I remember. I knead my fingers into her thigh and she shudders again, her whole body quivering.

As my hand drifts higher up into the towel, my thoughts wander to how it would feel if my fingers were inside of her. Fucking good, I'm sure. Way too fucking good. I could find out. I know she'd probably let me, but the fact that she would so easily makes me feel guilty. She lets just about everyone touch her, but not because she's a slut. I don't believe for one second that she is. There's something hidden inside her that she's trying to cover up with sex. I can see it in her eyes sometimes, when she gets really quiet. Sadness. Self-doubt. Self-torture, even.

She's not like that now, though, seeming more content and subdued than anything. My hand lingers on the top of her thigh, my fingers brushing toward the inner section, which is even softer. I can feel warmth radiating off her and wetness. God damn it, she's getting wet and I can feel it, which only makes me want to feel more. As my fingers make a path inward, just about to brush across her wetness, she grips down on the armrest and moans. Actually arches her neck, tips her head back, and fucking moans. My pulse hammers as my fingertips press down into her skin. *Fuck.*

"Ethan...God..." Her hair falls back from her shoulders, her chest bowing upward, and I nearly attack her with my lips, lick a path up her leg, slip my tongue inside her, something I've wanted to do since the first day I laid eyes on her.

My fingers dig deeper into her skin, as confliction settles inside me. *Pull my hand back. Keep going.* Somehow I manage to snap my thoughts away from my cock and swiftly pull my hand away. I can't believe I've screwed up again. I've always had my rules about fucking around with girls who I had any sort of feelings for.

I'm practically sweating as I get to my feet, digging my keys out of my pocket, hoping she doesn't notice my cock bulging in my shorts. "I got a few things to do, but I'll check up on you a little bit later." I wait for her to say something about what just happened, that I almost stuck my fingers inside her, but all she does is frown up at me.

"You don't need to check up on me." She adjusts the bottom of the towel over her thighs, crosses her legs, and covers herself up a little. "I'm perfectly okay by myself." She smiles at me but it looks fake.

I move for the door. "I'll check up on you later," I repeat, then open the door and step out into the sunlight, angry with myself for messing up and extremely angry at the part of me that wanted to mess up and throw my rules right out the window. I set them for a reason. To stop myself and others from getting hurt.

As I head to my truck, my phone beeps from inside my pocket. I retrieve it and check the screen. Rae again. I think about texting her back and telling her that I won't go to Virginia. But part of me wants to see London again, even if she's not the same London I fell in love with. I want to say good-bye, yet I don't. And part of me wants to run back to Lila because for some reason, being around her makes me feel better. I'm so confused at this point as thoughts of both London and Lila clash in my head. Whom do I hold on to? London? The girl who I thought I once loved? The girl I lost and will never get back? The girl I walked away from, just left to shoot up? The girl who I wanted to know more than anything, but I missed my chance? Or should I just let her go? Release my guilt of walking away from her that day, just like that. Go around fucking girls, living life, doing whatever I want? Deep down I know I should have never walked away from her that day and that if I'd stayed instead of thinking solely of myself then things might have been different today. Perhaps I'd still be with her.

I can't let her go yet—can't let go of my guilt. I should just be alone. It's for the best.

I end up skipping on sending back a text to Rae, knowing

that by doing so I'm allowing myself to continue to hold on to the idea of London and continue to think of Lila sitting up in her apartment in the hand towel at the same time.

My fucked-up thoughts are giving me a headache. "Shit," I mutter, kicking the tire.

I really fucking need a drink.

Chapter Two

Lila

I'm sitting on the couch alone, wearing a towel, stunned and slightly ashamed of myself. I don't know what the hell happened. Well, actually I do since it's happened before, but it still doesn't make it any easier. One minute Ethan's hand was wandering up my thigh and it felt so good but then he just up and left, totally blowing me off, and it frustrates me because I *want* him. Badly.

Ever since I met Ethan, that's how he's been toward me. He'll flirt with me all the time, yet for the most part he never acts on it, teasing me but never fully following through. I'm always hoping he'll surprise me and finally do something, like show that he's attracted to me. Something tells me that he might be a little different from the other guys I've slept with, sweeter, softer, or maybe rough, but in a good way. Usually, I'm strictly a collared shirt, slacks, nice car, money kind of girl. But there's something about Ethan and the mysteriousness in his brown eyes, the intricate tattoos on his arms, and the way his black hair is always all over the place that makes me burn with curiosity. And part of me thinks that maybe, just maybe I'd finally feel something besides unworthiness and humiliation after I had sex with Ethan. Although, I'm really starting to wonder if I just have a broken vagina. And heart. And head.

After he leaves me high and dry, the two pills I popped before I took a shower quickly kick in and fortunately everything—even being alone in my empty apartment after Ethan blew me off—feels okay. The pills keep away the memories and feelings of what happened last night, along with many other nights in my past. And not remembering them is important. Pain equals unwanted emotions, meltdowns, embarrassment. As much as I hate the blackouts the pills give me, I also hate temporary blackouts where bits and pieces come back to me in sharp, disgraceful images. All that does is remind me of what I've become and how empty and insignificant I feel inside. Sometimes it feels like my body doesn't belong to me, like I lost it a long time ago and I'll never get it back. I wonder if this is how everyone feels after sex. If they feel so dirty and unclean.

It does seem like I've been getting worse lately, but life seems to be getting harder. In the last year and a half my roommate and best friend moved out to go live her life and now I'm alone. I tried to stand up for myself to my parents, telling them I wouldn't come home and live the life they want me to live, and in return my dad took away my car. A few months ago he also canceled all my credit cards and now I'm running out of money and can't even come up with enough to pay my tuition. Being poor isn't something I think I can live with. So to escape the painful, shameful reality of how pathetic my life has become, I've started sleeping around more and downing more and more pills.

I first started taking the pills when I was fourteen because my mother encouraged me to, saying they would help erase the shame and dirtiness I'd been feeling. I'd just had sex for the first time with a guy who pretty much used me and it turned out the pill worked brilliantly, numbing almost all of my emotions. So I've been taking them ever since.

Sighing, I get dressed in a light-blue sundress, twist my hair up with some clips, and head to the kitchen to clean up the floor. Last night I spilled a bunch of wine on it, but I was too drunk to clean it up and now it's stuck to the tile and is stinking up the house. I grab a barely touched sponge and some cleaner out from under the sink, then try not to gag as I put a pair of rubber gloves on and get down on my hands and knees.

I hate cleaning up the house and try to avoid doing any sort of cleaning at all cost. I'd been having someone come clean the house since Ella left, but I'm running low on cash and can't afford her anymore. I get down on my hands and knees with a bucket of water and a sponge. As I'm scrubbing the floors, my mother calls me and I almost laugh to myself, wondering what she would do if she saw me on my hands and knees scrubbing dirt off the floor with a sponge.

I turn around and sit down before answering my phone, noticing that I've missed a call from Ella, like Ethan suspected. "Yes, mother," I answer.

"Have you changed your mind about coming home?" She's been saying the same thing to me ever since I announced my sudden decision to move to Vegas and attend UNLV over a year and a half ago. I'd just graduated from boarding school and had returned home for the summer. My family thought I was going to Yale in the fall, only because I'd lied to everyone and told them I was. I felt ashamed and I was angry at myself for feeling that way, like I couldn't just admit that I wasn't smart enough to go to a fancy school. I'd felt ashamed for the last four years and I didn't want to feel that way anymore. I knew eventually I'd have to tell everyone that I didn't get accepted to Yale or any other Ivy League school, so instead of facing it, I left. I packed my shit, opened a map, and pointed to a random place, which ended up being Vegas. I said goodbye to my mother and she fought me the entire way, yelling and screaming and saying that I'd never make it on my own. But I had money and decent grades and UNLV accepted me in a heartbeat.

"No," I respond with the same answer I always give her. "And I already told you I wasn't going to change my mind."

"Well, I was hoping that your mind decided to be smart," she counters. "But then again, I guess I should know better. You've proved over the last many, many years just how stupid your decisions can be." She sounds more and more like my father the more time goes on. She's almost like clay, easily pliable and shapeable.

I pick at my nail polish, debating whether to go to my room and take another pill. She's taking a jab at me for the huge mistake she'll never be able to forgive me for, not only because of what it made me look like but because it made her and my father look like they raised a slut.

"Did you call for a reason?" I ask calmly "Or to just complain about me?"

"Your father wants you to come home," she states in a subdued voice. "He says if you do he'll give you back your car and credit cards."

"As always, I'm going to have to decline his offer."

"Well, as always you're going to make dumb choices that make this entire family look bad. Between your sister being a waitress and having an illegitimate child and your living in Vegas in an *apartment*, we look like the low-lives of the community."

"Well, maybe you should just tell everyone we're dead, then." I feel numb as I say it and I'm thankful for the medication in my system. "I mean, we both know how great you are about making up cover stories when one of us screws up."

She laughs cynically into the phone. "Well, I've had good practice. I have one daughter who's an ex-junkie, and another daughter who's been a little slut since she was fourteen."

"I was confused and didn't completely understand what I was getting into." I swallow hard, trying not to think about where my journey of being a slut started. "And you did nothing to help me. Nothing beneficial anyway."

"You made a choice, Lila," she retorts derisively. "No one made you do anything. You *chose* to do it."

"I was fourteen," I mumble, the detached feeling in my body starting to lift as the walls close in on me, shrinking me into a ball, just like they did to me when I was a child. My mother has that effect on me, even with a simple phone call. I cradle my knees against my chest and rest my chin on my knees.

"Excuses are for the weak. And if you'd just admit that you made a mistake, and that you continue to make them, then maybe you'd finally be able to clean up your act." She sighs. "You're a beautiful girl, Lila, and your looks could carry you really far in life. Imagine what kind of man you could get if you'd try to date one instead of sleeping with them all."

"Wow, have you ever considered becoming a psychiatrist?" I ask sarcastically. "Because you'd be great at it."

She hangs up on me.

I'm not surprised and I was hoping she would, otherwise she would have started lashing into me about how much of an utter disappointment I am. I press END, glad that I no longer have to talk to her. At the same time I'm hurt that she views me like she does, that she hates me, wishes I was someone else, someone other than who I am. Although I don't even know who that is, so I can't figure out how she does.

I give myself thirty seconds to wallow, and then I call Ella to see what she wants.

"Hello," she answers cheerfully and I can't help but smile because she used to be so sad. I'm glad she's happy, although part of me envies her.

"Hey, did you call earlier?" I ask, lying down on the linoleum floor and staring up at the ceiling. I miss Ella and everything, but it's nice to live alone, too, because I'd never just lie down on the floor in front of her.

"Yeah, I figured you might need to talk," she says and I hear Micha shout something in the background.

"We can talk later," I tell her. "If you're busy."

"No, we can talk now," she insists. "Micha's just yammering in my ear for no reason." There's laughter in her tone and Micha shouts out something else, but it sounds murmured through the phone. "Ethan made it sound like you needed to talk."

"Huh...He called you?"

"Yeah, just a little bit ago."

I bite down on my lip, slightly irked, wondering if he called her to tell her to check up on me because I haven't been paying the rent. The last thing I want to do is tell Ella my problems when she has so many problems herself. Plus, I don't like talking about my issues—it's what I've been taught. The only person I've told anything to is Ethan and even he doesn't know everything. "Well, sorry to waste your time, but I don't really have anything to talk about."

She hesitates. "That's okay. I've been meaning to call you anyway."

"About what?" I'm trying to force the irritation out of my tone, but I can't quite get there. The pills need to kick it up a notch so I can feel artificially happy.

"Maybe I should call later," she says. "You sound annoyed right now."

I sigh heavily, stretching my legs out. "I'm sorry. I'm just a little hung-over and taking it out on you. Sorry."

"That's okay," she replies very cheerfully and very unlike the Ella I first met. "You've put up with a lot of crap from me over the last couple of years."

"God, have we known each other for that long?" I manage to keep my voice light and cheery, even though my head is aching.

"Yeah, we're getting so old, right?" she jokes, but she sounds kind of nervous.

"What are you not telling me?" I say, pushing up on my elbows. "You've got that tone...the one you use when you have a secret."

"I don't have a tone." She pretends she has no idea what I'm talking about, but her overly nonchalant attitude suggests otherwise.

I pinch the brim of my nose, trying to alleviate the pain in my head, and luckily my voice comes out sounding as if I'm the cheery Lila, the one everyone needs to see. "All right, spill your guts."

"Well…" She takes a deep breath. "I kind of moved the ring."

"What!" I exclaim and suddenly all of my crankiness diminishes. Ella has been wearing a ring Micha gave her on the opposite finger as the engagement one. The deal between the two of them was that when Ella felt ready to get engaged, she'd move the ring to the other finger and it's finally official. "When?"

She dithers. "Actually it was a while ago…the day Micha and I left Vegas."

"You bitch," I say, half joking, but kind of angry at the same time. "Why didn't you tell me earlier?"

"I don't know…I guess because I was still getting used to it."

I absentmindedly turn the ring on my own finger, thinking about how sick and twisted it is that I won't get rid of it. I swear the God damn ring still owns me—*he* still owns me. "You could have gotten used to it by telling me."

"I know and I'm really sorry. You know how I get about this kind of stuff though."

"I do." I really, really do. Ella shuts down and keeps things hidden. I didn't know that when I met her so it was a surprise when I got to see this whole other side of her. She went from a quietly, orderly, good girl, to this loud, reckless, badass, and I sometimes wish I could be the same way. Carefree and outgoing and just living life exactly how I want in the moment, without having to be intoxicated.

Micha, her fiancé now I guess, shouts something in the background and then Ella lets out a squeal in the phone. I hear a loud thump and then there's a lot of giggling. I wait for her to come back on, but the giggling only gets louder as she argues with Micha through her laughter about letting her go.

I roll my eyes, officially hating her for the beautiful relationship that she has and deserves. "All right, I'm going to go. If you can hear me, congrats and I'll call you later."

I drop the phone onto the floor and the quiet sets in. The sunlight sneaks through the cracks of the blinds and I can hear my next-door neighbors arguing about something. It's really loud and annoying and I yell, "Keep it down!" while banging on the wall.

They don't hear me though and keep shouting. The longer I lie there, the more the loneliness catches up with me, like a wave ready to slam into the shore. I want someone who will love me like Micha loves Ella. I want someone—anyone—just to love me. I've been trying the best that I can to find that kind of love, but it never seems to work out and I'm really starting to believe that I'm beneath being loved.

I thought I had love once, very stupidly. I should have known better. He was too old to actually love a fourteen-year-old and after it was all over, after he'd used me, he left me, brokenhearted, feeling dirty inside and confused over what I—we—had just done. Even now, when I look back at it, it doesn't make sense to me, at least from an emotional aspect. But the pills make it easier to accept.

"I really did think he loved me," I mumble, feeling the tears sting at my eyes as I rotate the platinum-banded diamond ring around on my finger. "He seemed like he did."

I get up and walk out of the kitchen, heading for my room, wanting to escape my mistakes and the emptiness. The problem is that every time I do, I only add more mistakes to the list and I always end up alone. But I'll probably keep doing it over and over again because it's what I'm good at—screwing up, being a slut, sleeping around, praying I can find someone who will fall in love with the worthless bits and pieces of me and take care of me like my mother is constantly telling me should happen.

I open my nightstand drawer and stare down out the prescription bottle, twisting the ring on my finger, knowing that any more pills will send me into blackout mode. But I want to be in that mode right now because it momentarily makes me feel happy and content. I pick up the bottle and open it. As the pills slide down my throat, numbness slides through my body and I fall back on the bed with my hand placed on the scar along my stomach, my one flaw, both inside and outside.

❧

I'm not sure how boarding school is going, whether I like it or hate it. It seems weird living at a school at fourteen years old. Plus, I'm having a hard time making friends. But I'm trying.

"You see that older guy over there?" Reshella Fairmamst, the girl I'm working on becoming friends with, says, pointing at the

table across the library, at a man wearing a suit. He's sitting in a chair, reading an old tattered book.

Reshella Fairmamst isn't my friend, but I want her to be—need her to be, otherwise I'll end up lonely and friendless. But becoming friends with her is tricky, because she's the richest, most entitled and popular girl in school. "You mean that old guy?"

"He's only twenty-two and he's part of the Elman family, who are totally wealthy." *She flips her honey-blonde hair off her shoulder and holds her nose in the air as if she's smelling a bitter aroma. She does this a lot and I've often wondered if it's out of arrogance or the fact that she's trying to make sure she doesn't have BO.* "He's totally acceptable."

"But I'm only fourteen," *I say stupidly as I twirl my hair around my finger.* "He's not going to want me. He's like eight years older. "

She looks me over from the seat beside mine. She wears a lot of makeup and always has gray eyeliner on because she says it brings out her sharp features. She wears a strand of pearls daily and insists none of the Precious Bells wear them. The Precious Bells are her clique and to get into the clique you have to be the best of the best of the best.

"Maybe you're not a good fit to be a Precious Bell," *she says snidely.* "Because to be one of us you have to be willing to date older men. We never, ever date guys in our school."

"But you're sixteen."

"So."

"So . . ." *I struggle against her condescending gaze.* "It's easier for you."

She rolls her eyes. "Oh please. It'll be easy for you if you just stop thinking so much like a child. It's time to grow up, Lila, unless you don't want to." She turns her head toward the group of girls and guys sitting at the round table in the corner, the ones everyone have deemed nerds and social outcasts, and my mother would never in a million years approve of me hanging out with.

I think of the last words my mother said to me before she dropped me off at boarding school to live out the rest of my high school life: "Do not embarrass us like your sister did. You will not hang out with crowds your father and I won't approve of and you will excel in your studies. Succeed, no matter what. Screw up, and we'll throw you out on the streets just like we did Abby." It was like she was reading a cue card written by my father, but I know it's the truth, because his threats always are. And I really don't want to live on the streets.

I sigh, straightening my posture. "What do you want me to do?" I ask Reshella.

Her glossy pink lips curve to a grin. "I want you to go over and get his number."

My jaw drops. "How?"

"Figure it out," she says simply. "And then, when you do, you'll officially be a Precious Bell."

Nodding, I get up and step back from the table, nervous and near fainting as I make my way over to him. When I reach his table, he instantly looks up. His beauty throws me off guard, along with the hungry, intense look in his eyes.

"I'm Lila," I say quickly, sticking my hand out like a spastic moron for him to shake. "Lila Summers."

His lips quirk, but he doesn't smile. He reaches over and takes my hand, but instead of shaking it he brings it to his lips and delicately kisses it. He has stubble on his chin and it grazes me, feeling both good and bad.

"Lila, that's a beautiful name for a beautiful girl," he says thoughtfully as he looks back at me.

I notice he has a ring on his hand, a platinum band encrusted with diamonds. It's on his ring finger, too, and I wonder if he's married. I wonder if I should ask. I feel so nervous right now, I'm starting to sweat.

I grin, though, kind of smitten by his dazzling smile, my heart throbbing inside my chest at the way he's looking at me. It makes me feel kind of special. And I've never really felt special before. For a moment I can be just a beautiful girl standing in front of a gorgeous guy, thinking she's the most amazing person in the world.

What I really should have been thinking, though, was how stupid and naïve I was.

Ethan

I can't get up from my fucking bed, not just because I drank a six pack of beer, but because I really don't want to. I've got the damn bracelet out again, the one she gave me so I would always remember her. It's on my bed beside my journal, both of them haunting me with memories. I'm lying flat on my stomach, moping like a pussy over a girl who doesn't exist anymore and shouldn't exist to me anymore. I need to let her go. But I can't seem to. I've always hated the idea of relationships—still do. I'd seen them at their grand ugliest and pretty much made my mind up that love and commitment were faulted, fictional, but then London came along and my views changed—I changed. And I don't understand why, what it was about her that made me think differently. And now she's gone and I've yet to find anyone else who makes me reconsider my warped, yet insightful view on eternal and never-ending love.

I haven't been able to take my eyes off the bracelet since I lay down. It's there in front of me, reminding me of everything that happened between London and me and everything that didn't.

"You are such a beautiful guy," London used to say all the time. In fact, she'd pretty much sing it to me. "Which is why you can pull off wearing a bracelet."

I'd shake my head. "No fucking way am I ever going to wear a bracelet."

"Even if it's from me?" she questioned with amusement as she traced her fingers down my face.

"Even if it's from you." I was such a douche to her, totally in my father's asshole character and I'll always hate myself for it. The thing is she never really did seem to care. I never knew what she was thinking or feeling and she never got to see me wear the bracelet. I could put it on now, but what would be the point? It doesn't have any meaning anymore, no connection to anything real. It's pretty much just a piece of leather with "E&L" imprinted on it.

I lean forward, observing it closely, realizing that it could also stand for Ethan and Lila, which makes me hurt only more because I'm thinking about Lila instead of London. What I really want is to not be thinking about anyone. I want silence. Solitude. I want my God damn thoughts to turn off.

Shaking my head, I toss the bracelet aside, out of my line of vision. I need to get out of the house, otherwise I'm going to drift into that place where I get stuck in my own head and pretty much lock myself in a box. My mother always called it being unsociable and a few shrinks referred to it as social anxiety and I call it knowing too much. A couple of shrinks wanted to put me on something for it when I was about fourteen and got super stressed out about the idea of starting high school, not because I was afraid but because it seemed like there were so many people just moving together in herds. All I could think about was the loss of the peace and quiet I'd gained over the summer and all the other stuff I'd rather be doing.

I've always loved the quiet, although I've never really gotten much of it. When I was growing up, I had my brothers always pounding on me. Then they moved out and I was left with my dad constantly yelling at my mom and sometimes he would even hit her. I tried to interfere and ended up taking a few blows myself, which was fine except both my dad *and* my mom ended up mad at me. My mom told me that I didn't need to interfere with things that weren't my business. I was, like, thirteen and it totally confused me. When I asked her why, she simply said, "Because I love your father more than anything and he's just going through a rough time in his life." Just like he was when I was in second grade and he was addicted to pain pills. Sometimes I worry I'm going to turn out like him, that eventually I will end up with someone and this ugly, abusive person will manifest itself inside me.

Eventually my dad stopped hitting my mom—although to this day he walks all over her—but I still saw enough of the ugly, and how easily it was forgotten, that I really question why relationships are so important. Even with London, I didn't see the importance of us declaring that we were together. We never said "I love you," even though I think we both felt it. Sometimes I think I still do…maybe…I think so anyway. Shit, I have no idea.

"I really need to get out of here." I push off my bed, grab my phone and keys, and head out the door. I think about going to a club, but I hate the noise. I consider a bar, which is lower key, but honestly I just want to walk, move forward, stop sitting still.

I take a cab to the strip, order a drink from this building that's a smaller replica of the Eiffel Tower, and then walk up the crowded sidewalk, shoving my way through the crowd, wishing I was some place else instead. It's as loud as being in a club, but I'm outdoors so it's easier to breathe through it. I wander around sipping my drink, watching the neon lights blink. For a while I consider calling Lila and asking her to come meet me, but I'm afraid of what would happen if she did. I feel bad for blowing her off, but I'm in one of my need-to-get-laid moods, which is the best way to turn off my thoughts, and with Lila around, I might end up breaking the rules I set with her. Then what? We'd fuck and things would get awkward and all those fun, light talks that we have, and the rescue missions, would get awkward and probably vanish.

Everyone's all wound up on the sidewalks and in the clubs, talking, chatting, smiling, groping the shit out of each other. While I'm throwing my empty cup away, I spot a few girls in ridiculously short dresses. One's eyeballing me and I think: *Now there's the distraction I've been looking for.* I shove any emotions out of me before approaching them. Micha used to do this shit with me all the time, which made it easier.

I pick the brunette in a red leather dress for no other reason than she seems more interested in me than the other two. I flirt and I smile at her and we walk up and down the strip together. She keeps running her fingers up and down my chest and batting her eyelashes.

"We should go back to your place," she finally shouts over the noise as we reach the heart of the casinos.

I nod, but make sure to play by the rules: always let them know where I stand. "We can do that, but just so you know, I just want to fuck. I'm not looking for a relationship." I'm blunt, but I have to be. The last thing I want is to be misleading and either hurt someone or have them cling on to me.

She grins up at me as she traces my bottom lip with her pinkie nail. "That's all I want, too."

About an hour later I'm screwing her in my apartment and there is no meaning behind it. She's using me and I'm using her. We're just two shells of people with body heat that have absolutely no substance to them at the moment other than what we're searching for—peace and calm. I never find it, though. But that might be because I never allow myself to.

Somewhere I lose track of what she looks like and picture her with short black hair, like London, and the more it continues the more she starts to look like Lila. It's completely messed up and defeats the purpose of having sex and trying to forget my problems. I don't want to be thinking of Lila—I don't want to be thinking of anything. I just want a clear head, and when it's over I go back to being alone, following my rules so I don't have to get close to anyone and move on. Let go. Accept the reality that London's never coming back to me and that she isn't because I chose to let her walk away.

Once we're done fucking, she gets up and tells me thanks while getting dressed and thoughts of London drift away as exhaustion overtakes me, yet Lila remains in my head as I wonder what she's doing right at this moment. I mutter a "you're welcome" and then she leaves, without giving me her number. I roll over in my bed, feeling alone, yet quietly content on the inside, exactly how I want to be. I glance at the clock and realize it's only nine o'clock, though. Fuck. What the hell am I supposed to do for the rest of the night?

Shaking my head, I turn over and take my journal out, doing the only thing I can do to pass the time and try not to think about London and the last time I saw her. I can never forget it, how I just walked away from her. I end up writing about the morning when I found out she was gone, even though I promised myself a long time ago to forget about it. But it can't seem to forget me.

The phone rings. It's like a song. A very annoying song that has a sullen tune and lyrics full of angst and remorse. I'm not even sure how I know it's bad news. I just do, and when I answer the phone and hear the sob, I know she's gone, but not in the way I expected.

She's gone.

But she's not.

She's in between death and life. Lost. Maybe forever. Maybe not. Who knows? No one really seemed to know much, and in the end the real London was gone, her mind always dying, veering closer and closer to death, but right at the last second it fleetingly starts to thrive again before starting the whole process over. She was always half starved, famished, unhealed, yet healed at the same time. It never made sense. None of it did with her.

None of it ever does.

Chapter Three

Lila

I love shopping, probably way too much. Spending money and buying clothes, for whatever reason, fills the void inside my heart. My mom used to drag me along with her all the time while she shopped. She'd go on these outrageous spending sprees every time my father would upset her. Instead of confronting him, she'd buy stuff and then put it all on and make herself look pretty. I remember watching her put new dresses on, shoes, and jewelry, and then she'd stand in front of the mirror and admire herself with a smile on her face.

"Don't I look pretty?" she'd ask me and I'd always nod because she always did look gorgeous and glamorous to me. She'd turn toward me and look me over, like I was a doll, sometimes even letting me try some of her stuff on. "One day, when you're older, you'll be as beautiful as me, Lila."

"But what if I'm not?" I'd asked, because some of the older people around the neighborhood that I'd seen weren't pretty like my mother. "What if I don't turn out as pretty as you?"

She clipped on a pair of diamond earrings that shimmered in the light flowing from the chandelier. "You'll have to make sure you do, Lila. No man wants an ugly woman."

Even at the young age that I was, I can remember thinking how strange her response was, especially since my teacher was always telling us that beauty lay more on the inside than the outside. Still, something about her words stuck with me and, whenever I get a new outfit and put it on, it temporarily makes me feel beautiful. If only the feeling would just last. Then I could stop spending so much money and wouldn't be going broke, nor would I have to take the pills. I'll figure something out, though. One day.

"Seriously, Lila," Ethan complains as he follows me through the mall. He's been in a downer mood the last few times we've hung out, but today he's extremely down because he hates shopping. "No more shopping. I can't take it anymore."

He's got a loose pair of jeans on that are frayed at the bottom and there's a hole in the hem of his green-and-black plaid shirt. He has an array of leather bands on his wrist, all of which look handmade. If only he'd try to dress nicely, then he'd be so sexy it'd be impossible for any girl to turn him down. Not like a lot do. "It's not that bad," I say, weaving around the shirt section in the men's department. I'm on a shopping high, not to mention the fact that I popped three pills before I left. I feel euphorically happy at the moment, so happy in fact that I think my smile might be real. "We've been out for only, like, a few hours."

He exaggeratedly widens his eyes as he turns his wrist toward himself to check the time on his watch. "We've been out for a few too many hours then."

I rummage through the clearance rack because Ethan will never buy anything that's not on sale. "I'm sorry, but I hate riding the bus and I needed to go shopping."

He sighs, letting his hand drop to his side. He's carrying my bags for me, which I'm secretly smiling about. He didn't even say anything when I handed them to him, as if he's gotten used to the fact that I'm going to ask him to help carry them. "Fine, but can you please hurry up? I have things to do."

I slip a hanger off the rack and check the tag on the shirt. It's a little high-priced for him, but I'm going to try anyway, because it's this light shade of pale pink that I love. "What things?"

He shrugs. "Anything besides shopping."

I hold the shirt up to him. "You should totally get this. It'll bring out the color in your eyes." I dazzle him with a sunny smile.

He sticks out his tongue and makes a gagging face. "The only time I would ever wear a shirt like this is if for some insane reason I wanted to get my ass kicked."

"It's not that bad," I say, angling my head to the side as I position it higher on his chest.

"It's pink." His expression is neutral.

"A pretty pink," I point out, grinning at him.

He just stares at me.

"Oh fine, whatever." I roll my eyes, but smile as I put the shirt back where I found it and turn to face him. "I try to help, but you never let me. You could dress so much nicer." I flick the hole in his shirt with my finger.

"I don't need to dress nicer," he says. "What I need is to get the hell out of here. I hate shopping, malls, crowded places where everyone is acting all money crazy. Besides," he says and arches his eyebrows, "have you even paid your rent yet?"

"Yes," I lie, frustrated with him for ruining my cheery mood created from the perfect balance of pills and new clothes. I hurry around him, though, hoping he won't notice my abrupt sunken mood.

His fingers wrap around my arm and stop me from going any farther. "Lila."

I roll my head back as I let out a frustrated sigh. "Oh, fine. I haven't yet, but I will."

"With what money?"

"Money that I have."

He holds on to my arm, refusing to let go. "You're being cryptic."

That's because I don't have an answer. I crane my neck and look at him. "Look, I'm going to pay it. In fact, these clothes I'm buying are so I can go apply for jobs." A huge lie, but I don't want him hassling me when I'm actually feeling good inside.

He doesn't look like he believes me, but he lets go of my arm. "Do me a favor, pay for the stuff you have and then come with me somewhere."

I have a few shirts draped over my arm and a skirt. "Where?"

"Somewhere I want to go," he says, leaning his elbow on the rack next to him. "I figure if I can spend the day shopping then you can spend some time doing what I want to do."

"It's not a strip club, is it?"

"Would it matter?" he asks curiously. "Would you go with me if I wanted to go to a strip club?"

I can feel my cheeks heat, which doesn't happen that often. "I don't know. Can't I get herpes or something just from going in there?"

He snorts a laugh. "That depends on what you're touching."

My cheeks flame hotter, something only Ethan is capable of causing. "I won't be touching anything."

He eyes me over quizzically and then his eyes darken. "But you'd go with me, then?"

I bite on my lip. I'm not sure why, but the idea of going to a strip club with him seems naughty and kind of sexy. I can picture him getting turned on and the look on his face would be totally hot. Jesus. I'm getting hot just thinking about it. "I'm going to go pay for my clothes." I hastily head for the cash register, dodging the subject.

His laughter hits my back and I have the urge to wind around and slap his arm or something. Honestly, what I have the urge to do to him should never be done in the middle of a store. It would be something that could happen only in the bedroom. His bedroom probably, since I'm going to end up getting evicted from mine.

Crap. What am I going to do? As the pressure of reality crashes on to my shoulders, I almost put the clothes back because I know I shouldn't be buying them. But then I think about how good I'll look in them and how, really, my looks are all I have. So I put the clothes on the counter, doing exactly what I was taught to do.

Ethan

I'm making her pay me back for dragging me around the mall. I hate shopping, watching people buy stuff they really don't need. It's so pointless. Give me a T-shirt, jeans, and a pair of boxers and I'm seriously good to go for a week.

"I can't believe you're making me do this," Lila complains after I take her to where I want to go. "I hate getting dirty."

"I can't believe you made me carry your bags," I reply, smiling up at the clear, blue, unpolluted sky. "I hate shopping."

We're out in the middle of the desert, the city far, far away in the distances, along with the noise and chaos of it. The sun is shining down on us and there's a little bit of sand on the blanket we're spread out on. We're side by side on our backs, squinting up at the sun. Lila has her arm draped over her forehead, acting overdramatic and I have my hand tucked under my head, feeling totally in my element. The quiet. The bare space. I love it. It makes all the crap jumbled in my head clear out. I just wish I could hold on to it.

"I didn't make you carry my bags," she protests. "I just handed them to you and you took them."

"You're right," I say, shutting my eyes as the cool air blankets me. "I guess I'm a sucker, then."

"You totally are," she muses. "But a sexy sucker."

It grows quiet between us. It's not news that Lila thinks I'm sexy. She's hit on me way too many times for it not to be evident, but it still makes things tense between us and the sexual tension builds.

"One day I'm just going to pack up my shit and take off," I say, casually changing the subject. "I seriously want to spend a year just driving around the country, sightseeing."

She's quiet for a moment, mulling something over. "But where would you live?"

"In my truck."

"In your truck?" she says. I feel her shift and I open my eyes, blinking up at her as she hovers over me with an astonished, almost horrified look on her face. "How is that even possible? I mean, where would you sleep?"

I shrug. "It's got a backseat. What more do I need?"

"Um, running water, a toilet, a fridge. Clothes. Shoes. Jesus, I could go on." She sits up straight, tucking her legs under her to raise herself up on her knees. "And where would you keep all your stuff, like your television?"

I shrug again. "Honestly, I'd be okay with leaving them all behind, but I'd probably just get a storage unit so I didn't have to start over if I ever decided to settle down again."

She seems angry, her face sharp, her gaze nearly cutting into me. "But you tried the whole loner thing already when you took that road trip and it didn't work out."

"It did work out, but Micha asked me to move to Vegas with him so he could be close to Ella and he couldn't afford to do it alone." I prop up on my elbows. "I was doing just fine being on the road alone. It was my niceness that got in the way of it."

She raises her eyebrows as she gathers her hair at the back of her neck, fanning her hand in front of her face as her skin dews with heat. "You're always telling me you're not nice." Her voice is tight and her face pinched.

"I'm usually not." I sit up and brush some sand out of my hair. "Why is this bothering you so much?"

"It's not," she snaps, turning her back to me. "I was just wondering why. That's all."

I stare at the back of her head as she rests her chin on her knees, staring out at the desert land. "It seems like you're bothered," I point out.

Her shoulders lift and descend as she shrugs. "If you leave, then I'll be alone." She mutters it so quietly I can barely hear her.

I'm silent for a while, unsure what to say or if there's anything I can say—want to say. "You can come with me." It slips out and I want to smack myself on the head. Taking her with me would defeat the purpose of escaping the noise and people, yet at the same time I know I'd miss her if I left her behind.

She glances over her shoulder with skepticism on her face. "Could you imagine me living in your truck, because I sure as heck can't."

"Why not?" Again, what the hell is wrong with my mouth? Why can't I just let it go? She's giving me such an easy out to a huge commitment I shouldn't be taking.

"Because."

"That's the silliest reason I've ever heard."

"Because I don't understand why anyone would want to take off from a city where you have everything at hand and live in a truck where you have nothing but a backseat. It's pretty much like being homeless."

I kneel behind her, inching close to her, then hesitantly place my hand on her shoulder. "Shut your eyes."

She leans away, like I'm scaring her. "*Why?*"

"Because I'm going to prove what's so awesome about my idea." I wait for her to do what I ask and she stubbornly drags it on for longer than necessary, then finally surrenders and turns around.

"Fine." Her voice softens a little. "Show me what's so great about a backseat."

"There's a lot of great things about a backseat," I joke in a low voice, and then dip my lips toward her ear and whisper, "Now shut your eyes."

I expect her to argue, but she very willingly obeys, shutting her eyes the second I utter the words. I shut mine, too, but only because being so close to her, breathing in her scent, feeling the warmth emitting from her body is driving my body into a frenzy.

"Now picture nothing but mountains," I say softly, picturing it myself. "No city. No noise. No crazy-ass parents who act like children and treat their children like shit. No nothing. Just the quiet."

"It seems like an awfully lonely place, if you ask me," she tells me. "Just me and the dirt and the quiet. Although I wouldn't mind the being without the parents part."

"You wouldn't be completely alone." I sweep her head to the side and rest my chin on her shoulder. "You'd be with me."

She pauses for an eternity and her breathing is ragged. Or maybe it's mine. "What would we do at this mountain place together?" she says.

"Anything we wanted."

"Hike?" There's disdain in her voice.

"Maybe," I say. "Or maybe we'd just sit and enjoy each other's company in the quiet."

She shifts her weight and situates her hands underneath her legs, leaning back against my chest. "That kind of sounds nice."

"Yeah?"

"Yeah."

As strange as it is, and as much of a pain in the ass as

Lila can be, I can actually picture us sitting together up on the mountains in the noiselessness, living in my truck, driving anywhere and everywhere. Together. And the comfort in the idea is kind of frightening because it means I'm thinking about our future. Together. Shit.

I think about moving away from her, putting a little space between us because obviously I'm heading down a road I shouldn't be headed down. The dream of living on the road has always been one I'd planned to live out alone and now suddenly I'm telling Lila she should come with me. God knows what would happen between us if we lived in a truck with one another. We'd either grow really close or end up hating each other. Or maybe both. But I can't bring myself to move and break the peaceful moment. So instead I sit down and wrap my legs and arms around her and we just sit there in the sun, enjoying each other in the quiet.

Chapter Four

Lila

It's amazing how one moment in life can be beautiful, and then you return home—to reality—and remember that beauty isn't everything and that the ugly painful part will always exist in the form of unpaid bills, bad choices, and tiny white pills.

At what point do you finally admit that your life is falling apart, not to just yourself but to the outside world? When should I finally tell someone what's really going on? That I'm penniless pretty much, soon to be homeless, carless, jobless, everythingless. That my mother was right. I was nothing without their help.

I thought about telling Ella once, a couple of months before she left for California, about some of my money and even my pill issues, but then I remembered what I'd been taught and decided it was best to keep my mouth shut. Besides, now she's got her own life with Micha. And I'm here, wondering what I should do with my life because I want to do something—anything. I wonder how long I can keep going like this, blacking out, having unmemorable sex, like I did the other night with some random guy I met at a club. It was after Ethan suggested our road trip together, even though I'm still not certain if he was being serious. Afterward he had to drop me off at my apartment because he had stuff to do and the emptiness and silence wore me down and I went looking for someone to fix it, after I'd taken a few pills. I've even considered telling Ethan about my problems a few times because I know he's done drugs in the past and might understand what I'm going through, maybe just a little. Although, it's not really the same. I mean he did weed and stuff and I just do pills.

"Earth to Lila." Ethan waves his hand in front of my face. I blink and then direct my focus to him. He shakes his head in disbelief as he shoves up the sleeves of his black-and-red plaid shirt that has a torn front pocket. "You totally just spaced out for, like, five minutes straight," he says, resting his heavily inked arms on the table.

"Well, maybe it's because you're so boring," I tease with a grin, stirring my Long Island iced tea with my straw. We're in a quiet bar with dim lighting and small lanterns on each table. Music plays from a jukebox in the corner near the restrooms and we have a platter of mozzarella sticks, jalapeno poppers, and hot wings in front of us. It's not usually my kind of scene—I like more glitz and glamour with a more sparkling atmosphere, classy music, fancier food, and top-shelf drinks. But I'm enjoying it for some bizarre reason, maybe because I feel heavily subdued. Or maybe it's because of Ethan. "You've barely said two words to me."

"Actually, I think it was five," he says indifferently, but the corners of his lips quirk. He picks up his glass of ice water and takes a sip.

"Since when do you drink water?" I remark and wrap my lips around the straw, taking a swallow of my drink.

"I think I need a break from drinking." He ogles some blonde wearing a tacky leather skirt and a bright pink tube top at the bar and I have to resist the urge to slap him against the back of the head. "It's getting exhausting."

"I hear you," I say and he crooks an eyebrow, staring at the drink in front of me. "No, not about drinking. About other stuff."

"Like what?" He picks up a mozzarella stick and dips it into the cup of marina sauce.

"Like stuff," I respond vaguely, and then reach for a jalapeno popper. It took me a while to actually try one, because the idea of eating something that had the word "popper" in it seemed repulsive. But they are really good. Way better than the appetizers at the restaurants I grew up eating at.

"Care to share the stuff?" He has a string of cheese on his chin from the mozzarella stick.

Biting my lip to restrain from smiling, I extend my arm across the table and pick it off, letting my fingertips graze the stubble on his chin, pretending it's by accident, when really I just like touching him.

His brown eyes widen and his lips part as I lean back. "What are you doing?" he asks.

"You had cheese on your chin," I explain, flicking it to the ground. He quickly wipes his chin with his hand and I laugh. "I just got it off. Duh."

He rolls his eyes. "I was just making sure you got all of it."

I dip a stick into a cup of ranch. "I got it all, so relax. I would never let you walk around with cheese hanging off your face," I tease. "Although, it would be kind of fun to watch you go hit on the slut over at the bar with cheese on your face."

The corners of his lips quirk as he watches me chew and he leans back in his chair. "I'm sure I could still get her to let me fuck her."

I throw a mozzarella stick at him, but he ducks so it misses his head. "You are such an ass."

"Why? Because I say the truth?"

"In the foulest ways."

"What? Saying *fuck* is foul?" he asks. "Would you rather me say *let me screw her*? Bang her? Let her ride me? Give her the hottest, sweatiest, lip bitingest, best orgasm she'll probably have?" His voice is getting louder and people are watching us, which seems only to amuse him while it embarrasses me.

"Ethan, please keep it down," I hiss, glancing at the tables around us, embarrassed, but a giggle escapes my lips. "People are watching us."

"Do the dirty nasty with me?" he continues, unbothered, his brown eyes darkening as he leans back in his chair, watching me with an arrogant grin on his face. "Fuck her brains out? Or should I just make the noises for you so you really get the picture?" He tips his head back, his black hair falling back out of his eyes, and he starts making little moans. Even though it's embarrassing, it's also turning me on. Especially how his lips hypnotically move and the way the light reflects in his eyes and makes them look lustrous.

Stop thinking about him like that. He made his rules for a reason. Shaking my head and the near-orgasmic feeling out of my body, I lean over the table and cover his moaning lips with my hand. "Okay, I get the picture. Will you stop now?"

His grin broadens against my hand and I withdraw, sitting back down in the chair. "I win," he says and winks at me.

I shake my head, but smile brightly. "For the record, fucking her and fucking her brains out are pretty much one and the same."

He covers his mouth with his hand, containing his laughter, because he always seems to think it's funny when I say the *F* word. In fact, he blames it on his bad influence on me. "Oh, I completely disagree. A lot more effort goes into fucking someone's brains out."

I want to argue with him, but I stop myself, because even though I've had a lot of sex, I've had a lot of meaningless sex, which doesn't make me an expert. I've often wondered what sex would feel like if I wasn't high on alcohol and/or pills. Would it feel different? Would I feel different, less worthless, or would I feel more? Would it finally feel good for once? Hot, sweaty, and lip biting? I wonder what it would feel like with Ethan…

I dive into the wings, eating one after another, trying to contain my sex-driven thoughts. Ethan devours the jalapeno poppers and continues to check out the slut at the bar, who's now noticed him, probably because of his moaning and groaning. She looks interested and he'll probably go home with her, which is fine. I've seen him do it a ton of times.

Ethan finally tears his attention off her and it looks like he wants to say something but is wary about it. I figure he's probably about to ask if he can go do his thing with her and I prepare myself for the stomach punch I always feel when he does this sort of thing.

He blows out a breath and wisps of his hair flutter to the side of his face. "Did you ever get your rent thing taken care of?" he asks, completely blindsiding me.

"Um…what…oh, yeah I did," I lie, licking some barbecue sauce off my lip.

He cocks an eyebrow at me with skepticism on his face. "Lila."

"Don't *Lila* me." I sound whiney and I clear my throat, reaching for a napkin. "Okay, so I haven't yet, but I'm working on it. I just need to get a job, but they're really hard to find."

He hitches a finger over his shoulder, pointing at the bar, where a guy is wiping down glasses with a towel. "They're hiring here."

I eye the bar as I wipe the barbecue sauce off my fingers. "Yeah, for a waitress."

"So?"

"So, I can't be a waitress."

"Why? You could end up being good at it." He inclines forward, resting his arms on the table, and amusement dances in his eyes. "And think of all the tips you'd get if you wore a short, low-cut dress that showed off all your goods."

I roll my eyes. "You know I don't dress like that."

"Well, you could always wear that towel of yours," he says in a husky voice. "You looked good in that."

It feels like I'm falling, air gets trapped in my lungs and my heart flutters at the hooded look he's giving me. I'm about to ask him if he liked the towel, because I would seriously put it on for him right here, right now, when he sputters a laugh.

"Relax, I'm just messing with you." He scoops up a wing and takes a large bite. "I'd rather you not dress like that out in public."

I swallow hard, feeling like an idiot. Of course he's just teasing. He always is. And that's how it's supposed to be between us. Just friends. But then what the hell was that hyperventilating, falling-off-the-cliff feeling then? "I knew you were," I lie, sounding pathetically disappointed and feeling strangely conflicted inside.

His expression falls a little and he forces the bite of chicken down his throat. "Are you okay?"

"I'm perfectly okay." I tuck a strand of my hair behind my ear as I lean forward in the chair and dunk a wing into the ranch, biting my tongue hard as I struggle to keep the tears back. *Stop it. You don't ever get upset over a guy like this. Get it together.* "I'm just thinking that you're right and I do need a job, but not here." My heart is aching inside my chest and I don't know why, but I feel furious. "And just because I like sex doesn't mean I'm going to use my body for money."

"I told you I was just joking about the towel." His eyebrows lower as he studies me. "I've already told you I don't think of you that way."

"What way?" I snap, dropping the wing back into the basket. "A slut. An easy lay. A *whore*." I hate the word *whore*. Hate it! But it sums up what I am really well.

He throws up his hands exasperatedly. "Look, I don't want to fight with you. I'm just trying to help, but clearly I'm not doing that so I'll back off."

"Well, I don't want your help because I don't need help." I shove away from the table, my heart racing. *Is it time for another pill yet? I feel like I'm crashing.* I wind around the table, picking my purse off the back of my chair, then storm for the exit and shove out the front doors, stepping out onto the street. I start to walk down the busy sidewalk, searching the streets for a cab since I didn't drive here. I start twisting the platinum ring on my finger as my emotions take over and the need to medicate burns inside me. I know I'm acting ridiculous and probably look nuts because of my abrupt switch in moods. I could try to blame it solely on the fact that I need a pill, but it's much deeper—like the fact I have so many bills and no money left, that I'm proving my parents right and I can't take care of myself, that I'm going nowhere with my life and have no idea how to change it. And then there's Ethan. God damn him for being so sexy. Seriously. I've liked him since the first day I met him and it gets harder to be around him when it's clear he doesn't want me, at least not how I want him. He just teases me. Plain and simple.

I reach the corner of the sidewalk and look left and right before I step off the curb. The evening sky is cloudy and there's the faintest scent of rain in the air. I hope it doesn't start raining because I don't have a jacket on and I'm wearing opened-toed satin high heels and water will ruin them.

"Lila!" I hear Ethan shout as I reach the other side of the street.

Having no desire to talk to him right now, I pick up the pace. I hear the sound of his footsteps rushing after me, but I only walk quicker, balling my hands into fists, and the platinum ring digs into my skin. I clench them even tighter, hyperaware of the pain as the metal indents into my skin and of each scar on my body, all linked to the damn ring.

"God damn it, Lila." He's getting irritated. "Slow the fuck down."

"Ethan, just leave me alone," I call out over my shoulder, wrapping my arms around myself. "I'm not in the mood to talk right now."

The sound of his footsteps gets closer as I zigzag around a group of people standing in front of one of the older casinos. "I know you're not, but that doesn't mean I should leave you alone walking down the fucking strip by yourself."

I pause near the street post beside a mob of people waiting to cross and I deliberate if I should turn around. I don't move as his footsteps arrive beside me, but I don't turn my head to look at him either.

"Look," he says, panting. "I have no idea what the hell happened back there, but whatever I did or said to make you mad, I'm sorry." In the year that I've known Ethan, I've never heard him give a genuine apology.

With my arms crossed over my chest, I peek over at him, feeling the slightest bit embarrassed over my outburst. Ethan looks sincere, his eyes dark and slightly wide underneath the flashing fluorescent lights, and his chest is moving rapidly as he works to regain his breath.

"You don't need to be sorry." I sigh as I uncross my arms. "I'm not mad at you."

He rakes his fingers through his hair. "Then why the heck did you take off?"

I shrug, shuffling my shoes on the sidewalk. "I don't know...I guess I'm just feeling a little down lately and I was taking it out on you." I put my fake, pill-induced game face on and smile at him. "It's really not a big deal."

He takes a deep intake and releases it. "Stressed out over bills?"

"That among many things." I push my finger against the crosswalk button on the pole.

"Is it your mom again?" He folds his arms over his chest, and I can't help but notice how his muscles flex beneath the vibrant artwork on his skin. "Has she been hounding you to move home? Or is it your dad? He's not being a douche to you again, is he? I swear to God, Lila, you need to just tell them to fuck off if they are. They don't deserve to even know you with the way that they treat you."

I bite down on my lip, trying not to stare at his lean muscles or his luscious lips or the fact that he just told me one of the sweetest things I've ever heard. "No, I haven't even talked to him in months. My mother's been calling me all the time to come back home, but that's not what's wrong."

"Did you finally tell her off?"

"As much as I always do."

"Was she mean to you?"

I shrug. "It doesn't even matter. At this point it barely affects me." I'm such a liar and I think he can tell.

His forehead creases as he studies my face. "Do you want to just tell me what's bothering you or should I keep guessing?"

The light flashes to go ahead and cross the street and I step off the curb. He walks with me, keeping close to my side as we maneuver through the crowd coming at us. I want to tell him what's wrong, but I'm not one hundred percent sure what's bothering me just yet. If it's money, the loneliness I've felt for the last month, the fact that I need a job but don't even know how to get one, or if it's the feelings I have for him.

"Did you know that Ella and Micha are engaged?" I say, changing the subject and stepping up onto the curb.

Traffic rushes by us as we walk past the towering, uniquely shaped buildings that glimmer and shine. Each building is so different from the other: a replica of the Eiffel Tower, a massive pirate ship, a pyramid—you name it and it's probably here. Neon lights flash across billboards and marquees, trying to entice people to come gamble their money away, see flamboyant shows, or drink drinks while staring at tits. There are a lot of people whisking around and the heat, the dancing, the skimpy clothing, and the music playing make the atmosphere erotic and steamy. The combination makes me want to dance and have fun, instead of thinking about stuff.

"Yeah, Micha told me a couple of weeks ago." He slips his arm around my shoulder and draws me closer as a guy tries to hand me a card with a picture of a naked lady on it. "Sorry I didn't mention it. Micha wasn't even supposed to mention it, because Ella wasn't ready to tell anyone, but he let it slip out."

"She told me the other day," I say, breathing in his scent. *He smells so mouthwateringly good.* "And she sounded so happy."

"I'm sure they are." He slants his head down to meet my eyes and inquisitiveness sparkles in them. "Is that why you're upset? Because they're getting married?"

"No, I'm just…honestly, I'm not sure what's bothering

me. I think maybe I'm just tired. I haven't been sleeping well lately."

He searches my eyes a moment longer, the lights on the marquee above our heads reflecting in his pupils. "Do you want me to take you home?" he asks. "So you can get some rest?"

I shake my head, even though I'm exhausted. I don't want to go home to my empty house. "Can we go to a club or something? And I mean a really nice one." I grab his arm and pretty much beg. "I need to do something that's fun."

He dithers. "You know how I feel about clubs. They're too God damn noisy and packed and fancy ones are even worse."

"Please." I pout, exaggeratedly sticking my lip out. "I'm not ready to go home just yet."

"Can't we just go to a bar?"

"I want to do something that's my kind of fun."

"You mean spend money you don't have?" he says bluntly.

I glare at him. "Fine. I'm sorry I even tried." I start to stomp away, but he pulls me back.

He sighs. "Fine." He gives in to me, then lets go of my arm and offers me his elbow and I take it, even though I know I shouldn't, because I'm getting too attached, dangerously one-sidedly attached. He guides me across the road, talking about how hot it is. So simple. So easy.

Too bad he doesn't want me because I would love to let him have me.

Ethan

I really hate clubs. There are too many people packed in a tiny area and the music is always turned up to the point where it vibrates in my chest. But Lila didn't want to go home and I don't want her out and about when she's obviously upset about something.

We're sitting on barstools at the bar that probably cost more than my truck. The bartender keeps hitting on Lila, even though she seems uninterested. It's annoying to watch, but it's always hard to watch her get hit on. In fact, it's harder than it used to be and I can't help thinking she's mine, even though she's obviously not.

"Are you sure you don't want a shot?" she asks me over the music as she slams down her fifth shot of top-shelf vodka, which I'm sure she can't afford. I remember when I first met her how much of a lightweight she was, barely able to drink beers, but now she's fucking crazy, reckless even. It makes me a little nervous and I'm seriously considering taking her fake ID and cutting it in half so she can't use it anymore to go out, but then again I'd be a fucking hypocrite if I didn't get rid of mine so I could stop going out.

"Then who would drive home?" I ask loudly, glancing at the dance floor. There are a ton of women out tonight, dressed in short dresses, tight pants, their tits pretty much bulging out of their tops. It's usually a nice sight, but I'm not feeling it tonight. I wasn't even feeling it back at the bar with the blonde eyeing me. I kept staring at her, deciding if I wanted to hit on her or not, but Lila and my worry for her kept pulling me back and finally I'd decided just to focus on her.

"We could get a cab." She spins the empty shot glass around on the bar. I open my mouth to protest, but she interrupts. "You don't have to. You're just always so tense when we come to these kinds of places and alcohol usually relaxes you."

My forehead creases as I assess her. Typically, people don't notice my uneasiness and it makes me question why she's been paying such close attention to me. I remember the countless times London used to drag me to noisy places, either not noticing that I hated the noise or not caring.

"What?" Lila touches her hair self-consciously and then glances down at her dress that brushes the middle of her legs. She has a sweater jacket thingy over it, which makes no sense to me since it's hot as hell outside. She also has a pearl bracelet on and a diamond necklace and everything about her screams money, a rich princess pretty much. We're so opposite, yet I can't seem to stay away from her.

"It's nothing," I say, patting the bar with my hand. "I'll take a few shots with you, but you have to order them."

She lowers her hand to the bar. "Why?"

I restrain an eye roll. "Because the bartender is obviously into you and I'm guessing he might get the shots for you faster."

She glances over at the bartender talking to a group of women. "He's not my type," she says nonchalantly, looking back at me with curiosity. The lights from the dance floor flash across her face and there's no use trying to deny how beautiful she is, princess or not.

"Not preppy enough for you?" I tease, but underneath my skin, irritation surfaces.

She props her elbow on the bar and watches me, not saying anything. It's making me uncomfortable. I want to ask her what the hell she's thinking about and why she's staring at me like that, but I don't because I'm afraid of the answer. "What do you want to drink?" she asks.

I shrug, taking an uneasy deep breath, hating how unsettled I feel inside. *When did things get so complex between us? How did I let it get that way?* "I'm going to have to go with tequila."

She giggles under her breath. "To kill ya coming up."

She raises her hand, leans over the bar, and flags down the bartender. She slips off her jacket, the thin straps of her dress revealing her shoulders and the low-cut back showing her smooth skin. I'm not sure if she does it on purpose, to get the bartender's attention, but it works. She orders a shot of vodka and a shot of tequila. He grins at her, drinking her in, and I want to punch him in the face just for looking. I'm not much of the jealous type, so the feeling throws me off a little.

The guy on the barstool next to Lila starts flirting with her a few seconds later, eying her lips as she chews on the straw. He's older, at least twenty-five, wearing a black suit and ridiculously shiny shoes. Lila seems vaguely interested in him, not laughing at his jokes, yet she lets him place his hand on her thigh and inch it up north.

I'm getting pissed. I've never had much of a possessive side—I've seen my father overreact too much with my mother, even if she was just talking to the mailman—but right now my jealous, controlling side is coming out. As the bartender sets the shots down in front of us, I grab the top of her barstool and spin her in my direction so the guy's hand falls off her leg.

Her eyes widen as the guy shoots a glare at me. "What the hell, Ethan?"

I have an arm on each side of her and my hands are just beside her hips. I lean in so she can hear me. "If you want me to stay here with you and take shots, your attention needs to be on me." I wince at my own words, but it's too late and I can't retract them.

Her expression is calm, yet her eyes carry interest. "Okay," she says simply and gathers the shot from the counter. She raises it in front of her, giggling. "To paying attention."

I shake my head, rolling my eyes at her drunkenness, but a laugh slips through as I collect the shot glass. "All right, Lila." I raise the glass upward. "To paying attention."

I'm about to clink our glasses when she pulls back. "That goes for you, too," she says and when my expression slips to confusion, she adds, "You have to pay attention to me tonight, too."

Why do I see this going very, very wrong? "Okay." *I'm an*

idiot. "You have my one hundred percent undivided attention, Lila Summers."

Her lips curve to a smile and then she clinks her glass against mine. We both pull away and tip our heads back, devouring our shots.

"Now what?" I ask, slamming the empty glass down on the bar while she gags on the drink—she always does.

Her grin is almost devilish. "Another one?"

I sigh and shrug, feeling slightly better as the alcohol burns its way through my body. "Why not?"

❧

"Why do you think it's so hard to be alone?" Lila asks, struggling to keep her eyes open as she gazes out at the night sky through the cab window.

I'm turned sideways in the seat, with my knee up, so I'm facing her, even though she won't look at me. I lost count of how many shots we had hours ago and I can barely comprehend how we got to a cab—stumbling, laughing, as she rubbed her hand up the front of my jeans. No, that can't be right, can it?

"I think being alone is fan-fucking-tastic...well, maybe... sometimes..." I mumble, draping my arm on the back of the seat. I stare at her for a moment, taking in her bare skin in the moonlight. I want to touch it. Lick it. Even bite it.

I'm bursting with sexual energy and I channel it to my foot on the floor, bouncing my knee. There's something different about tonight, something out of the ordinary, this strange need to keep getting closer to Lila. It could be the alcohol. Or it could be something else, but there's no way my tequila-soaked mind is going to reach any sort of answer.

Lila turns her head toward me, her pupils wide and shiny. "Why are you staring at me like that?"

I keep tapping my foot on the floor, trying to think of a better answer than the first one that pops into my head, but I can't find one. "Because I'm thinking about you."

She glances at the cab driver, a thirtyish guy wearing a baseball cap, and then her gaze lands back on me. She sucks her lip into her teeth and I have to bounce my knee faster or I swear I'm going to fucking lose it. "Thinking what about me?" she asks, looking wary, interested, and exhausted.

Don't say it... "I was thinking about what it would be like to lick you... or bite you... either one really." It seems like I should regret it as soon as I say it, but regret is nowhere in my reach at the moment.

Her breathing quickens and her voice comes out shockingly unsteady for someone who has sex so much. "Then do it."

I blink, wondering if I heard her right through the massive amount of alcohol consuming my thoughts. "What?"

She holds my gaze steadily, even though she seems really nervous, her voice trembling. "Then bite me. Or lick me... whatever you want."

Every part of me is screaming not to do it, that I'm breaking my rules—rules I set for a reason. But desire and fucking tequila rampage the rational side of my mind. Drawn by a needy current, I lean forward, sweep her hair off her shoulder, keeping our eyes locked the entire time, and she quivers as my fingers brush her collarbone. When I reach the curve of her breast and trace a line above it, she bites her lip and groans. It's way too much. My body feels like it's going to combust. Before I can even acknowledge what I'm doing, I duck my head forward, slip my tongue out, and lick a path from her collarbone to the arch of her neck, grazing my teeth softly along the path.

"Oh God... Ethan." She shivers, clutching her hands at her side. "That feels way too good."

My eyes close and my breathing becomes ragged as I battle to pull back, keep my hands to myself, fearing that if I touch her, I'll rip her clothes off right here in the back of the cab. And I can't go there. It's not the same as when I hook up with random women. I can feel a connection with Lila and sex will ruin it, especially when I bail out afterward.

"Lila..." I trail off as her hand glides up the front of my shorts. "I think..."

I bite down on the sensitive spot right below her ear, just above her neck, not enough to break the skin, but enough that her shoulder jerks upward, and my hands clamp down on her waist, my fingertips delving into the fabric of her dress.

"Do it again," she whispers, breathless, her hand rubbing me hard. "Please."

I remember how she told me she never begged, and

suddenly all my doubts dissipate into the sea of alcohol swimming around in my head. I move my mouth upward to the tip of her earlobe, breathing hotly on her skin the entire way, and then I graze my teeth along her earlobe, slide my tongue out along it, and taste her just like I wanted to.

"Oh...my...God..." She releases a slow breath that's echoed by a whimper, her chest curving forward and pressing against mine.

I'm a little stunned by how much she's enjoying it and by how much I'm enjoying it, too, my moves fueled by an adrenaline surge and yearning in my body. I swear all the sexual tension inside me is pouring out in my motions. I've lost control. I place my hand on her bare leg and glide it up until it's fully underneath her dress, her skin searingly hot against mine, and my fingers graze the edge of her panties. The warmth and wetness that I felt when she had the towel on is there and all I want to do is say fuck my rules, slip my fingers inside her, and lay her down on the seat.

"Shit, Lila..." I sound choked as I squeeze my eyes shut, trying to decide what's right and what's wrong—what I *need* to do and what I *want* to do. "I think we should—"

The cab jerks to a stop and Lila and I quickly pull back, looking stunned. I'd seriously almost forgotten that we were in a cab. We're at the entrance of her apartment, the lampposts lighting up the parking lot. It's late, the neighborhood quiet, and the cab driver looks really pissed off.

"Jesus," she whispers, blinking her eyes open, and then she

aims her attention at the door. Her hand is still on my cock and my hand is still up her dress.

Reluctantly pulling my hand out from underneath her dress, she follows my lead, so we both have our hands to ourselves. I inch my legs out of the way so she can squeeze through and climb out, but she doesn't budge, looking at me expectantly.

"What?" I ask, confused.

"Aren't you going to come in?" Her voice carries confidence, but her slackened posture and uneasy demeanor portray self-doubt and the doubt makes me hesitate.

"Maybe I shouldn't," I say, torn between the good side of me and the bad, the drunken side and the sober side. *Rules. No relationships. What am I doing?* "It might not be a good idea… maybe…"

"Oh." Her eyes widen in horror and it surprises me. With all the flirting we've done and the guys Lila has slept with, I'd never expect her to look so hurt. And maybe that's why I decide to do it. Or maybe I'm just really, really stupid, but somehow I find myself getting out of the cab with her.

After we pay, we run in a drunken stupor to her complex, laughing about God knows what. When we reach her door, she fumbles with her keys, until finally she gets it open. She trips over her own feet, laughing as my fingers fold around her waist, catching her before she falls.

"You're a clumsy drunk," I say as she stands up straight, steadying herself by clutching on to my shoulders.

"And you're sexy when you're drunk," she says, biting her lip as she turns to face me.

My hands are still on her waist, my fingers gripping at her skin, wanting to feel more of it, but I'm still hesitating to take it any further. I know Lila—like *really* know her—and afterward, I'll have to see her again. What if it changes things between us? Do I care? As soon as I think it, I realize I do care about her more than I want to admit. She knows more about me than anyone. Jesus, she really does. I've told her shit about my parents, my druggy past, and my future loner plans and she's told me a lot of stuff about her and how her dad is verbally abusive and cheats on her mom all the time and her mom just accepts it. We know stuff about each other and I never even got that far with London.

Looking anxious and uncertain, Lila grips the front of my shirt and tugs me with her as she walks backward toward the hallway. Neither of us says anything. We don't turn on the lights. We just breathe loudly with each step, our eyes fastened together as we move our legs in sync.

Minutes, or maybe seconds, later, we're falling onto her bed. I brace myself with my arms, catching my weight so I don't crush her, and she gazes up at me, not saying anything, just breathing, her chest brushing against mine with every inhale. I want her so damn bad and I know she can tell since my hard-on is pressed up against her hip. Unable to tolerate the tension anymore, I lower my mouth toward hers, ready to kiss her, but she turns her head at the last second and my lips brush against her cheek instead. At first it's kind of weird, but then she slides her body upward, so her neck is in my face and I understand what she wants.

I press my lips to her skin, rolling my tongue out, and then drag my teeth gently across her neck as her hand finds the top of my shorts and she undoes the button and zipper. I shiver and groan as she grabs my cock and starts to rub me hard again. I bite down on her skin, maybe a little too roughly but she trembles with me, enjoying it, but she doesn't moan, which is disappointing because the sound of it in the cab nearly drove me crazy in a good way. I want to make her moan so badly that it becomes the sole focus of my thoughts. Moving my body downward, I create a path of kisses and gentle bites, nibbling soft skin until I reach the top of her dress. Then I suck the curve of her breast as I reach up and slip one of the straps down her shoulder.

"You are so beautiful," I mutter. The sight of her skin right there for me to taste is driving me fucking crazy and I don't think I've ever wanted to be inside someone as much as I do right now. I'm about to yank her other strap down so I can get a full view of her breasts when I realize how still she's gone. At first I think she's passed out, but when I pull back, she's just lying there motionless as she stares at the ceiling, fiddling with the platinum ring on her finger.

"Lila," I say, trying not to worry over what it could mean. That maybe I'd misread her and she really wasn't into this. Did I force her to do something? Shit. I didn't even remember to ask if she wanted this.

"Yeah," she answers numbly, without looking at me.

"Are you okay?"

"Yeah, I'm fine." She sounds as hollow as she looks. "Keep going."

I blink at her, stunned, and then I sit up, disconnecting the fiery connection between our bodies. "Keep going? Are you even into this?" I try not to sound upset, but it shows through the unevenness in my voice.

She still doesn't look at me, and when she speaks, her voice is flat. "Yeah, I want it."

"You sure as hell don't sound like you want it." I climb off the bed and zip my shorts back up. "How wasted are you?"

She finally meets my eyes and I'm taken back by the emptiness in them. And it's not because she's drunk. She knows what's going on, yet it looks like she feels nothing about it. As much as I hate to admit it, it stings, tears at my heart a little.

"I'm just going to go," I say, backing toward the door, pissed off at myself for getting into this situation to begin with. I knew better than to come here with her and now I can't take it back.

She sits up, the moonlight filtering through her window, illuminating her pale skin. Her eyes look black in the shadows. "If that's what you want," she says emotionlessly.

I have no idea how to take her right now. I could ask her questions, but we're both drunk, and honestly the hurt inside me is intensifying. "I'll call you tomorrow." It's all I say—all

I can say at the moment because I have no idea what's going on and I despise how freaked out I'm feeling over it.

I leave her in her room and she doesn't chase after me. By the time I reach the curb, I'm chewing myself out for ever going there because I know there's no way we can go back to what we were before. This is irrevocable.

Chapter Five

Lila

November is pretty much over and I'm running out of money and ways to escape the landlord. I know I need to get a job, but I've never worked before and I'm not qualified for any decent jobs. I guess I never really thought the whole being-on-your-own thing completely through. I feel like I'm standing at this fork in the road and both paths lead to places I don't want to go. I could go backward, but I don't want to go there either. My past is full of irreversible mistakes. I'm sure anyone who looked at me, when I was medicated anyway, wouldn't think I had any problems. But I'm seriously considering breaking down and asking someone for help. Asking Ella. My sister even, although she can barely take care of herself. I even went as far as calling her, but she cut the call short, saying she had to go to work. I could hear her son crying in the background, the one I've met only once because I moved away and haven't been back to San Diego since. We barely talk anymore, and when we do, the conversation is casual and rushed because she's always too overwhelmed with bills or her job as a waitress.

I could talk to Ethan, but I haven't really seen much of him since the whole club fiasco. I'm not even really sure what happened. I mean, he'd finally given me what I wanted, touching me and kissing me, and even through the alcohol it'd felt different, good for once, like I was safe and maybe worthy of being touched like that. But it lasted for only a moment and then the past caught up with me. The second we reached the bed I knew what was going to happen. He'd fuck me and then leave me and I'd be completely alone this time because Ethan is pretty much my only friend anymore and now I don't even know if he's that.

So I let the off switch flip me into a state of numbness and I moved through the motions, knowing what I was supposed to do but making myself disconnect from my emotions. What shocked me though is that he was upset about it. No guy has ever been upset about how I act. Then he'd left without finishing and I haven't talked to him since. I'm a little afraid too, afraid of what he saw in me that night or didn't see in me.

The last week has been really depressing and the only company I've really had is a random friendly call from my sister and my mother's phone calls that leave me feeling emptier than I did before them. She keeps making threats, telling me she's going to disown me if I don't get my ass back to San Diego. It's not too late, she keeps saying. Brentford Mansonfield is back from his six-month trip to Europe and he's looking to settle down. I could win him over, start again, and turn myself into someone worthy of the Summers name. I asked her if she really thought Brentford wanted used goods for a wife.

"Well, you're almost twenty-one, Lila," she'd said. "No one expects you to be a virgin."

"True, but I'm also kind of a whore," I'd responded, mainly because I'd had a couple glasses of wine and was feeling a little bit tipsy.

"Lila Summers, watch your mouth," she replied sharply. "You will not utter such things aloud."

"Why? It's true."

"I know it's true. I'm the one who had to come clean up the mess in New York."

"How can I forget," I said. "Since you're always reminding me."

"Lila, quit being a little bitch. I didn't raise you to be that way. I raised you to keep your mouth shut and to do what you were told."

I couldn't take the frustration building inside me anymore, so I let it explode and screamed into the phone, "Like you do with Dad and his slutty mistress!"

She called me a spoiled bitch and told me she was going to hang up. I told her okay, because I didn't really have that much more to say and she hasn't called me since.

It's overwhelmingly hot today, but I couldn't turn the fan on since it would rack up my already overdue power bill. I open the candy cane slash pill drawer again, reaching for the bottle at the bottom. Ethan gave me the candy canes as a Christmas present after I told him I'd never had a candy cane, and it was seriously the sweetest moment I've ever had with a guy.

"Are you fucking being serious right now?" he'd said. We were in his truck and it was late, the midnight sky above us as chilly winter air filled the cab and frosted the windows.

"Um...yeah...What's the big deal?" I'd wondered, turning sideways in the seat to face him.

"Because it's a fucking candy cane." He'd gaped at me unfathomably. "It's like the most common Christmas candy there is. My mom even puts them all over our tree every year."

"Oh, I've never had a Christmas tree either," I admitted, which made him gape at me only longer. "What? She thinks that the pine needles on real ones are too messy and artificial ones are too tacky."

Later that night, he'd given me an entire box of them. He didn't wrap them or anything, just dropped them on my lap when I'd been sitting on his sofa in the living room of his parents' house.

"There you go." He'd said it like it was such an inconvenience for him as he flopped down in the recliner.

I'd smiled, then leaned over and gave him a hug before I unwrapped one. As I started sucking on it, I told him it was delicious and he'd made a dirty remark about my lips. I made a comeback about the zipper on his pants being undone and that I could see his special man parts bulging out. He'd rolled his eyes, but then checked his zipper anyway. I started to giggle and ended up dropping the candy cane on my leg. I was wearing a dress and the candy stuck to my thigh.

"Okay, maybe I don't like them," I'd said, pulling a disgusted face as I picked it up from my leg. I tried to wipe off the stickiness with my hand, but that only made everything stickier.

"Here, let me help you," Ethan muttered, his eyes locked on my leg. I thought he was going to go get me a paper towel or something, but instead he got up from the recliner and dropped down on his knees in front of me. His dark hair hung in his eyes as he peered over my knees, smirking at me.

"What are you doing?" I asked, intrigued but slightly nervous. I mean he was super hot and everything, but I was fully sober and could feel everything going on, like my accelerating pulse and the weird flip my stomach did.

His eyes darkened as he ran his hand up my leg and it made my skin instantly ignite with stifling, overwhelmingly passionate heat. It was a new sensation for me since foreplay was pretty much absent with any of the people I'd hooked up with. The feeling was piquing my curiosity so I let my legs fall open just a little and suddenly he seemed like the nervous one. I kept thinking about how much I wanted another pill because I could feel way too much, but then I'd have to get up and break the moment.

Ethan had paused with his hand resting on the top of my thigh. I traced the lines of the tattoos on his arms, biting my lip as my heart leaped inside my chest. His breathing became ragged and his palms were starting to sweat the longer we sat there, unmoving in the silence and glow from the twinkly lights on the Christmas tree. Then he did it. He angled his face down, his lips parted, and his tongue slipped out as he licked the candy cane stickiness off my skin.

I dug my fingernails into the arm of the chair and moaned, a loud, blissful moan that surprised me, along with the burst of warmth that flashed through my body. He responded with a sharp intake of his breath and I quivered uncontrollably. I wanted to run my fingers through his hair, touch him, push his face up just a little bit farther, and make him lick me in places that would send me into a euphoric, uncontrolled spiral. But then he quickly sucked my skin, nipping at it before pulling away.

I frowned disappointedly up at him. "Seriously?"

He shrugged, dropping down into the chair. "What?" He eyed me over, like he was waiting for me to announce that he'd gotten me all hot and bothered. "Is something wrong?" He'd pressed back a smirk, like he was the funniest person in the world. "I'm just waiting around for my Christmas present."

Two could play at this game. Smirking back, I unhooked the front clasp of my red lacy bra through my top, then slid the straps down my shoulders, managing to get it off without flashing him. Then I threw it at his face. "Merry Christmas."

Most guys would have grinned or said some dirty comment, but Ethan just flicked the little red bow on my bra, then shrugged and set it down on the armrest of the chair. "I've seen sexier," he said, his grin shining through his eyes.

With my mouth hanging open, I tossed a candy cane at him and it hit him in the head. He laughed, picked it up and unwrapped it, and then popped it into his mouth. "Damn, these are good," he said, smiling as he rolled the candy along his tongue.

I think that's when I realized how much I liked him. Not because he was being an ass or because he gave me candy canes, but because he'd stopped kissing my thigh. He knew enough about me—how easy I was—to know that he could have pretty much gotten me to do whatever he wanted, yet he didn't. Even if it was because he didn't like me, I still kind of liked that he stopped, even if it left me sexually frustrated. I'd had sex with guys before who later made it clear they didn't even like me, yet they still had sex with me because I was an "easy lay." And I was left with self-hatred stirring inside me because deep down I knew they were right. I'm good for only one thing. A one-night stand, a good lay, a moment of distraction, and I'll pretty much do whatever they ask, even when I don't want to.

But now the good thing I had with Ethan is gone, thanks to my fucked-up head. It makes me loathe myself even more, knowing just how good of a guy Ethan is. He'd stopped it, refusing to have sex with the numb version of me. I'm still baffled over it.

Sighing, I force myself out of the memory and return my attention to what's under the pile of candy canes and pick up the orange bottle. I take a couple, then lay down on the bed, on my back with my legs and arms out to my side, just like they were that day my life changed for the worst six years ago, when *he* used me and then abandoned me. I've been on a downhill decline ever since, but the good thing is I've barely been able to feel it. I feel the soaring rush from the pills and then the crash from the wine as the two substances mix and collide inside me. They're diluting each other, so I turn on my side and take a few more pills and somewhere between the sixth or the seventh my thoughts start to melt together. Until I feel empty.

Alone.

And I desperately want to find someone to fill the void.

❧

I'm way too out of it to be out here, but I can't find my way back to my apartment. So I keep wandering aimlessly around the parking lot with no real destination, and I can't even remember why I came outside in the first place. I think it might have been the fear of being compressed between the shrinking walls in my house that made me go outside, but I'm not sure.

This older guy comes up to me as I make my way over to a carport and he tells me about this party up the street. I mutter something about not really wanting to go with him, but then he takes ahold of my arm and kind of guides me along, or forces me (I sometimes have a hard time distinguishing between the two) toward the street.

He keeps talking about swimming or hitting or something, but the grogginess in my head barely allows me to decipher half of the words he's saying. His lips keep moving and he has nice, soft, full-looking lips, and there's this scar on the bottom one. I thought his eyes were green, but when we step into the house, underneath the light, I realize they're blue. His hair is way too long for my taste and he's wearing this ratty-looking T-shirt that makes me crinkle my nose with distaste.

"I think I have to..." I try to say *go*, but my lips have gotten really numb. I stumble over my shoes, which aren't fastened.

"You look really beautiful tonight," the guy whispers in my ear and I'm relieved I caught the whole sentence.

"Thanks..." I trail off as the stereo is cranked up and the floor starts to vibrate beneath us. Everyone starts dancing and shouting as they drink beers and grind against each other.

There are people crammed into a small living room and the furniture has been pushed out of the way. The kitchen to my right is lined with empty beer bottles and there's a large bucket filled with ice and drinks on the table. The loudness and chaos kind of reminds me of being at Ella's, where everyone could just roam free and do whatever they wanted. The first time I witnessed it I thought it was insane, but now it kind of feels like maybe this is the kind of place I belonged the whole time.

"Do you want a drink?" the guy shouts over the music as he holds on to my arm.

I nod, relaxing. *He doesn't seem that bad.* "Yes, please!"

Then he smiles and it's a dark smile, one masked with an alternate meaning. I've seen this smile before right before *he* tied me to the bed. I'm not sure what the alternate meaning is but I can't seem to concentrate on it for long enough to care. He releases my arm and I brace my hand against the wall nearby so I don't fall down. I want to dance, because I love to dance. But I'm dizzy and vomit burns at the back of my throat. I try to recall how many pills I'd taken. Two...No, I took more, didn't I? After the landlord knocked on my door? Yes, but how many did I take. Four...five...eight. God, I've completely lost track and things are starting to get dark and chilly, not just around me but in my head. The song switches and I try to focus on the beat. The guy who brought me here returns. He hands me a beer. I drink it. Somehow I end up dancing with him. He's grabbing me roughly, forcing me against his body as he grinds against my hips. I'm not sure if I'm into it, so I try to back away.

"Where you goin'?" he wonders, pulling me back.

"I want to..." *What do I want?*

He shakes his head and probes his fingernails into my arms. I feel the skin puncture and the pain spans throughout my entire body. I try to shout, but the sound is lost in the music. He grins, all desire and need, just like every other guy who exists on the planet.

"Come here, baby." He presses me against his chest, his hand sliding underneath my back, and I find myself wishing he were Ethan so I wouldn't feel so unsafe. He grabs at my butt, touches me, and just like that a switch flips off inside my head. Like always, I become numb, every emotion draining out of me. Suddenly, it feels like I'm watching the guy as he gropes my ass, feels my breast, kisses my neck, presses our bodies together. I can't feel a single thing, don't want to. I don't deserve to. I'm worthless. *A whore*, like everyone always tells me.

He starts to lead me through the crowd, to the hallway, and I'm pretty sure he's going to take me to a room and do whatever he wants to me, when my eyes roll into the back of my head and my legs start to give out as my stomach burns.

"I think I'm going to throw up," I say and groan and the guy scoots back faster than the beat of the song with his hands out in front of him like he's afraid to touch me.

I take off, shoving through the crowd, and run out the front door, leaving it open as I stumble outside, then hurry down the stairs. One of my shoes gets caught in the bottom step and I can't get it out, so instead I wiggle my foot out of my shoe. Then I hunch over and fall to my knees in a bed of tulips and bushes. My shoulders jerk as I dry heave, feeling like I need to throw up, but nothing will come out of my mouth. My heart is beating rapidly, slamming against my ribs, and my skin is coated in sweat. I'm having a hard time keeping my eyes open and I fall back into the bushes, landing in the moist dirt on my back. I see the stars. They're gorgeous. I wish I could touch them. It feels like I can.

I lie there forever, feeling my heart beat faster as my

stomach vines into painful knots. Then my butt starts ringing, or maybe it's my head...no, it's my phone. Yes, definitely my phone. Rolling to my side, I feel the back pocket in my dress and retrieve my phone. I let my thumb fall on the talk button and then put the phone to my ear.

"Hello." The sound of my voice hurts my head.

"Seriously?" Ethan says, sounding more pissed off than he usually does. "Again?"

"Huh..." I clutch my pulsating head.

"What do you mean, huh?" he snaps. "I can tell you're drunk again, which means you probably need me to come pick you up from some guy's house." He sounds venomously jealous, and in the pit of my stomach, I like it.

"No, not drunk," I mutter. "I'm out of it."

"I can tell."

"I think...I think...I took too much...this time." It's becoming harder to breathe, my chest constricting and it's bearing weight down on my body.

"Too much what?" he asks and I think I hear concern in his voice. Maybe, but I could be wrong.

"The stuff..." I try to snap my fingers, attempting to think of the word, but I can't tell if I still have fingers. "Those pills I have."

"What pills?" His voice sounds all high and abnormally off pitch.

"Nothing...never mind...I'm really tired...I'm going to go..." I start to let my arm fall to my side.

"Lila, don't hang up!" he shouts through the phone and I can hear a lot of banging in the background. "Where are you? At your place?"

"No...I'm in some bushes...and tulips." I swat my arm at this blurry spot forming above me. "Ethan, it's really cold."

"It's not that cold." His voice is harsh and makes me feel even colder inside. "Now just tell me where you are and keep your God damn eyes open."

"Okay..." I blink fiercely, struggling to get my eyelids to stay open. "But I don't know where I am."

"What do you mean?" he asks and I hear the engine of his truck roar. "How the hell can you not know where you are?"

"Well...this guy took me somewhere...and I don't remember where..."

"Can you recognize anything?"

"Stars...and..." I trail off, letting the sleepiness overtake me. He says something, but I'm too exhausted to answer.

"Lila!" he yells.

My eyes snap open. "Yeah..."

"Tell me what's around you."

"Bushes...and stars...and a building..."

"What does the building look like?"

"Like every other building out there..." My head flops to the side. "There's this really weird flashing pink bird thingy at the entrance...That could be in my head though."

"Thank fucking God." He sounds a little relieved. "I know where you are." He says a bunch of other stuff, but I can't tell what he's saying, so I just drop the phone because it's too heavy anyway. Then I gaze up at the stars and let myself fall into the darkness and numbness that I've become so familiar with. In fact, it's really starting to feel like home.

～

"You're so beautiful," he says, sliding his hand up my thigh. "Your skin's so soft, too."

I force a smile, even though the way he's touching me feels wrong. Everything about the situation feels wrong, but at the same time it feels right, because the way Sean's looking at me right now makes me feel worshipped and loved. "Thank you," I say, which makes him grin this adorable grin that makes him look younger than he is.

"You're welcome," he says and leans forward, giving me a soft peck on the nose. "You're amazing," he whispers against my skin, peppering kisses down to my jawline as his fingers drift up my plaid skirt. "I want to touch you everywhere . . . kiss you all over."

I place my hand on his chest, holding him back just a little so that I can look him in the eyes. "Why don't you ever touch me in public? Is it because you were lying about not being married?" I eye the ring on his finger.

His eyes turn cold, his mouth setting in a firm line as he leans away, leaving his hand on my upper thigh, but his fingers stiffen. "No, I told you I'm not married. It was a gift and you know why we can't be seen in public. Age matters to people, Lila."

I run my fingers through his soft hair, worried I've pushed him too far. "You're not that much older than me and it doesn't matter to me anyway."

He stares at me like I'm incompetent. "Lila, don't be stupid. They would rip us apart. Everyone would." He starts to reach for the door handle of his car. "Maybe I should go."

"No, don't." I grab a handful of his suit jacket and pull him back to me, terrified that he's going to leave me. "I-I'm sorry I brought it up. Please, just go back to what you were doing."

He narrows his eyes, looking like he's deliberating whether he should stay or go, whether he's too good for me or not. He is. I know that.

"You want me to do back to what I was doing?" he asks, cocking his head to the side as he assesses me. There's something in his eyes that is both thrilling and terrifying and makes my skin tingle in a way that it never has.

I nod, but with a lack of confidence. "Yes."

He places his hand back on my thigh. He slowly starts to travel upward to the bottom of my skirt, briefly lingering at the hem before slipping his fingers underneath the fabric. I instinctively tense and he seems pleased by it. "Are you sure, Lila?" He reaches the fabric of my panties. "You really want me to go back to what I was doing?"

I open my mouth to say that I'm not sure and that he's making me feel dirty, but then he forces his fingers inside me with a rough, almost violent movement. I'm not sure what to do because it hurts and feels wrong yet it also feels good.

He starts to move his fingers inside me, almost forcefully. I think about telling him to stop, but the wonderful and horrifying feelings of bliss and need silence my lips. Then he moves his free hand around to the back of my head and grabs violently at my hair.

"Ow, that hurts," I mutter through a moan with my neck being forced to arch back.

"Good," he says, his eyes darkening with pleasure. He pulls even harder on my hair and pain and pleasure flood my body.

My feelings become hard to decipher as I reach forward and clutch on to his arms as my body heats up and I can't breathe. When he pulls his finger out of me, I'm not sure whether I enjoyed it, regretted it, or both. I'm not sure how I'm supposed to feel.

Ethan

At first I think she's at some guy's house and even though I don't want to go to that jealous place inside me, I do. It pisses me off because only a week ago, I was touching her and all was great until she zoned out and it seemed like she didn't want to do anything with me.

But then I notice the dazed sound of her voice and none of that matters. I've heard the distance and dazed sound in London's voice many times and in my own, too, when I used to get smashed. An alarm goes off in my head and all I can seem to think about is walking away from London the last time, right after the needle entered her arm. Then Lila starts talking about pills and I remember the prescription bottle in the couch cushion. That's when I really start to freak out. I'm trying not to panic as I try figure out where she is, but she seems to have no idea. Then she mentions the pink bird and a small amount of relief washes over me. I drive by that damn pink bird twice a day to and from work. It's not too far from my house, only a few minutes away. I keep talking to her to make sure she stays awake, debating whether I should call an ambulance or something.

I can still hear her voice when I spot the pink bird in front of the apartment complex that's tucked between a house and a gas station. But when I'm pulling in, there's a thud on the line and then it goes silent. For a split second all I can think about is how I'm never going to see her again, that she's gone, and I almost become paralyzed. I've never felt so much adrenaline rush through my body and my heart starts to slam against the inside of my chest.

"Shit." I swing a hard left and slam on my brakes, stopping on the curb, the tire ramping up onto it. She said she was in the bushes, but there are bushes everywhere. I hop out of the truck and shout. "Lila!" No one answers. I run around the two-story brick buildings situated inside the fenced parking lot, shouting out her name as I unlock my cell phone screen to call 911. I spot a flashy high-heeled shoe near the bottom of one of the stairways and I pick it up, wondering if it could be Lila's. It looks like something she probably wouldn't wear and more like something a stripper would own and there are a lot of those around here.

When I turn around I see feet sticking out of the shrubbery

and one of them is missing a shoe. I run over and drop to my knees beside Lila, sprawled out on the ground, taking in the paleness of her skin and the glossiness in her eyes. Suddenly a feeling rushes over me, rams me square in the chest, gut, legs—everywhere. Looking at her, like this, makes the possibility of losing her much more real.

"I feel sick, Ethan," she murmurs and then rolls onto her side, tucking her hands under her head and closing her eyes.

I carefully slide my arm underneath her neck and slant her head up, patting her cheek so she'll open her eyes. "Lila, what did you take? Can you remember the name?"

"What I always take," she slurs, blinking her eyes open. "That stuff in my drawer."

Shit. Shit. Shit. "And what's that?"

"That stuff...you know...those pills that make you all awake...God, Ethan, I can't...I can't remember the name of them. It's a really...*really*...big word."

I glance at the dirt and the bushes around us. "Did you throw up?"

"No..." She slowly sighs, her chest rising and falling. "I feel like I need to, though. My stomach hurts really, really bad."

I help her sit up, holding on to her arms, which have red welts on them that look like marks left from someone's fingers digging into her skin. "Okay, I'm going to turn you around and I want you to throw up, even if you have to stick your finger down your throat."

Her head bobs up and down as she nods. "Okay."

I guide her to the side and help her turn so she's hunched over on her hands and knees. I keep my arm underneath her stomach, supporting her weight. She stays still for a minute with her mouth open, and then she finally shoves her finger down her throat. I angle my head to the side, staring at the parking lot as she pukes in the bushes. By the time she's finished, she's shaking and her skin is sweaty and paler than it already was.

"All right, let's get you to the hospital," I say as she sits down and rests her head against my chest.

"No, no hospitals." She shakes her head and peers up at me. In the glow of the streetlights, her eyes look black, or maybe it's because her pupils are dilated.

"Yes, to the hospital." I get to my feet and scoop her up in my arms, bearing her dead weight as she nuzzles her face against my chest.

She gripes about going to the hospital, but only until we make it to the truck. Once I get her in the passenger seat, she relaxes and I buckle her seat belt over her chest. I drive straight to the hospital, knowing that there is no room for mistakes in the state she's in. It's why I stopped doing drugs. Why I went back to overthinking everything, even though I didn't want to. I learned firsthand what can happen. How one slipup can take you away forever, and thinking about the fact that Lila might be reaching that point terrified me more than I would have thought. It scares me to death, the thought that I might lose her. At that moment, I realize that Lila has become more than a friend. Much, much more.

Chapter Six

Lila

I wake up unable to remember what happened the night before. I should be okay with the confusion, since I'm used to it, but for some reason I feel more dirty and ashamed than I normally do.

The scent of cologne flowing from the blanket that's over me is familiar. I've smelled it before and it comforts me. I force my eyes open and instantly recognize the band posters and drum set in the corner of the room. I sigh with relief. I'm in Ethan's room, lying in his bed.

"Thank God," I mutter, gradually sitting up and my stomach muscles constrict in protest. I wrap my arm around my stomach and realize that I'm wearing one of Ethan's shirts.

Holy crap, did I sleep with him? I run my hands through my tangled hair, sifting through my hazy memories. But the only things I can remember are stars, bushes, beeping machines, and the smell of cleaner.

"Feeling better?" The sound of Ethan's voice makes me jump and my stomach churns from the motion.

"Ah…" I moan, hunching over and clutching my tender stomach with my gaze fixed on the comforter in front of me. "What the heck happened last night?"

I hear him walk toward the bed and then the mattress bows as he sits down on the foot of it, making sure to keep some space between us. "You can't remember anything at all?"

I shake my head, still looking down, feeling mortified for reasons I can't explain. Then I notice the hospital band on my wrist. "No…I can remember wandering around the apartment complex…Then this guy took me somewhere…" I pause, daring to peer up. "And then all I can remember are stars and the smell of cleaner."

He's wearing a black-and-red T-shirt, his hair is damp, like he just got out of the shower, and there are holes in his jeans. "You pretty much overdosed," he says, cautiously watching me.

He thrums his fingers on his knees, considering something. "You know, I've never been one for pressing people about their problems." He slides his knee on the bed, turning sideways so he's facing me. "I've never been a big fan of talking about my own shit and so I usually avoid trying to make people talk about theirs unless they're being stupid and right now every single part of me is screaming at me to make you tell me what happened." He pauses and I start to speak, but he talks over me. "And don't try to tell me that you're taking that prescription because of a doctor's orders. You told me last night on the way to the hospital that you've pretty much been abusing them since you were fourteen, something I probably should have just told the doctors, but I didn't want to get you into trouble." He stops and waits for something. A thanks? An explanation? The truth? I honestly don't know and I don't want to tell him anything either.

"I don't know what to say." I shut my eyes and summon a deep breath, chanting in my head not to cry. But I feel disembodied from my emotions and my stomach feels like I've done an infinite amount of sit-ups. All I want to do is lie down, sleep, and forget that all of this happened.

"How about the truth?" Ethan states cautiously, sounding less angry, and I feel him shift closer to me on the bed. "You know I get the whole substance-abuse thing."

My eyelids snap open at his awful accusation. "I don't have a substance-abuse problem," I say, seething and tossing the blankets off me. "It's a prescription. Doctor's orders." I swing my legs over the bed and push to my feet. A rush of blood flees from my head and my knees instantly buckle. I reach for the metal bedpost as I collapse, but Ethan jumps up and catches me in his arms right before I hit the floor.

I blow out a breath, looking at the wall beside me as he holds my weight up. I feel like an idiot. "Let me go. I can walk."

"You're supposed to be resting." He helps me back to the bed and I begrudgingly sit down. "*Doctor's orders.*"

I press my lips together, shaking my head. "Ethan, please just don't. I don't need this from you right now."

"Please don't what? Talk about what I saw last night? Because I'm not going to do that. It fucking scared the shit out of me, Lila...seeing you trashed out of your mind like that." His eyes are wide and filled with panic as he sits down on the bed again, leaving a little less space between us as he roughly rakes his fingers through his hair. He looks stressed out and exhausted. "And as much as I hate to push you to talk about it, I feel like I have to. I can't...I don't want anything..." He's fumbling over his words and it seems to be frustrating him. He's acting very out of character and I wonder if something else is wrong.

"You don't have to do anything," I mutter, frowning down at my lap. "I'm not your girlfriend or anything—you don't owe me anything. You should have just told the hospital I tried to kill myself. Then they could be dealing with me and you wouldn't have to."

He pauses, contemplating what I said. "You're my friend and that's equally as important, if not more important... You're important..." His forehead creases as he says it, like he's confused himself as much as he's confused me. He starts to reach for me, as if he's going to put his hand on my cheek, but then pulls his hand back.

I cover my mouth and shake my head as tears start to form in the corners of my eyes. "I can't."

He raises his eyebrows inquiringly. "Can't what?"

"I'm not supposed to talk about stuff like this."

"Like what?"

"Like this." I wave my hand down in front of my terrible state. "All messed up and not put together."

His head cocks to the side as he crooks his eyebrow. "Lila, I've told you some of my fucked-up stories about drugs and sex and you've seen where I live—you know what kind of a home I was raised in and what my parents did to each other. Messed up is nothing new to me."

"That doesn't matter," I say exasperatedly as I gather my hair around the nape of my neck. "I'm not supposed to be this way, or at least no one's supposed to know that I'm like this."

"You keep saying *like this* but I'm still trying to figure out like what?" His eyes scroll over my body carefully, as if he's searching for visible wounds. And there are a few, on my ankles and waist and even a very faint one on my wrist, but most people never notice them. "As far as I can tell, the only thing you're acting like is someone who needs to talk about their problems." He's being nice and it's only making me feel worse.

"It'd be easier if you just yelled at me," I say, releasing my hair and spanning my arms out to the side. "Or left me alone. That's what you usually do."

"Easy is overrated," he replies. "And I can't leave you alone this time. Not about this. I'll hate myself if I do."

"Ethan, please just take me home," I plead, wrapping my arms around myself. "I just need to go home."

"No," he responds stubbornly. "I'm not going to just let you run home and pop a pill. You need help."

My body and mind are yearning for a pill and only one thing is going to make it better. I keep running my fingers through my hair, trying to subdue the anxiety overcoming me. When I raise my head back up, I force a neutral expression on my face. "Look, Ethan, I appreciate your help and everything last night, but seriously I'm okay. I just need to go home and get something to eat and shower and I'll be better."

"Pftt, don't try to bullshit me," he says callously, folding his arms and leaning against the footboard. "You can't bullshit a bullshitter."

"You're not a bullshitter," I argue, slamming my hands down on the mattress, wanting to scream at him. "At all."

"I was once," he reminds me. "Over stuff just like this. It's what people with addictions do. You'll do whatever you can— say whatever it takes—to get to the next high."

My mouth plummets to a frown and I clasp my hands out in front of me, desperation coursing through my body more toxically than the pills do. "Ethan, please, pretty please just take me home and forget about this." My voice is high and pleading. "Then you don't have to deal with it."

He considers what I said, then gets to his feet, and I think I've won. "No, I'm not going to just forget." He backs for the door and grabs the doorknob as he steps out of the room. "You know where the shower is when you're ready to take one."

"I don't have any clothes!" I shout and then throw a pillow

at him, feeling the angry monster inside of me surfacing. I'm plummeting into a dark hole filled with every negative thing that makes up my life and I don't have any pills on me to bring me back up to the light. "Why are you doing this to me?"

"Because I care about you," he says matter-of-factly and then he shuts the door.

No one's ever said they care about me, not even my sister, Abby, and his words should make me feel better. But they don't. If anything, the craving and hunger for another pill amplifies, ripping through my body, leaving abrasions that only a dose will heal. Because I don't deserve for him to care about me. Everything I've done, I've done to myself. Everything—where I am and who I am—is all my fault.

I sit on the bed for a while, stewing in my own anger as I stare out the window, rocking my body, trying to still the nervous energy inside me. It's a sunny day, the sky blue and clear and breathtaking. I should be out suntanning by the pool, but no, I'm stuck in here, feeling like I'm going to rip my hair out. And the longer I sit, the more desperate I become until finally I get up from the bed. Fighting the pain in my stomach, legs, and head, I search his room for my clothes. I find them draped over the stool in back of the drum set.

"Jackpot," I say and wind around the drums, picking up my white dress, and then I frown. It's caked in mud and some sort of gross green stuff and it smells like puke. I tap my fingers on the sides of my legs, trying to figure out what to do. Half my instincts are screeching at me not to put the filthy dress on and go out into public looking so disheveled, but the other half of my instincts, the ones connected to the pills, are conflicting with how I was brought up.

I ball my hands into fists, gritting my teeth, constraining a scream, and then slip Ethan's shirt off. I put the dress on, and then pull the shirt back on. I comb my fingers through my hair and then glance in the mirror. I look like death: pale skin, bloodshot eyes, and makeup smeared everywhere. Again, I'm torn. Run to what I need or hide what I am?

Turning in a circle, I search the floor for my shoes. I look under the bed, in the closet, near the dresser, but they're nowhere to be found. I give up and head for the door. There's only one way to get out of Ethan's house without jumping out a window or off a balcony and that's to walk through the living and out the front door. I wonder if he's in there, if he'll argue with me again. It doesn't matter, though. I'm a grown woman and I can walk out of a house if I want to.

I straighten my shoulders, open the door, and step out into the hall. There's music playing from the stereo in the living room, so I'm surprised when I walk in the room and he's not in there. He isn't in the kitchen either. For a second I wonder where he is, but then I realize it doesn't really matter. All that does matter is that I'm free to leave without further confrontation.

I open the door, step outside, and blink fiercely against the sunlight. Shielding my eyes with my hand, I hurry down the stairs and walk swiftly for the bus stop. I know I look crazy, with no shoes on, a baggy T-shirt over my dress, and my hair and makeup all ratty. But for the first time in my life I don't care about my looks. All I care about is getting home, so I can sedate the hungry beast waking up inside my chest.

Ethan

I'm wondering if I'm seriously in over my head. I realized this when she admitted to me last night while she was in the hospital waiting to get her stomach pumped that she's been taking the pills since she was fourteen to numb her pain from something. I probably should have just told the doctors the truth and that she was an addict or even that she was suicidal, but I was afraid she'd get in trouble. Plus, she'd thrown up quite a few times by the time we got there, so there was little proof of what happened left in her. All she had to do was dazzle them with a smile and feed them a bullshit lie of mixing too much wine with a little too many pills and they let her go. Although, I wonder if they really believed her, or if the insanely busy emergency room aided her easy release.

Part of me wishes I would have spoken up. Then maybe they could have assisted her with the approaching withdrawals. When my dad came off of them things got really intense and the medication he'd been taking was dangerous to quit cold turkey so he had to come off it in low doses. My mom helped him through it, battling with him every single God damn day when he'd ask for more, and only giving him a little, slowly weaning him off them. And I start to wonder if that's what I'm facing—if this is how it'll be when Lila comes off the pills she's been taking. If so, can I do it? Can I help her get better? Especially if she doesn't want to? Part of me wants to just walk away and leave the drama behind, but the feelings I have for Lila, the ones I realized I had when I saw her on the ground like that, beg me to help her.

But I'm not a fan of drama and helping with other people's problems, partly because it's overwhelming and partly because I'm worried I'll mess up, like I did with London. And Lila's is an addiction. I've seen it many times. Felt it. Had it consume every single cell in my body, mind, and fucking soul. I had to get over it myself and it was one of the hardest things I've ever done. And I did drugs for only a year. Lila's been popping pills for over six years. That's a fucking deep addiction. Plus, I know nothing about what's even behind her addiction. What I do know is the wounds behind the addiction are even harder to heal.

After I walk out of her room, I crank up some music and sit down at my computer in the living room. Then I start researching opiate addiction and find the name of the one she told me she was taking when she was barely awake. What I find out pretty much describes what I saw with my dad. Anxiety. Irritability. Vomiting. Tremors. Confusion. The list is pretty long. And it says for long-term drug abusers either medication should be used during detox or the user should gradually be weaned off from it, like my dad was.

Jesus, it would be so much easier to check her into a facility. Although I'd have to convince her to check herself in and that seems fucking complicated, too. Everything does at the moment. I'm not sure if I can do this.

I try to figure out what to do—what kind of person I really am, the kind who can just walk away from a situation like this and not help her or the kind who wants to do the right thing and help her overcome the very hard obstacle of quitting. I think about the last time I walked away and what resulted from it. I don't want to go down that road again, but I also don't want to help her and fuck up her recovery because I did something wrong. What I need is some advice from someone who's helped someone get through a tough time in their life.

I crank up some music and then wander back to Micha's old room and lie down on the floor. I retrieve my cell phone from my pocket and delete all the text messages Rae has sent me over the last three days—the ones I've refused to read—before I open up the dial screen. I hesitate for probably ten minutes before I finally dial Micha's number. It's weird to be asking advice from him—usually it's the other way around. But he's been through something like this with Ella, who'd run away and completely changed her identity after her mom committed suicide. She had a lot of psychological problems, but Micha stuck by her side and never gave up on her even when things got hard.

"What the fuck?" he answers with a laugh. "You hardly ever call me."

"Yeah, I know." I rub my forehead with my hand, totally out of my comfort zone. Normally, I'm the one listening to his problems. "I have a question…about Ella."

"Okay…" He sounds really lost and I don't blame him. I'm acting like a weirdo right now.

"All those problems that you went through with her…was it hard?"

"Um, yeah. Problems usually are."

I know I'm not verbalizing myself very well. I do better with a pen and paper. "Yeah, I know that, but was it hard to help her out with stuff when you knew it was going to be hard?"

It takes him a second. "Are you asking if I ever considered bailing out and not helping her?"

"Kind of," I say. "But not bailing out so much as worrying about even getting into it with her because you knew it was going to be a pain in the ass to help her get past her problems and you weren't sure if you could handle it or even really help her."

"Not really," he answers guardedly. He's never been too comfortable talking about Ella's problems. "I mean, in the beginning I hesitated to be with her, but that's only because I knew she wasn't ready for anything more than friendship."

"Well, what if you were just trying to help her as a friend?" I ask. "And you knew you were just going to stay friends. Would you still have helped her then, even if you knew you'd have to deal with a lot of shit?"

"Of course," he says straightforwardly. "I know I'm going to sound all stupid and cheesy here, but isn't that what friends are for? I mean, you've always kind of been there for me."

I snort a laugh, rolling my eyes. "You know you sound like some kind of cartoon special, right? The ones with bouncing kangaroos that talk about how wonderful and neat it is to have a friend."

"Bouncing kangaroos?"

"Hey, I've never been a cartoon person so how the hell should I know what kind of characters they have now?"

"I'm pretty sure there aren't any kangaroos."

"Okay, well, it doesn't really matter." I waver. "So you'd still have helped her?"

"Absolutely," he assures me. "And I've never once regretted doing it."

I'm not sure if I feel better or not now. "All right. Well, thanks I guess."

"Not what you were wanting to hear, huh?" he asks.

"No . . . honestly I'm not really sure what I wanted to hear." I sigh as I sit up, dragging my fingers through my hair. "But anyway, I'll let you go."

"What? You're not going to explain where this really random phone call came from?"

"I can't just yet."

"All right, gotcha." He hesitates. "Totally off the subject, but you aren't by chance coming to San Diego anytime soon, are you?"

I rub the back of my tensed neck muscles. "No, why?"

"It's nothing," he replies and I hear a door shut. "It's just that Ella and I are thinking about having the wedding in a month, around Christmas time, and I was thinking that maybe you and Lila could fly or drive out together."

"In a month?" I question, lowering my hand to my side. "Isn't that, like, really soon?"

"Soon for two people who've known each other for almost seventeen years?"

"Yeah, good point, I guess." I try not to roll my eyes because I think marriage is ridiculous. Look at my father and mother. They are prime examples of what can happen to a couple if they forever bind themselves to each other.

"So will you?"

"Has Ella talked to Lila about this?" I ask. "Or talked to her at all lately?"

"I don't think so," he says, sounding confused. "Why? What's up?"

"It's nothing." I get to my feet and head for the door. "I'm down for California, but I'm going to let Ella ask Lila if she thinks she can go."

"Sounds like a plan, man." He turns on some music, letting it play quietly in the background. "Talk to you later, then."

"Sounds good." I hang up and take a deep breath before going out into the hall and veering to the left toward my bedroom. The door is open and I know right away that Lila's gone and I don't doubt for one second where she's going. I've been in that desperate place before and it's an overwhelming place to be trapped in. It makes not wanting to help her feel easy and wanting to help her feel hard, but the feelings that I have for Lila, ones I didn't know existed until I saw her laying on the ground completely out of it, also make it impossible to turn my back on her.

I hesitate for a moment, thinking about everything Lila and I have been through, the long talks, the flirting, the touches that almost led to something but never fully did, the way she makes me feel, the fact that I've broken my rules with her a ton of times, the fear that overtook my body when I saw her in the bushes. As I remember it all, it makes it slightly easier to make my decision. I snatch my truck keys off the dresser and head for the front door, knowing I've got to beat her to the apartment, otherwise this is going be even harder than it already is.

As I trot down the stairs, gripping my keys in my hand, I try to mentally prepare myself for what I'm diving into so hopefully I'll be able to handle it. At the bottom of the stairs, I take out my phone and call my mom to get some advice on the right way to try to wean someone off an opiate addiction, since she's done it herself. I just pray to God Lila and I won't turn into what they turned into during it, yelling and fighting and my mom always crying secretly in her room over the things my dad said to her. I can't picture this happening, at least the crying part, but I can't erase everything I saw when I was a kid.

There're so many emotions crashing through me at the

moment as I make the final decision to be there for Lila, but out of all them, what really gets to me is the fact that I'm going to help her, because I care about her—more than care. That in and of itself is fucking terrifying, more than running head-on into traffic. More than walking into a room and looking at the girl you thought you might love, only to find out she has no idea who you are anymore and that you might have never really known her and never will.

Chapter Seven

Lila

I'm sweating and it's not from the heat. In fact, I think the air is kind of chilly, but it feels like I'm drenched in sweat. I need to get to my apartment and I *need* to take a pill. Now. Before I lie down and die in the middle of this bus. God, this is the worst I've ever been and if my mom and dad saw me they'd be so embarrassed they'd probably never call me again. Which doesn't seem so bad—yet it does. Sometimes I hate them so much I want them to leave me alone forever, but then I'd feel even more alone in the world and that's scarier.

I hop off the bus and sprint for my apartment complex across the street, the asphalt rough against the bottom of my bare feet. I'm panting and nauseous, but I know as soon as I get to the drawer everything will be okay again.

But when I turn the corner of my building, I slam to a stop at the bottom of the stairway. "What are you doing here?" I put my hands on my hips and narrow my eyes. "God, Ethan, can't you take a hint?"

Ethan stands up from the top step, putting a hand on the railing on the side of the building. "What? Did you seriously think I was just going to let you go?" he asks, arching his eyebrow. "After what happened last night?"

"Yes," I say with honesty. "You always let me go after I mess up. You've picked me up how many times and never said a word? That's what you do. You let me be and you don't judge me. You even walked out on me that night after we made out and almost had sex. You just walked away." I can't believe how blunt I'm being at the moment and I should be embarrassed, but I have more important things to worry about, like getting to the damn pills.

Ethan briefly winces at my words, but stays composed, making sure to stay on the subject. "Yeah, but this is different." He trots down a stair and tips his head down so he can look at me. "This isn't sex. This is drugs."

"I don't take *drugs*," I snap, rather loudly. I'm making a scene, but at the moment I can't care because every solitary nerve in my body *needs* to get into that house. And Ethan is the only thing blocking my route. "It's just a prescription."

"A prescription that you abuse." He steps down another stair and then another, closing in on me like the damn walls always do. "Lila, look at yourself." His eyes sweep my body and I glance down at his shirt and the bottom of my dress showing out from under it, stained with dirt and vomit.

"So what?" I cringe, knowing I don't mean it. He arrives at the bottom of the stairway and stuffs his hands into the pockets of his jeans, looking uncomfortable and scared to death. "I want to help you."

"I don't need help," I snap, stepping back. A few of my neighbors are outside on their balconies and near their cars and they pause to watch the scene unfold. "You were never supposed to see me like this. This isn't who I am. And as soon as you let me go into my house, I can clean up and we can forget about all of this. I can go back to the smiling, happy Lila."

"No, you won't," he argues. "Sorry to break it to you but I haven't seen that Lila for a while."

"Well, I can at least give you the illusion of her," I retort hotly.

He scratches his unshaven chin with a doubtful look on his face. "After you clean up and take a pill?"

I shake my head multiple times, but I can't seem to answer him with words. "Please just let me through."

"Nope," he says simply, and then his hands come out from his pockets and he reaches for me. "Lila, I want to help—"

I cut him off as I skitter around him and sprint up the stairs, skipping steps even though my body aches and the metal of the steps burns the pads of my feet. Thankfully, I left my door unlocked last night and I get into the house easily. I make a bolt for my bedroom without so much as looking over my shoulder. All I need is one, just one dose inside my bloodstream and all will be forgotten. Everything will be okay and I'll be back to the normal, happy, full-of-sunshine Lila.

When I reach my room, I jump over my bed to get to my dresser drawer. Right as I get my fingers around the bottle and relax, I hear Ethan enter my room.

"Don't fucking do it, Lila." His voice is unsteady, which is really strange for him. He's usually full of humor and radiating calmness in unnerving situations. "Just give me the bottle and we can talk."

I shake my head and slam my trembling palm on the lid, pushing down to twist it off. "No, please just go away. I didn't ask you to be here or follow me. I don't want your—"

His arms snake around my waist and I let out a spastic wail as his fingers come down over my hands. He tries to pry them off the bottle, but I wrestle my arms away, slipping out of his hold. I bend my knees to jump over the bed, but he catches me midleap and hauls me down onto the mattress.

"Ethan, stop it!" I cry as he holds me down with his body. I writhe my hips and jerk my shoulders, attempting to escape. "You're hurting me!" It's a lie, but I'm desperate, needy, obsessed with what's in that bottle.

"Stop being a baby," he says, kneeling up so my waist is trapped between his knees. "I'm barely putting any weight on you.'"

I hug the bottle to my chest. "Yes, you are!"

"No, I'm not." He grabs my hands and then pins them down above my head, pressing his forehead against mine. With his free hand he pries the bottle out of my frantic grasp.

"No, please, Ethan. Please, stop it. Please…please…

please…" I start to cry and hyperventilate and I despise it because I already look ridiculous as it is.

He doesn't say anything as he climbs off me and then off the bed. I leap up from the bed, begging and pleading with him to give me the pills back.

"I'll give you whatever you want," I say, with my hands overlapped in front of me as I stand vulnerably before him. "Anything, you want. *Anything.*" I know it's low to offer myself in exchange for a bottle that's mine, but that bottle is worth more to me than any part of my used body, worthless mind, and empty heart.

"I don't want *anything* from you, Lila," he says, staring undecidedly at the bottle in his hand. "Except for you to get better."

I lunge for him, but he rotates to the side, so I slam into his back. He thrusts out his arm and holds me back as he grips the bottle in his hand. The longer they're out of my reach, the more I feel like I want to claw out of my own skin. I start to tremble as my blood pressure rises. "Please, please just give them to me," I mutter as I start to sweat. "Help me, please…I don't want to feel like this.

He suddenly lets go of me and for a second I think he's giving in. Then he pushes down on the lid with his hand and twists it off.

"What are you doing?" I ask, my mouth salivating as he dumps one tiny pill into his hand.

I notice his finger tremble a little as he breaks the pill in half with his fingers and hands one of the pieces to me. "Take this."

I shake my head at the tiny piece that's not going to do shit for me at the moment. "I need more than that."

He shakes his head. "That's all I'm going to give you and I'm only giving it to you so you're body won't freak out from withdrawals."

"They're not yours to hand out!" I shout and lunge for him again, but he catches me in his arms and holds my weight as my legs give out on me. "They're mine! Not yours." I'm shaking from head to toe as my mind screams at me to take the half and then do whatever it takes to get more from him. "Ethan, please just give me the bottle. I'll do whatever you want..." I shut my eyes and take a deep breath before I offer him something I've offered other guys before in exchange for pills. "I'll let you fuck me. And I mean fuck me, without any of the relationship, needy crap afterward that I know you hate."

His arms tighten around me as he presses me closer to his chest. "Lila, stop. I already said I don't want anything from you except for you to get better." Then he moves the insignificant-sized pill into my line of vision.

I hate him so much right now I can't stand it. I can't stand myself. I can't stand a lot of things, but I still take the pill, and once it touches my tongue, the bitter taste spreads through my body and for a brief second I feel slightly better. But then I remember he has the rest in his hand and I can't get another bottle until Monday, which is two whole days. Two very, very long, tiring, emotional days.

A switch I never knew existed flips inside me and unwanted emotions spring loose. "I hate you!" I shout. Fear and rage pound through me so badly and all I want to do is hit him. I start hitting him in the chest, over and over again as tears slip down my cheeks. He doesn't do anything, which makes me angrier. At least if he hit me or something it'd distract me from the aching pain growing inside me. "I fucking hate you!" I yell it over and over again until my arms and legs are so sore I sink to the ground, clutching on to his shirt. Every emotion I'm feeling cuts at me like a knife.

Ethan silently scoops me up and carries me to my bed, even though I protest. I turn on my back with my head on my pillow and stare up at him through a veil of tears.

"I hate you so much," I say, even though I don't. "I really do."

"No, you don't," he replies imperviously as he stands at the edge of the bed, staring down at me.

"Yes, I do," I lie and flip to my side so I don't have to look at him anymore. I turn the ring around on my finger, over and over again as I stare at the wall.

I think he's going to leave me there in my bedroom alone, which I don't think I can handle—at the same time, I'm fuming with so much rage that I don't want him to be there. There is no good solution to the situation. No matter whether he leaves or stays, the pills are with him and I can't get a refill for two days because the guy who writes the prescription for them for me is gone for the weekend.

Ethan doesn't make a sound as he stands beside my bed, like he's waiting for me to say or do something. I shut my eyes and pretend he's not there. Finally he shifts and I think he's leaving, but then the mattress sinks down and a second later he's lying beside me. He drapes his arm over my side, his muscles tensing, and then he inches closer so our bodies are perfectly aligned.

"I'm sorry," he whispers against the back of my neck, brushing my hair to the side so he can trail his fingers across the base of my neck.

I'm not sure exactly what he's sorry for, but nonetheless I start to sob as I roll over and bury my face into his chest. He smoothes my hair down as I cry my heart out, and even though every single part of my body and mind wants to wither and die, for the first time in my life, I don't feel utterly alone in the world. And the strange thing is I can feel the emotion behind it—I can feel everything.

Ethan

I'm completely out of my element. I've never been one for affection, even with London, but London wasn't affectionate either. She liked to kiss and have sex, but other than that, the touchy-feely thing was nonexistent in our relationship. She'd cried a few times in front of me, but she always pushed me away or diverted to sex when I tried to comfort her. And she never ever told me anything about the cause of her problems and sometimes I wonder if she didn't trust me enough.

As Lila clings on to me, crying her heart out, trusting me completely, I feel more awkward than I ever have. But a few things make the awkwardness bearable. Like knowing that I'm making the aching need inside her the slightest bit less painful, and that's what keeps me in the bed with her.

She cries for half the night and then sleeps until midafternoon. I get up around ten when a text message goes off on my phone. Sighing, I delete the message from Rae and then tuck my phone and the bottle of pills into my pocket. Then I wander out to the refrigerator to get a snack, trying to shake the rising emotions inside me. All that she has is some expired milk and a rotten sandwich and the fridge isn't even on. I shut the door and check the light switches and sure enough the power is out.

I knew she was having money trouble, but this is way worse than I thought. I start to question why she didn't tell me just how bad things were getting, but then I realize that I'd probably do the same thing. In fact, at this point, I'd probably have packed my shit up and hit the road, living in my car or something, which actually doesn't seem so bad at the moment.

As I slam the cupboard shut, there's a knock on the door. I debate whether to answer it, but then they knock again so I open the door. There's an old dude wearing a T-shirt with the sleeves ripped off and a pair of cargo shorts, and he has a piece of paper in his hand.

"Is Lila…" He glances down at the paper. "Summers here?"

"No," I lie breezily, leaning against the doorway. "You just missed her."

"Can you give her this?" He shoves the paper at me.

"I guess." I take it from him and he walks down the steps as I shut the door, reading the paper over. It's an eviction notice. "Shit."

I remember when I was coming down, after I'd decided to make the decision to stop doing drugs, I was very touchy about everything. I even remember yelling at my mom because I couldn't find any socks. Everything pissed me off and upset me, and an eviction notice…I can't even imagine what that would have done.

As much as I'd just like to pay her past-due amount for her—because that's the easiest solution—I don't have the funds. I could ask her to ask her parents, but from the stories I've heard about them, I don't think they'd help her. They might make her come home, but I don't think she'll go and I kind of don't want her to. There's only one more solution, one I'm not very fond of, because of the many things that can go wrong. Still, I ball up the eviction notice and toss it into the trash.

When I go back to her room with a glass of water and half a pill in my hand, she's awake, curled up in a ball, hugging a pillow. I linger near the doorway for a while, trying to figure out what to say to her. "So," I start, realizing it's probably the stupidest thing to say at the moment, but honestly anything that comes out of my mouth is going to annoy her.

She frowns and scowls at me. "Who was at the door?"

I step into the room and sit down on the foot of the bed. "Your landlord, I think."

She gradually sits up, blinking her eyes and clutching on to the pillow. "What did he want?"

"He dropped off an eviction notice," I explain and her face crumbles. "Your power's off, too. Did you know that?"

She shakes her head and rests her chin on top of the pillow. "It was on last night."

"Well, they must have turned it off this morning," I say. She smashes her quivering lips together and I scoot closer to her and hand her the glass of water and the pill. At first she just stares at it with a disgusted face, but then reluctantly she takes it, popping the pill in her hand and then taking a gulp of water. For a second she looks relieved, but it quickly erases and she starts glaring at me again. But that's okay. The half doses of pills aren't supposed to numb her pain, just keep her body from freaking out on her.

"Here's what we're going to do," I say, setting the glass of water down on the nightstand when she hands it back to me. "You're going to get cleaned up and then you're going to come with me to find some boxes. Then we're going to pack up your stuff and get you out of this apartment."

Her lip pops out as she frowns even more. "Where am I

supposed to go, Ethan? I barely have any money left and even if I pawned my ring"—she raises her hand in front of her and wiggles her finger—"it still wouldn't cover a new deposit and rent for another place."

"Yeah, but you're not going to get another place," I say, giving her leg a gentle squeeze before rising to my feet. "You're going to come stay with me for a while."

"What!" she exclaims, throwing the pillow aside. "Why?"

"So that you don't have to go home or go live on the streets," I say, bringing my hand away from her leg. She clamps her jaw shut and starts to pick at her fingernails. "I don't want to live with you."

I bite down on my tongue, getting pissed off. "Why the hell not?"

"Because I don't." She looks away at the wall with aggravation burning in her blue eyes. "I'd rather live on the streets."

"You wouldn't last a God damn day on the streets and you know it." I lean in front of her line of vision. "You don't want to because you think I'm going to make you stop taking those stupid pills."

"No, I *know* you're going to make me," she snaps back, her head whipping in my direction. "Because apparently you're an asshole who will give me only half a dose, when clearly it's not helping me at all."

"Damn fucking straight I'm an asshole," I retaliate. "And those half doses are going to help you not freak out while you quit." I grab her arms and pull her to her feet. Steering her by the shoulders, I move her in front of the mirror. "Look at yourself, Lila. In the last month you've completely fallen apart. You're not the girl I met a year ago."

"Yes, I am! I've been falling apart for years, and just hid it better than I have lately," she says and then her eyes enlarge as she bites down on her lip so hard it instantly starts to swell. "I didn't mean that. I'm fine, so stop telling me things to try to get me to see clearly." She steps forward to move away, but I pull her back.

"Look at yourself," I repeat, because it's important for her to see what she really is at this moment, when everything the drugs have done to her is showing. "When I was doing drugs I never really saw what I'd become until I was pretty far into it. I'd lost a lot of weight and my skin looked like shit. Plus my personal hygiene was nonexistent. This"—I gesture at her filthy clothes and matted hair—"is what you look like because of those pills. Can you handle that?"

"This is an exception," she argues, glancing in the mirror. Her hair is all over the place, her makeup smeared, and her lips are chapped. "I usually don't look like this. The other night was an exception . . . a minor slipup."

"No, you look like this every morning that I've had to pick you up. I always thought it was a morning-after sort of thing, since every other time I saw you, you always look so put together, but now I'm kind of realizing that you just hide it well and that the mornings I had to pick you up were just slip-ups." I take a deep breath. "And this wasn't a fucking slipup.

You could have died if I didn't find you. Do you realize that? How close you were to dying?"

Her eyes enlarge for a split second, but then narrow on my reflection in the mirror. "I hate you," she says, her shoulder shaking under my hands.

"No, you don't." And I know she really doesn't. She's just furious, not even at me, but at the fact that whatever she was masking with the drugs is probably surfacing. "And FYI, that's getting a little old."

She glares at me, fire scorching in her eyes. "Then leave."

I shake my head. "As your friend, it's my duty to not leave you alone for a while, at least until we can get you down from the half doses to no doses."

She laughs sharply and crosses her arms. "What? Are you just going to follow me around all the time then, until you get sick of me? Didn't you get the hint the other night that I don't want you?"

It hurts like a knife slashing into my skin, deep, violent thrashes, but I know enough to know that she's desperate right now and will say anything to get me to leave. "If I have to." I realize as I say it that I actually mean it and the feeling is bluntly real. "If that's what it takes, then that's what it takes."

She drags her hand down her face and then she notices the small blue-and-purple bruises on her arms. "Where'd these come from?" She touches them lightly with her fingertips.

I shrug, removing my hands from her shoulders. "I have no idea. You had welts there when I found you in the bushes.

If you ask me, it looks like someone got a little rough with you."

She winces and then glances at her reflection. "I'm going to take a shower."

I sit down on the bed and cross my arms. "Okay, I'll be right here when you get out."

"What? Aren't you going to come take a shower with me?" she asks derisively as she yanks open the dresser drawer.

I notice there are candy canes in it and it makes me mentally smile, thinking about when I gave them to her, but I quickly shake the thought away. "Nah, I'll wait for you here."

She scowls at me as she snatches a pair of black lacy panties out of the drawer. "Fine, but how do you know I don't have any pills hidden in the bathroom?"

"I'm guessing you don't since I'm pretty sure you would have gone after them last night," I tell her.

Her face reddens with rage. "Whatever." She storms for the door and I follow her out into the hall, staying at her heels, making sure she doesn't try to make a run for the front door. She slams the bathroom door in my face and I sit down on the couch to wait for her.

I'm trying not to panic about what the future holds, but I can't help it. Excluding the fact that I'm taking a big step with another girl besides London, I'm actually going to have to live with her, too, and I could barely stand living with Micha. I like my personal space and if I don't get enough of it, I start to feel like I'm caged in. I mean, I like Lila and everything, but I'm not even sure if I've seen the real her yet, just the drugged-up illusion of her. Drugs are like that. They make someone a different person. With me, I was calmer on the inside, so on the outside I had an easier time talking to people. Lila's always seemed happy enough, except for the last few weeks. What if she turns into a completely different person and I end up not liking her? I've enjoyed all the time we spent together, the bantering, even the sexual tension, the inappropriate touching, and I'll even admit it, despite the fact of how it ended, that night on her bed made me feel things I never knew existed. But what if that's all gone after this?

Chapter Eight

Lila

I'm a bitch. I've been snapping at Ethan and saying mean things even though he helped me out when he didn't have to. He let me move in with him, and even went as far as helping me pack up my apartment. But I can't help it. It's like there is this foul thing living inside me, this famished monster that wants nothing more than to be fed, and Ethan is getting in the way of the feast, only giving me broken pieces of pills, and he's giving them to me less frequently each day. I haven't felt this shitty since my mom and her driver picked me up from boarding school after the incident. She wasn't there to rescue me, though, like I hoped. She was there to talk some sense into me.

"Well, I have to say that I'm very disappointed in you," she'd said, staring out the tinted window as we drove through the city, the tall buildings shadowing the streets and the car. "Although, I'm not surprised." She angled her head to the side to look at me and slipped her sunglasses onto the top of her head. "As much as I hate to admit it, I expected nothing less of you."

The indignity and mortification of what happened at school still burned inside me and yet I still couldn't control my tongue. "And why's that, mother?"

"Watch your tone," she snapped. "Just because your father isn't here doesn't mean you can disrespect me."

"Why? You let my father disrespect you." I was sitting on the opposite side of the backseat, looking at her with such animosity for making me come to the city and the school. If I'd been in California then maybe I would have made better decisions. I wouldn't have felt so lonely and therefore wouldn't have gone looking for something to fill the emptiness inside me. I would have never met him and never have done things, disgusting, unimaginable things that I'll forever regret.

Her eyes snapped wide and before I had time to register what she was doing, she slapped me hard across the cheek. Heat and pain ignited across my face and inside my heart, too. But I didn't cry. I wouldn't give her the satisfaction of crying in front of her.

I cupped my cheek with my head hung low so she couldn't see the hurt in my eyes. "You're acting like this was entirely my fault, but I didn't even know what I was doing. I didn't understand...I didn't..." I shook my head, discouraged at myself, but still able to will myself to sit up straight. "It really hurts."

"Hurting and crying over something a guy did to you is pathetic, Lila Summers," she said and I had to resist an eye roll because she was seriously one to talk about being pathetic. "And it is your fault. You made the decision to be with him, even though you knew he was older, and now we have to deal with the consequences."

"We?" I questioned.

"Yes, we," she said in a calm voice as she tugged off her leather gloves. "Everything you do is done to this family. Your father has family here—you know that. You have cousins and some of his business colleagues' kids go to the school. How do you think I found out about this to begin with?" She tossed her gloves onto the seat, then reached for her purse. She took out a prescription bottle and read the label. "And the outburst in the middle of class...you're making us look like we've raised some kind of lunatic."

I'd balled my fists. "The other kids are tormenting me, though. Those stupid Precious Bells told the entire school, and now everyone keeps saying what a little slut I am and how I threw myself on Se..." I trailed off, unable to utter his name. "A-And I haven't been sleeping very well...I've been having nightmares about waking up underneath...underneath him." I summoned a deep breath, wishing she'd hug me or something, or try to make me feel a little better. She used to give me hugs when I was little, but then my father got a mistress and she got her pills and wine. When she was taking them, which was almost always, they became the most important things to her, and everything else, including me, didn't seem to matter.

She stared at me with a little bit of sympathy as she twisted the cap off the pills. "Take one of these a day until you're feeling better." She grabbed my hand and dumped a pill into my palm.

"What is it?" I held the tiny white pill warily.

"It's something that's going to make this all better," she insisted, screwing the cap back on. "For everyone. You, me, and your father."

I knew it was wrong, yet she was watching me expectantly, and all I really wanted to do was make the heavy, humiliating, filthy, self-loathing pain vanish, so I tipped my head back and swallowed the pill.

"Good girl," my mom said like I was a dog who had just done the correct trick and had been rewarded with a treat. She handed me the bottle and then pulled her sunglasses back over her eyes and crossed her legs. "And if you run out, let me know and I'll get you more."

And she did. Every time I'd run out, she'd get me a refill. Sometimes when I was visiting at home, she'd share her stash. We'd take the pills and then go shopping or something, the only visible things inside either of our bodies were the shallow, materialistic, shadows of our true selves.

I've been spending a lot of time in Micha's old room, which is my new temporary room. And a lot of that time I spend staring in the mirror, not vanity or anything, just looking at my reflection and trying to figure out who I am without pills in my system. The blue eyes that stare back at me are not recognizable, too wide and confused, instead of blank like they've been for years.

As sobriety starts to seep in with each passing day, I try to figure how I got to this exact moment when it felt like I'd been okay just a few days ago. In four days' time it feel like a thousand bricks have tumbled down on my chest and are pinning me to the bed. And I wonder if I'll ever be able to stop them from crushing me.

Ethan

What the hell am I doing?

I'm not looking for a relationship. They're ugly, raw, brutal, painful, life destroying. They exist only in the hearts of the needy and I don't need anything from anyone. I'm perfectly content being alone, hiding in the desolate place inside myself. It's what I need to exist because I don't think I can handle anything else. Even with London, I made sure to keep as much distance as I could and I'm glad. If I hadn't, I might have broken apart that morning when I got the news. But instead I felt numb, barely feeling a thing about it, almost like it never happened. And being in that place is a great place to be. It's quiet and still and peaceful. There's no yelling inside my head, no commotion, no anxiety. I don't have to worry about being walked all over by someone, being controlled, or losing myself, or trying to take away the identity of another person, pretending to love them, when really I just want to own them.

Within the loneliness inside me, I don't have to worry about turning into someone I don't want to be, like my mother or my

*father. I'm just Ethan. And I can live with that. But with Lila…
Jesus fucking Christ, I'm turning into a person I barely recognize.
A nice guy who cares way too much, who's breaking his rules and
getting involved.*

*Yep, I've become everything I promised I never would be after
I lost London.*

"Your couch smells like old cheese." Lila walks into my
room with a scowl on her face. It's the same scowl she's been
wearing for the last four days, ever since I learned about her
habitual pill popping habit. "And your fridge has mold in it."

"Well, at least it runs." I put my pen away and shut the
notebook, toss it on the nightstand, and lean against the headboard. "It could have no power *and* be growing mold."

Her forehead creases as her scowl intensifies. Her hair isn't
combed, and she still has on the pair of boxer shorts and the
tank top she slept in. "What were you just doing?" She eyes the
notebook. "Writing about what a bitch I am?"

I cross my arms and stretch my legs out on the bed in front
of me. "Why would I have to write about that when I can tell
you in person?"

Her blue eyes turn cold. "You're an asshole."

"You know, you've said that about twenty times in the last
few days and it's getting really old, especially since most ass-
holes wouldn't just let you move in with them."

She shakes her head and huffs with frustration. "It's time
for you to give me another stupid piece of my pill."

I glance at my watch and then shake my head. "Not yet."

She lets out a scream through gritted teeth and then flips me off before leaving my room. My head flops back against the headboard and I stare up at the crack in the ceiling. I'm not sure if I'm doing anything right, whether I'm helping her or harming her. She's so much different, more closed off and stubborn and bitchy. She won't talk about anything and complains about everything. She's driving me fucking crazy.

I rub my forehead, cursing the nonstop headache I've had for days. Finally, I can't take it anymore. I need to relieve the stress and there are only two ways for me to do that. Sleep with someone or play the drums. Usually, I'd go with the first, but I'm not feeling it at all.

I get up from the bed, take my shirt off, and sit down on the stool beside my drums, scooping up my drumsticks from off the floor. I reach over to my dresser and grab my iPod from the dock. I select "Gotta Get Away" by Offspring, put the iPod back in the dock, and crank the volume, wanting to drown out the noise of my thoughts and any more potential Lila drama.

Once the song clicks on, I slam the sticks down on the drums and start pounding to the rhythm with more force than usual. I'm usually considerate of the neighbors, but right now I need to let off some steam. The longer I go, the more into it I get. Midway, I just close my eyes and let myself drown in the music and beat, my skin covered with sweat and my pulse hammering against my chest. I feel myself getting dragged away from my problems and life. For a moment, I'm alone in the apartment, in the world, and all the worries that surround me cease to exist. Then the song ends and I open my eyes and nearly fall off the stool.

Lila is sitting on the edge of my bed, watching me with what looks like a disinterested look, but I think it's a mask to hide the fact that she's curious.

"Jesus, Lila." I try to catch my breath, sweeping my fingers through my sweaty hair. "You scared the shit out of me."

She crosses her legs and stares at me impassively. For a second I think she's going to ask me for another pill, maybe even try to bargain with me, something she's done a lot over the last few days. But instead she says, "How do you think I feel? One minute I'm sitting in a quiet room and then suddenly the whole place is shaking?"

I clutch on to the drumsticks, rotating them in my palms, gripping them so forcefully the wood rubs coarsely at the skin. "Sorry, but I had to do it, otherwise I would have done something really stupid."

She elevates her eyebrows. "Like what?"

"Like leave the house."

"Good, I wish you would have." She pauses contemplatively. "Wait, why would you leave the house if you didn't play?"

"Because I needed to let off some steam." I wipe some sweat off my forehead with my arm. "And it was either this or go get laid."

I catch the faintest flicked of annoyance in her neutral

expression. "You should have gone with the getting laid. It works a lot better." Her tone is clipped and she's breathing stridently, working hard to keep the oxygen flowing.

I study her, really missing the smiling Lila I first met a year and a half ago, the one who I thought was my complete opposite, but now I'm reconsidering this idea. In fact, the more I get to know her, the more she does kind of remind me of London, erratic and full of secrets. I thought I knew Lila but I guess I was wrong and I'm not really sure what to do with it or how I feel about it yet. "How do you know? Have you ever played before?"

"You know I haven't."

"How do I know anything that you can't and can do? Because I'm learning pretty quickly that those little heart-to-hearts we had for the last year weren't real."

"They were too," she says, looking hurt, and I relax at the sight of emotion in her face, even if it is sadness because at least it's something. "Everything I told you was true. I just didn't tell you everything, which I'm sure you did with me, too."

I don't bother trying to deny it. Sure, she knows stuff, like how my parents were and are, but she doesn't know about my fear of being with someone because I'll turn out like them or about what happened to London. "All right, fair enough."

We sit in silence for a little bit and she's either staring at my drumsticks, which are on my lap, or my dick.

Finally, she asks, "Is it really therapeutic?"

I wipe the sweat off my arm with my hand. "Is what therapeutic?"

She catches my gaze and she looks helplessly lost for the first time since I met her. "Banging on the drums. You said it was good for letting off steam."

"It's even better than punching a bag." I collect the drumsticks from my lap. "Do you . . . do you want to try?"

She leans back, shaking her head, like she's afraid of them—or me. "I don't know how to play. You know that."

"No, I don't know that since I never got around to asking you." I inch back in the stool. "But I can help you if you want. It might help with your"—I press my lips together, trying not to grin—"bitchiness."

I wait for her to get all riled up, but instead she stands up with confidence and weaves around the drums toward me and I can't help but think, *Now there's my Lila.* But I quickly shake the thought away because she's not my Lila. She's my *friend*.

"And how are you going to show me?" she wonders, eyeing the sticks in my hand.

A thousand dirty comments run through my mind, but I bite them back and scoot away just a little bit more, making room for her, and then pat the spot on the stool that's in front of me. "Sit down."

Her eyes sweep the small space, and then biting her lip she tucks locks of her messy blonde hair behind her ears and tentatively squeezes between my knees and the drums. She drops down in the seat and I realize just how bad of an idea this is as her ass presses against my cock. I try to keep my dirty thoughts to a bare minimum as I reach an arm around each of her sides and hand her the drumsticks.

"What song do I get to play?" she asks as I slant to the side to grab the iPod. "One of your crazy rock songs?" She sounds amused and it makes me smile.

"Not too crazy." I select "1979" by Smashing Pumpkins, then quickly place the iPod into the dock, press my chest against Lila's back, and wrap a hand around each of hers so that my fingers are folded around her wrists.

"You're sweaty," she remarks. "It's gross."

"Well, you haven't taken a shower in, like, four days. Imagine how *you* smell," I retort, but she actually smells good—fruity, like watermelon. I swiftly sweep her hair to the side and lean over her shoulder, resting my chin on it so I can see what I'm doing. The song starts playing and before I know it the drum section is starting.

"We missed the intro," Lila says, stating the obvious. "And this song is really fast anyway. I can't keep up with this."

"Never say can't." I lift her arms in the air. She's still holding the sticks and my fingertips are pressing against her hammering pulse. She's nervous, which surprises me. I expected her to be more subdued, because that's how she usually is. But then again, this is a whole different Lila, one without drugs in her system. "You ready?" I ask her and I have to momentarily shut my eyes when she shudders against the feel of my breath against her shoulder.

She nods and I open my eyes. "I'm ready," she calls out over the music.

I take a deep breath, feeling uneasy. Thankfully I know it will clear as soon as I start playing. The song is reaching the chorus, the perfect time to jump in and start playing. We wait and we wait, breathing in and out until it feels like we're going to combust, and then finally the song approaches the perfect moment. Gripping her wrists, I bring her hands down to the drums. I hear her laugh as the sticks hit and don't quite match the beat. It's a little harder to play like this, but I make it work, because playing well isn't the point. Playing from the heart is and letting her tune out her thoughts with something else other than the overwhelming desire I know she's still feeling.

She continues to laugh, a few times trying to take over on her own. It sounds terrible, nail-scratching, ear-clawing terrible, but it's making her happy and relaxed, completely out of her own head, and honestly I feel the same way.

Lila

Once I take a seat, I know I'm in trouble. His sturdy, tattooed chest is crushed against my back, radiating heat through my thin shirt and making it hard to breathe. Something about the feel of him melts the starvation inside me and suddenly my thoughts are sidetracked. I've seen him without his shirt on before, once when we were playing strip poker. But I was drunk and medicated, and truthfully I'm not sure I was seeing very clearly because he looks so much sexier now. All the guys who I can remember being with have been clean-cut, with perfectly tanned skin and chiseled abs. They looked like good guys who use manners in public, although behind closed doors it was usually a different story.

I've never been with anyone who played the drums, had scraggily, untrimmed hair, a five o'clock shadow, or lean, tattooed arms that rippled as they slammed drumsticks down on the drums. I mean, I knew Ethan had tattoos, but I'd never paid enough attention to how many. And God, they look good on him. There's one in particular going across one of his pecs that's always caught my attention. It looks like letters from maybe another language that go around in a circle, sketched in jet-black ink. The only other language I can speak is French, so I'm not sure what language it is. But by the unique shapes of each letter, I'm guessing it's not a very common one. I wonder if I'm right. I wonder what it means. I wonder if he'd tell me if I asked him.

My palms are sweaty against the drumsticks and my heart thrashes up as he holds his fingers around each of my wrists. I know he can feel my pulse jolting against his fingertips, but he doesn't say anything about it, either to be nice or because he's getting too caught up in playing. I'll admit it's liberating, slamming the sticks to the rhythm of the music and I even manage to laugh.

As he continues to move my hands, I dare to steal a glance

over my shoulder at him. He looks so peaceful and in harmony with the song, like he's thinking about nothing but the beat and lyrics. His eyes are shut and he has this euphoric look on his face. It's fascinating, watching him match the beat of the song, moving my hands right along with his. He's really getting into it and it's sexy and hot and, oh my God, I have to bite down on my lip to restrain unwelcomed noises escaping from my lips as I remember how it felt when his tongue and teeth were on my skin.

It's the most amazing feeling I've ever experienced, like all of my negative emotions are channeled into slamming the sticks and I wish I could keep doing it forever. But then the song comes to an end and the moment of freedom disappears.

I quickly look away from him before he opens his eyes and catches me watching him. I'm panting and so is he, the movement of his chest and my back harmonized.

"That was fun," I say, breathless, my skin damp with sweat. Everything inside me is so scorching, but in a mouth-wateringly good way, and unlike usual, I can feel it, taste it, breathe it, want it. *Want him. Good God, I want him.* I'm sober, completely coherent, and I want him, like I had him that night we took shots at the club and then I just laid in my bed, feeling my usually self-induced numbness, only this time he wouldn't stop and leave and I wouldn't shut down, instead letting myself feel everything.

His chin is on my shoulder and when he tips his head to the side, his breath caresses my neck. "I think you're a natural," he says, amusement in his voice. "Maybe we should get you your own set."

I chew on my lip, slanting my head to the side to look at him and almost end up kissing him. "A pink set, maybe?" I wet my lips with my tongue, noting the close proximity of his mouth, feeling this new, unfamiliar pull toward him as sensations of heat and tingles course through my body.

He laughs at me, his breath warm against my cheek as he shakes his head. "Pink? Why am I not surprised?" He leans in, pressing his chest harder against my back, but I'm unsure if he even realizes he's doing it.

"What's wrong with pink?" I ask, the feeling of desire and hunger leaving my body.

"Nothing's wrong with pink." Smiling, he climbs off the stool and holds out his hands, and the desire in my body fizzles. "I just think it's funny that now you want a set when just a little while ago you came in here to complain about the whole house shaking."

I swallow the lump in my throat as I place the drumsticks into his hands and climb off the stool. "Sorry," I mutter, feeling bad, remembering how I was acting like a bitch. Usually I wouldn't care, but right now I feel like I'm on the verge of tears, my emotions all over the place. I swing around him, banging my hip on one of the cymbals. "I'm just going to go back to my room."

"Lila, wait." He snags my elbow as I reach the foot of the bed. "Look, I'm sorry. I was just teasing, but I really shouldn't be. Right now is not the time or place." He takes a deep breath and his chest sinks as he releases it. "I know how you're feeling, and teasing is the last thing you need."

I close my eyes, taking a cleansing breath and mentally clearing my head of any sexual feelings I have for Ethan, before I turn around and look at him. "Don't be sorry. All of this is my fault. I should have never called you that night and brought you into my secret train-wreck life."

His fingers leave my arm and he deliberates something, chewing on his lip while he does. I wonder if he knows he's doing it, or if he knows how crazy it drives me when he does it. "What do you want to do today?" he asks, throwing me off guard.

I stare perplexedly at him. "What do you mean?"

"I mean, what do you want to do today?"

"What are my choices?"

"Anything."

I hold on to the bedpost, feeling light-headed for no reason as I consider what I want to do. "I think maybe you better choose," I say. "Because everything I'm thinking involves things you're not going to let me have." *Pills. Alcohol. You.*

He presses his lips together, looking strangely happy. I'm about to ask him why when he says, "Go take a shower and get dressed in something comfortable."

I put my hand on my hip. "Why? Where are we going?"

"It's a surprise." He reaches for his shirt draped on the bedpost and I have to step back so his arm doesn't brush my breast. "And no questioning. It'll take all the fun out of it."

I'm skeptical, but curious enough that I obey his instructions and start to head out of the room to take a shower. But I pause in the doorway, my mind going back to his tattoo as he goes to slip his shirt on.

"What does that mean?" I ask, pointing at his chest.

He glances down with his shirt half on around his neck. "This?" He touches the tattoo lightly with his finger, then glances up at me through hooded eyes. "It means solitude in Greek."

"Solitude?"

He nods, slipping his arms through the sleeves. "It's a dream of mine."

"To be alone?" I question. "Like on your little road trip thing, because I thought you were going to take me with you." I try to say it lightly, but I'm feeling too low and down.

He shrugs. "Dreams change, I guess."

"Then maybe you shouldn't tattoo them permanently on your skin," I joke.

His lips tug upward. "Whenever I put a tattoo on my skin it always means something to me at the time, and I've never regretted getting one."

I bite on my already chomped-off fingernails as he makes his way over to the dresser. "Maybe I should get one."

He glances over his shoulder at me through hooded eyes and slowly scans my body, making me feel naked. "Maybe you should."

It gets really quiet between us as we stand there staring at each other, my body heating with each second his eyes are locked on me. Finally he clears his throat and the tension crumbles.

"Now go take a shower so we can get going," he says, picking up a bottle of cologne from off his dresser.

I nod and go take a shower, wishing the water would wash off the untamed emotions flustering inside me, along with cleaning me. But I pretty much feel the same way when I get out, all riled up inside. I try to shrug it off the best I can and put on my one and only pair of jeans and throw on a pink tank top. I braid my damp hair to the side since I'm not in the mood to curl it. Then I slip on my sandals and head out into the living room where he's lying on the couch reading a book.

"You read more than any other guy I know," I say, sitting down on the arm of the couch. "It's weird."

Without looking up at me, he turns the page. "Good. I like being originally weird."

I cross my legs and fiddle with my braid. "Do you now?"

"Absolutely." His eyes return to the book, like he can't quite break himself away from the story. His hair is swept to the side and he's wearing a gray T-shirt, accented with a black-and-white-pinstriped shirt and a pair of black cargo shorts. He has leather bands on his wrists and boots on his feet.

I sit there for a while, waiting for him to put the book down, but I'm starting to grow bored and restless. Finally he sets it down on the coffee table, marking the page by folding the corner over. "Sorry," he apologizes, getting to his feet. "I had to get to the good part."

I eye the worn, bent, torn cover as I rise to my feet. "It looks like you've read it, like, a hundred times."

"I have." He scoops up his keys and wallet and then opens the front door, holding it for me. "But that doesn't mean that the good parts get any less good."

I roll my eyes and walk out into the sunlight. "Whatever. I've never understood what the big deal is about reading."

He shuts the door and locks it, turning for the stairs. "Going to another place. Getting lost in time. Pretending that you're living a different life." He heads down the stairs and I follow him. "What's not to love?"

"Is that why you're reading all the time? And writing?"

"Who said I read and write all the time?"

"I said so," I say as we arrive at the bottom of the stairs. We head for the carport where his truck is parked. "I've seen you reading and writing in that journal a couple of times, but now that I'm living with you"—I grab the door handle of his lifted truck—"you do both a lot."

He beeps the truck unlocked and we open the doors and hop in. It takes me a little bit more effort, considering how tall his truck is and I'm barely average height. We slam the doors simultaneously and he starts up the engine, giving the gas a few hard revs.

"Okay, I have to ask," I say, securing my seat belt over my shoulder. "What is it with guys and their cars or trucks or anything with an engine, really?"

He shrugs as he shoves the shifter into reverse. "I grew up

around cars so it was kind of a given that I'd love them." He backs out, cranking the wheel to the right. "As for every other guy out there, you'll have to ask them."

I rest my elbow on the console. "So, what? You guys don't ever discuss your love for engines or whatever?"

His forehead furrows as he straightens the truck and drives for the exit. "You mean, do we sit around and dig into the depths of our dark hearts to figure out why the power of an engine is so appealing?" Amusement dances in his eyes.

I aim an annoyed look at him, but when he smiles, I hopelessly lose the battle and grin. "Dark hearts?"

"Oh yes," he says, pulling out onto the main road beside his apartment. "Us men have very dark hearts. Isn't that what you women talk about all the time?"

"Maybe." I sit straight forward in my seat, staring at the towering casino buildings of the main area of the city that's out in the distance in front of us, the lights of the marquees so bright I can read them, even though they're a little ways away. The sun is gleaming and the sky is a flawless blue as we head toward the freeway. "Some really do have dark hearts, though."

He arches a brow. "What do you mean?"

I shake my head. "I mean exactly what I mean. That some men have dark hearts and some women, too."

As he slows at a red light, it looks like he wants to say more, but I look out to the side window, not giving him the opportunity. I haven't made any promises to him about whether or not I'll stop taking the pills. I've just chosen not to contact the guy who writes the prescriptions for me yet. I could any time, but part of me feels guilty since Ethan's helping me out by letting me live with him. But talking about dark hearts and thinking about the men and women who I know have them makes me want to race to a place where I can get some pills, and not a half of one. I want a full dose, maybe even two or three, so that maybe my own heart doesn't seem so dark.

Chapter Nine

Ethan

I know it's really not her thing, four-wheeling in a truck and doing outdoorsy stuff, but the fact that it isn't might be good for her. Maybe doing something completely out of the ordinary will help her feel better and make it a little bit easier on her when I bring up my rules of living together, ones that are going to be hard to discuss but that need to be discussed, otherwise this is going to end up being disastrous.

"The desert?" She gapes at me, completely thrown off by where I've driven us. She gestures at the sandy hills out in front of us that are marked with tire tracks. "This is where you brought me? To the middle of the desert? Why do you keep bringing me to dirty places?"

"It's not dirt. It's sand." I unclip my seat belt and turn down the music. "And I don't know why you sound so surprised since I've brought you here before."

She crosses her arms and taps her foot on the floor. "Yeah, but it's weird that you keep doing it."

I silence the engine. "Why?"

Her lips part. "Because it's out in the middle of nowhere and there's nothing to do here but talk."

"There's plenty to do here," I insist. "And being out in the middle of nowhere is the best place to be." The corners of my lips quirk. "Remember, we already talked about this. You, me, the mountains, and the quiet."

Her plump lips tug upward. "Oh yes, you and your mountain-man obsession."

"Don't judge me," I say. "Just because I like a little bit less of a materialistic life doesn't mean there's something wrong with me."

She unfolds her arms and leans over the console, propping herself up on her elbows, and the curves of her breasts rise up out of the top of her shirt. "I never said there was something wrong with you. I just don't get why you would bring me out here to distract my mind."

I blink my eyes and tear my gaze from her tits. "Because it's the perfect place."

Her lips curl to a smirk. "Are you enjoying the view?" She presses on her chest a little harder and I know her tits are popping out even more, but I don't look down, even though I know it's going to be a fucking amazing view, one I've almost seen and still want to. There's no use denying it.

I maintain my gaze and gesture out at the desert. "Of course, what's not to love about the view?"

She frowns and then turns forward in her seat, fidgeting a little. "So show me what's so fascinating about the desert."

I climb out of the truck and stroll around the front of it, knowing she's confused as hell. When I open her door, sure enough, she has a perplexed expression.

"What are you doing?" she asks, staring me down with her arms crossed.

I wave my hands at her, motioning her to scoot over. "Showing you a good time," I say. She rolls her tongue in her mouth and scans me over, looking like she wants to rip off my clothes, and I realize I'm giving her the wrong idea. "Scoot over into the driver's seat, Lila," I clarify cautiously, reminding myself that now is not the time to try anything with her. She's too vulnerable at the moment and I already decided I wasn't going to go down that road.

Her cheeks redden with embarrassment as she swings her leg over the console and sits down behind the wheel. As she's pulling her other leg over, I notice that she has a scar looping around the bottom of her ankle.

"How'd you get that scar?" I ask, hopping in and shutting the door. "I've never noticed it before."

She places her hands on the top of the steering wheel, sighing. "It's just from something really stupid I did a long time ago." She lowers the steering wheel and scoots the seat forward, even though I haven't told her she's driving anywhere yet.

"Are you going somewhere?" I joke, strapping my seat belt on.

She frowns, blowing out a breath and wisps of her blonde hair flutter around in front of her face. "Isn't that why you asked me to scoot over?"

I nod, deciding to let the teasing go. "Yeah, put your seat belt on, though."

Sighing again, she reaches around and grabs the seat belt. "I don't see why you're having me drive," she states, clicking the seat belt.

"Because it's therapeutic."

She glances at me from the corner of her eye. "Like your drums?"

"Were they not therapeutic?" I question. "Because it seemed to me like you relaxed."

She looks me over from head to toe and for some dumb reason I find myself squirming like a fucking moron. "Ethan, why are you doing this?"

My eyebrows knit. "What? Letting you drive my truck?"

She shakes her head. "No, helping me. I know…we've talked and hung out enough that I know it's going to drive you crazy having me live with you. I know you like your alone time."

"Yeah…I do, but I guess I'm making an exception for you."

"But why? I mean, all I've done for the last few days is be a bitch to you and I know you lived with Micha and everything, but living with a girl is way different."

"Are you insulting your gender?" I tease.

She shrugs, picking at her fingernails. "Not insulting. I'm

just stating the obvious. We do things, you know. Like want to talk and watch sappy movies and leave our bras and panties hanging in the bathroom because we can't machine dry them."

I fidget uncomfortably, trying to figure out what to say. "Well, you and I talk a lot anyway and I don't mind sappy movies every once in a while, as long they're poetic, and the bra and panties..." I dither with a waver of my head. "I mean, why the hell would that bother me?"

Her cheeks flush a little and I wonder what she's thinking about. "But you never said why you're doing it."

"Because...I like you, Lila. You're a good friend and you need help." *Friend*. I need to remember that.

She mulls over what I said, which was nothing but the truth. "Poetic, sappy movies, huh? Do those even exist?"

"I guess you'll have to figure that out." I grin. "Otherwise, I guess no movies."

She sucks her lip between her teeth, her blue eyes brighter than I've seen them in the last few days, which makes my heart speed up a little. "I might just have to live without them, then." She faces forward in the seat and the fading sunlight glows against her face, her skin soft, her lips full, and she doesn't have any makeup on, which is rare for her. And honestly, I prefer her without it because right now she looks fucking gorgeous in the realest way possible. "So what am I supposed to be doing here exactly?" She motions at the sandy land in front of us.

The sound of her voice tears me from my thoughts of her and I focus on the windshield. "You're going to drive."

"Drive?" She seems hesitant. "Like back to the apartment?"

"Eventually." I extend my arm over the console and push the four-wheel-drive button. The truck grinds and then locks in. As I lean away, my arm grazes her chest and it takes a lot of energy not to lean over and touch her more. "But first I want you to drive around here."

She blinks at me, stunned. "Are you joking?"

"Do I look like I'm joking?" I stare at her with a serious expression.

She shakes her head with reluctance, looking horrified. "No, and I'm wondering if you lost your mind or something. Maybe when you hit that hard bump in the road on the way up here and you hit your head on the window, which is going to be a mild injury compared to what could happen if you let me drive."

"Don't worry about crashing it," I reassure her and relax back in the seat. "You'll be fine."

Her jaw drops as she grips the wheel. "Are you being serious right now? You *have* driven with me before."

"I remember." I laugh under my breath, thinking about how terrified I was as she recklessly weaved in and out of traffic. "I seriously thought I was going to fucking die."

She lightly punches me on the arm and I wince, but laugh. "Oh, *now* the asshole is going to make a grand appearance."

Stifling my laughter, I rub the spot where she hit me. "I'm just stating the obvious." I reach over and turn the key, then lean back in the seat. "Now come on and drive. As long as you stay on the straightaway and keep the acceleration up, we'll be fine."

"And what if I don't go fast enough?"

"Then we'll get stuck."

She looks worried, and even though I'm not letting on, so am I. There are so many things that could go wrong right now, but it's fun and adrenaline pumping and that's what she needs. Good, reckless fun, without the pills, because right now, she'll be able to feel the exhilaration of it and I'm not sure how long it's been since she's felt anything at all besides need.

Her shoulders rise and fall as she attempts to release the stress, and then finally she shoves the shifter into drive and presses on the gas. I try to stay calm, but when the truck lurches forward, I tense and grip the handle above my head.

"Easy," I say, grinding my teeth. "Just go slow."

She huffs in frustration and then lets off the gas a little. The truck gradually inches forward, the engine lagging a little. She starts to smile as she maneuvers the truck up the sandy slope, but then her face plummets as the tires protest against the lack of traction and the truck rolls back.

"Push on the gas harder," I instruct, waving at her to go forward.

"But you just said not to give it a lot of gas," she says, placing her hand on the shifter.

"Except when we're going uphill."

She frowns and then floors the gas way too much and we lurch forward. I slam my head on the headrest and hear something on her side hit something hard. When I glance up, she has the heel of her hand pressed to her forehead.

"Is your head okay?" I ask as I rub my own.

She nods. "Yeah, I think so."

I cringe as the engine cuts in and out. "Lila, go, before we get stuck."

She throws her hands up exasperatedly. "I don't know why you're having me do this."

"For fun," I explain. "You need to have some fun in your life."

I must have said the magic words or something because she places her hands on top of the steering wheel and hits the gas way too hard again, the truck jerking forward. This time I'm ready and I grip the door handle, keeping myself in place. She whines in discouragement, but continues driving. The longer she does it, the more relaxed she gets and so do I, even when she hits the ramping hills and some of the bumps in the road. As she drives over a particularly large bump and the truck rumbles, bounces, and shakes, she starts to laugh.

When the truck gets on flat land again, she laughs harder and the truck starts to slow down. Ultimately, she stops it completely near the edge of the rocky road and rests her head on the steering wheel. Her shoulders shake as she sputters laugh after laugh. I remain quiet for as long as I possibly can, until I can't take it anymore.

"Care to share what's so funny?" I ask, flipping the visor down.

She shakes her head from side to side without looking up at me. "It's nothing."

"Come on, share. It's driving me crazy."

"Well, if I tell you, then you're going to think I'm crazy."

"If you don't, I'm going to think that anyway," I joke, but I'm being sort of serious.

She sighs, disheartened, and raises her head up. Tears stain her blue eyes and I have a hard time telling if they're from the laughter or if she was crying while her head was down. She dabs the corners of her eyes with her fingertips and blinks the tears back.

"It's just that . . . this is the most fun that I've had in a long time." She shakes her head like she's disappointed with herself. "Which is just silly."

"It's not silly," I say, resisting the urge to wipe her tears away. "I think it's fun, and trust me, I'm not silly at all." I flash a grin at her.

She gazes at me intently. "No, you kind of are, but in a good way."

I'm not sure how to respond to her since it seems like she's being genuine, but genuine about my being silly. "Lila, there's actually a reason why I brought you out here."

She pushes the truck into park and presses down on the parking brake before rotating in the seat to face me. "I figured as much."

"I just want to know what your plans are," I say, staring at the sky. The sun is setting and the lights of the city in the far distance illuminate the skyline.

"Plans for what?" She sounds confused.

I focus my attention on her. "Just with stuff."

"You're already getting sick of me, aren't you? Look, Ethan, I can totally move out. I have a few friends I can stay with until I find somewhere else."

"And how are you going to pay for this other place?" I ask. "And who are these other friends you'll be staying with? Guy friends?" *Why the hell did I just ask that?*

"Hey, I have other friends." She presses her hand to her chest, offended. "You're just my favorite." She's not joking when she says that, and for some reason it makes me happy and also makes me mentally roll my eyes at myself.

"That doesn't answer how you can pay for your own place," I say, unbuckling my seat belt.

She tips her chin down and twists the platinum ring on her finger. "I have no idea."

I reach over and fix my finger under her chin, forcing her to look up at me. "Hey, you're totally taking me wrong here anyway. All I want to talk about is our plans for moving forward."

"*Our* plans?" she asks, assessing me with skepticism.

"Yeah, you and I and the place we now both call home," I explain, removing my finger from her chin.

"Oh, you want me to start paying rent." She frees a trapped breath.

"Yes and no...I know you're going to probably need a little more time to heal and what not, but I think we should probably discuss how this is going to work a little further down the road." I flip the handle of the door, hating to say it but knowing it has to be said. "Like maybe when you're feeling better, you could get a job and start helping out." I'm trying to be subtle, but it's hard. "I just think that maybe if you were doing just a little bit more stuff, like working and finding some kind of hobby, things might be a little easier."

"I know that," she says quietly, her brow puckering as she stares at the scars on her wrist. I asked her once where they came from and she said it was from something really stupid she did, which makes me wonder if she got them when she got the ankle one. "But I have no idea where to start."

"I'll help you," I assure her, reaching over and giving her knee a gentle squeeze. "I'm not going to let you go at this alone. And when you're ready, we can talk more...about anything that you want to. I'm an excellent listener."

"I know you are." She stares at me for an eternity, searching my eyes, like she doesn't quite believe I'm real. When she finally opens her mouth, I have no idea what she's going to say. "Thank you." She unlocks her seat belt and leans over, giving me a kiss on the cheek.

I'm stunned. Despite all the touching we've done, this feels different. More intimate and personal and I realize that despite the fact that we've touched each other in places most friends don't, we've never actually kissed each other, a *real* passionate, lips-devouring kiss. And I want to kiss her so much it takes a lot of inner strength to keep my hands to myself. My instincts shout for me to jump out of the truck and run through the desert back to the apartment, far, far away from her. But the need to help her keeps me in the seat. I need to help her, like I didn't help London. This is my second chance to get things right and I want to make things right with Lila and with us. It's an overpowering, binding, magnetic feeling, one I'm unsure what to do with other than keep going.

When she leans back in the driver's seat, the look on her face is unreadable. "What do we do now?"

I shrug and then my mouth turns upward. "How about we go home and watch a sappy, poetic movie?"

"Home?" She says it like it's unreal, like homes don't exist. "Yeah, let's go home." She opens the door and jumps out into the sand, then turns around and aims a finger at me. "But you're driving. I'm so flipping scared I'm going to wreck your truck." She blows me a kiss and then slams the door, acting just like the Lila I met a year ago, only she's not because the Lila I met never really existed. She was a mirage created by pills.

Strangely enough, I'm not the same person when I met her because what I'm doing right now—what I'm feeling at this exact moment—is something I never thought I'd do or feel. Dependency—the thing I hate. I've seen it in action, through drugs and through relationships, like my mom's dependency on my dad, but I'm letting her be dependent on me, and in a weird way, I'm kind of relying on her to let me help her and trusting her to get better.

Even though she's been a pain in the ass for the last few

days, the thought of Lila moving out, living with another friend, annoys me. I kind of want her to live with me and that leaves me confused because it means that for the first time since London, I want someone to be in my life. I want Lila, more than I've ever wanted anyone.

Chapter Ten

Lila

I've been living with Ethan for two weeks and I've been pill free for two days, not even taking my half pills anymore. It's a strange feeling, one I'm still adjusting to and learning how to handle. I'd never realized how altered things would get when I was popping pills. Even the heat of the sun feels a little more blistering. Plus, I haven't slept with anyone. I think it's a record for me. Even when I dated guys, like my fleeting relationship with Parker a year ago, the relationship was based solely on sex that I barely felt, barely remembered. This has been my life since the first time I had sex. Even then, I had no idea what I was getting into, and when I finally did, it was too late. The things that happened forever changed who I was and how I saw things. I've pretty much never looked at guys the same way since, except for Ethan. He's a genuinely nice guy, which is rare, and makes our situation complex. Ethan and I have always had an interesting relationship, one that's pushed the boundaries of friendship yet hasn't quite crossed it. Now that we spend so much time together we barely touch each other, despite the fact that we're constantly defying friendship boundaries. Like when he walked into the bathroom while I was taking a shower this morning.

"What the hell are you doing?" I'd yelled when I heard the door open and shut.

"Relax, I'm just getting my toothbrush," he'd replied and then I heard him rummaging around in the medicine cabinet.

"If you don't get out of here, I'm going to pull back the curtain and flash you." I said, feeling squirmy about the fact that the curtain was very thin and nearly clear, almost see-through.

The water turned on and then he busted up laughing. "Okay, best punishment ever."

My stomach fluttered with butterflies as I smoothed back my wet hair and cracked the curtain back, peering out at him. "You know just as well as I do that you do not want to see me naked." I'm not even sure why I said it—whether I'm challenging him to admit something I hope exists or if I really do believe he doesn't want me that way.

He was wearing a pair of plaid drawstring pajama bottoms and no shirt. He had a toothbrush in hand and he was leaning over the sink, staring at the curtain. "Do you not know me at all?" He cocked an eyebrow as he stuck his toothbrush, coated with toothpaste, into his mouth. "I love seeing naked women." His voice sounded funny and he waggled his eyebrows, completely cool and casual.

I narrowed my eyes, wondering just how much he could see of me through the curtain, and wondering if I cared. "Yeah, but you made the friend line between us for a reason." I was being blunt and I didn't know why. I blamed it on withdrawals because I was learning quickly that they could make me insane and turn me into a crazy, emotional mess. "And you..." I almost bring up that night when we touched each other, but I'm scared.

His eyebrows knitted and he leaned over the sink, spitting out a mouth full of toothpaste. "No, we both agreed on that line, I thought." He rinsed off his brush and returned it into the holder near the sink. Then he turned around, leaned against the counter, and crossed his arms. "Am I wrong about that? Do you...do you...What do you want?"

Why is he asking me this? What does it mean? Why am I asking myself so many questions?

Water ran down my eyes and face as I discreetly gazed at his body. He's so beautiful in a way I'm not used to. A rough beauty, one that has substance, the kind that's real, not masked by tans, perfectly sculpted bodies, and fancy suits and ties. He's art, pure and simple—wispy hair that always falls into place right over his dark, smoldering eyes, creating the perfect shadowy look and those tattoos...dear God, the tattoos. He is the kind of art you really have to look at to get what it means—to understand what he's thinking.

I suddenly realized just how out of character I was. I was noticing him more than I normally do and I could feel it through every inch of my body, the pulsating urge to fling the shower curtain back and beg him to take me now. Beg him to. I never do that with sex. Usually guys just take it from me and I shut my feelings off. But I was contemplating going there with him, asking him for the first time, and being sober. It was making me wonder if I really knew who I was. All these years, the person I'd become was based on pills and this crazy need to feel loved.

We stared at each other for a while, and then Ethan cleared his throat and stood up straight, heading to the door. "If you want, we can pack up the rest of your clothes and go down to that consignment store and see if you can get anything for them." His voice sounded a little off pitch, but his expression was unfaltering.

I nodded, trying to stand motionless through the steam and the heat coiling up my inner thighs. "Sounds good."

He smiled, and then winked, his gaze skimming to the curtain hiding my body, and then he walked out, shutting the door behind him. I released the curtain, moving back below the showerhead, allowing the water to wash the heat and want off my body and down the drain, telling myself I'd get over it—get over Ethan. But for some reason, the idea seemed unlikely and very out of reach.

❧

"So how much do you think I can get for all of this?" I ask Ethan as he loads up the back of the truck with boxes of my clothes. My beautiful clothes I never want to let go of, but I know I need to in order to buy things like, say, food. I thought it would feel horrible to do this, and it kind of does, but there's also simplicity in it, like I'm getting a do-over, which I know isn't real, but at the moment everything feels real. Like the heat and the way my clothes stick to my damp skin. How my hair is in a messy ponytail, tugging at the nape of my neck. My hair has never been this messy and my cuticles never this dry. But I'm in simplicity land, where BMWs and designer purses and platinum rings don't exist and I'm trying to figure out what kind of person I am and where I fit in all this. Can I handle being poor? Taking care of myself? Who do I want to be? Who is Lila Summers?

Ethan heaves the last box into the bed of the truck and then slams the tailgate shut. "How the fuck would I know?" He wipes the sweat from his brow with his arm. He has on a green T-shirt and a pair of black shorts secured by a studded belt, along with an array of leather bands on his wrists. He's sweaty and kind of cranky, but beneath the sunlight he's freaking hot and I'm fixated on him.

"What?" he asks, noting my staring.

I press my lips together, shaking my head. "It's nothing."

"It's something. Otherwise you wouldn't have a goofy grin on your face."

I self-consciously rub my hand over my mouth like I can erase my smile or something. "I don't have a goofy smile."

His lips curve up into a playful grin, and for a moment his

grumpy mood vanishes. "Yeah, you're right. Now will you tell me why you have that beautiful smile on your face?"

"It's nothing." I shrug, trying not to let my smile broaden at the fact that he called it beautiful. "I was just lost in how nice you look today," I say, telling him the truth in the most casual way that I can.

He glances down at his sweaty T-shirt, then peers up at me warily. "You think I look good?"

"Sure." I shrug again, not really wanting to delve into the details of the fact that I think he's ridiculously hot looking and I want him to touch me. This feeling has become a growing desire over the last week. Living with him has seemed to sprout it like a flowering blooming on a tree. It's annoying and I wish it would go away because apparently without the pills I am one sex-starved person. Plus, Ethan has gotten a glimpse into what lies beneath my makeup, jewelry, and designer clothes—he's seen the *real* me at the ugliest times. I fear that having sex with him would be different, carrying more depth, at least for me, and I'd become emotionally involved. And then what would happen when our relationship ended? I'd probably pretty much be where I was at after Sean, the first and last guy I cared for and who used me and discarded me like trash.

He slants his head to the side, assessing me with a quizzical expression on his face. "Really?"

"Yeah. Why are you acting so weird?" I shield my face with my hand as the gleaming sunlight reflects off the metal roof of the apartment building.

He doesn't say anything, opening his arms and stepping forward. "Are you really, really sure you think I look good right now? So good that you want to touch me?" He does this weird thrusting thing with his hips that causes all my attention to center on his manly area.

I roll my eyes even though I shiver on the inside. "You're so weird sometimes."

"Weird, huh?" He comes at me, giving me little to no warning.

I try to gracefully sidestep out of his way, but I step on my own toe instead and trip over my ankles. I stumble to the side and he catches me in his arms, laughing under his breath as he intentionally rubs his sweaty body against mine.

"Oh my God!" I squeal, wiggling, attempting to get away. "You're all wet and gross."

"You're the one who said I look good." He lifts my feet off the ground and I stay straight as a board, trying to maintain distance from his sweaty body. He rounds the back of his truck, heading for the passenger side and somehow he gets the door open without letting go of me.

"What are you doing?" I yell, trying to sound like I'm turned off by his sweaty touch, but the pleasure of the moment is evident in my voice.

He drops me down on the seat and then grabs the seat belt. He leans close as he moves the strap over my shoulder to buckle me in.

"You still think I look good?" he asks with a dark look in his eyes, his face so close I can see the faint freckles on his nose.

I nod slowly, swallowing the lump in my throat. "Yes, but I also think you smell."

"I smell like a man," he says, grinning at himself. He leans in, getting his chest closer to my face so I can get a whiff of his man scent.

"Blah!" I scrunch my nose, turning my face to the side, even though the smell of him isn't that bad. He actually smells like cologne and sweat and heat. Very nice. Very manly. I discreetly breathe him in, letting the scent of him saturate my lungs. He must notice the rise and fall of my chest, because he leans back and looks me in the eyes, sheer perplexity burning in his pupils.

"So apparently you like the smell of sweat." He tries to joke but his voice cracks and I wonder why. Ethan never gets nervous. I've seen him hit on women many, many times, and he always gets them to come home with him.

I don't say anything and I'm not sure why. I just keep staring into his eyes and it feels different—I feel different, giddy, alive, and not numb for once. That switch that always flips off stays on. I'm not sure if I like the feeling—the vulnerable, misplaced emotions swarming inside my chest—or not.

Without even realizing it, I hitch my legs around his waist. The need to feel someone close to me, connect with me, touch me, is conquering anything else within me. I haven't been touched in a while and it feels good—better than good.

Ethan's breath hitches in his throat and it startles me. He's nervous. I'm nervous. I feel this strange shift between us, the heat between us intensifying, and I get excited, my nerves bubbling up inside me. Suddenly I'm a completely different person. I'm not broken. Lost. Numb. Confused. I'm a girl enjoying a moment with a guy I really, really like.

I close my eyes as he leans in. He's going to kiss me. I can tell. And I mean really kiss me this time instead of almost kissing me. I've been waiting for this more than I realized and despite all my concerns about my new feelings, ones that I'm sure existed before this moment but I was too medicated to feel anything, I want him so much it consumes every part of my body. I can feel all the warm, hot, overpowering sensations, and I breathe in his delicious scent, taste the anticipation. *Kiss me. Please God, kiss me. Don't back away.*

I moan from the heat of his breath and trace my hands up his back as I arch into him. I wait for it. Wait for the kiss, feeling his cheek touch mine. He rests it there, pressing our skin together, and I know that next he'll touch his lips to mine. I wait as he moans my name under his breath. And I wait. Seconds later his cheek leaves mine. *Break me. Throw me away. You don't want me. Of course you don't. No one does.*

Even though I don't want to, I open my eyes, feeling angry and humiliated when I realize he's watching me. This is a first for me. Usually, when I get to this point with a guy, they're staring at my breasts, ready to rip my clothes off, like I'm an object they're ready to devour.

"We should get going." That's all he says.

I'm struck dumb. Speechless. And feeling more unloved and undesirable than I ever have. "Yeah, I guess." I force a tight smile as I sit up, the inside of my body shaking with anger and disappointment. Tears actually start to sting at my eyes, something that's never happened to me before. I'm not sure how to handle it as I struggle to suck them back, twisting the ring on my finger as I remember everything I used to be.

"Are you sure?" He steps back from the door, farther away from me, and the sunlight hits his face. He looks sad and in pain, almost as if he's trying not to cry, just like me, and very un-Ethan-like.

I nod, adjusting my pink tank top over my stomach. I feel defeated, unwanted. Honestly, I have no idea what I feel and it's scaring me. I've lived my life moving through a string of very similar guys, ones who are polite in public, buy me nice things, have nice cars, and always tell me what I want to hear, at least until we screw, but I've never felt a single thing with them. And now there's Ethan. He's poor, drives a truck, and I'm pretty sure that every word he's ever said to me is real. He didn't bail on me, even when things got tough—he actually tried to help me, something no one's ever done. What does that say? That all this time I've been looking for the wrong person in the world? One who I thought I was supposed to look for? The type of guy my mother has always told me I needed. Is that what I've been doing all this time?

I feel like I'm about to burst into tears, not just from

rejection from Ethan or the lack of confidence flowing inside, but because I'm worried that all this time I might have been doing what my mother's wanted and was too blind to realize it. All I want to do is pop a pill and make everything I'm feeling go away. I want my confidence back, at least my fake confidence. I want my blissful, numb, never-having-to-experience-shame state because it's easier than reality.

Luckily, Ethan walks around the truck and climbs into the driver's seat. This seems to break the strange, depressing desire bubble that's formed around us.

"So to the store then, right?" he asks, turning the key.

"Where else would we go?" I say it softly as if it doesn't matter, but somehow it does.

He nods again and then backs away and the simplicity that I'd been feeling just moments ago evaporates and I'm left with a massive void in my chest and only one thing will fill it.

One tiny, fit-into-the-palm-of-my-hand, forbidden pill.

Ethan

Things are getting weird between us, just like I guessed they would. I'm not even sure what the hell the problem is. I mean, one minute she's taking a shower and for some damn reason I go in there, pretending I need to brush my teeth when really I just want to flirt with her. And then the truck thing. What the fuck? I seriously almost kissed her and then cried about it over all the emotions pouring inside me, emotions that I haven't felt since London. I have strong feelings for Lila and I know it; it's getting hard to handle. And we live together now, which makes things even more complicated. What happens if we end up doing something? We just live together? Kissing and touching and fucking, and if relationships go how I've seen them, we'd ultimately end up fighting.

But for a brief second I look past the idea of turning into my parents and actually like the idea of Lila and me kissing all over the apartment . . . fucking all over the apartment . . . having a relationship.

No, I can't go down that road. Yes, I want to help her, but as a friend, because that's what both of us need right now. I need a break from all of this, my emotions for her and my overanalyzing thoughts. What I need to do is go back to what always helps me clear my head and go get laid, yet the idea of sleeping with someone else makes me feel guilty, and not over London. Over Lila, even though I don't belong to her and she doesn't belong to me. I'm free to do whatever I want, yet for some stupid reason, it feels like I'd be cheating on her if I hooked up with someone else.

This living-together thing is seriously screwing with my head.

After we sell off her clothes, we wander around the secondhand store for no other reason that it helps avoid awkward time alone in the closed-in truck and then in the apartment.

"Ethan, what do you think?" Lila holds up this really tacky pink fluffy rug with flowers on it. She flashes me a teasing grin, totally trying to work through our awkward moment in the truck.

I make a face, but I'm seriously distracted by my thoughts, which are stuck back in the truck, wishing I'd kissed her. Yet at the same time wishing I could kiss London again. What the fuck is wrong with me? "It looks like a nineteen seventies shag rug that a lot of people probably had sex on."

Awkwardness builds around us at my use of the word *sex*. She shifts uncomfortably and I clear my throat.

"So should we go?" I ask, stepping to the side as a man walks up the aisle. I grow anxious and I need to get the hell out of here.

She lets out a breath and then sets the used rug back onto the shelf, seemingly depressed. "Yeah, I guess."

I feel like an ass. She doesn't need this right now. She needs a friend. *Why can't I just keep my hands to myself? Why can't I just be her friend?* The answer that pops into my head frightens me to no end. Because I want Lila and not just as a one-night stand.

I try for a lighter mood and subject. "We could go get some ice cream before we go home."

She shuffles to the end of the aisle, shrugging. "It's fine. I'm kind of tired anyway." She heads for the door, looking down at her feet, a broken version of the person I first met, and yet she's probably even more whole now. The brokenness just isn't hidden inside her anymore.

The drive home isn't any better. It's quiet and she keeps

picking at her nails and won't look at me. I'm about to drop her off at the apartment, ready to bail out for the night and get my mind out of depression land and my stupid thoughts of being with her. It's getting late, the sun is setting behind the sandy hills, and the Technicolor sky looks like a watercolor painting, beautifully unreal.

"Aren't you coming?" she asks, holding the truck door open, ready to climb out. Her blonde hair is slipping loose from her ponytail, her tight white tank top and shorts showing off her curves, and her blue eyes looking sad.

I shake my head, pressing my foot onto the brake, ready to bolt. "Nah, I got somewhere to be tonight."

Her eyes shadow over as she narrows them. "You mean you're going to go find someone to fuck you?" Her voice is sharp and she's clenching her fists so hard I think her fingers might break.

I feel like the biggest douche who's ever existed, but I'm also very confused. About everything. How I got to this place where every rule I set for myself I've managed to break. Where I'm looking past London and my guilt and all I want to do is be with Lila. "Yeah, probably."

She nods her head vigorously and then hops out, shooting me a heated look before slamming the door. I back away and before she even makes it to the curb I am spinning the tires. I head straight for the strip, parking as close as I can get and hop out. I wander over to the busiest section of the town, where the lights are glowing all over people's faces and pictures of half-dressed women litter the sidewalks. I search the crowd and nearby buildings for a potential hook-up. Because I need to fuck someone. Now.

I start searching for someone who looks like they'd be good for a one-night thing. There are too many people out tonight, so I end up going into one of the casinos and searching around the slots until I spot a group of women around my age laughing near the front of the building. I head over to them, knowing it's not the best scenario because they're in a group, but I need to clear my fucking head and screwing is the best way when my thoughts get this mixed up, because it distracts me. Not even the quiet will give me that right now.

A shorter woman with curves and tits that bulge out of her leopard-print dress starts eyeing me the closer I get. She whispers something in her friend's ear and then giggles as she starts twirling a strand of her blonde hair around her finger. I'm trying to decide if she's really my type, and if I even have a type anymore, when she starts to approach me.

"Hey," she says, smiling at me. She has some pink lipstick on her teeth and her eyelashes are a little too long, but she'll do, at least I think she will.

But as soon as I think it, my thoughts drift back to my apartment where there's already a beautiful blonde. I wonder what she's doing. If she's okay. Why did I just leave her like that?

"Hello, are you listening to me?" the blonde in front of me says and I blink out of my daze.

"No, sorry, I can't hear you over all the noise." I gesture around at the machines flashing around us.

She nods, biting on her lip. "Well, maybe we could go somewhere quiet."

I want to but all I can think about right now is how I bailed on Lila because my emotions were getting the best of me. Because I wanted to kiss her in the truck and then take her upstairs and fuck her. I want to be with her and for it to be more than just a one-time thing. I want to break my rules for her. The last person I broke my rules for was London, and I wanted her to be my last, at least I did at one point in my life, but now I'm not so sure.

The sounds of the slot machines are driving me crazy, along with the music playing. I could go with this woman somewhere that's less noisy, like a hotel room. Stay there for a few hours until I'm sweaty and temporarily content. Yeah, I could do that.

"Sure, we could go some place else." I smile at her, but I feel anything but happy on the inside.

She tells her friends she'll be back in a while and we head up the strip, weaving through the people. She starts telling me about her life, but I barely listen. I just keep nodding my head, thinking about Lila and how I feel about her, and every time I reach the same conclusion. That I don't think I can think about being with her completely yet, not without thinking about London as well.

I've always been good at controlling my actions and

emotions, but they're out of control at the moment, a wild reckless tornado sweeping through my body. I can't think straight. Lila. London. Lila. London. The slutty girl in front of me. I have no idea what I want and the truth is, whether I want to admit it to myself or not, I've been dependent on the idea of London, holding on to her and on to the guilt I felt for walking away from her that day. I can pretend all I want, but all the sex and numbness I've been seeking, just like I'm about to with this girl, was just covering it up, not getting rid of it. And now I'm trying to do the same thing with Lila because I feel guilty over having feelings for her. I think until I can let London go, I won't ever really be able to be with Lila on a complete emotional level where I'm just thinking of her. And that's what she deserves. Not my halfhearted attention or my moodiness where I run off to avoid what I'm feeling through sex. It's a revelation. A big, painful revelation and I have no idea what to do with it, although my original instincts say to go fuck this woman and forget about stuff for a moment.

I suddenly stop in the middle of the strip and people run into me.

The woman I've been walking with slows down, looking confused. "What's wrong?"

I blow out a breath, raking my fingers through my hair, thinking about how bad I just want to fuck her and momentarily feel better and how Lila is probably at home feeling the same way about taking pills, especially with how sad she looked when I bailed on her. "I have to go," I tell her, backing away from her through the crowd. I may not be able to have a relationship at the moment with Lila, but I can be her friend and I can walk away from having sex with this woman because I really don't want to be with her.

"What do you mean you have to go?" she calls out, but doesn't follow after me, probably because she doesn't care enough to try. We were simply two people looking for something in the wrong places and we didn't even bother to get each other's names.

When I make it back to my truck, I try to call Lila but she doesn't answer, so I make tire-ripping veer onto the road and floor the gas pedal, pushing the speed limit until I get back to the apartment. I'm worried about what I'll find and feel guilty that I've bailed out on a girl *again*.

When I open the door, my nostrils are instantly flooded with the scent of paint thinner. Or nail polish anyway. Lila peers up at me from the couch, her damp hair a veil around her flushed face. She has her foot propped up on the coffee table and she's painting her toenails as music plays in the background. My eyes instantly go to the half-empty beer on the table.

"It's just a beer," she quickly says as she swipes the paintbrush on her toenail.

"Is it the only thing?" I hate asking, but I need to know.

She blows out a breath, her bangs fluttering up from her face. "What do you think?"

I shut the door and toss the truck keys next to the lamp.

"Whatever you tell me, I'll think." I hope though that, like me, she was able to stay away from the one thing that helps her numb the stuff she doesn't want to feel. I hope she still feels her emotions right now, like I am. Because seeing her sitting here makes me realize that even though I still have a lot of shit to work on, mainly with figuring out how to let London and my guilt for her go, walking away from that woman on the strip was the right thing to do.

She puts the brush into the tiny bottle and twists it on, screwing it tightly closed. Then she sits back in the sofa, staring at me with an unreadable expression. "I didn't take anything, if that's what you're getting at."

I lower myself down onto the armrest and I'm overwhelmed with the scent of nail polish and her shampoo. "I'm not getting at anything, Lila. I just walked into my apartment."

"Yeah, but that's why you came back, right?" She scoffs. "Because you thought I was going to do something stupid."

I let out a stressed breath. "Look, I know things have been weird between us, but—"

"Weird," she says, cutting me off and throwing her hands into the air exasperatedly. "Ethan, you almost kissed me in the truck and then that night...that night we refuse to talk about..." She shakes her head, discouraged. "I don't even know where we stand anymore."

"I don't..." I struggle for words, surprised by how she tossed it out there so openly. It throws me off and I struggle to get my balance back, but I'm hopelessly falling to a place I'm unfamiliar with and I need to regain my footing before I do anything drastically life-altering. "I don't know what you want me to say."

"I don't either," she says. "And it's been driving me crazy, because I have no idea what I want or what you're thinking. I'm going so crazy that I seriously thought about using again. Every single thing is driving me crazy!" She balls her hands into fists, about to scream. "I can't take it anymore. I'm going to lose it. I seriously think I'm losing my mind. I mean, maybe I need to be on pills. Maybe they were what was keeping me sane and now all of my insanity is out there for the whole world to see."

She doesn't have to explain. I know what she means. I thrum my fingers on the side of my leg, racking my brain for something that will make this situation better. I need to calm her down and make her understand that she's not in this alone. "Did I ever tell you about the time I ran my truck into the ditch?" I have a vague idea of where I'm going with this, but honestly I just might be rambling.

"What?" She gapes at me, dumbfounded. "How does that have anything to do with what I just said?"

I slide off the armrest and down onto the cushion, leaving a little distance between us as I kick my feet up onto the coffee table. "It happened two days after I decided to clean up my act. I was pretty much insane and my mind was all over the place. I seriously thought I was going crazy." I omit the fact that a major part of this had to do with London, because even though I've realized my issues with holding on to London, I'm still not ready to talk to Lila about her. "I ended up dozing off and ramming my truck into a ditch. I was completely sober, and that in and of itself can be even more complex than getting high. It's distracting, you know. And hard."

She taps her foot on the ground, refusing to look at me. "Why are you telling me this?"

"Because"—I lean closer to her and start to shut my eyes when I get a whiff of her perfume, but quickly blink my eyes open—"I want to let you know that I understand how you're feeling and that sometimes things do feel all crazy, but it'll fade."

She sighs begrudgingly. "How long?"

"Until what?"

"Until it goes away completely?"

I stare ahead at the wall in front of us. "I'm not sure it ever does go completely away. It's always kind of there, you know. Like a sleeping beast or something, but the intensity of the cravings fades away."

She turns her head toward me. "Did the beast ever wake up for you? I mean, have you ever slipped up?"

I nod. "Once. About a year after I stopped doing drugs." The day I saw London again. It was too much to see her like that, a shell of her old self.

"And then what?" Lila asks. "You just fixed yourself again?"

"Pretty much," I say, again omitting the truth. That I was afraid of myself when I do drugs. Afraid of what I might become. Afraid I'd lose my mind, too, and end up jumping out a window, following in London's footsteps. The people at the house had said they had no idea she went upstairs. That they didn't see her. That's because they were out of it and I should have been there for her. And she shouldn't have shot up the damn heroin in the first place. What really gets to me though, and I'll always wonder, is why did she jump? Was it because of the drugs? Or was it for another reason? Did she want to jump? If I hadn't left her, then I'd know. If I hadn't left her, then she might not have jumped. But she still might have. I'll never really know."

Lila bites on her lip, soaking my words in like a sponge and I pray to God I've said everything right. She looks at me, her eyes big and blue, and she frees her lip. "You're seriously like Mr. Miyagi or something."

My eyebrows shoot upward and the dark tone of the night flips to amusement. "Did you seriously just reference the *Karate Kid*?"

She shrugs. "What? It's just an old movie about kicking ass."

"Yeah, but..." I shake my head. "It doesn't seem like something you'd watch."

"Well, I'm full of surprises." She rolls her eyes like she's saying the most ridiculous thing that's ever existed, but really, it's the truth. Good and bad, Lila has been surprising me over and over again and I wonder just how many more surprises I'm in store for. Good and bad.

"Yes, you are," I say, truthfully, remembering how different she was when I first met her. "You really are."

Chapter Eleven

Lila

Ethan's teaching me how to take care of myself, like how to shop cheap at the grocery store and pretty much spend as little money as possible wherever I go. It's a little bizarre, not just because I need to be taught these things at the age of twenty, but because what he's teaching me goes against everything I've been taught. I grew up in a home with maids, nannies, dry cleaners, chauffeurs, and money always on hand. Then while I lived with Ella, when I couldn't pay someone to do these things for me, she'd do them. Looking back at it now, I feel guilty. I should have never let her be responsible for cleaning up after me. Now I'm broke and doing my own laundry. It's weird and kind of sucks, yet at the same time there's this strange gratification of being able to take care of myself, like I'm finally not completely worthless.

"I have a job interview tomorrow morning," I announce as I walk into the apartment, shutting the door behind me, feeling a little proud of myself, despite what position the interview is for.

Ethan glances up from the book he's writing in at the kitchen table. His hair is swept back out of his eyes and sticks up everywhere. "Oh, thank God. Finally. I was beginning to think I was going to have to kick you out on the streets." He grins, amused with himself, but there's an underlying pain in his expression, almost as if he's forcing his humorous self to come out to disguise something else.

I'd ask him about it, but after the whole truck fiasco I'm deciding it's better if we keep a little bit of distance between us, until I can figure out where we stand.

"Rude much?" I toss my purse on the couch and chuck the keys at him. He ducks, laughing, and the keys miss him and hit the wall behind him. "And I know you would never put me out on the streets." I grin as I enter the kitchen. "You like me way too much."

"Do I now?" He sits up straight and humor dances in his eyes. "But I'm glad you finally got an interview. You've seriously applied for, like, a hundred jobs."

"I know." I sigh and head to the kitchen, opening the fridge. "But apparently if you're twenty and have never worked before, no one wants you to work for them." I grab a can of soda out of the fridge and bump the door shut with my hip. "They all kept looking at me like I was worthless, and I'm not." I tap the top of my finger against the can as I sink down into the chair. "I've got skills, you know."

"Mad finger skills?" He laughs as he eyes my finger tapping insanely against the top of the can.

I flip him my middle finger. "You would be very surprised at what I can do with my fingers."

He clenches his fist and places it in front of his mouth. "Oh, I'm sure I would."

We both go silent. I can hear the loud roar of an engine outside and the clanking of the refrigerator. It's an awkward silence, which is becoming more common the longer I live here with him. I'm not sure what's causing it. Sexual tension? Probably from me, but I'm assuming Ethan's managed to maintain his playboy lifestyle, bringing his women home late at night and sending them home as soon as he's done with them, because that's what he's always done. I haven't actually seen any of them, but none of them in the past have stuck around very long anyway. I'd be disgusted by his behavior, but I've done the same thing time and time again, only I'm usually the one leaving the house in the early hours of the morning.

Ethan clears his throat and then shuts his book, shoving back from the table. "So should we go celebrate?"

"Celebrate what?" I take a gulp of my soda to cool down my body.

He scoops up the keys without taking his eyes off me. "The job interview." He stands up straight, closing his fingers around the keys. "By the way, where is it at?"

I set the soda can down on the table. "It's at that bar." I try not to go into the details on purpose because I'm not sure how he's going to react.

"What bar?" He pushes the chair in and tucks the keys into the back pocket of his jeans.

"The one down on that street by the old section of Vegas," I say evasively, pushing away from the table. I collect my can and head for the hallway. "I'm going to go to bed early, so I can get some rest for tomorrow." I glance over my shoulder as I step through the doorway. "Rain check on the celebration? I only want to celebrate if I get the job."

He scans me over quizzically. "Where's the job interview, Lila?"

"Nowhere." I walk quickly down the hall to avoid any more questioning. Once I make it to my room, I shut the door and breathe in the silence, but as soon as I step away from the door it opens and Ethan comes walking in.

"Where's the interview, Lila?" he repeats, standing in the doorway, looking vexed.

I place the soda can down on one of the boxes I haven't unpacked yet and then cross my arms. "Why is this bothering you so much? I thought you were just happy I finally had an interview."

He shifts his weight and then sweeps his fingers through his hair, brushing it out of his eyes. "Because...you're not..." He's struggling and I'm twistedly finding it amusing. "You're not applying to be a stripper, are you?" His gaze locks on me and fury burns in his eyes.

Without taking my eyes off him, I sit down on the foot of

my bed. "Why would it matter if I was? I thought you *loved* strippers."

He shrugs, casually leaning against the door. "It doesn't matter, but it's not the place for you. You're too…" His gaze skims my entire body, making even the coolness of the air conditioning feel stifling.

"Too what?" I press.

His attention lingers on my chest and then he blinks, fixing his eyes on my face. "It's nothing…you just don't fit in a place like that."

I bend my knee and unfasten my sandal, wiggling my foot out. "I think a lot of people would disagree with you." I shake my chest and then roll my eyes. "What else am I good for?"

He remains by the doorway, grasping on to the doorknob. "You're good for a lot of things, you just don't see it."

Okay, so that was a little bit sweet. "Like what exactly?" I toss my sandal into the closet without getting up. "I can't do anything by myself. I mean, you had to teach me to work the dishwasher for crying out loud."

He lets go of the doorknob and sits down beside me on the bed while I take off my other sandal. "So what? Everyone has to learn sometime. You're just learning a little bit later than most people."

"Because I'm a spoiled brat who had a maid."

"You don't anymore, though. You're becoming an independent, strong Lila." He winks at me and gives me a lopsided grin. "And that Lila doesn't belong in a strip club."

I think I may have just fallen in love with him. No one has ever said something so nice to me or put that kind of confidence in my character. In fact, I've been told the opposite for as long as I can remember. *Lila, you'll never make it. Lila, you're worthless. Lila, you're messing up this family. No one will ever love you if you don't change into something they can love. Be perfect. Be beautiful. Because no one will want you if you're not.*

"Even though I know you're going to get annoyed with me for saying it," I begin, slipping my foot out of my sandal, "you're seriously really sweet when you want to be."

He frowns with annoyance. "I'm not sweet. I'm actually really, really mean."

"You're so full of it." Once I get my shoe off, I flop back on the bed, not bothering to tug my shirt down when it rides up over my stomach. "I have to take more of my clothes down to that store tomorrow because I'm running out of money. Can you give me a ride? Or can I borrow your truck?"

He lies down beside me on the bed, surprising me, and turns his head toward me. "You say that like it's the most tragic thing that's ever happened to you."

"It kind of is." I pout with my arms overlapped on my stomach and my gaze fixed on the ceiling. "As shallow as it's going to sound, I love my clothes."

"You'll get over it." He runs his finger along my exposed stomach, right above the scar hidden behind the waistband of my shorts, and I fight back the urge to shiver and moan. "Besides, you're not dressed up all fancy now." He props up on his elbow, keeping his fingers on my stomach, although I'm not even sure he realizes they're there. He peers down at my tight, purple T-shirt that Ella left behind and my denim shorts I've never worn until today. "And you look pretty fucking good."

"I'm dressed this way because of where I applied." I have to work to keep my lungs moving as he continues to trace his fingers back and forth across my stomach. The insides of my thighs are starting to shake, more than any other time a guy has touched me. "I had to play the part."

"And what part is that?" He cocks an eyebrow and then playfully pinches my stomach right above my belly button and a hot sensation coils deep within me. "Come on, just tell me where you might be working because I'll end up finding out anyway."

I begrudgingly sigh. "Fine…at Danny's Happenin' Bar and Entertainment."

His fingers stop moving and his eyebrows arch. "The one on the old strip?"

I nod, avoiding eye contact with him. "Yep, that'd be the one."

His fingers stay on my stomach for what seems like forever, blinding me with heat and deafening me with desire. I'm so relieved by the time he pulls them away because I swear I'm seriously on the verge of having an orgasm. "You dance?"

I tilt my head toward him, finally encountering his gaze. "Why do you sound so surprised?"

He wavers, chewing on his lip. "It's just hard to picture you dancing...like that."

"What? Slutty? I don't see why you'd be surprised about that."

"It's not slutty," he says, still seeming puzzled as his eyes do a quick sweep of my body. "It's...sexy and kind of erotic, at least from what I can remember. It's been a while since I've been down there."

"It's not that sexy...I mean, I don't take my clothes off or anything," I explain. "It's just dancing at a bar and sometimes on the bar, depending on what night. I get to wear normal clothes...well, normal tight clothes. And eventually they'll teach me how to bartend."

"I know what it is, Lila." His hand lazily scrolls up my body again and I swear to God I'm going to melt from the heat emitting from his eyes. Then he catches sight of his fingers on my stomach and, blinking at them, he quickly pulls his hand away.

I sit up, no longer wanting to be on the bed with him because I'm seriously about ready to straddle his lap and force myself on him. "Look, I really need to get some rest." I climb off the bed and backtrack to the door, opening it wider so he'll get the hint to leave and let me be horny for him in peace.

He doesn't get up, only pushes up on his elbows. "You want me to leave?" He fakes a sexy pout, trying to be mocking, but it comes off more mouthwatering than anything. "I thought you were going to show me the moves you used when you applied."

I place my hand on my hip and give him an overdramatic look of aggravation. "Ethan, seriously, stop teasing me. I only had to fill out an application so far. Besides, you really don't want to see me dance. You just want to try to make me blush or something."

"Why would I ever want to do that?"

"Because . . . I have no idea. You tell me."

He sits up and crosses his arms, his muscles flexing. "It's just something to think about. You could practice on me." He smirks. "I'm an excellent judge."

I roll my eyes. "I'm sure you are."

He chuckles under his breath, totally pleased with himself, and then he stands up. "Are you sure you want me to leave? I mean, I'm assuming that's why you're standing by the door, looking all hot and bothered."

I open my mouth to say, "Get out please," but nothing comes out. I never want him to leave, which is really bad. I could blame it on the fact that I like his company, but the fact of the matter is that I need him. "You want to watch a movie or something?"

He smiles broadly. "A sappy, poetic one maybe?"

I point a finger at him. "You know they don't exist. We tried to find one on Netflix, remember?"

He sits up, ruffling his hair into place. "I'm sure one exists, we just haven't looked hard enough…but we can watch a movie."

"Which one?"

"Whatever you want?"

I raise my eyebrows to express my doubt. "And what if I say the girliest movie ever?"

He yawns, stretching his arms above his head, showing off his rock-hard abs and the artful ink on his skin. "Then I guess I'll finally get a nap. I've been wanting to take one all day."

I roll my eyes, but smile. "I secretly think you like girly movies," I say as we head out into the living room.

He shakes his head, but I hear him laugh under his breath. "Not the movie, just the company that comes along with it."

I don't say anything, because I can't. I've never been around guys before who have complimented me on anything besides my tits and my ass. I situate myself on the couch while Ethan boots up the Xbox so we can stream Netflix. Grabbing the remote, he sits down on the couch beside me. He sits closer than I anticipated, his knee resting against mine and it feels almost painfully good, to the point where my body feels like it's going to explode from the tension and heat, and while I hate it, I also love it because I've never felt it before. It's crazy and strange, like I'm a virgin again or something, and it alters my entire thought process. For the first time in my life, I picture myself sitting next to him, doing this exact same thing ten years down the road. We would be living in the same shitty apartment and Ethan would still be working his job in construction because he never graduated from college and I don't think he cares enough to do anything more with his life. And I won't be going anywhere, since I could barely get a job as a dancer at some skanky run-down bar. I would still be wearing an outfit I got off a clearance rack and we would have the same crappy furniture because Ethan hates fancy stuff and we couldn't afford it between our crappy salaries. But despite poverty, everything would be okay. In fact, I can actually envision myself happy, even if I were poor. I've had everything before, material-wise at least, and look where it got me. Addicted to pills, struggling to take care of myself, and bearing all the emotional trauma I couldn't deal with because I'd been taught it was wrong to show emotions that were anything but perfect and pretty. I feel so content right now and I want to keep feeling content. Genuinely content.

Ethan drapes his arm on the back of the sofa and his fingers brush my hair away from my neck. He starts searching through the movies, asking me questions about them, and I answer with minimal responses because I'm too engulfed in what's happening to my body and mind. There's so much clearness in it and I'm hyperaware of everything, from the way his lip is slightly swollen from where he chews on it to the intoxicating scent of him. I can even feel the heat flowing off his body, enflaming my skin and he's not even touching me. It's amazing. Clear. Undiluted. Is this what I've been missing? All these years? Is this what things are supposed to feel like?

Warm and heart pounding, instead of cold and silent. If it is, though, then what the heck am I supposed to do with it?

A little bit into the movie Ethan falls asleep and he slumps over, putting his head onto my shoulder. I'm fairly sure he has no idea that he did it and I wonder what he'll think when he wakes up. I let him stay there, running my fingers through his hair, across his nose, his jawline, his lips, like a creeper touching someone in their sleep. I can't help it though. He's got such soft skin and amazing lips. I wonder what they'd taste like if our mouths finally came into contact with each other.

I'm smiling at the thought when he starts muttering in his sleep. At first it's really quiet and it almost sounds like he's saying "Lila." But then he starts to get louder and I realize he's saying "London, don't leave me... Please, stay... I need you..."

London? Is it a person? If so, Ethan's never mentioned a London before. Who could that be? A girlfriend? But if so then why has he never introduced us? An endless list of things runs through my mind and I realize that even though he sleeps around, the idea of him having a girlfriend is like a knife to the heart. Sex is meaningless, but a girlfriend he could care about.

Maybe even love.

Ethan

"Oh, Ethan," London singsongs as she skips through a field. There's a bonfire burning near the trees in the distance and the smoke rises to the starry sky. There's a party going on and people are laughing,

shouting, drinking, having sex and London is out in the field skipping like the strange girl that she is.

"What are you doing?" I ask, drinking my beer as I walk slowly behind her, watching her move through the field of tall grass and weeds. "You're going to get us lost."

She spins around and around, with her head tipped back, her dark hair blending with the night. "I'm having fun." She spins again and then stops as I reach her. "How about you?" she asks, breathless.

I knock back the rest of the beer and then crush the cup, throwing it into the dirt. "What about me?"

She grins, walking toward me, swaying her hips. "Are you having fun?"

"I'm having a blast," I say flatly, placing my hands on her hips.

She frowns. "Well, that sounds convincing."

I sigh, letting my head fall forward so it's pressed against hers. "Sorry, I'm just tired. And there are too many people over at the party for my taste."

"You can be such a party pooper," she says. "But only half the time. And then sometimes you're totally into it."

"I'm totally into it when I'm either drunk or stoned," I admit. "But when I'm sober, it drives me crazy."

She pauses, hooking her finger through my belt loop. "Sometimes I think you're going to just pack up and leave and go wandering off on your own."

I don't answer right away, moving my forehead away from

hers so I can look her in the eye. "*I sometimes think about it. Just packing up and hitting the road.*"

"*Would you take me with you if you do?*"

"*Would you want to go with me?*"

"*Maybe... I don't know.*" *She doesn't look like she wants to.* "*Would you want me to go with you?*"

"*Maybe,*" *I say, but honestly I'm not sure. I really like her, more than any other girl out there, but there are times when I do think about leaving not just my life behind, but everyone in it.*

"*You're such an ass,*" *she says.* "*I can't believe you wouldn't want to take me with you.*"

"*I never said that,*" *I tell her.*

"*But you didn't completely deny it,*" *she retorts.*

Silence grows around us and she holds on to me, wrapping her arms around my waist. "*Okay, I take my 'maybe' back. I want to go with you but only so you can take me away from this place—my life.*" *Her voice is flat, saddened, devoid of any emotion. She gets this way sometimes when she's talking about her life.*

I kiss the top of her head. "*What's so bad about your life?*"

"*What's so bad about yours?*" *she says, dodging the question like she always does whenever I try to dig deep into her psyche.*

"*Nothing, except that I don't want it,*" *I reply, pulling her against my chest.* "*London, if you want me to take you with me then I will.*"

"*Okay, well, I'll need notice before we go,*" *she jokes, the sadness leaving her voice.* "*And I'll have to check my calendar. I'm really busy this summer.*"

I pinch her ass hard and she squeals, backing away from me. She takes off running through the field and I chase after her, but somewhere along the line I lose track of her and the darkness swallows her whole.

"London," I call out, but she doesn't reply. I hear her laugh from somewhere, but I can't figure out where. "London…"

Someone is shaking my shoulder and I'm snapped out of my dream. I feel hot, burning up, like I have a fever and my heart is racing erratically.

"You're totally a lightweight," Lila says when I open my eyes. I'm lying on my back, my head resting in her lap, my feet kicked up on the armrest.

I'm very aware of how comfortable I am on the outside, but on the inside I'm a mess as memories of London float around in my head. Once again, I'm stuck somewhere between Lila and London and I don't know how to get over London completely so I can just be with Lila.

Lila hovers over me with a hurt look in her blue eyes, like she's upset about something. "You passed out, like, ten minutes after it started."

"I made it ten minutes?" I instantly crank up my humor, trying to shut down my thoughts of London as I blink up at Lila. "I should get a medal for that or something."

She rolls her eyes and sits back on the couch so that I can sit up. "It wasn't that bad."

"No, it was terrible." I stretch my arms above my head and yawn as I lower my feet to the floor.

She watches me with this strange look on her face, like she's trying to unravel a puzzle. "Who's...who's London?"

My heart just about drops into my stomach as a shock pulsates through me. "*What?*"

"London." She repeats, relaxing back in the sofa, with an intent look on her face. "You were muttering it in your sleep." The corners of her lips quirk, but it looks forced. "At first I thought you were saying my name and I thought, ew, gross, he's having sex dreams about me. But then I realized you were saying London and I'm starting to wonder if you have a secret girlfriend or something."

"She's no one," I snap, not meaning for my voice to sound so clipped, but I've never talked to anyone about London because talking about her makes everything real. "So don't worry about it."

She shakes her head. "Don't get all snippy with me. You know a lot about me—things I'd rather you not know—and I think it's only fair that I know a few things about you."

"You already know things about me," I say, trying not to snap, because it'd be bad, both for her and me. "Now drop it."

She considers this and then her expression darkens in a very un-Lila-like manner. "No, it's bullshit." She inches closer to me on the sofa. "You've gotten into my head so much over the last few weeks and it's not fair that I don't know a lot about you."

"You know enough." My voice is tight and packed with a warning for her to not go down this road.

"Apparently not, since I've never heard of this London, yet she seems to be important to you."

"Lila, drop it," I warn, sitting up and stretching my arms above my head. "You don't want to go there."

"Yes, I do." I'm not sure why, but she seems like she's looking for a fight.

Anger crashes through me, a ripple of fire, ready to burn anything in its path. I'm a very controlled person, except for that one time, right after I heard about London—the one time I lost it. The one time I turned into my father and shouted at everyone, broke stuff, showed my rage. "Shut the fuck up." My voice is low, but the deep, heavy tone is worse than me yelling.

Her eyes water over, like she's about to cry. "You shut the fuck up! I just asked you a God damn question."

I take a few deep breaths, and then I stand up. "I'm going to my room." As I walk toward the hall, she watches me, looking enraged, irritated, and the slightest bit hurt, just like how London looked the last time I saw her, the last time I walked away from her.

But I can't bring myself to turn back to her. I'm too worked up over London, and the emotions surfacing inside me make me want to run out and find someone to fuck. But I can't. God, I haven't been able to since the incident on the strip, and honestly I've been pretty content about it until now.

My head is in such a weird place right now over the dream. I try not to think about London, but she always catches up with me, whether I'm awake or asleep. Plus, Rae won't stop texting me, so that doesn't help. Three to four times a day, every fucking day, she texts me or leaves me a voice mail. I've been screening her calls, refusing to answer until I'm certain about what I want to do.

I lock myself in my room and do the only other thing I can think of to try to clear my thoughts. I write.

I'm afraid. More than I want to admit. Fear has never been a feeling I have been comfortable with. I always adopted the artificial, subdued, and in-control demeanor, because I don't think anyone needs to know what really lies inside me. Like the fact that I still feel torn apart, ripped in half, my soul split, because the only girl I thought I wanted to be with is an outer shell that still exists in every aspect down to the mole she has above her lip. That's still there, along with her hazel eyes and the scar above her mouth. Her skin is still flawlessly smooth. Her looks still exist, but she doesn't. The London I knew—the London of the past—is no more. She's forgotten her life, and life for her now is only about the future. Everything else is lost to her.

But what I really worry about is if I do go and see her, I'll finally have to let her go. Forever. And the scariest thing is I both do and don't want to. I want to move on, maybe with Lila and yet I want to hold on to London because it's easier than feeling everything that comes along with letting go. But deep down, I'm realizing that eventually I'm going to have to finally say good-bye.

Chapter Twelve

Lila

It's been a little over a week since I brought up this London person and Ethan will still barely talk to me. He avoids me most of the time, but when we do cross paths, he keeps it very business-like, as if we're only roommates and nothing more. Whoever this mysterious London girl is she obviously means something to him. At first I thought it was just a secret girlfriend, with the way he whimpered out her name after he fell asleep on the couch. It hurt. A lot. I'd always been okay with him sleeping with women, or at least I could live with it. But a girlfriend? The idea was clawing at my skin like overly manicured nails.

When I started questioning him about it, though, the spark of anger and discomfort and pain in his eyes led me to believe she might have been someone he loved. But getting to the bottom of it seems nearly impossible when all he'll say to me is hello. It's annoying me a little, because he knows so much about me. But when I think about it, Ethan's always been more of a listener than a talker, and he keeps a lot about himself to himself.

I got the job at Danny's and I'm still figuring out if I like it or not. Honestly, it hasn't been too bad, but then again, I haven't gotten up on the bar and danced yet. Today is supposed to be the big day.

After I check out my reflection in the mirror for what seems like ages, I finally head out. Ethan is sitting on the couch, watching the news, although his glazed-over expression means he's probably daydreaming about something other than the weather. He's got no shirt on and a torn pair of cargo shorts. His hair is a mess and his eyes are red, like he's high, but I know Ethan enough to know he's not.

I collect my purse and a jacket off the table and his eyes wander over to me. Usually, he immediately disregards me, but tonight my outfit sets him off, which I expected.

"What the fuck are you wearing?" He sits up, giving me a dirty look as he takes in my tight white tank top that shows off my stomach, my breasts, and the leopard-print bra I am wearing underneath. I have a pair of really short cutoffs on that reveal the bottom of my ass when I bend over, which one of the waitresses told me I'll be doing a lot since the guys usually throw the tips onto the floor.

"I could ask you the same thing," I retort, swinging the handle of my bag over my shoulder. "There's a thing called a shirt, you know."

He narrows his eyes. "What the hell did I do to you?"

"Besides ignore me for the last week?" I say, jerking the front door open. "Nothing."

"I'm not ignoring you," he calls out. "I'm just opting not to spend time with you. Something roommates do a lot."

I stick my head back in the door. "You're being an asshole and I don't know why. I didn't even do anything to you besides ask a God damn question."

His eyes soften and I think he's going to apologize as he stands up and struts over to the door. But then he says, "You look like a whore."

That strikes a nerve, severing my connection with him. I raise my hand to slap him or shove him—I'm not even sure which. But then I decide against it and, shaking with rage, I walk down the stairs. "I don't even know what I did!" I holler, unconcerned that I'm making a scene. I've spent my whole life trying not to make a scene and I'm so sick and tired of it. Nothing feels right anymore.

"You didn't do anything…This is all my fault…I'm sorry," Ethan calls out after me, but I'm already running across the parking lot so his words hit my back.

I have no traveling options other than to take the bus or walk. It's a long walk, so I take the smelly, gross bus. I sit in the back, stewing in my anger, zipping my jacket up over my slutty clothes. I've never cared that I was a slut before. I've been called it since I was fourteen. But that God damn word—whore—sends me back to a time I've tried to forget.

"Just lie down on the bed," Sean says in a sultry voice that makes me feel warm and loved inside. "I promise, Lila, it'll feel good."

He'd just put the platinum ring on my finger, saying that he was waiting to give it to someone special. My head feels a little hazy, due to the few shots I had before I came to his place. I hate drinking, but my friends told me it was necessary for tonight, especially if I was going to lose my virginity. All the cloudiness evaporates as I blink up at him and I can see the love in his green eyes, even if he hasn't said it aloud yet. I know he loves me, because no one has ever looked at me like that—like they want me.

"Take off your clothes," he whispers, leaning in to give me a soft kiss on the mouth.

I nod as he leans away and I start to unbutton the crisp white shirt I have to wear every day at school. I keep my eyes on his as I fumble with the buttons, both loving and fearing the hungry look in his eyes.

"You have such gorgeous eyelashes," I say as I slip my arms out of my sleeves and let my shirt fall to the floor. I'm standing in my plain white bra, plaid uniform skirt, and knee-high socks, the standard New York Reform School attire. I've never been topless in front of a guy before, but Sean isn't just some guy. I gradually walk toward him, trying to look sexy and confident, but my nerves are bursting inside. I slide my fingers up the front of his shirt, feeling his rock-hard chest beneath it, pretending that I'm not terrified at all of what's about to happen—pretending I'm more experienced than I really am.

His muscles constrict as I reach his neck and for a flicker of a second the caring softness I've always seen in his eyes ices over. But the oddly cold look quickly vanishes as he reaches up and places his large hand over mine. "Guys don't want to be told they have gor-geous eyelashes, Lila," he says in a blank tone. "Think of something better."

I swallow hard, worried I'm turning him off. I rack my brain for something to say to him—anything that will get him to stop looking at me as if I'm just an inexperienced, naïve girl. But I can't seem to think of anything witty and sexy through the massive sea of alcohol in my head.

Sensing my panic, he gathers my hands in front of me. "Relax, Lila. I'm not going to hurt you."

"I never said you were." I sound choked and I know he can feel my pulse pounding through my wrists that he has pinned beneath his hands.

He smiles, glancing around his dimly lit bedroom. He has candles burning on the nightstands and in the windowsill, creat-ing the perfect glow and lavender scent to make love in. The bed is decorated with rose petals, there are chiffon curtains enclosing the elegant four-poster bed, and soft music flows in the background. Everything is perfect. Perfection. I can feel it, which means this is right. The thing I'm supposed to achieve. I have the perfect guy, older and more mature, with stubble and a firm jawline, and he's wearing a fancy suit. These are the things my mother always told me to look for in a guy. Yes, he's been a little rough with me, and when we're around other people, he ignores me, but only because he has to because he's older.

He strokes his finger delicately down my cheek and all my

reservations melt like the wax dripping from the candles around the room. "You trust me, right?"

I nod, gazing up at him. "Of course."

An artful smile curls at his lips. "Good." He leans in, putting his lip to my ear, and breathes on my skin. I try not to shudder because I know it will make me seem immature, but I can't help it and my shoulder drifts upward. "Lie down on the bed for me," he says softly and then grazes his teeth across my ear.

"O-okay," I say breathless.

He leans back and his eyes almost look black in the inadequate lighting as I back toward the bed and he slowly drinks me in. My knees are shaking as I sink down onto the mattress, remaining on the edge.

"Do you—do you want me to leave my skirt on?" I sound so nervous, but he's so experienced and I'm not and I'm doing a terrible job of hiding it.

He walks back and forth in front of the foot of the bed, tracing his finger along the footboard. "Leave it on for now." As he reaches one of the bedposts, he stops and begins unwinding a frayed rope I hadn't noticed was there until now.

My eyes are fixated on it, my body filled with uncertainty as he unravels the rope from the bedpost and winds it around his hand. "You look nervous," he observes, rounding the bed back and coming to me. "I thought you trusted me."

"I-I do," I stammer, unable to take my eyes off the rope. "You just seem different tonight."

He puts a finger under my chin and forces me to look up at him. "Lila Summers, listen to me. I'd never do anything to hurt you, understand?" He pauses, waiting for me to nod, and I do, almost certain that I mean it. He smiles. "Good, now lie down for me please."

I obey, telling myself I love him, even when seconds later he calls me his little whore as he ignores my pleas for him to stop and he ties me to the bed…

I jump up from my seat, even though the bus is stopped nowhere near my destination. The doors open and I rush out into the heat and dusty air, trying to shake my head of thoughts of lavender and the aching memory of how the rope felt. I make a right instead of a left, heading toward a house I know I shouldn't be going to, but it's hard—too hard. Remembering the things I've done—the dark things I did—is making a vile feeling pollute my stomach.

The house is located a few blocks down from where I got off the bus. The neighborhood is nice, homey, each two-story stucco house surrounded by lush green lawns dotted with plants and small trees. Each two-car driveway has a midsize sedan, sleek, but not too sleek. There's an illusion of middle-class perfection in this neighborhood, but behind some of these closed doors lives a darker way of life. I know because I'm headed to one of them.

At the end of the street, I make my way up the driveway and rap on the door that has a decorative wreath on it and a welcome mat below. I fidget anxiously as I wait. My phone goes off, notifying me that I have a text message, but I reach into my pocket and silence it. I want one thing right now and only one thing and when the door swings open, that's what I say.

"I need one right now." I sound panicky and it's going to give Parker all the power, but I don't give a crap at the moment. I just need to feel okay.

He leans against the doorway, looking handsome, his sandy-blond hair perfectly in place, the sleeves of his black button-down shirt rolled up to his elbows. He has dimples and his smile is flawless. He seems perfect with his charm and a PhD. Perfect. Perfect. Perfect. *Isn't this what my mother wanted for me?*

"You know instant hits cost more than a blow job," he says, nonchalantly leaning against the doorway. "But I guess you do know that, since you were pretty much a little whore for our entire relationship."

I want to tell him a thousand things, like how I hated every second we dated. Or how I wanted to break it off with him after our first date, thought about it a ton of times, but the fact that he could write prescriptions kept me coming back. But saying so would piss him off and I need him happy at the moment.

"I know what it costs," I say, letting the foul feeling take me over because I know it'll be gone soon. "But can we make it a quickie? I'm in a hurry."

He grins like a freaking greedy, disgusting thief and I

both hate him and love him for it. Hate him because of what he's making me give him but love him for what he gives me in return.

Ethan

I know I've messed up, yelling at her like that, just like my father always did with my mom, but it wasn't to belittle her or to purposely hurt her. I told her she looked like a whore, which she did, but I hated that she's dressed like that and how good she looks dressed like that. I hated that every guy in that damn place she works at is going to be thinking the same things as me.

I've been doing my best to keep my distance from her, especially after she mentioned London's name. I've never talked about London with anyone and suddenly Lila was asking me to talk about her. It scared me because I was afraid of what I'd say, that I miss her, but not really, that I feel guilty for walking away from her, but I don't want to, that I want to let her go and move on—move on with Lila.

After I call Lila a whore and she runs off, I realize just how badly I've been fucking up for the last week. The look on her face was toxic. Dangerous. I need to make it right. I need to not screw up again. I try to text her a couple of times and finally decide just to go down to her workplace, hoping I don't have to see her dancing up on the bar. I need to apologize for messing up.

When I arrive, however, I can't find Lila anywhere. The place is filled with ogling guys, drooling all over themselves as they stare up at the half-dressed women shaking their asses on the bar. It's the first time I've showed up at a place like this not looking for entertainment and it's strange seeing it from an outsider's point of view. It makes me think kind of poorly of myself for being here and loathing myself for letting Lila work in a place like this. Why didn't I stop her? Sure, she needs a job, but not like this.

I stop one of the waitresses as she whisks by wearing a see-through dress and carrying a drink tray. "Hey, there's a girl named Lila who works here. Have you seen her?" There's panic in my voice.

She looks me over from head to toe and then tries to dazzle me with a grin. "No, but whatever you're looking for, I can sure as hell give it to you."

"No, thanks," I say, walking away from an open invitation. And I haven't had sex with anyone since Lila moved in— twenty-two fucking days. Jesus, I'm getting blue balls.

I'm making my way to the bar when my phone vibrates from inside my pocket. I reach in and take it out, checking the text message.

Lila: I messed up.

Shit.

Me: What happened?

Lila: I did something bad... I think I might need your
　help.

Me: Where r u?
Lila: At work.

I glance around at the packed tables, the dancers, and the crowded bar area.

Me: Where?
Lila: In the bathroom.

I scan the room until I spot the restroom sign. I shove through people, pushing anyone who gets in my way. Finally, I stumble into the hallway and the voice and music quiet down a little bit. I walk up to the bathroom door and text Lila.

Me: I'm right outside.
Lila: Why???
Me: Because I wanted to see if you were okay.
Lila: Okay…can you come in here then…I need u…

Need. It's a very strong word. Taking a deep breath, I push the door open. There are two women fussing over their reflections in the mirror. When they spot me, their eyes widen.

"Ladies." I grin charismatically at them.

They seem unimpressed and scurry for the door, one of them calling me a pervert, but I ignore them. I scan the stall doors, all of them shut.

"Lila," I call out.

It takes a second before I hear her muffled voice. "I'm in here."

It sounds like she's in the last stall. I make my way over and when I put my hand on the door, it swings open. She's sitting on the grimy floor, hugging her legs to her chest, her chin resting on her knees. She's still wearing the outfit from earlier, but she has a jacket pulled over her.

"What are you doing?" I ask, cautiously stepping inside the stall.

"I messed up," she mutters, frowning at the floor.

I take another step in and shut the door behind me, gliding over the latch to lock it. "Did you…did you take a pill?" My heart pounds in my chest as I wait for her answer.

She glances up at me and her eyes are red and swollen, like she's been crying. "Would you hate me if I did?"

I crouch down beside her, brushing her hair out of her eyes, trying to get a good look at her pupils so I can get a better assessment of her state of mind. "I could never hate you, Lila. I…I already told you that I messed up while I was trying to recover, too, but it's important that you tell me the truth so that I can help you."

She takes an unsteady breath and then her hand trembles as she removes it from around her leg and stretches it out in front of her. Inside her palm is a tiny white pill.

"Fuck." I run my fingers through my hair, relief rushing over me so powerfully it's hard to stay upright. "Did you… did you take another one?" I'm afraid to find out, fearing that we're going to have to start over.

She shakes her head, her whole body quivering. "N-no but I want to take this one. So bad, Ethan. I can't even…" Her chest heaves up and down as she fights to breathe. "It's driving me crazy, it even being in my hand."

Blowing out a breath, I take the pill, pinching it between my fingers as I straighten my legs and stand up. She doesn't say anything, fiddling with the ring on her finger as I make my way over to the toilet, but her eyes are fixed on me.

I hold my hand over the bowl, waiting for her to yell at me, but she just watches, horrified and relieved at the same time as I open my hand and let the pill fall. When it hits the water, I flush the toilet and then turn back to her, finally able to breathe again.

"Are you okay?" I ask.

She nods, tears pooling in her eyes. "I'm so sorry."

I squat down in front of her again, needing to get closer to her, like a magnetic current is guiding me to her. It's overwhelming how much I want to be close to her and how much I regret driving her to this place on the floor. It's all my fault and I know it. I fucking screwed up and now I need to fix it.

I look her in the eye so I can see what she's feeling, let her know what I'm feeling. "Sorry for what? You didn't do anything wrong. I'm the one who yelled at you."

She lets out a sharp laugh as tears slip out of her eyes. "Didn't do anything? I went over to my prescription-writer drug dealer, or whatever the hell you want to call him, totally ready to fuck his brains out so I could get one single pill."

My heart tightens in my chest and it feels like a knotted, warped, thorny vine is winding through my body and stabbing at every single inch of me. I feel like I'm being ripped apart from the inside, a feeling I've never felt before and can't quite comprehend the entire meaning of. "It's okay," I say, even though it's not. She fucked some guy for drugs. She fucked him. *Fucked him.* I take a deep breath and unsteadily let it out.

"No, it's not okay," she says, sniffling as tears fall down her cheeks. "I messed up. Really, really bad."

I hook my finger under her chin, so she'll have to look at me. "No, you didn't. You didn't take it and that's good. Really, really fucking amazing."

"I know that," she says, puffing out a frustrated breath. "That's not what I'm upset about."

I slant my head to the side, confused. "Then why are you? Is it...is it because of what I said back at the apartment? Because I'm really sorry I said it. I was just..." I glance at her body hanging out of the barely there clothes she's wearing. "I don't like you dressing like that. At all."

Her shoulders rise and then slump as she inhales and exhales, looking ashamed. "I stole the pill while Parker was going to the bathroom. I didn't sleep with him like I promised."

"Parker?" I state, my eyes wide. "That preppy jerk you used to date? That's where you get the pills?"

She nods. "And the prescriptions." She blinks and then

panic fills her eyes as she quickly stands up, nearly smacking her head against mine and I have to lean back on my heels to get out of her way. "Look, it doesn't matter. He's going to be pissed, Ethan. He'll come looking for me, wanting to collect what I took. And I'm going to have to sleep with him." She starts to pace the stall as I stand up. "Normally, that was never a problem but normally I was medicated." She anxiously chews on her fingernails. "It felt so wrong, just from him kissing me. I could feel it..." She shakes her head, her eyes widening with whatever revelation she's having. "I could feel *everything.*"

"That's a good thing, though." I lean back against the stall, very aware at how relieved I'm feeling over the fact that she didn't sleep with Parker, but also furious that that asshole was her pill provider. I seriously want to beat him. "Feeling stuff is a good thing."

She lets out a heavy sigh as she continues to pace. "I know, but I never have, you know. All those times, meaningless sex, it always felt like a routine." She sticks her hands out to the side and stops in front of me, looking me in the eye. "I mean, I don't even really like it."

"Not like sex?" Okay, that concept is foreign to me and makes me wonder what she felt when we just about had sex. Were all those sparks I felt a one-sided thing? Is that why she just lay there?

She nods, her blue, mascara-stained eyes so wide they're practically popping out of her skull. "Yeah, it's just something that I do, not something that I really want to do. It doesn't even feel good."

A lot of inappropriate thoughts creep into my mind at that moment and it takes a great amount of energy to hold them back. "We should get you home," I say and move to take her hand.

She shakes her head, turning out of my reach, and strands of her hair curtain her face. "I think I might have lost my job."

"I'm glad," I say honestly, stepping forward and brushing her hair back because I want to see her face. "This place isn't somewhere you should be working."

"But I have to pay rent."

"We'll figure it out. There are a ton of jobs out there."

She shakes her head again, wrapping her arms around herself as tears begin to slip down her cheeks. "You're too nice to me. You need to stop. I don't deserve nice."

It's like she thinks she's unworthy of nice. I want to ask her about why she thinks this, but I don't want to set her off again. She needs to relax.

I aim for a joke. "That's funny, because a few weeks ago you couldn't seem to stop calling me an asshole." I smile at her, trying to lighten the mood.

"Stop it," she says, wiping the tears and smeared mascara off her cheeks with the bottom of her shirt. I can see her stomach, perfect, smooth, and almost flawless, except for that scar going around the middle. "Don't joke. You're being too nice again and I'm so messed up."

"Everyone's messed up." I reach forward and slowly wipe away some of the tears running down her cheek with my fingertips. "In their very own fucked-up way, a lot of people just won't admit it aloud and then try to change it." I reduce the space between us and place a hand on her arm. "But you've done both of those, which makes you so fucking strong, Lila. I wish you could see that. You're strong and amazing and beautiful and you deserve so much more than sitting on a bathroom floor in a skanky bar. You deserve to have an amazing life." I mean every word I say and even though I'm being really emotional, I don't regret anything I said.

She tries to wipe some of her tears away, but more pour out. She starts to sob and rushes toward me, throwing her arms around my waist. I tense, but then circle her in my arms, hugging her tightly against me as she buries her face in my chest and a strange sense of calm comes over me. I feel comfortably at peace with her in my arms, and if I could, I'd just keep holding on to her forever, comforting her, making her feel better in every way that I could. It takes me a minute to grasp what it might mean. I might be falling in love with Lila. And the moment I realize this is the moment I realize that I'm not sure if I was ever really in love with London. Infatuated with her, maybe. Love, I don't think so. Because what I'm feeling right now, this terrifying, cliff falling, heart dropping, thoughts racing, plunging into the unknown was far from anything I ever felt for London.

Lila cries in my shirt for an eternity and I trace my fingers up and down her back, telling her that it'll be okay, while I kiss the top of her head over and over again, feeling my life— feeling myself change. The longer she stays in my arms, the less I want to let her go. I want to hold her. Smell her hair. Kiss her cheeks until I can't feel my lips, only her. I want to do a lot of things to her, very slowly and deliberately so I can feel every sensation.

But then she pulls back and peers up at me with bloodshot eyes. "What am I going to do about Parker?"

"What do you mean, what are you going to do?" I keep my arms around her shoulder, still not wanting to let her go. "If he comes near you then I'll kick his ass."

"I don't want you to get hurt," she whispers. "You don't need to be fighting anyone for me."

I laugh again, louder, until my whole side aches. "I'm pretty sure I can handle Parker. In fact, he looks like the kind of guy who likes to bitch slap and pull hair when he fights."

She restrains a smile. "He's not that much of a wimp."

I roll my eyes again and shake my head at the absurdity. "We are talking about the same guy, right? The douche you dated for a while?"

She nods her head and I detect a hint of an amused sparkle in her eye. "And you were so excited when I broke up with him."

"I was drunk when you did."

"And we were playing strip poker. I remember."

I smile, because it's a perfect moment, a light after a dark episode. "Ah, strip poker," I say, tucking her hair behind her ear. "If I remember right you never did take your bra off when I won that hand."

"Only because I knew you couldn't handle the goodies." She shakes her chest and her tits bounce against my chest. She pauses and then lowers her cheek against me, breathing quietly. "Thank you, Ethan . . . for everything."

I could tell her she doesn't need to thank me. That I was glad to do it. That I loved helping her. But I'm not. I wish it'd never happened. Instead, I wish she never had to go through all of this.

I mutter, "You're welcome." Then lace my fingers with hers and tug her toward the door, ready to take her back to our home and get her the hell away from this place. I'm ready to take her back home.

To *our* home.

Chapter Thirteen

Lila

It's been four days since my little episode and for the most part, life has been fairly normal, except for my relentless need to fixate on Ethan. Ever since he found me in the bathroom stall, I can't stop thinking about him. It's worse than before, an intense growing obsession. I'm not even sure what it is. The way he looked at me, touched me, spoke to me, joked with me, forgave me, and then took me home. They're such little things, yet they mean so much. He may be rough, blunt, somewhat perverted, and completely imperfect according to my mother's standards, but I seriously wouldn't have it any other way. I've had the supposed perfect guy before, the one who gave me rings, told me I was beautiful, told me he loved me, that I owned his soul, and that he'd do anything for me. But it was a bunch of shit. Unreal. Perfect doesn't exist. Realness does. Realness is what I need. And Ethan is as real as anyone I've ever met.

I'm trying to figure out what this all means in terms of my feelings for him. I thought I understood love once, but it turned out I was wrong. Could the feelings I have for Ethan possibly be love? I have no idea, but eventually I'm going to have to figure it out, instead of wandering around analyzing everything.

I'm also looking for a job again, one that's Ethan approved, and I'm still getting used to that fact. No one has ever thought highly enough of me to think I deserved something better. Sure, my mother wouldn't approve of the job at Danny's either, but not because she thought I was better than that. She would think the Summers's name was better, but not my character. In fact, if she was basing it solely on my character she'd say I belonged there, something she made pretty clear during one of her phone calls.

"You did what?" she practically screams into the phone and I have to hold the receiver away from my ear as it rings against her voice. "You moved in with some guy?"

I put the receiver back to my ear and balance it between my head and my shoulder. "Yes, that's what I said."

"I know that's what you said," she replies curtly. "But what I don't get is why the hell you did it."

I'm rinsing off the dishes as I load up the dishwasher. I also vacuumed, swept, and cleaned the toilets, and even though it sucked, I also took a bit of pride in doing it. "Because I needed a place to live."

"Is this guy rich?"

"No, he's normal."

"Normal isn't acceptable, Lila Summers. Normal will get you nowhere but pregnant and living in a shack and wishing your life was better."

"Normal is perfectly acceptable." I smile at myself, saying it aloud, as I scrub some green stuff off the plate underneath the stream of water. "And besides, what makes you such an expert on normal. You don't even know anyone who is."

"Your aunt Jennabelle is."

"I didn't know I had an aunt Jennabelle."

"She's my sister and you don't know her because she lives in a studio apartment with her three children and had to take a job as a secretary to make ends meet after she left her husband when he started screwing a woman he worked with. And no one ever wants to visit a poverty-stricken, single-parent divorcee who lives in a crappy apartment. If she would have just stuck with her husband and overlooked his one flaw then she wouldn't live in the run-down part of town with a bunch of drug addicts and criminals."

"Just because they live in the run-down part of town doesn't mean they're drug addicts and criminals," I say. "And I would love to visit her," I argue, rinsing off a glass. "She sounds like a strong woman who was brave enough to leave a man who obviously didn't love her enough to treat her well and she's been able to take care of herself."

"She's poor, Lila," she harshly snaps like the word is so filthy it has no right to even leave her lips. "She can't even afford a new car."

"Neither can I," I state, sliding some silverware under the faucet and scrubbing the gunk off with my fingers.

"Well, that's your own damn fault for being so stubborn. You could have everything you want in life, Lila. The perfect life, but you keep messing it up for yourself. Instead of doing what I've told you to do and come home and live with us until you can get back on track and meet a nice, wealthy guy who will take care of you, you're living in poverty, probably taking the bus."

"I'm not living in poverty," I reply. "Not yet, anyway. Thanks to my normal friend, who's letting me stay here with him because he's nice. Money and cars and nice clothes aren't everything, mother. And I don't want to sacrifice being around people who I like just to have a glamorous life." Wow, when did I get to this place? "I want to be around people I care about and who care about me. That's all I really want in life." God, I care about Ethan. I really, really do.

"Well, that's a lovely way to look at life. Maybe you should go visit your aunt Jennabelle and get a real taste of what life is like," she says, and then adds, "And what on earth is that noise? That water noise in the background."

"Water." I put the plate in the dishwasher.

"Well, I know that," she snaps. "But what's it from?"

I turn off the faucet and close the dishwasher door. "It's from the sink." I press the power button and wipe off my hands on a towel. "I just got done doing the dishes."

"You what!?" she shouts into the phone so loudly my ear rings. "That's it, Lila. This kind of behavior is unacceptable."

"Why? Because I'm cleaning up after myself?" I walk into the living room and flop down on the couch. I have some vanilla-scented candles burning and the whole house has a shiny, polished look to it. It looks good and I hope Ethan will appreciate it when he gets back from work.

"Summers's do not clean up after themselves," she snaps. "They hire maids for that."

"Well, since I'm broke, a maid really isn't an option." I sit back in the chair and comb my fingers through my hair. It's still long and perfectly trimmed just like I was taught to maintain it. "God, with the way you're acting, you'd think I'd just told you I did drugs or something."

She laughs into the phone. "Quit being a little bitch and be grateful for everything I've done and given to you. Without me, you'd be worse off than you are now. And that's going to end quickly because I'm coming down to get you."

"Good luck finding me," I say, inspecting for split ends. I should really just cut my hair off, like I wanted to when I was a kid. "Vegas is a very big city."

"What is wrong with you?" she cries. "You're being rude and inconsiderate. I don't get it. I don't get any of this, like why you're even living in Vegas in the first place."

"Because it was the first place I pointed to on the map," I mutter to myself, remembering how I got here.

"What are you talking about?" she seethes hotly. "Are you even listening to me?"

"Nope, not really."

"Well, you need to," she snaps. "If you'd just listen to me then you'd quit messing up your life. Being with a guy because he *cares* about you is going to get you nowhere, especially if he's some low-life like the guys your sister dates. He'll end up screwing you over and then you'll be left alone, probably pregnant and poor."

"That's not going to happen, so quit being overdramatic."

"Yes, it is. You wait and see. You'll get pregnant and guys like that won't take care of you. And I sure as hell won't help you."

"I don't want your help," I tell her, fuming with aggravation. "I want to be right where I am, living with Ethan. I don't want to be with anyone else. Ever." Wow, this conversation with my mom is getting productive in a very scary, life-altering way.

"You are really starting to piss me off," my mother says sharply.

"And you're pissing me off." I hang up, tossing the phone onto the coffee table. I feel so strange. So light, even after talking to her because of what the conversation revealed. I want to be here. With Ethan. And I don't ever want to leave, at least as far as I can see into the future.

"I want to do something exciting," I mumble to myself, coiling a finger around my long blonde hair. It's the same haircut I've had for years and I've never dyed my hair, yet I've always wanted to. "I want a change."

Change. I want to change who I am. I want to be better. I want to be a person who I can love, not hate and despise. Smiling, I get up and grab my purse off the table, and then I head out the door, knowing I'm going to have to take the bus, but it feels okay today and that in and of itself is another change. I wonder how many more are to come.

〜

I'm really starting to walk on the wild side, well the wild side for me. I got my haircut at a discount hair salon and not just a trim or anything. I cut it off so it's shoulder length and I added black streaks to it. I'd always gotten pretty much the same haircut, always at this expensive, appointment-only place down in the main area of the city. Turns out discount places aren't that bad. Shelia, the lady who cut my hair, was really nice. She told me how she ended up cutting hair, how she'd been going to school to be a lawyer because her parents wanted her to. But when she was sitting in class one day, listening to her professor ramble on and on about the law, she realized how much she couldn't care less about law and that really she'd rather be breaking some laws instead of learning about them. She left class, traded her nearly new car in for a motorcycle, and drove across the country. Just like that. Then when she got back she decided to try beauty school, simply because it was the first place she came across when she entered town. Her parents never forgave her for messing up what they deemed a perfect life, but she didn't care. She was happy. Still is. And that's all that matters.

I loved her story and it gave me hope that one day I'll figure out what I want. Although, I do know one thing that I want. My very sexy roommate/drummer/savior. Although, he'll never admit it, Ethan saved me. Many, many times. If I could just have him now, then life would be good. Because I want him. *Want him.* I really, really do.

After my head fills like it's going to burst from overthinking, I decide to call Ella to distract myself and to maybe get some girl advice with my guy problems.

"Hey," Ella says, answering after a few rings. "I was actually getting ready to call you!"

"Oh yeah?" I stare out the bus window at the street, the smell of fast food from the takeout bag on my lap overwhelming me. "Maybe you read my mind, then."

"Maybe." She pauses. "Okay, I was trying to figure out how to ask you, since every time I've ever brought you and Ethan up, you always deny there's anything going on, but I'm just going to be blunt. Are you living with him? Because Micha said you were."

"Umm..." I let out a breath, unsure why it's always been so hard for me to talk about my relationship with Ethan aloud. "Yeah, I have been for a while."

"Why didn't you tell me?" she asks with a hint of humor in her tone. "Are you...are you two together?"

"Not together like that," I say quickly. "And I didn't tell you because the reason I moved in with him isn't the kind of stuff I'm used to talking about."

"I get that," she says. "But I still wish you would have at least given me a heads-up."

"Heads-up?" I reply in a teasing tone and she laughs. "I am really sorry. The next huge news I have is yours first."

"Good." She clears her throat, sounding nervous. "And now I have news."

"Oh my God, are you pregnant?" I sit up straight in the seat, trying not to laugh at my joke.

"What! No!" She gives me an elongated pause. "Why would you think that?"

"Why wouldn't I think that? You and Micha are always going at it, even when you're not together. The walls were very thin in our apartment and those late-night chats you two had while he was on the road were very, very loud."

"Oh my God," she says, mortified. "You should have said something."

"Like what? Quit having such loud phone sex with your boyfriend." I laugh and then lean closer to the wall, shielding out the sunlight with my hand. "But anyway, what's your big news?"

She takes a deep inhale. "Micha and I are getting married."

"I already knew that."

"I know . . . but in, like, a week."

My jaw drops as my hand falls to my lap. "Are you sure you're not pregnant?" Now I'm being a little bit serious.

"Quit saying that. You're scaring the shit out of me." She steadies her anxious breath. "I'm *not* pregnant. We just wanted to get married and figured why the hell not, since we're already living together. We've practically been living together since we were four."

I smile, because even though I'm jealous, they are cute enough that the jealousy is worth it. "Did Micha give you that speech?"

She laughs. "Is it that obvious?"

"Um, yeah. It always is with him," I say, coiling a strand of my much shorter hair around my finger. I pause, because even though I've been a cheerleader over their relationship from the start, as a best friend, I still have to make sure. "Is this what you want?"

"Yeah, it really is." She sounds so happy and the jealousy in my chest builds.

"All right, then, I'll get over there," I say. "But I have to point out that I really hate San Diego, so my going there means I really must love you."

She's quiet for a while and with Ella, that means she's really thinking. "Lila, thank you," she finally says. "For everything."

"Oh, whatever. I didn't even do anything really."

"Yeah, you kind of did," she insists. "If it wasn't for your little pushes, telling me that I'd be giving up the kind of love that shouldn't exist—letting me know how lucky I am—then I'm not sure I'd be where I am, but I don't think I'd be getting ready to marry the love of my life."

"That's not entirely true," I say. "Things still could have worked out for you."

"I doubt it, but maybe . . . maybe I would have finally come to my senses on my own and quit fighting the need to make myself miserable." She sounds like she's getting choked up, which is strange for her. She pauses and then clears her throat. "You're coming, though, right? And you'll be my maid of honor?"

"Of course. I've actually always wanted to be one." I pause, contemplating whether I should ask, since her family is such a serious subject for her. "Ella, who else is coming?"

"You and Ethan."

"And your dad?"

She hesitates. "I know things have been going pretty good between my dad and me and even my brother, but this is kind of something I want to be simple. Just me and Micha and you and Ethan, of course. Then there won't be any drama."

I sigh, sad that that's how she feels. But then again, if I ever did get married, I'm not sure I'd want my family there either because they'd probably ruin it for me, especially if the groom wasn't up to their standards. "Well, I'm totally coming, but you'll have to ask Ethan."

"Micha already did."

"When?"

"A few days ago," she says hesitantly. "He said he'd go."

I'm kind of hurt. Why did he not mention this to me? "Okay, then I guess I'm going." Usually, I'm good at sounding happy when I'm not, but the hurt shows through in my voice.

"Are you okay?" she asks. "I mean, with Ethan...is everything okay between you two?"

"Why would I not be okay?" I stand up from the seat as the bus reaches my stop, growing nervous over the idea that Ethan said something about us.

"I don't know...because you two have a weird relationship."

I grab the handle as the bus lurches to a stop. "Did Ethan say that to Micha?"

"No." She sounds like she's lying.

"Ella, please just tell me if he said anything." I step off the bus and onto the curb feeling very insecure.

"Look, Lila, just relax," she says and then I hear someone shout in the background. "Look, I got to go. Call me later after you've talked to Ethan and let me know when you'll get here and stuff."

"Fine." I look left and right and hurry across the street toward my apartment. "Wait for me to shop for your dress, though."

"Okay, I will, but I'm telling you right now," she says, "that I won't in any way shape or form be wearing a frilly white dress. It needs to be rock-star-ish or something."

"Oh, we'll find you something very Ella-like." I step onto the sidewalk and enter the apartment complex entryway that's situated between a broken fence and a desolate section of sandy land. The sun is setting so the air isn't nearly as hot as midday, yet it's still blistering and I'm starting to sweat. "I'm an excellent shopper."

"It's a deal," she says cheerfully. "Talk to you later."

"Okay, bye." I hang up and seconds later I realize that I never got around to the reason why I called her.

Sighing, I take the house key out of my pocket, frustrated at myself because I really could use some girl advice about Ethan and what I should do; she probably would have given it if I'd just been brave enough to ask her, but my initial instincts to keep my mouth shut got the best of me. Although, I remember in high school how far girl advice got me. Just sleep with him. It'll feel good and he'll be less likely to break up with you. Sex means commitment. Sex means you're older. Sex. Sex. Sex. I'm not even sure if they were ever really being sincere or if they were just toying with me.

When I enter the apartment, Ethan's still not back from work. I settle down on the couch, with the takeout bag in front of me on the coffee table, trying not to think too much about the past, otherwise I know where I'll end up heading—what I'll end up doing. I turn on some of Ethan's music, which I'm still getting used to, feeling nervous for some reason, like I can feel that I'm about to do or say something really stupid. Because I'm seriously considering telling him that I *like* like him. It's time to be bold and blunt. It's time to let him know how I feel. That I like him. I might even love him. My eyes widen as I realize that I might really do it and then double widen as I run my fingers through my now-chin-length hair that's even shorter in the back. And as if that wasn't a big enough change, I had black streaks put in.

"Who am I?" I whisper. I really don't know anymore. A girl who chops off her own hair? Feels things for Ethan? A girl who wants to tell Ethan about her feelings? And that is very, very scary.

I'm deciding what I should do, run away or stay put and face my fears, finally be brave, when someone knocks on the door. I get up and open the door, then swiftly step back. "Parker?"

He looks me over and his face twists with disgust when he notes my new hair. "What the fuck did you do to your hair?"

"Cut it." I shrug, praying to God he's not here for the pills, even though deep down I know there's no way that could be true. "What are you doing here?"

He's wearing a navy-blue polo shirt, slacks, and a Rolex. "Don't act like you're surprised to see me." His tone is sharp, his posture very rigid and threatening.

Suddenly I'm very aware that I'm alone in the apartment. "How did you know where I live?" I ask, gripping the doorknob tightly.

"I asked around." He takes a deliberate step toward me, inching his way into the doorway. "You fucking stole from my stash, Lila. *My* fucking stash. Now I know you're used to getting your way with me, but not with this. This is business."

I step back, moving to shut the door, but he slams his hand against it. "I'm sorry, Parker," I say, attempting to stay calm, but my palms start to sweat and my heart is beating wildly inside my chest. "I didn't mean to. Really. I was just having a rough day and I messed up."

He stalks closer, stepping over the threshold and onto the small section of chipped linoleum in the entryway. "Don't try to feed me your sob story. You didn't mean to? Seriously. What?" He starts swinging his hands animatedly as he speaks and it makes me wince. "You just accidentally opened the bottle hidden in my nightstand drawer and then accidentally poured a pill into your hand. I checked after you left, Lila, and there was a pill missing. And you know I keep track of that shit. You've seen me count them after I make a deal. Although, I'm a little surprised you took only one, seeing as how I've seen you pop four at a time without even hesitating."

Shaking my head, I stumble back into the living room and inch around the coffee table, knowing I'm in serious trouble. "Look, what do you want me to say? I'm sorry, okay? I messed up. But I can't bring the pill back. I can pay for it, though." I reach for my wallet that's next to the television.

He laughs darkly, walking all the way into the apartment. "You're going to pay me for that fucking pill, Lila," he says, shutting the door with his foot, keeping his eyes fixed on me. "But not with money. You know I don't accept cash for pills."

I glance at the hallway, contemplating running into the bathroom and locking myself in there. This is bad. Very, very bad. I can feel that something bad is about to happen and I'm not sure how to get out of it.

"Don't even think about it," he says and then unzips his pants. "Now, you can either fuck me or suck my dick, but either way I'm going to get something out of this. I'm not just going to let you steal a pill from me and get away with it. You know me better than that."

"You're right. I do," I say, my voice unsteady as I search around the room for my phone. Where did I leave it?

This evil ugly monster is about to come out of him. I know because I've seen it with every other guy out there. Try not to give them anything and they'll break you. Give them what they want and they'll take everything you have and then they'll leave you in the dirt.

I press my lips together, feeling a slight tremor inside my heart, but deep down I know I can probably do this if I need to. Just screw him and get it over with. I've done it before, but that was when I felt nothing. But right now it feels worse than wrong. It feels icky and twisted and warped. I'm scared, just like I was when Sean tied me to the bed, ropes around my ankles, wrists, even my stomach. I didn't want to do it. I even told him that. Once. But once wasn't enough and he took what he wanted.

"I think I—" I start, my hip bumping into the corner of the television stand as I try to back away more.

Parker hurries forward, his fly undone and before I can move he grabs a handful of my hair, wrenching on the roots so hard my scalp stings. "Get down on your fucking knees and be the whore that you and I and every other guy out there knows that you are."

I raise my hand to slap him, but he catches me by the wrist, jabbing his fingers into my skin as he slaps me across my face. Tears sting at my eyes and my ears ring as he shoves me down onto the floor, pressing on my shoulders until I'm kneeling at his feet. I whimper pathetically as the rough carpet scrapes against my knees and my neck bends in an awkward position. "Stop it, Parker... You're hurting me."

"Good." Cupping the back of my head, and still grasping violently on to my hair, he shoves my face toward his open fly. "Open your mouth and be the whore that you are."

I remember when I was dating Parker I never felt a single speck of emotion. My mind and body were blank, just like almost every other single sexual encounter. I want the blankness right now—crave it. But it's not coming. The switch that flips is staying stubbornly in place. I can feel the shame, terror, and embarrassment way too much. I start to cry because this is real. I'm not drunk or on pills and I don't want to do anything with Parker, like I really didn't want to with Sean. I was just too afraid to admit it and worried that if I walked away he wouldn't love me. And I wanted—want—to be loved for once in my life.

But I never said no. All those years and not once did I refuse anyone who wanted me. I worried that no guy would ever listen to me, and really, I just didn't think I was good enough to say no. In a sickening and perverse way, I've never felt good enough for anyone. So I just popped pills and did things I thought other people wanted me to do and waited for them to accept me, to love me, yet they never did. I thought Sean loved me, but he hurt me and now I'm scarred inside and out. I'm scarred and I don't want to be. I want to feel like a whole person again. I want to go back to being fourteen and not make stupid choices, not have sex with an older guy who ties me to the bed after I say I don't think I want to, that I don't think I can, and then he screws me so hard the ropes cut into my skin and I bleed all over the bed. Then I'm left feeling guilty because I let it get that far and I'll always feel like I didn't put up enough of a fight. But I was lost. Confused.

A painful wave rushes over me as my past slams down on my shoulders. I don't want to be this girl anymore. This lonely, hollow girl. I want to feel like I deserve things and not hate myself so much. I'm deciding whether to open my mouth and scream or just bite down really hard when the door opens and Ethan walks in, carrying his tool belt.

"Oh, thank God," I say with relief and realize I'm trembling.

Parker turns around and looks over his shoulder, and then his fingers immediately leave my hair and I fall to the ground on my ass, cupping the side of my face that he struck me on.

"Dude, she wanted it," he tells Ethan with his hands up in front of him.

I get to my feet, clutching my tender cheek as Ethan assesses the situation, taking in Parker with his pants undone, then me and my swollen cheek, before his eyes land back on Parker. He's still dressed in his work clothes, torn cargo shorts, a black shirt stained with dirt, and he has his work boots on.

He looks all bad boy from the wrong side of the tracks who kicks people like Parker's ass just for fun. And I love it.

"Is that true, Lila?" Ethan glances at me, slowly taking the hammer out of his belt like he's going to use it to beat Parker. I can tell he's not going to, nor does he think what Parker said is true, but he's messing with Parker's head. "Did you want this loser to unzip his pants and force you down onto your knees?"

Parker cringes, eyeing the hammer as Ethan holds it in his hand, but he doesn't say a word, inching back against the wall, trying to creep toward the doorway.

I wipe the drying tears from my eyes and swollen cheek as I shake my head. "No, I didn't want it at all." There's this strange kind of freedom in saying it, like this secret I've kept hidden drifts out into the open, even if I'm the only one who understands.

"She's a liar and a slut," Parker argues, glaring at me, and then his gaze returns unsteadily back to Ethan. "Come on, man. You know her, so you must know what she's like."

Ethan shakes his head as he tosses his tool belt onto the couch, keeping ahold of the hammer and tapping it in his hand. "The Lila I know isn't a slut."

Parker's eyes widen, and then he crosses his arms. "Well, the one I do is."

"Well, that's too bad for you." Ethan chucks his keys onto the table, but doesn't budge from the doorway.

I love Ethan. I seriously do. I feel the brave side of myself emerging and I take a small step forward. "Parker, as much as I would love to stand around here looking at your small penis, I'm sure Ethan doesn't, so please zip up your pants."

His gaze drops to his slacks and he quickly tucks himself in, then zips up the zipper. "Whatever," he says, raking his fingers through his hair, attempting to tidy himself up. "I'm just going to leave. You two can go to hell." He moves to the right to step around Ethan, but Ethan matches his move and blocks the doorway and his path.

"You're not fucking leaving this house until Lila says what to do with you." He looks at me with intensity burning in his eyes as he places his hands on the door frame. "Do you want me to beat the shit out of him or call the cops?" He raises the hammer in Parker's direction.

"Fuck you," Parker says, but he doesn't dare move. It's clear how easily Ethan could kick Parker's ass, even without the hammer. He's taller, stronger, rougher, and way, way more intense looking, like he's been through things, which he has. He's been beaten by his father and watched his father hit his mother, while he tried to stand up for her. He's real. And I want real, not the deception of it that sometimes comes with wealth and money. I'm not going to sacrifice my life like my mother did just so I can have nice clothes and a roof over my head. I like the cracked one that's over my head now perfectly fine.

I unintentionally smile, especially when Parker makes this

weird noise that sounds like a strangled cat. "I'm not sure what I want you to do."

Ethan shrugs and then winks at me. "It's up to you, beautiful."

I can only imagine how broad my smile is at this moment because I've never had this—protection. I've never had someone in my life who would stand up for me and tell me that it was okay, that people make mistakes and it doesn't mean you have to suffer eternally for them. I look over at Parker, who's waiting expectantly for me to chime in and save his ass. I study him forever, until he squirms and looks like he's about ready to piss his pants.

"Lila," he says, his eyes pressing. "Help me out here."

"Why?" I ask, folding my arms over my chest. "You seemed tough enough to handle yourself a few minutes ago."

He glances at the hammer in Ethan's hand, and then frowns back at me. "Lila," he pleads. "You know I hate fighting."

I roll my eyes. "Unless it's a girl, right?"

His eyes narrow at my divulgence. "God damn it, Lila, I swear to fucking God…" He trails off, his jaw tightening as Ethan steps forward, patting the head of the hammer in his hand again.

I shake my head and sigh, knowing I'm not really going to let Ethan kick Parker's ass, but only for Ethan's sake. Parker's the kind of guy who would either try to sue and press charges or come back with a group of his friends and have them all beat Ethan up. And if I call the cops, Parker's daddy will probably just get him out, since he's a lawyer. "Fine. Whatever. Ethan, just let him go."

Ethan doesn't budge. His eyes are locked on me, and his arm snaps up to the side when Parker tries to head toward the door. "Are you sure?"

I nod, hugging my arms around myself. "Yeah, he's not worth it."

Ethan firmly holds my gaze as he steps to the side of the door and toward the couch, leaving a tiny bit of space for Parker to squeeze through. "Fine, but I'm letting you walk out of here bruise-free only because of her." He nods his head in my direction as he glares at Parker.

Parker narrows his eyes at Ethan but doesn't say anything as he turns sideways and squeezes between Ethan and the doorway. Every muscle in Ethan's body tenses, his knuckles whitening as he tightly grips the handle of the hammer, and I can tell it's really hard for him to let Parker walk out of here.

When Parker steps outside, he pretty much takes off running, and Ethan kicks the door shut hard, like he's locking out the bad by doing it. He turns around and faces me, tossing the hammer aside, then leans back against it with his arms crossed.

"So what really happened?" He studies me intently, taking in every square inch of my body, and it makes my skin ignite. His gaze lingers on my cheek and I know he's wondering: *Did he hit you?* It makes my skin even hotter, because I can see in his eyes that he cares.

It's a minor sensation, the slightest bit of heat in all the right places, but it's enough to make me notice the difference between the way I feel around Ethan and the way I felt with Parker. Around Parker my skin was chilled like ice, basically numb. It's the sensation that I've felt with most of the guys I remember hooking up with.

"It's a long, stupid story like most of my life is." I sink down on the edge of the coffee table and place my hands on my lap, focusing on them instead of Ethan because I do feel ashamed of what just happened—what he just saw—because it's not the first time I've been in that kind of a situation and it's my own fault it happened. "He came to collect my debt for the pill I stole. I said I'd pay him, but since I'd promised at his house that I'd fuck him for one, that's the payment he wanted. So he...well, what you saw."

The muscles of his arms flex and his jaw is taut. "You say that like it's no big deal."

I shrug, examining my fingernails, once again feeling like he's seeing the real, rare sight of me that I'm so used to keeping hidden from people. "It's not anything I haven't had to deal with before. You know that...you know what I'm like."

Shaking his head, Ethan walks over in front of me and kneels down, splaying his hand on top of my thighs. His skin is seductively hot, yet comforting. "Would you stop thinking about yourself like that? So you screwed some guys. So fucking what? People have sex and that doesn't make you a slut. And it sure as hell doesn't give rich douche bags an excuse to rape you or make you do anything you don't want to do."

"He wouldn't have raped me," I say, with my chin tucked down. "I would have given in before it became rape."

He frowns, his face reddening with anger. He huffs out a breath and then cups my face between his hands. "Don't ever say that again. If a girl says no even once then a guy should stop. Hell, if she shows a single sign of not wanting it, the guy should stop. You should never, ever have to have sex with a guy when you don't want to."

Tell that to the many guys I've been with throughout my life. "Okay."

His frown deepens. "Lila Summers, where is that perky girl I first met?"

"I think she died at some point."

"So bring her back."

I sigh, discouraged. "I can't. She takes too much energy and pills. And honestly, I'm not sure I want to be her anymore."

"And that's fine. Be whoever you want to be, but please, please stop thinking so poorly of yourself. You barely even smile anymore and I...I fucking miss it." He gives me an adorable, lopsided grin. "You have a very beautiful smile."

I'm not even sure what overtakes me. His words. The bluntly, beautiful, realistic moment. Or if it's just him. Whatever it is, I quickly lean forward, letting my emotions drive me to him, which is a first for me. I press my lips to his and it's amazing. Undiluted. And I feel it all, from the way my heart rate accelerates to the swift flow of my blood rushing to my head, the heat of our contact, the soft, wetness of his lips.

I've kissed more guys than I can count, but the emotions freed in this kiss are new because there's *real* emotion behind it. Even though I was having a hard time deciphering it earlier, because I'm pretty sure I've never felt love toward anyone ever, or been on the reciprocating end of it, I realize now what this is.

Love. I'm completely, one hundred percent, truly in love with Ethan.

Ethan

It took a lot of energy not to slam my fist into Parker's face. I wanted to really, really badly. I remember a couple of times when I walked in on my dad beating the shit out of my mom. My dad used to be a fairly big guy, with bulky arms and a really thick neck, but he looked so pathetic as he shoved my mom down to the ground and then backhanded her across the face.

One moment in particular always sticks out in my mind because it was the first day I realized how bad things were between them.

I'd just gotten home from school, a little earlier than usual, and I let my bag fall to the kitchen floor as I took in the sight of my mom cowering on the ground and my dad raising his hand to slap her. "Dad, stop!" I didn't even think. I just ran up to my mom, ready to protect her.

"Ethan, stop!" she cried back right as my dad swung his arm around without even looking and struck me across the face.

He hadn't hit me since I was eight, so it kind of took me off guard a little, although I wasn't that surprised. That's the funny thing about being beaten by someone who's supposed to love you. It's hard to see how wrong it is, because the idea of love can be blinding. Which is exactly what happened to my mother.

She got up from the floor and hurried over to me as I cradled my cheek with my hand. "Ethan, what are you doing here? School isn't out yet."

I peeked up at her, shooting a glare in my dad's direction as he rubbed his hand. "School got let out early today. I gave you the note on Monday."

"Oh yeah." There were tears running down her face and her cheek was inflamed. She looked a little lost for a minute and then she patted me on the shoulder. "Go do your home-work in your room."

I glanced at my father, who looked remorseful. He always did, though. It was like he'd get caught up in the heat of the moment and turn into a monster, his eyes glazed over with rage. When it was all over, he was always sorry and kept telling everyone that over and over again.

"Maybe I should stay out here with you," I told my mom, wishing I was big enough that I could actually hurt my dad back for her.

My mom shook her head and ruffled my hair, like everything was okay. Like none of this was messed up. Like her face wasn't swelling, or all the kitchen chairs weren't tipped over, or the veins in my dad's neck weren't bulging. "Ethan, go to your room and do your homework. Everything is fine."

I swallowed the lump in my throat and collected my backpack, swinging it over my shoulder. They both watched me as I headed to the doorway and the entire situation felt wrong. I felt confused, afraid, and terrified, yet I couldn't figure out why.

I glanced over my shoulder when I reached the doorway, looking back at them. "Are you sure, Mom?" It felt like leaving wasn't the right thing, yet I couldn't figure out what else to do.

"Ethan, your mother's fine," my father replied. "And I'm really sorry that I accidentally hit you...I didn't realize you were there."

Sorry. Sorry. Sorry. Always sorry. I nodded and left the room, locking myself in my bedroom. A few minutes later they started yelling at each other and I cranked up the music to drown them out.

Walking in on Lila and Parker, I felt the same kind of fear and fury that I did when I was younger. The sight of it—the control he had over her—rammed me hard in the stomach. Yet, unlike when I was a kid, I knew I could kick Parker's ass. And I wanted to so much I could feel it raging through my bloodstream. I wanted to beat him so hard he couldn't see straight. A flood of emotions rushed through me and not only was I pissed that he was making a girl do something she obviously didn't want to do, but he was making *my Lila* do something she didn't want to do. And as soon as I saw it—felt it—I knew that whatever I'd been trying to deny was going on between us was obviously something I couldn't run away from. But I'm worried because the amount of anger in my body matches the amount of anger I've seen in my dad's eyes.

The rage continues to amplify, burning inside my chest until suddenly and completely unexpectedly, Lila kisses me. And that kiss, the single touch of our lips, the slight elevation of heat in my body, the flood of mixed emotions, erases my anger and changes my life despite the fact that I don't know if I want it to.

I don't react right away, partially from shock and partially because I'm afraid. My mother and father's turbulent relationship is fresh in my head and so is the fear of turning out like them. This isn't just about sex. There is so much more to it than that. We have a connection. We have since the day we met. I just refused to feel it, but now it's forcing its way on me, controlling, owning me—she controls and owns me—which means I'm dependent on her in a lot of ways.

I'm freaking out, but then she starts to pull away and I realize that I don't want her to, so I open my mouth and sweep my tongue into hers as I cup the back of her head and bring her back to me, all my worries and fears briefly dissipating.

Jesus fucking Christ. This is so different from what I'm used to. I'm both curious and terrified to explore it more. But desire and want push me forward and I comb my fingers through her short blonde hair that's streaked black. "You changed your hair," I murmur. "I like it…" I gently tug it back as I explore her mouth further with my tongue, massaging it, caressing it, searching every inch of it.

Her eyes shut tightly. "Ethan," she says, clutching my shoulders, her nails piercing through the fabric of my shirt and into my skin. The roughness of her touch surprises me and adds fuel to my very eager body. Before I even know what I'm doing, I stand up, disconnecting our kiss.

Her breath falters and her cheeks turn a little pink as she opens her eyes, like she's embarrassed. Before she can say anything, I grab her by the hips, digging my fingers into her skin, and swiftly pick her up. I've never been much of a carrying-a-girl-around kind of guy, but I'm feeling different with her. I want to hold her, hug her, have her so damn close to me that I can't tell where she starts and I begin. Every inch of my body is blazing, adrenaline spiking as it crashes through my body. I'm light-headed, burning up, wanting her more than I've ever wanted anyone. Feelings soar inside me, ones I knew existed but refused to fully feel before. I seal our lips together before any words can be uttered and before I can start analyzing what this is going to mean.

I kiss her deeply and passionately as I carry her back to my bedroom, feeling my way blindly down the hallway, bumping us into walls and into door frames. I interlace my fingers around the back of her, bearing her weight as she latches on to me by crossing her ankles behind my back. She keeps groaning, her tongue tangling forcefully with mine, sending my body into a spiraling frenzy of yearning, need, and ultimately fear of how much I want to be with her and not London anymore. I want Lila more than anything at the moment. I trip over some stuff on my floor and manage to bang my hip into one of my drums, and then I finally stumble into the bed. We bounce when we hit the mattress and she laughs against my lips but keeps her eyes shut.

I pull back a little and her eyelids flutter open. She looks perplexed and lost, among a thousand other emotions that probably match my own.

"What?" she asks, self-consciously. Her legs are still fastened around me and her arms are locked around my neck. "Is something...is something wrong?"

A thousand things are wrong, I want to say. I'm feeling too much for you, Lila. I can't do this. I'm getting too caught up in you and if I keep going eventually we'll hate each other. I'll break you. Ruin you—us. I'll mess up. But my voice refuses to work and so I kiss her instead. Fiercely. Forcefully. With heat, desire, and hunger suffocating both of us as we drown in each other's feelings. Our bodies align and press together as I kiss her with all the pent-up energy I've been collecting since the first day we met. I've lost all control over my actions.

Rules don't exist. The past and the future dissolve and only this moment exists.

Between deep kisses and throaty moans, I manage to get my filthy work shirt over my head and I toss it on the floor. Her eyes snap open as I lower myself down onto her and she gasps. She traces her fingers up my chest, her fingers shaking, and I realize how nervous she is. Maybe she doesn't want this. Maybe she's just doing it because she's afraid to say no. I'm worried she's going to shut down like the last time we ended up on the bed touching each other.

"Lila," I start, conflicted, because if she does reject me, it's going to hurt. "Are you okay with this? I mean, you...do you want this?"

Her lips part and her breath falters as she curves her body into mine, a sea of emotions pouring through her eyes. "I do... but if you...if you don't want to then you can stop." She seems to be struggling with words as she gets lost in whatever she's feeling.

It's not the answer I'm expecting. And she looks so fucking nervous, almost like she's having sex for the first time. I'm not sure what to do, but then she props herself up on her elbows, bringing her mouth to mine, and sucks my bottom lip into her mouth as she closes her eyes, and I feel her entire body shudder beneath me.

"Shit...Lila..." I groan as she grazes her teeth down the inside of my lip. My eyes shut involuntarily as I dip my head down and our lips collide roughly, to the point where I wonder if we're going to have bruises.

I move my arms to the sides of her head to support my weight as she keeps pressing her chest against mine, like she's starved—been starved forever. Our tongues tangle as I slip my knee between her legs, causing her to clutch on to my upper arms. Her fingernails jab into my skin as her body scoots down a little and meets the top of my leg. She starts rubbing against my leg, her eyes glazed and her expression hitting a euphoric state. I lose it completely and shove my hand up the front of her shirt, slipping it beneath her bra. I rub the pad of my thumb over her nipple and it instantly hardens as she whimpers, her entire body quivering as she continues to rub herself against my leg. I'm blown away. I've never enjoyed seeing a girl so responsive to my touch, but maybe that's because how I feel about Lila is very different from how I've felt before. It's different. We're different. I'm different.

I keep rubbing her nipple as she grinds against me, her head tipped back, and I know she's close. So am I. Fuck. Really, really close.

"Harder," she breathes as I watch her on the verge of falling apart.

I give her what she wants and pinch her nipple harder. She groans loudly in response, her entire body rising up as she gasps in ecstasy. I'm on the brink of losing it myself and work hard to stay in control. After a moment of panting, she lies flat beneath me. Her skin is beading with sweat, her expression content, and she's more beautiful than ever. Her hair is scattered above her head, her skin damp, her breathing ragged.

"That was good," she says and breathes in and out, her chest moving up and down. "God, that was really good."

"The best you've ever had?" I try to joke, but my voice comes out breathless in reaction to the fact that I'm hard as hell and it's actually starting to hurt.

She shakes her head from side to side. "I can't even compare it to anything…I've never felt anything like it before."

I'm still cupping her breast and I can feel her heart racing and I count each beat to calm myself down. "I'm not sure what you mean."

She shakes her head. "Neither am I and it doesn't matter." She leans in to kiss me and her whole body starts trembling before she even reaches my lips.

I'm worried she might be going into shock or something over what just happened with Parker. I bring my hand out of her bra and cup her cheek. "Maybe we should stop," I say, searching her eyes for what she's really thinking.

Her eyes widen in horror. "Oh my God, you don't want to." She starts to roll to the side to move away, but I put my arm next to her so she can't get too far.

"That's not what I'm saying," I tell her as she turns her head to look at me. "I want to, Lila…God, I want to so fucking badly. In fact, I'm pretty sure you can feel how bad I want to."

Her cheeks turn a little pink, shocking me again. "Yeah, kind of."

I fight back a smile. "I'm just worried you're in shock over what happened with Parker and maybe you're not thinking clearly."

"I'm thinking more clearly than I ever have," she insists. "I want this. I want you."

"Are you sure? Because I don't—"

She cuts me off, tracing her fingers up the front of my chest. "Yes... God, yes, I'm sure," she says, her voice alarmingly off pitch. "Please don't make me beg, Ethan. *Please.* I can't... I don't... I never *wanted* to be with anyone like this before. *Ever.*"

I let out a slow, tension-filled breath, fighting the urge to rip her clothes off, needing to be sure where she stands. And where I stand. Where the hell do we stand? "I'm just trying to be a good guy here, Lila, but you're making it really..." I trail off as her fingers reach the top of my jeans. "Really... really... difficult."

"Good," she says and then rises up on her elbows and crashes her mouth against mine. Her movement is sloppy and very inexperienced, the kind of kiss that carries doubt. She's throwing herself out there in front of me, and despite how terrified I am about what this move will mean for us I decide to do the same thing and kiss her back with equal, if not more, desire.

We kiss until our lips are swollen, until our bodies are covered in sweat, and then I sit up, only so I can take her shirt off and reach around to unclasp her bra. Then I lean back and take in her body. She's beautiful, amazing and nearly perfect, except for the scars on her stomach. But in a way it almost makes her more perfect, because it shows she's flawed and real. I just wish I knew where she got them from, wish I understood her better.

I trace my finger along her scar and she shuts her eyes, looking like it's hurting her. My hand travels upward to her breast and grazes her nipple and she sucks in a sharp breath.

"This feels so good," she whispers, breathless as she brings her hands up to my shoulders. Cupping my shoulder blades, she draws me down to her so our chests are pressing together. She inhales and exhales, like she's savoring the moment and I lean down and kiss her neck, softly at first, but the more excited and breathy she gets the rougher my kisses become. I make a trail of kisses to her breast and then I suck her nipple into my mouth, tracing circles around it with my tongue. She cries out my name and it makes my heart pump with adrenaline. I can't take it anymore. She's driving my heart and body crazy. I pull back and kick my shorts and boxers off and to the side, and then I unbutton her shorts and practically rip them to get them off her. I reach for a condom in my nightstand, feeling this new sensation build up inside me.

I want Lila. Just her. No one else. I want to be with her.

Seconds later, I slip inside her, knowing that whatever we had before will forever be changed. I know when it's over she'll mean more to me than any other girl ever has. The surprising thing is, I really don't care. In fact, I'm glad.

Chapter Fourteen

Lila

I'm not sure if it's the fact that I realize I love him or the fact that I'm sober, but every touch, kiss, every time our skin comes into contact, I nearly lose it. I'm on the verge of combusting, feeling as though I'm tumbling into a wonderful, divine, unknown place. I'm starting to wonder if I've ever had a real orgasm. Probably, I'm sure, but I've never been coherent enough to fully feel it.

I can barely breathe and every single one of my nerves is pulsating with dread, desire, and bliss. I've never let myself be so exposed before, not since Sean, and even then I didn't know myself enough to show who I really was. I'm starting to understand myself more, who I am, what I want, what I need. And it all ends with Ethan.

I can barely think straight as he pinches and sucks on my nipples, touches me all over, feels me from the inside and the outside, head to toe, bathing kisses all over my body. I don't know how much more of this I can take before I'm going to explode, and he must feel the same way because suddenly he's ripping the rest of our clothes off and throwing them onto the floor. When he slips inside me, I scream out his name as heat courses through my body, my insides trembling as he fills me. He starts thrusting inside me and I keep waiting for my mind to shut down, but I don't want it to and thankfully it never does.

His muscles are taut, his arms beside my head as he rocks into me and I curve my back inward, bringing myself up to meet him, wanting more, needing more. I swear to God it feels like I can't get enough as our bodies keep connecting, in tune with each other. The way he watches me every time I gasp in pleasure makes me feel beautiful, not filthy; wanted, not used. I wish it could go on forever, but I also want to reach the end because I feel like I'm going to lose it. As he gives one last hard thrust, I feel myself letting go of everything, the past, the shame, the worry, and it's so blindingly intense, so over-powering, that I stab my fingernails into his shoulder blades, needing to channel the forceful energy somewhere. I feel his flesh split apart as I hold onto him, knowing I'm letting the rough side of me show through, but for once I just embrace it, embrace who I am. *This is who I am.*

He lets out a deep groan, his face contorted with pain and pleasure, and seeing the effect I'm having on him makes me rise higher until I completely lose touch with reality all together. When I finally return to reality, he's stilled inside me. He's situated between my legs, his head lowered onto my chest, and I can feel his pulse throbbing inside me.

He lays motionless forever, breathing against my chest, and the longer it goes on, the more nervous and insecure I get as I wait to see where this is going to go. Will he leave me like Sean did? Should I get up and walk away before he does? I don't want to. I want to be with him. Forever maybe.

When he raises his head, I see something in his eyes I've never seen in any other guy's eyes before. Ethan cares about me and he looks just as nervous as I do.

"That was…" He breathes in and out as he brushes my hair away from my damp forehead. "Amazing."

I nod, because I'm speechless and way too out of breath. He smiles, kisses me delicately on the lips, then slips out of me and rolls onto his back, lying beside me with his arm tucked underneath my neck.

"Are you sure you're okay?" He rotates to his side and places a hand on my bare stomach. "About the Parker thing?"

I turn my head to the side and take in his firm chest, his damp, heavily inked skin, his dark brown eyes that are actually looking at me instead of through me. "Yeah, I really am, I think… You made me feel better. Much, much better."

He smiles, seeming nervous, and I'm trying not to think about how having sex is going to change our relationship. It could end up ugly. Or beautiful. Although, I'd love to be optimistic, all I've ever seen is ugly, with my mom and dad, with every guy I've met. There is only one exception to this and that would be with Micha and Ella. I want what they have, but is it possible for someone like me to have such a beautiful, pure love?

"Tell me what you're thinking about?" he whispers as he affectionately combs his fingers through my hair.

"What's going to happen between us?" I ask honestly and he presses down on my wrist, feeling my pulse, and right beneath his fingertips is one of my scars.

He pauses, searching my eyes, for what I'm not sure. "What do you want to happen between us?"

I swallow hard, reluctant to put myself out there, fearing I'll be rejected. "I don't know. What do you want?"

He inhales slowly and then lets the breath ease out of his lips. "You know about my parents. How they were, right? I've told you."

I nod. "Yeah, you've told me stories. Honestly, they sound a lot like my parents. My dad might not hit my mom, but he cheats on her and yells at her all the time."

He shuts his eyes, breathing in before opening them again. "I don't want us to turn out like either one of them...I love being with you, even when you're being a pain in the ass." He tries for a light tone, but fails. "What if a relationship ruins what we have? What if we ruin each other?"

My chest tightens and I'm finding it hard to breathe. It seems like my scar on my stomach is getting more distinct and I wonder if he can see it more clearly. "But what if it doesn't? What if..." *Jesus, breathe, Lila.* "What if we end up having something really good, like what Ella and Micha have?"

He presses his lips together. "But what if it does ruin us? Then what? We just walk away from each other? I sure as hell don't want you out of my life. And I...I worry about you. The stuff you've been going through...It's still so new and relationships can be very dangerous."

Tears sting at my eyes as the feeling of being rejected builds inside me. I could stand by and just let it come like I did the last time, but unlike Sean, Ethan seems like he's worth fighting for. "I don't want how I'm feeling to go away." His lips part, about to say something, but I interrupt him, deciding that it's time to let him know who I really am on the inside, without the pills, the shots of Bacardi, without the makeup and fancy clothes.

"When I was fourteen and I went off to boarding school, I met this guy," I begin, summoning every speck of courage I've kept locked inside me. "Actually, I kind of made us meet. I was feeling really lonely and this group of girls—the Precious Bells"—I roll my eyes at how ridiculous it sounds—"said they would be my friend if I hit on one of these older rich guys who liked to hang out at the library for some reason." I can feel the ring on my finger weighing a hundred pounds. The ring Sean gave to me, telling me he loved me, whispering a false promise of loving me forever. Suddenly, I don't want it on my finger, branding me and what we did together. I don't want to remember his love anymore. Or him. Who I was with him. I want to move on, become a different person—a stronger person—so I slip it off and toss it onto the nightstand next to me.

Ethan watches me with curiosity, trailing his fingers back and forth across my stomach. "Are you okay?"

I nod, returning my wrist to his hand, and continue with my story. "I hit on him and he seemed to be interested. At first, things moved really slow, a few texts and e-mails, but then we finally met up and everything changed. We kissed and for the first time in my life...I felt loved." I pause, catching my breath. Ethan looks like he wants to say something, his forehead furrowed as he swallows hard but I keep going because I need to get it all out. "Anyway, to make a long story short, I was really stupid and pretty much would do anything he told me to do because I thought he loved me." I pause. "The first and only time we had sex"—I bring my free wrist up, the scar on it matching the one on my other wrist—"he tied me to the bed with ropes, even though I wasn't really into it." I nod at my stomach and he follows my gaze to the faded scar traveling across the bottom section of my stomach. "And then...well, I'm pretty sure you can probably figure out what happened next."

His skin turns white as he stares at the scars on my stomach and then his gaze returns to mine. "Those are from the *ropes* because some fucking guy tied you to a bed?"

I nod and then shrug. "It was my own damn fault. I told him no once, but he said it'd be okay, so I believed him and went through with it." Tears burn at my eyes as I remember how confused I felt, how lost, how disgusting and yet at the same time loved I felt. "And it kind of felt good at first, but then when he..." I breathe out, letting the words rush out. "Well, he got really rough with me and I was too afraid to ask him to stop, too afraid I'd lose his love." I suck back the tears, forcing myself not to show the shame I feel on the inside. *Keep it trapped*. "Afterward, he left me and I never saw him again. I guess his girlfriend, who I didn't even know about, found out about me but honestly I'm pretty sure he was done with me... I could see it in his eyes when he finished fucking me that he was done." I pause, taking a deep breath. "What made it worse was that everyone found out about it and told me that I was a slut." I give Ethan a moment, because he looks like he's about to freak out. "I should stop, right? This is too much." I start to sit up, ready to go and give him some breathing room from my sluttishness and depressing story.

"How old was he?" he asks through gritted teeth as he gently pushes me back down on the bed. "This guy."

"Twenty-two," I say and feel him cringe. "Anyway, it was a long time ago and I'm sure he's completely forgotten about me at this point. I'm just trying to tell you why I am the way I am. I've spent the last six years popping pills and having sex with random guys because I seriously feel like I don't deserve anything better." I'm about to cry and I hate myself for it. I feel so ugly right now, but Ethan deserves to know who I am, what he's going to get into if he chooses to be with me. "I'm fucked up, Ethan. I never feel loved, yet I always keep looking for it, hoping that somehow it really exists."

He watches me for an eternity. "The guy who was twenty-two was fucked up. He should have never been with you, let alone tied you to a bed your first time."

"I instigated our relationship . . . It wasn't entirely his fault."

"I don't give a shit who instigated it. You were fourteen and didn't know any better."

I roll my eyes, more than anything to keep the tears from escaping, because he's saying everything I wished my mother would have said when I told her, but instead she told me it was my fault and made me feel more like the whore everyone was telling me I was. "I didn't put up very much of a fight when he was tying me up."

He scoots closer, placing a hand on top of my rib cage, just below my breast. "Lila, everything about that story was wrong on the guy's part. He was way too old to be messing around with a fourteen-year-old. It's disturbing and wrong and illegal."

"My mother didn't think so," I say, speaking more to the ceiling than to Ethan, my eyes locked on a crack running from the top of the wall to the fan in the middle. My vision is still blurred with tears, but thankfully no more are forcing their way up. "She said that she expected nothing less from me and then she handed me a pill so I wouldn't have to feel all the guilt and shame I'd been feeling."

He rolls to his side, putting his body above me, so his face is directly in my line of vision. "Are you being fucking serious right now?" Anger flashes in his eyes. "Your mother's the one who got you started on those pills?"

I nod, startled by the fury in his eyes. "Sh-She thought she was making me feel better."

"Your mother's an idiot," Ethan says, shaking his head. "Lila, seriously. That's not normal at all. God, I hate this. I hate how parents are supposed to be the adults, and yet they act like children and bring their children down with them. It happens all the time and it's ridiculous."

I'm not sure what to do, all I know is now I'm worried he's going to leave me because of how fucked up my family is. "I... it was my own fault for taking it."

He shakes his head resolutely as he cups my face and grazes his thumb across my cheekbone, staring intensely into my eyes. "No, it wasn't. None of what happened was your fault." He stares at me for an eternity and I have no idea what he's thinking, whether he's going to leave me, what he's going to say. Then he slides his hand down my shoulder, rests it on my side, and he pulls me against him as he turns, hugging me against him, our bodies pressed together. And it feels so amazing, just to be hugged, to know that someone cares about me, that he's not going to run away and leave me.

"You deserve so much better than what you have," he whispers against my head. "You really do."

A few tears fall from my eyes, not just over my mother or what Sean did to me, or even how I spent the last six years of my life. I cry because Ethan's holding on to me and for the first time in my entire life, I feel like someone wants to hold me just as much as I want to hold on to them.

Chapter Fifteen

Ethan

I would have never guessed. Looking at Lila, I'd always seen a beautiful girl, one who I thought had been spoiled most of her life. She seemed to always get what she wanted and did whatever she wanted. There were a few brief moments when I saw sadness in her eyes, but I never, ever thought it would be from something as dark as what she told me.

I hate her mother for starting her addiction to pills and I really, really fucking hate the perverted bastard who started this mess. I have a lot of hate floating around inside of me. It worries me, because my father has hate in him, too, and it nearly cracked my mom. But the moment Lila and I kissed I knew it was going to be very hard to let her go. And when we had sex, I knew I was done for. But what really did me in was when she told me her story, when I saw the pain in her eyes, the fear of being unloved and unwanted. Right then, I knew I wanted to take all that pain away from her. I think I can finally understand what Micha was always ranting about whenever

I'd question his refusal to let Ella go, despite her problems. And I think that's because I'm falling in love with Lila. Really falling in love.

There's one thing I need to do, though, before I move forward with her. I need to see London, not to try to bring her back or hold on to her, but to say good-bye like I never did so I can finally move on. I've been clutching on to the idea of her for years now, over my guilt of walking away and the sheer fact that I wanted her, broke my rules for her, but never did fully understand her, no matter how hard I tried. I'm ready now, though, to say good-bye to London and Rae completely. Ready to move forward in my life instead of being stuck. And move forward with Lila.

I'm supposed to be booking a flight to San Diego for Ella and Micha's wedding, but as I'm searching for flights I change the destination from California to Virginia. I search through the flights, feeling a lump form in my throat and it only grows when I click on one of the cheaper flights.

I'm seriously going to do this. I'm going to let go.

And hopefully move on with Lila.

Lila

It's time to say good-bye to the ring. I haven't put it on since I took it off while lying with Ethan and I haven't wanted to. Now I want it gone. Forever.

I decide to go to the nearest pawn shop, which is in walking distance from the apartment. I walk into the run-down brick store pretty much shaking at the idea of setting it down on the counter, not because I am afraid but because I am so excited to be letting go of it and everything that it represents.

I have my hair down, barely touching my shoulders, and a tank top and frayed shorts on. I look so much different than the girl the ring was given to, and not just because I'm older but because I'm stronger. I'm not some girl searching for love in all the wrong places. I'm a girl who found love in the right place.

I set the ring down on the glass counter, my fingers trembling, the cashier guy looks at me like I am a crack addict, but it is okay because I am getting rid of the damn ring.

"How much can you give me for this?" I ask, wiping my sweaty palm on the side of my shorts.

He picks it up and scans it over, pretending to only be half interested. Honestly, I probably would accept a dollar, even though I need the money, because it would mean the ring is gone from my life. Luckily, though, he gives me enough that I could afford part of the rent, food, and a plane ticket to San Diego.

I tuck the cash into my pocket, smiling as I head for the door. When I step out into the sunlight, my smile only broadens and it's the realest smile I've ever had because finally I'm free from my past.

Ethan

I return home from work the afternoon Lila and I are supposed to be flying out to San Diego prepared to tell Lila about who London really is and that I'm going to fly to Virginia before I head to California to see her. Normally in these kinds of situations, I'd just pack up my shit and go. I'm not used to telling anyone what I'm doing, but bailing out on Lila isn't an option. I don't want to hurt her, and I want her to understand and be okay with it and for her to know that I want to be with her.

"Hey," Lila says when I walk into her room, all sweaty from the heat of the desert sun beating down on me all day. She has her suitcase opened up on her bed and she's folding clothes and putting them into it. Her hair is pulled up and she's got a thin tank top on that hugs her curves and for a moment I just stare at her, mesmerized by how beautiful she is. "You should go shower and pack your clothes. Our flight leaves in, like, five hours."

I walk up to the foot of the bed, watching her move back and forth. She's gorgeous and still so sad, but the sadness disappears every time I hold her, kiss her. It's been a long damn time since I've spent so much time with the same girl, or with anyone really, and it's nice, new, and uncomfortable.

"I have to tell you something," I say cautiously. Panic immediately floods her eyes as she looks up at me and I quickly take her hand. "It's not bad. It's actually good I think. But you're going to have to trust me."

"Okay." She sounds very distrustful but sits with me as I guide us to the bed, our fingers threaded together. "What is it?"

I take a deep breath. "I never booked the ticket to San Diego like I told you I did."

Her expression falls. "What? Why?" She pauses, looking uncomfortable. "Was it because you couldn't afford it? Because I still have some extra money from some of the jewelry I sold off."

"No, it's not that. I have enough saved up." I rub my free hand down my face, blowing out a stressed breath. "You remember how I told you I stopped doing drugs very abruptly, but I never said why?"

She nods, her eyes scanning my face. "Yeah..."

"Well, the reason why was because of something that happened to this girl I was dating," I say, massaging the back of my neck. "We were pretty serious. In fact, besides you, she was the only girl I've considered my girlfriend." I pause as she tries not to smile. At first I don't get why, but then as I retrace my words it clicks. I just declared she was my girlfriend and not even on purpose. I could take it back, but it seems really stupid and not what I want to do.

"She was into drugs," I continue, trying to stay focused. "Heavy drugs, like heroin." I swallow hard as images of that day surface. Needles. Sadness. Pleading. Me walking away. "The last time I saw her she was shooting up...I tried to talk her out of it, but once London made up her mind it was very hard to change it." I inhale and exhale probably a thousand times before I can continue, the emotions I've kept trapped inside pouring out of me. "I got a call the next morning from her mother, saying she'd fallen out the window of a two-story house. No one at the house supposedly knew why—whether she jumped or fell. She had some serious head trauma...amnesia to be exact, but her mom was really hopeful that'd it be temporary." I pause, remembering what it felt like to know London was alive but that she couldn't remember anything about me—us. It hurt worse than being beaten, yelled at, watching your mother go through torture just so she could stay with your dad. It was like London had died but her spirit was still walking around haunting me. "It wasn't temporary, though, and she never remembered who I was or a lot about herself."

Lila swallows hard, her blue eyes massive as she grasps my hand. "Is she still...is she still like that?"

I nod, feeling either her pulse or mine throbbing in my fingertips. "Her name's London, which I'm sure you remember from when you caught me muttering in my sleep. Rae—her mother—keeps asking me to go there, hoping that after four years I can help London remember something, even though the doctors told her it's pretty much impossible—that the damage is irreversible."

Lila stares at me forever and it drives me insane because I need to know what she's thinking and how she feels about what I just told her because quite honestly I'm perplexed as hell over what I feel. Strangely, I almost feel liberated, like I'm finally letting everything I felt out.

"She must have meant a lot to you," Lila finally says, holding my gaze.

"She did," I admit, tracing my finger across the inside of her wrist. "She was the first girl I ever really thought I might love."

Lila swallows hard again, biting her lip, looking like she's tearing up. I want to tell her that I think I might be in love with her. I want to let her know how I feel and that she means the world to me. I don't want her to cry or hurt. I want her to be happy, like the Lila I first met, only this time her happiness will be real, not pill induced.

"Are you going to go and see her like her mother wants you to?" Lila asks nervously and I feel her hand tense in mine.

I press my lips together and nod. "I think I have to, for a lot of different reasons. One being that I never really said good-bye to London. I was always kind of too afraid to."

Lila smashes her lips together so hard they turn purple. "Okay..." It comes out breathy. "I understand."

Shaking my head, I bring my free hand up to her face and brush back her hair. "Lila, it's not like what you're thinking. It's just something I have to do. I have to say good-bye to her, because I never really did. I just kept holding on to her, which is part of the reason why I've felt so stuck in my life. If I go see her, then maybe I can quit living in the past and move forward." I take a deep breath. "With you." And there it is. The truth.

I can tell she's struggling with whether to be happy or sad. She tips her head back, attempting not to cry. "You'll be there for Ella and Micha's wedding, though, right? Because it's in, like, a few days."

"Of course. Micha would fucking kick my ass if I didn't show up," I say, wishing she'd look at me, wishing I knew what she's thinking. "Besides, I take credit for the fact that their dumb asses are even getting married. If it weren't for me, they'd still be trying to please each other instead of actually telling each other how they feel."

That gets her to look at me and laugh and the sound of it is so amazing, I swear I could fill a thousand pages with words describing the beauty in it. "You're probably right. They are both very stubborn."

"So are we," I say, thinking about how hard I fought against my feelings for her.

She nods, agreeing. "Yes, we are."

"Yeah...we definitely are..." I drift off as I lean in to kiss her, wanting to lick and bite her again—wanting to be inside her again like I was the other night. We haven't had sex since then, not because I don't want to. I want to so fucking bad my cock gets hard just thinking about it. But after what Lila told me, I'm not going to push things until I know she wants it. Plus, I want to go say good-bye to London first so I can hopefully have a completely clear head.

Lila meets me halfway, brushing her lips against mine and she instantly groans and clutches on to me. By the time we finish kissing, we're lying on her bed, my body pressed on hers and I'm sweatier than I was when I got home from work. "I'm going to go take a shower and pack," I say, my lips hovering over hers. I bite at her bottom lip and then suck it into my mouth before I force myself to move away and get up from the bed.

"Are you sure?" she asks, batting her eyelashes up at me as she grips my arms, trying to pull me back. "We could keep kissing and see where it will go."

"Oh, I know where it will go," I assure her. "But I also know that I need to pack and if I start kissing you again, I'm not going to be able to stop. I'll probably want to keep going all night, over and over and over again." My voice drops to a husky growl and she blushes.

Trying to pretend she's not all hot and flustered, she gets to her feet and returns to her suitcase. "Are you flying to Virginia today?" She folds a pair of shorts up and places them in the suitcase.

I nod from the doorway with my hands braced on the door frame. "I'm flying out about the same time you are and then I'll fly to San Diego on Friday."

"So you'll be spending two days in Virginia?" she asks, fighting a frown as she folds up a shirt.

I nod. "Yeah."

She's obviously uncomfortable with the idea and I feel bad

that she is. But I need to do this. I know it's going to be hard, finally letting go of London and my guilt after all these years of holding on to it. But I know I can do it, because I want Lila, want to give her what she deserves, needs, more than I've wanted to do anything else in my life.

Lila

I'm trying to be strong, but it's difficult. I've finally opened myself up to someone and then he tells me about his one and only other girlfriend, who has amnesia apparently. I can see in his eyes that he still really cares for her and I wonder if he might still love her. It feels like my heart is breaking, until he calls me his girlfriend. That helps a little. As much as I want to be secure about our relationship, I'm still battling with my inner self-doubting demons. I'm still figuring out who I am and who I want to be. All I really know is that I love Ethan and haven't told him that yet. And now he's going to see his ex-girlfriend.

I'm feeling very bummed out and defeated by the time we arrive at the airport. It isn't very crowded today and we get through security pretty quickly. His flight leaves a half an hour before mine though so he drops me off at my gate and then heads to leave.

"All right, you can call me for anything," he says as he slings his bag over his shoulder.

I nod, trying not to pout as I stand near the seating area with my suitcase at my feet. "I know."

He walks backward, dodging to the side to get around people. "Especially if you feel the need to."

I force a smile, pretending I'm more okay than I really am. "Stop worrying about me," I say. "I'll be fine."

He returns my smile, but he's worried about me. I can see it in his eyes. "All right, I'll see you in two days." He turns around and walks away, and it makes me sadder because he didn't even kiss me good-bye.

I watch him with a giant frown on my face. He's dressed in faded jeans secured by a studded belt, a dark plaid shirt, and there are leather bands on his wrists. His dark hair is all messy because he took too long in the shower and we had to rush out of the house before he had time to do anything with it, although he didn't really care. He's so gorgeous and I wish I knew for certain if he was mine, but I don't know that yet. These things take time to fully understand.

Once he's out of my sight, I turn toward the section where I'll board with my ticket in my hand. I'm used to flying first class, but I can't afford it.

I'm on the verge of tearing up when I feel someone grab me from behind. I open my mouth to scream bloody murder, but arms encircle my waist and I catch a scent of a very familiar cologne and relax into Ethan's touch.

"I forgot something," he whispers in my ear, turning me toward him. His eyes are dark, his hair hanging in his face as his gaze drinks me in slowly, deliberately. I forget to breathe as he leans down and kisses me. And I mean *kisses* me, the kind of kiss that rips my breath right out of my lungs, makes me forget where I am, who I am. As our tongues entwine, it makes every single struggle I've been through worth it because they've gotten me right here to this moment—they've gotten me to him.

His hands comb through my hair and I breathe in the scent of him as I clutch on to his arms, wishing he wasn't leaving me. By the time we pull away, we're panting, my heart is slamming against my chest, and everyone is staring at us with silly smiles on their faces that I'm certain match my own.

"I'll see you in a few days." He kisses me on the cheek before backing away.

I nod, breathless and flushed. "Okay."

He smiles and then picks up his bag, turning around and walking away for real this time. I still feel sad, but I'm twenty times lighter now, knowing I can make it for three days.

"I love you. I really, really do," I whisper so softly no one can hear. I want to tell him. I do because I think it'll be different from when I told Sean I loved him, but I can't quite get there yet. But I can feel myself headed in the right direction and that's got to mean something and gives me hope that when I do finally tell him, things will be different because Ethan's different.

And so am I.

Chapter Sixteen

Lila

Ella and Micha's house is adorable. I would have thought I'd dislike the place, seeing how small it is and that it's perched at the end of this really bumpy road that weaves through a neighborhood where all the houses look different. It's pretty, though, the way the yellow shutters stick out from everything else around and how the grass is covered with a variety of flowers, none of which go together but make it colorful and lively. It's Thursday morning and the sun is hot, but in a bearable way, unlike the stifling desert air in Vegas.

"I really love your house," I remark for probably the third time as Ella and I sit on the back porch beneath the sunlight. We have shorts and tank tops on. My hair hangs down to my shoulders and I haven't put my makeup on yet, but no one's around so it doesn't really matter.

"Thanks." She stretches her feet out in front of her. "We got it dirt cheap, too, thanks to Micha's mom," she says and when I glance at her funny, she adds, "An old friend of hers works out here as a Realtor and she hooked us up with this place. The lady who owns it is really old and probably bought it back in the 1940s when it was built so she wasn't asking a lot for it. We were really lucky."

"I'm glad," I say. "You guys needed some good luck."

"We did?" She crooks her eyebrow, questioningly.

"I think everyone does," I say, hoping that I'll get some good luck soon and finally work up the courage to tell Ethan how I feel about him. That would be the best luck ever. "So," I say, changing the subject, "you're really getting married on Saturday."

Ella nods, sipping her coffee as she stares out at the fence that divides her yard from the next-door neighbors, who apparently collect wind chimes, since there's a collection of them trimming the entire back end of the house.

"I really am. Totally weird, huh?" she asks, seeming a little nervous, but that's just how Ella is. When I nod, she adds with a discreet glance at me from the corner of her eye, "About as weird as your new hairdo."

I touch the ends of my hair, scrunching my nose. "It doesn't look that bad, does it?"

She shakes her head and sets her coffee mug by her feet. "No, I like it…" Her green eyes sweep over me as she readjusts the elastic around her auburn hair. "It just looks different— *you* look different."

I examine my nails, pretending to be blasé. "How so?"

She shrugs, staring at me with a quizzical look on her face. "You're dressing different...less fancy and more like me. And I don't know...you just look different. Happier or something."

That throws me off the slightest bit. "Happier? That's weird, because a lot of people have said I was the happiest person they'd ever met."

She reaches for her coffee, again tucking her foot underneath her as she brings the brim of the glass cup up to her mouth. "I can see why they'd say that, but I don't know..." She takes a sip, shaking her head. "You just look different for some reason. I can't put my finger on it." She rotates her cup in her hand, pressing her lips together, and it looks like she's trying really hard not to smile.

"What?" I finally say as I reach for my coffee. A little laugh slips through my lips because she looks so amused and I have absolutely no idea what's going on. "Why do you keep giving me weird looks?"

"Is there anything you want to tell me?" she asks.

I shrug, taking a gulp of the coffee. "That you have a nice house."

She gives me a tolerant look. "Lila."

I press back a smile, even though I have no clue what's going on. "Ella."

She grins, and then shakes her head, laughing. "Fine, if you're not going to fess up, then I'll just say it." She pauses, gripping the handle of her mug. "I heard a rumor that there finally might be something going on between you and Ethan."

I hold my cup in one hand and thrum my fingers on the wicker armrest of the chair. I haven't talked to Ethan since we parted at the airport. I texted him a few times, but he always gives one-word responses, so I decided to give him some space, seeing how he's probably really busy with London. God, even thinking about it hurts a little. "By rumor, you mean Micha told you about us."

She shrugs, grinning amusedly. "Maybe."

"What did he say exactly?" I ask curiously, a little worried about what he said, but the fact that he did tell him has to mean something, right? That he cares enough about me to tell Micha. "Or should I say, what did Ethan tell him?"

She turns her head toward me with a mischievous grin on her face. "Why don't you tell me your side and then I can compare?"

I set the coffee cup down on the ground again while she takes a drink of hers. "Fine, we fucked."

She sucks in a sharp breath and then quickly moves the mug away from her mouth as she spits coffee all over the deck in front of her feet. "Holy shit, Lila." She presses her hand to her chest, coughing as she works to catch her breath. "I was not expecting you to be so blunt about it."

I can't help myself. A big silly grin rises on my lips. "Me neither, but I think I'll have to do it more because it's really, really fun."

She wipes the coffee from her face with the back of her hand. "You're starting to sound like me."

"The new, fun you or the old, boring one who I first met?" I joke. "I need clarification."

She shields the sunlight with her hand. "The new one, which is the better one. Trust me."

"I do trust you," I say. "But the Ella I've always known, new or old, was still a good person and that's a great thing to be compared to."

She shakes her head, stifling a smile. "Are we going to have a moment here or something?"

"Maybe," I say. "We never really did have one in the entire two years that we've known each other. Maybe it's time. We can hug, cry it out, and tell each other how much we love each other."

"I'm not one for crying." She lowers her hand to her lap. "Or for throwing out the *L* word."

"I know and honestly I'm trying to cut back on it," I joke. "We could have a girl-bonding moment though and you could ask me how sex with Ethan was while we eat popcorn and watch a really sappy movie."

She makes a gagging face, pressing her hand to her chest like she's choking on the idea. "I never ever want to hear you talk about sex with him. Ever." She shudders. "So gross."

We giggle over it for a moment and then talk about lighter things, like how Micha and she have been over the last couple of months. She presses me for more Ethan details, asking me why he couldn't get off work to fly out with me. Apparently, Ethan never told anyone about London and I decide to keep it to myself, figuring Ethan must have his reasons. Other than that I don't have much to say, besides the fact that kissing Ethan is amazing and that only makes her dry heave. She understands my need to be vague for the most part, because she's pretty much the vaguest person I've ever met, and she doesn't press much, which makes me glad she's my best friend. I didn't even realize how much I'd missed being around her and it makes me feel happy that I have that kind of friendship with someone but kind of sad because I know I'm only going to miss her when I go back to Vegas.

"So what about your dress?" I ask as we head back into the kitchen, deciding for a subject change. I need to talk about something happy and clothes always do that for me.

She sets our mugs into the sink and rinses them off. "You want to see it?" she asks, shutting the faucet off.

I nod eagerly and clap my hands together. "Of course. I love wedding stuff. And the dress is the best part."

"I know." She frowns as she winds around the tiny island in the middle of the kitchen. "Which makes me reluctant to show you."

"Why?" My face scrunches up. "Ella, what did you do?"

"I didn't *do* anything." She sighs. "Which is why you're not going to like it."

I stare blankly at her, confused, and she sighs and motions for me to follow her as she walks toward the hallway. She takes me back to a small bedroom. The blue walls are covered with artwork and there's a wrought-iron bed piled with sheets of paper that are smudged with penned lyrics.

I pick up one of the sheets of paper from the foot of the bed. "What? Do you guys just sit around and write and draw together all day?"

"Kind of," she says, opening the closet door. "I mean, I'm not in school right now and I only work part time down at this art gallery, so I have to fill up my day somehow."

I nod and set the sheet down on the dresser. "I'm trying to find a job," I admit. "But I'm having no luck."

She's searching through the clothes hanging up, but pauses, glancing at me from over her shoulder with her eyebrows elevated. "Really?"

"Yes, really." I sit on the edge of the bed and cross my legs, but then pull a face and put my hands on my lap. "Wait, is this safe to sit on?"

She sifts through the small amount of clothes in the closet. "My bed? Why wouldn't it be?"

"Because God knows what you two do on it."

She rolls her eyes. "It's fine, just keep your hands on your lap."

Laughing, I lean over and examine a sheet of lyrics on the bed. "So, does Micha work every day?"

"Sometimes," she replies. "Sometimes he gets a week off at a time. Sometimes he's on the road all week. Right now, he's recording at a studio in town."

"And it's not hard for you?" I ask. "To be away from him like that, because I remember how hard it was for you two the first time around."

"I'd be lying if I said it wasn't, but I go with him to every performance I can and we spend every waking hour together when we're not working."

I sit up straight, leaning back on my hands. "I'm not really surprised that you guys are doing well."

She removes a hanger from the rod and turns around. "You aren't? Really? Because I kind of am."

"I already told you that you guys have the most beautiful relationship that's ever existed and although you're kind of crazy, you're not stupid and I knew you'd eventually get it all right." I make a swoony face, tipping my head to the side as I drape my hand over my forehead. "You guys are so dreamy together."

She rolls her eyes. "Whatever, Miss Smarty Pants. Maybe I should be giving you a hard time."

I lower my hand. "About what?"

"About whether or not you're in love with Ethan." She arches her eyebrows, waiting for my response.

I am! I want to scream, but I haven't told Ethan yet, so telling her first seems wrong. "So how about that dress?" I say, trying for a subject change and reaching out for her to hand it over. "Let me see it."

She lets my abrupt subject change go and slowly pulls out a plain black tank dress. "I hate white," she says, holding the fabric up to her body, "so I thought this could work."

It goes to her knees and has no detail at all. Plus, it has a really high neckline and the straps look really worn out.

"Are you going to a funeral?" I ask, pulling a face at the hideous dress. "Or a wedding?"

She sighs, defeated, lowering the dress to her side. "I don't like fancy stuff, okay. And besides, fancy dresses are expensive."

"It doesn't have to be fancy." I get to my feet. "But this..." I touch the fabric and then cringe at the roughness of it, like it's been washed a thousand times. "Ella, you seriously can't get married in this. It's hideous."

"Well, what do you suggest I wear?" she asks. "I don't have a lot of money and I don't have anyone to help me besides you."

I mull it over for a minute, wondering if I really want to go to where my brain's heading. How much do I care for Ella? A lot obviously, since I'm even considering what I'm considering right now. I mean, she's my best friend, and she deserves a really pretty dress. "I have an idea, but you'll have to trust me. And I mean really, really trust me."

"Why?" She's wary. "What are you up to?"

"I'm not up to anything," I tell her, heading for the door. "I just don't want you to be shocked."

Her mouth turns downward as she trails after me. "Okay, I'll trust you, but I have a few rules." She counts down on her fingers. "Like no ruffles, no pure white, no poofiness."

I laugh as we head out the door.

Ethan

It's Thursday morning, only about twelve hours since I left Las Vegas and Lila behind. I find that I'm missing her a lot more than I'd expected. She's texted me a couple of times and I want to call and talk to her, but I promised myself I wouldn't until after I talked to London. That way I could have a clear head. Maybe. Hopefully.

I'm at London's aunt's house, where London lives most of the time because it's closer to her doctor's office. I've been sitting in a living room that smells like cat food for about an hour, counting the ticks of the grandfather clock while drinking iced tea and listening to Rae talk about hope while we wait for London to come back from her doctor's appointment. I'm getting a little restless waiting, wondering what she'll look like and the stupid part of me believes there's a small possibility that she'll walk into the room and recognize me. It's making me regret coming here and making me really want to hop onto a plane and go back to Lila, just so I can hold her.

I'm just about to tell Rae that I can't do this when the front door swings open and London walks inside. It's mind-blowingly strange, seeing her again. She looks older, yet the same. Her black hair is still resting at her chin and streaked with purple, and she still has a scar on her lip and her nose is pierced. She also has a faint scar on her head where she hit it on the rock when she fell out the window, the thing that caused the brain damage. I swear, if I didn't know any better, I'd guess that I'd somehow stepped back in time four years.

There's this fleeting moment when I swear her eyes light up like they used to whenever she looked at me, but it vanishes so quickly I wonder if I was imagining it. She glances at her mother, who she does recognize, but not from her childhood. She can't remember anything from the past, except the basic functions of walking, talking, and breathing.

"Who's he?" she asks her mom in a robotic kind of voice.

Rae looks just how I remember her the last time I saw her right after London's accident. She's still the spitting image of London, only twenty-years older. She gets to her feet. "This is an old friend of yours."

London's eyes lock on me and I remember how she sometimes used to just stare at me with this thoughtful look on her face, like she was memorizing what I looked like. But now, well, she just looks lost, like someone who wandered off into the forest and can't find her way back.

"I don't remember him," she says, stepping back toward the door. "Why is he here?"

Rae quickly winds around the sofa and grabs London's arm, stopping her from bolting. "He came here to talk to you. A long way actually, so the least you could do is sit down and listen to what he has to say."

London glances at me and I force a smile. It's too weird. I just keep thinking about all the time we spent together and how I can remember it but she can't. I'm a stranger to her, but I realize now she was kind of like a stranger to me the entire time we were dating.

"What's your name?" she finally asks me.

"Ethan," I get up from the sofa and walk toward her with my hands tucked into the pockets of my jeans. "Ethan Gregory."

She considers this for a moment. "I have no idea who you are," she says and then shrugs like she's at a loss for words. "Sorry."

"I'm sorry, too," I reply, but I'm not quite sure what I'm sorry for. Whether it's for leaving the house that day, not ripping the needle out of her hand when she was about to shoot up, or for the plain and simple fact that I can't make her remember me. Or maybe it's because even though I'm standing here with her, I can't stop thinking about Lila, her smile, her sadness, and the fact that at the moment I really just want to be with her, not here.

"Why don't you two sit down?" Rae gestures at the sofas. "And I'll go get you some iced tea." She smiles at me with hope in her eyes as she walks past me, heading to the kitchen and leaving me alone with London.

London shakes her head and then sighs and sits down on the sofa. "I don't know why she tries so hard." She tucks her hands underneath her legs. "I can barely remember her and she's my mother."

"She just cares about you." I take a seat in the recliner across from her. "It's a good thing."

"Or a stupid thing, depending on how you look at it." She eyes me over as she leans back in the sofa. "What's your name again?"

"Ethan," I say, picking up the glass of iced tea Rae has placed beside me. She's disappeared back into the kitchen, and I can't help but wish I was back there with her. "Ethan Gregory."

"And we dated?"

"Yeah, pretty much."

"And we had sex?"

I'm in the middle of a sip and nearly spit the iced tea all over the floor. "Yeah, I guess you could say that," I say, setting the glass down.

"Was I any good?" she asks curiously as she leans forward. "I mean I had to be if you're here to visit me." Her feistiness resembles the London I remember so much it's kind of hard to take in.

"You were," I admit, wiping my lips with the back of my hand.

She arches her eyebrow. "The best you ever had?"

I open my mouth to answer, but then clamp my jaw shut because the answer is no. The best I've ever had is back in San Diego doing who knows what, hopefully smiling and being happy.

"Aw," she states, her eyebrows arching as she relaxes back in the chair. "There's someone else."

I nod slowly, sadly. "Kind of."

She seems amused by this, the corners of her lips quirking. "Are you in love with her?"

I lean forward, overlapping my hands on my knees. "You know, you ask a lot of questions."

"Only about things I can't remember," she replies. "You know it's a pain in the ass not being able to remember everyone, yet they're always looking at you, hoping you will."

"You can't remember anything at all?" I know the answer, but I still ask the question.

"Nope, not really."

"You seem so calm about it, though."

"Not calm. I've just accepted it. I can remember the last four years, so that's something. I'm not completely clueless and from what I understand—the fact that I threw myself out the window while on heroin—maybe I needed this."

"I'm not sure I'd go that far," I say uneasily. "Forgetting your past is a really big deal."

"Maybe." She pauses, crossing her arms over her chest.

I take a deep breath, preparing myself to say what I came here for. "About that day...the day you..."

"Threw myself out the window," she finishes for me bluntly.

I nod. "Yeah...I wanted to say..." I fidget with the sleeve

of my shirt. "I want to say that I'm sorry. I should have never left you in that house."

"You left me?" she asks. "Why?"

I shrug. "You were frustrating me because you were obviously upset about something, yet you wouldn't talk about it—you never would. You wanted to shoot up heroin instead and I didn't want you to."

She tucks her hair behind her ear, her analyzing gaze boring into me. "You told me not to do it?"

I nod. "A few times, but I should have tried harder. I should have made you stop."

"How would you have done that?"

"I don't know...ripped the needle out of your hand or something."

She thrums her fingernails on the armrest, considering something. "You know, if I've learned one thing through this whole ordeal it's that sometimes you can't make things happen, even if you want them to. You can't change things or make people do things they don't want to do or can't do."

I swallow hard, understanding what she's saying. "But I could have tried harder."

"And in the end I'm sure I still would have put the needle in my arm," she says. "And probably went out the window."

"Maybe not though."

"But maybe." She pauses. "But we'll never know. And it's not for you to feel guilty when I can't even remember you."

I shake my head. She's still so London and it's crazy. "I guess so." I get what she's saying. I really do. But it's hard to accept because we'll never know what might have happened or might not have happened if I'd just gotten her to put the needle down.

"I don't want to talk about me anymore," she says dismissively. "I'm always talking about myself—with my mom, the doctors, everyone I come across who used to know me. I get so sick of it."

"What do you want to talk about, then?" I ask, leaning back in the seat, feeling a little lighter and at the same time a little sadder because I know this is it. This is how things will always be between us and I can't change it.

"You." She crosses her legs and stares me down so hard I swear she's trying to burn a hole in my head. "Tell me, Ethan Gregory, this girl who's the best you've ever had, do you love her?"

"Love?" I ask. "You want to talk about love?"

She nods. "I do."

I shrug, feeling uncomfortable under her scrutiny. "What the fuck is love anyway?" Giving your heart to someone completely? Saying here, take it, I'm yours? Letting them love you, hug you, own you? Yell at you and tell you you're worthless? Hold you and tell you you're important? What is the definition of love? How can you tell?

I open my mouth and decide to just go for it, letting the first answer that pops into my head slip out. "I think I do." My mind is flying about a million miles an hour with the declaration and it's hard to process, especially since I just said it for the first time in front of my ex-girlfriend who has amnesia.

She tilts her head to the side, studying me. "Did you love me?"

I think about her question, knowing the real answer, but it's hard to admit it. "I think I did, but in a different way."

"What do you mean?"

"Our love was kind of chaotic and careless and we really didn't know each other enough to actually completely love each other." I reach into my pocket and retrieve the bracelet London gave me, the one with our initials intertwined. "But I think in some way or another we did have some kind of love for each other." I lean over the table, holding my hand out to give her the bracelet.

"But not as much as this other girl?" she asks, taking the bracelet from my hand. "What is this?"

"You made it for me," I say, leaning back. "You said it would always help me remember the time we spent together."

She runs her finger along the leather. "Was I going to break up with you when I gave it to you? Because it kind of sounds like I was."

I shrug and then shake my head. "You could have been thinking about it, but honestly I don't know. Half the time I never knew what you were thinking."

She grins as she looks down at the bracelet in her hand. "And now you'll never know." Leave it to London to have a sick and twisted sense of humor about the whole thing. But she's right. I'll never know what she was thinking, how she really felt, how I really felt, because we never got around to telling each other. I was so afraid of my feelings that I held them in and now the chance to tell her is gone. She'll never know whether I loved her or not. How much I cared for her. I'll never know if she felt the same way, whether she loved me so much she'd hang on to me if something happened to me and I was no longer part of her life. I will never know a lot of stuff about our relationship and there's no changing that. It's done. Final.

"I guess not." I offer her a small smile.

She continues to stare at the bracelet, looking sadder with each passing moment. Finally she sighs and sets it down on the table. "So tell me something happy," she says, shifting her mood in the amount of time it takes me to catch my breath. "And not about my past."

I take a deep breath and start telling her about the last few years of my life, which aren't really happy or sad, just neutral, because I've basically been stuck in the same mentality, never moving forward, always thinking about the past. Except in this very moment, I want to be moving forward to the other side of the country to be with someone else. By the time we're done talking, it's midafternoon. My flight doesn't leave until the morning, but the idea of waiting until then seems impossible. I need to see Lila now and I need to tell her how I feel so I don't miss my chance again.

Chapter Seventeen

Lila

"So I've come to the conclusion that I'm becoming a very bad influence on you," Ella says as she roams through my old room in my parents' three-story mansion located up in the greener, more luxurious side of town. The ocean rushes toward the shore from outside the window and the sun beams brightly against the pale pink walls.

"I guess so." I open my closet and walk into it, the immense space almost overwhelming because it's been a long time since I've seen it. So many memories overwhelm me, ones filled with loathing from my parents and self-loathing from myself. For a moment, I swear to God the damn walls feel like they're closing in on me again.

I run my fingers along the fabrics of each dress and shirt, remembering what it was like to have an endless amount of clothes, money, anything of material value. I was showered with things, and in return, I was not showered with affection and love. I would trade anything, live on the streets in a soggy wet box, just to have my parents genuinely love me.

Ella steps up behind me and evaluates my closet. "Are you sure your maid's not going to tell your mom or dad we snuck in here?"

I shrug as I sift through the dresses, the sight of each one making me sick to my stomach, because each one carries a memory of a time I wish I could forget. All the horrible things I've done in them, all the horrible things I felt. "I doubt it. She hates my mother and father almost as much as I do. It doesn't really matter, though." From the back section, I select a dress that flows to the floor. "I mean, what are they going to do? Kick me out?"

"How about make you stay," she says from behind me. "I know you don't want to be here."

"I don't." I glance over my shoulder at her, forcing a smile. "I guess you'll just have to owe me for this big time."

"I think that all kind of depends on why you brought me here." She wanders around, her eyes huge as she takes in the large selection of shoes on the back wall. "Because I'm really confused right now."

I smile at her and then hold the dress out toward her. "We're here for this."

Ella examines the dress with a wary expression on her face. "What is that?"

"You're such a goof sometimes. Seriously." I push the

dress at her. "It's for you. I thought you could wear it at your wedding."

She stares at the dress that has a shimmering black silk top, a red ribbon securing the back, and an elegant flowing white bottom bunched together in places by red and black sewn roses. She tentatively reaches out and touches the fabric with a stoic expression as she runs her fingers along one of the black flowers.

"Where did you get this?" she asks, touching the silk top.

"I wore it one year for... for Halloween," I say, choking down the images of what I did while wearing the dress. I drank drink after drink that night and chased them down with pills. I'm surprised I didn't end up in the hospital, although I probably would have been better off, instead of sleeping with two different guys in the same night and then throwing up alone in the bathroom afterward. I almost puke just thinking about it now, thinking about who I was.

She glances up at me. "*You* wore *this* for Halloween?"

I nod. "But it was actually just a dress I bought from a store and then turned it into a Victorian-style dress."

"I guessed that much." She lets her arm fall to her side. "But it looks so... unlike anything you would wear."

I laugh, because she's right, yet at the same time I'm also standing next to her in an old pair of shorts and a band T-shirt I stole from Ethan's room. "I guess, but it was also Halloween and I was supposed to dress up as something unlike myself."

"That's true." Her gaze returns to the dress and she bites back a smile. "Can I try it on?"

"Of course." I hand it to her and head for the door so she can change in the closet. "You're not offended I gave you an old costume, though, are you?" I ask.

She shakes her head, slipping the dress's straps off the hanger. "Are you kidding me? It's, like, the perfect dress, Lila. Seriously."

I smile. "I thought it might be."

"Lila?"

"Yeah."

She offers me a genuine smile and makes me feel good inside, like I did something right. "Thank you."

I return her smile wholeheartedly. "You're welcome."

I shut the door and sink down on the four-post bed. It still has the same satin white comforter on it that's trimmed with lace. There are fluffy throw pillows all over it and the same floor-length curtains hang over the French doors. Everything is clean and tidy. Everything looks perfect. When I turned thirteen my mom spent weeks redecorating this room as a birthday present for me. I told her I wanted a pool party with my friends. Hell, I would have taken letting my friends come over and hang out over curtains and pillows that made the room pretty in theory—but it'd always felt so overly empty and unwelcoming. This used to be my life, and even back then I didn't like it very much, yet I always kept going with it because it was what I was supposed to do. This kind of lifestyle, flourishing on the outside and no substance on the inside, was ingrained into my mind since the day I entered the world. I was pretty much doomed to be just like either my mom or my sister, and I would have probably ended up like one of them eventually, but I got lucky. Lucky because I met Ethan. He saved me not just from an addiction but also from myself. He showed me that I was worth getting clean. I'm worth more than self-destruction and emptiness.

I really wish I could talk to him at the moment. I just want to hear the sound of his voice. God, I wish I could kiss him again, feel his arms around me, feel him inside me, pushing me over the edge, making my body feel things I never thought were possible. He said I could call him whenever I needed him and it feels like I need him because this God damn house is getting to me and is surfacing the need to take a pill. It affects my emotions too much, the place where I endured my father telling me over and over again just how worthless I am. It's where it all began, where I entered the world, doomed to strive for perfection, even though it doesn't exist. I strived and strived, with everything I had in me, nearly killing myself to achieve something that I could never achieve because it's not real. This life I'm in now, with Ethan, with Ella, is what's real.

I decide to take Ethan up on the offer. I take my phone out of my back pocket and dial his number and put the phone up to my ear.

"Yeah?" he says quickly, answering after the fourth ring.

"Hey, it's me, Lila" I say stupidly, and then roll my eyes

at myself. We've talked to each other a thousand times on the phone, but it feels different now that we've had sex and I feel sort of nervous.

"Yeah, I know," he replies in a rushed voice. "Your name came up on the screen."

"Oh yeah, duh." I coil a strand of my short hair around my finger, unsure how to react to his standoffish attitude. "Sorry, I'm being a little bit spacey, aren't I?"

He doesn't answer right away and I can hear someone talking in the background. A woman. London probably. "Did you need something?" he finally asks, distracted.

"Not really," I say, unraveling my hair from my finger. "I was just sitting in my old room and suddenly thought of you."

"You're in your old room... why?"

"Because," I start, but there's a loud crash in the background and then it gets really loud with voices and rustles. "I'm sorry. You sound busy. I'll just call back later."

I expect him to argue a little, but instead he quickly says, "Okay, talk to you soon." Then he hangs up.

I try not to sulk or let it get to me, because I've been so accustomed to guys blowing me off, but I wasn't in love with them. And I had my pills. As the urge to cry over his brush-off overpowers me, I want to leave the room and go track down my mother's stash, because she has them hidden all over the house.

"Jesus, Lila," Ella calls out from the closet. "Is there a secret to putting the dress on... I can't get the ribbon to tie."

"Do you need my help?" I say starting to get up when the

closet door opens and she walks out, the flowing dress swishing with her steps. It's not tied and so it's loose in the front, but she still looks beautiful. I instantly place my hand over my mouth and shake my head, my eyes welling up. "Oh my God, you look so beautiful."

She swallows hard, glancing down at the dress, gripping some of the fabric in her hands. "I guess so."

I lower my hands from my mouth. "You don't sound happy. Do you not like the dress?"

"No, I like the dress." She glances up at me, confused. "It just feels like there's something missing."

I move forward and fiddle with her hair. "It's probably because you don't have any makeup on and your hair's not done, but we can get it done for the wedding."

She shakes her head again, turning it to the side and looking at her reflection in the full-length mirror on the wall next to the vanity. She stares at herself forever and I can tell she's about to cry. Sucking in a breath, she turns for the closet.

"I'm going to get out of it," she mutters and then disappears into the closet, shutting the door.

I stand there for a moment, deciding whether or not to go in there and find out what's wrong. She's obviously hurting over something and I wonder if it's something about Micha or her family. My best guess would be her family, since they've been the center of her problems in the past.

Deciding to go find out, I step forward toward the closet but stop when my mom walks into my room.

She's wearing an unwrinkled cream-colored pencil skirt and silver satin blouse. Her heels match her shirt and the purse draped over her shoulder, the purse that I know holds her bottle of pills. Her blonde hair is done in a bun and it's been a while since I've seen her, but the lack of wrinkles in her face probably mean she's recently had Botox done.

"Jesus." She stumbles back, surprised to see me and the heel of her shoe makes a streak across the shiny white-and-black marble floor. "How did you get in here?"

I clutch my hand around my phone, remembering the last time I saw her and my father and they both told me how stupid I was for moving to Vegas. That I was going to turn into nothing and that to my father I was already nothing, worthless, a huge massive disappointment that he wished had never been born. He didn't want garbage like me in his house. Those were his exact words and that's when I jumped into my car and drove back to Ella's, making the decision to never see them again. And I've been good on my promise until today.

"I walked through the front door," I say, regretting coming here, but Ella needed a dress. She deserves one, a good, pretty one that will make her feel special on her wedding day. Because whether she'll admit it or not, almost every girl wants the perfect dress.

My mother stands in the doorway, looking me over as she grips the doorknob. "You look like shit, Lila. That T-shirt..." She makes a repulsed face. "And that godawful haircut. What were you thinking?"

"I wasn't thinking anything," I tell her, eyeing her Botoxed face. "Other than I was sick of looking artificial."

"Watch it, young lady," she warns, letting go of the doorknob and stepping forward. "Or you won't get what you came here for."

I cross my arms and raise my eyebrows at her, unsure what she means. "And why did I come here?"

She waits, like she's expecting me to give her the answer, when I don't have a clue what's going on. "So you finally took my advice and came back. Honestly, I'm not sure how I feel about this, Lila." She walks into the room, her head held arrogantly high as she takes in my appearance like I'm a sideshow circus freak. "Do you know how frustrated your father and I have been with your life choices lately?"

"Probably about as frustrated as you've been with them since I was born," I say, my voice coming out sharper than I intended.

She purses her lips and places her hands on her hips as she reaches me—close enough, yet her eyes look so far away. "Lila Summers, you know the rules in this house. You won't talk to me like that while you're here."

I've always been taught to obey, but seeing her like this, my vision undiluted, I feel like I'm seeing her for the first time, along with everything she's done and said to me over the years. "Yes, I do, mother. Don't express anything, right? At least in a healthy way."

"What does that mean?"

"You know what it means."

"No, I don't." She rushes toward me and gets in my face. "If you're going to move back in here with me, there will be rules."

I smile at her politely, suddenly understanding what she thinks I'm here for. I'm about to say something when the closet door swings open and Ella walks out carrying the dress over her arm, her eyes red, like she's been crying. She stops dead in her tracks as she takes one look at me and my mother and tenses, eyeing the door like she's going to bolt. And I don't blame her. I'm thinking the exact same thing.

"Who are you?" my mother asks curtly, her gaze sliding over Ella's torn shorts and faded purple tank top.

Ella glances at me with a what-the-hell-should-I-do look and I can see the apprehension on her face. She doesn't do well with parents, and even though I don't completely understand why, I'm guessing that it's because her dad's an alcoholic and probably wasn't that nice to her.

"She's my friend," I state, swinging around my mom and grabbing Ella's arm. I jerk her toward the door a little harder than I meant to, but I'm trying to portray inner strength, even though it's hard to feel it whenever my mother's around. "And we were just leaving."

"Like hell you are." My mother's fingers snag my elbow and she yanks on my arm. The side of her purse brushes against my arm and I can't help but think how easy it would be to snatch it from her and steal her bottle of pills, knowing the instant one went down my throat, I'd feel better, but it'd be a fake better. "You aren't walking out of here, especially when you look like that."

"Look like what?" I wrench my arm away from her. *Inner strength. Do not let her get to you.* It's difficult, though, without the pills. "A normal human being?"

Her eyes turn icy as they narrow in on me. "I'm not going to let you screw up your life, even though you've been so determined to do so. It's time to start over." She cuts her gaze to Ella. "And get away from the people who aren't suitable for you."

Ella glares at her as she starts to open her mouth and even though I'm curious as to what's going to come out of it, I decide it's time for me to put my mother in her place, because I need to stand up for myself. "That's what I'm doing right now." I flash her my most beautiful smile, and then grab Ella's hand and hurry for the front door.

One foot in front of the other. Get the hell away from here and all the emptiness it holds.

My mother starts yelling at us as she follows us through the house, saying mean things about me and Ella, and she even tries to take the dress away, telling me that neither one of us is worthy of having it, not when we look so trashy. That's it. She can take jabs at me because I'm used to it, but not at my friends. It's ridiculous and pathetic. As we reach the entryway, I whirl around and threaten her with the one thing I know will make her stop.

"Walk away, Mother, or I'll tell everyone your secrets," I

warn in a low tone, walking toward her. I get in her face, surprising her and myself. "I will make sure everyone knows just
how great of a person you are outside and *inside*." I smile as she
frowns, her face draining of color, and inside I do a pleased
dance.

"Watch your mouth." Her voice trembles, but her face is
subdued.

"Oh, I will." I let out a sharp laugh. "I'll watch it as I walk
around announcing to anyone who will listen just how great
you and Dad are behind closed doors."

I'm putting her worst fears out there. Part of me wants to
keep going, slap her across the face, tell her how worthless she
is, beat her down like she's done to me for years, but I don't
want to turn into her either. Ella and I walk out of the house
and I make a silent vow to myself that I will never, ever return,
not to her, my father, that lifestyle, or the pills. There's nothing there for me. Never has been. Now that my head is finally
clear, I can see that now. See what I want.

I want a life of my own.

Chapter Eighteen

Lila

After we drop the dress off at Ella's house, we change into nicer clothes and then I take her out to a nightclub as a sort of bachelorette party. I asked her if she wanted anyone else there, but she told me no and that besides Micha, I was really the only person she wanted to hang out with at the moment. The nightclub isn't as fancy as the ones I'm used to, tucked in a corner of a run-down neighborhood, but the entrance fee was cheap and they have two-dollar JELL-O shots.

"Are you okay?" Ella calls out over the loud, booming music, crossing her legs as she spins back and forth in the barstool. She has on a short green dress and her hair is down and curled at the ends. She keeps getting texts from Micha and each one brings this lovey-dovey look to her eyes that I envy and want. "You seem really sad."

"Yeah, I'm fine. Why wouldn't I be?" I have a backless white-and-black dress on that hits halfway above my knees. It looks really fancy but I actually bought it at a discount store.

She takes a sip of her drink, looking uncomfortable. "Because of your mom?"

I shrug and sip my fruity drink. I promised myself I wasn't going to drink that much, but I'm walking in dangerous territory right now, having just got done with my mother and the fact that I haven't heard from Ethan since we had that awkward, rushed conversation. "Yeah, but I don't really want to talk about it if that's okay."

She flips her hair over her shoulders and fans her hand in front of her face. There's no air conditioning inside the club and there are way too many people in the compacted area. "Okay, what do you want to do then?" A devious grin appears on her face as she slams back the JELL-O shot. "Talk about Ethan?" She slams the little plastic cup down on the counter top.

I shake my head. I haven't been trying to think too much about Ethan and the phone call. I keep trying to tell myself that he's probably just having a hard time. I mean, it has to be hard seeing someone you care about who can't remember you at all.

"I don't want to talk about him either," I tell her, stirring my drink.

Ella sucks the last of her drink down, gagging as she swallows the alcohol piling up in the bottom beneath the ice. "Why not? You never used to be so closed off about guys. In fact, you told me stuff about Parker that I really didn't want to hear."

"Ethan's different from Parker." I shrug as memories of

what happened with Parker surface, but I swiftly shake them away. "Besides...I don't know...I think that maybe Ethan and I should just be friends."

Her forehead furrows as she props her elbow on the countertop. "Why?"

"I don't know," I say. "I worry he might not be as into me as I'm into him."

Ella muses thoughtfully over this with a trace of a smile playing at her lips and a drunken look in her eyes. "You think so?"

I tilt my head to the side, studying the strange look on her face. "You know something, don't you?"

"I know a lot of things." She spins around in her stool so she's facing the packed dance floor. "Like the fact that Ethan has never ever talked about a girl so excessively until you."

I rotate around in my stool, too, leaving my empty glass on the counter. "When has he ever talked about me?"

She smiles, the glow of the lights on the dance floor shining across her face. "For, like, the last month. Micha says he hasn't stopped talking about you."

"He's probably saying what a pain in the ass I am," I say. "I'm sure I'm driving him crazy, living with him." Plus all the drama I've brought into his life.

"He's both complained and gushed," she remarks, making an exaggeratedly swoony face and then rolls her eyes. "Would you quit worrying? Jesus. You've never been like this with guys before. Usually you don't give a shit."

"I *don't* give a shit," I lie, but it comes out so pathetic sounding that I give up and just say the truth. "All right, you know what, you're right. I do worry about how Ethan feels about me, but I also haven't felt this way about a guy before."

"What way?" she asks with interest, leaning in so she can hear me over the music.

"I can't tell you yet because I need to tell him first." I give her a halfhearted smile. "Now can we please have a subject change, perhaps something that doesn't have to do with me and my life?" I thrum my fingernails on the counter. "Like maybe you could tell me what had you all teary-eyed back at my house."

Her expression falls as she takes a deep breath and then, shaking her head, she grabs my hand and tugs me toward the dance floor. "Come on, let's dance and have some fun," she says, steering us through the crowd.

She's acting weird and I wonder why, but I decide to let go of both of our problems and have fun. I laugh as I trip in my heels and push my way to the center of the dance floor. I start shaking my hips and spinning in circles, enjoying the moment, but in the back of my head something is on my mind that I continue to grow restless over. Ethan. I can't stop thinking about him. I've never been so consumed by a guy before. Not even with Sean. With Ethan it's so much different. For one thing, I know him, more than I know any other guy who's breezed in and out of my life. He's a good guy, sweet, even though he pretends otherwise. He's been there for me, more than anyone else in my life. What if he doesn't want me how

I want him? Will I turn to pills? I'm not sure what the answer is to that and it's kind of scary. However, there is a thin spot of hope left. I haven't run to the pills again, even when I was in my mother's house and knew I had full access to them. It makes me feel sort of strong and confident.

Ella suddenly lets out a deafening squeal as a guy rushes up behind her and wraps his arms around her waist. When he swings her around I see it's Micha, and he's laughing as she works to catch her breath. It's the first time I've seen him since he moved away. I remember how sexy I thought Micha was when I first met him. He had these striking aqua eyes and this really soft-looking sandy-blond hair. His lip was pierced, too, and I remember thinking how I'd never kissed a guy with a lip ring before and the idea of doing so felt like I would be doing something naughty, like I was slumming it with a bad boy. Then I saw how he looked at Ella, the love in both their eyes, although Ella wouldn't admit it, and I knew there was no way I'd ever be able to even so much as hit on Micha. I remember how bummed out I was about it because I was heading home and I really did feel like doing something with a guy who was different from the other guys I hooked up with. Then I met Ethan and I remember thinking how hot he was and how much I wanted to hook up with him. I figured I'd get drunk, have sex with him, and return home feeling numb and content. The problem was Ethan wasn't like the guys I normally hooked up with and he wouldn't sleep with me. He insisted he'd only be friends with me.

"Hello, Lila." Micha grins at me and then kisses Ella's neck. "How have you been?" he asks between peppering Ella with kisses.

She shivers into his touch. "Stop, that tickles," she protests through laughs, but I can tell by her expression that she likes it.

Micha bites at her neck and laughs when her eyes close and she protests more. He gives her a soft, loving kiss on the cheek, and then his eyes focus on me. "You look good, Lila, especially the hair. I like it." Micha has always had this charming way about him. Ella said that before her he slept with a lot of girls and I can see why. Still, so has Ethan and he is anything but charming. In fact, he's very blunt most of the time and I guess that can be sexy, too, since it worked on me.

"Thanks," I shout out over the music as I touch the tips of my hair. "It was an impulse cut."

He winks at me. "A good impulse cut. It works on you."

I smile, glancing at Ella as she gets this weird look on her face, not looking at me but over my shoulder.

"Could you tone down the dazzling, man." Ethan's voice rises over my shoulder and the second the sound touches my ears heat, want, self-doubt, and excitement rush through my body. "Seriously, can't you turn it off for, like, two seconds? It's fucking ridiculous."

"I'm not doing anything," Micha replies in an innocent tone. "Besides giving her a compliment."

"Whatever," Ethan says and then his hands touch my waist.

I pretty much die of a heart attack. My heart is acting insane, crashing against my chest, like it wants to flee. I tilt my head back and look over my shoulder at Ethan. "I thought you weren't coming here until tomorrow?"

His expression is unreadable, his eyes dark, his hair all messy, and he's starting to get a five o'clock shadow. I love the look on him, but the reluctance in his eyes makes me wary. "Can we go somewhere and talk?" he asks.

"I…" I look back at Ella, who nods and motions at me to go ahead. I turn back to Ethan, who's trying to smooth the wrinkles out of his gray shirt. "I guess I can."

He smiles, but there's worry behind it, and suddenly my mind flips on, running about a thousand miles a minute. He's just seen his ex-girlfriend. What if it turns out he still loves her? What if he's come to tell me this? What will I do? Break? The idea of going back to pills seems so easy and yet at the same time so hard. The idea of going back to that girl who relied on medication and sex to make her feel better almost makes me sick. I don't want to be her. I want to be the Lila who's been developing over the last month: the pill-free, clear-headed one, who can live without money or fancy clothes. The one who felt every part of the experience with Ethan and didn't feel ashamed or worthless.

I don't want to die all over on the inside. I don't want beauty and money to define me. I want to thrive. And that's what I'm going to choose to do.

Chapter Nineteen

Lila

It's been a while since I've been this nervous. Right after the thing with Sean happened, one of the Precious Bells told the entire school. I remember sitting in my room the day it happened, dreading going to class, fearing what everyone would say. I was actually sick to my stomach. In the end I had to go to school and everyone started calling me a whore. It was all a big joke to them. They cut me apart, ripped me to shreds, but nothing hurt as much as the fact that Sean had never called afterward. He'd simply untied the ropes, zipped up his pants, grabbed his jacket, and muttered a "that was great," before slipping out the hotel room door.

As Ethan and I sit on the bed in Ella and Micha's quaint little guestroom, I feel like I'm headed to that same place, but I'm not sure why. Ethan hasn't really said anything. He was being standoffish on the phone. I need to stop overanalyzing.

"So how's everything been for the last few days?" Ethan

asks, leaning against the headboard. He looks tired, bags under his eyes, like he hasn't slept in a while.

I shrug, kneeling on the bed near where his knees are. "It's been going good…Although I did go to my house and ran into my mother."

He straightens up a little, his muscles tightening. "Why the hell did you go there? You should stay away from them. Your parents are fucking douche bags." He pauses, assessing me like he's afraid they physically broke me or something. "Are you okay?"

I nod. "As okay as I ever am."

"What did they say to you?"

"*They* didn't say anything to me. My father wasn't there."

"What did your mother say to you then?" he asks, looking unhappy.

I shrug, unable to keep a frown on my face from forming. "Nothing she hasn't said before."

He presses his lips together and shakes his head. "You need to stay away from them…the things you told me they've said to you…they don't deserve you."

I love you. God, I do. I sit down, crossing my legs, my dress riding up a little. "I know, but I didn't go there to see them. I went there to steal a dress out of the closet."

He arches an eyebrow. "A dress?"

I shrug and then tell him about the dress and what happened with my mom, surprised by how easy it is to tell him the truth, down to how I felt about knowing the pills were so close. I wanted to rip them out of her purse and devour them. I wanted to make myself feel better, but I didn't do it. I know now they don't make me feel better. They just make me not feel.

"It's normal," he says when I'm done. He sits up and turns to the side so he's facing me. "To want them when you know they're near. What's important is that you didn't take them."

I nod, trying to pick up his vibe, but he's stoic and it's frustrating me. "How about you? How was..." God, this is so hard. "How was seeing London?"

He waits a moment to respond, looking me over with his eyebrows furrowed as if he's perplexed. "It wasn't like how I thought it would be."

I take a deep breath, fearing the answer, fearing the worst, but ultimately telling myself that I have to handle it because I won't go back to being what I was. "And how did you think it would be?"

He keeps staring at me, not saying anything and it drives me crazy, to the point that I feel like I'm going to explode.

"Ethan, would you please tell me what you're thinking?" I kneel up in front of him as I wince at the neediness in my tone.

A breath eases out of his lips as he reaches for my hips, surprising me when he folds his fingers around me and brings me to his lap so I'm straddling him. "I'm thinking that I missed you." His forehead creases as he says it. "In fact, I was kind of surprised how much I was thinking about you the entire time."

I'm not sure whether to be happy or offended. "You weren't planning to think about me at all?"

He shakes his head, staring at me like he's lost. "I honestly thought I'd go there and be completely focused on saying good-bye and letting London go, but it turns out I think I already had in a way…I think it might have happened the moment I decided to be with you." He pauses, contemplating, his lips quirking. "I'm kind of sounding cheesy right now, huh?"

I try not to smile, but I'm failing. "Cheesy can be good, though. Like in the movies. Everyone always ends up happy."

"You think we're going to end up happy?" He seems wary.

"I honestly don't know, but…" I gather my breath and my courage as I place my hands on his shoulders. "But I'd kind of like to find out." I hold my breath while I wait for him to say something.

He plays with a strand of my hair, twirling it around his finger and then tucking it behind my ear. "I don't want to turn out like my parents…I don't want to hurt you."

"I don't either," I say. "I want us to be happy."

"Relationships can be ugly. I've seen it."

"So have I." I pause, not wanting to ask but needing to know. "But, Ethan, I don't get it. You say you don't want to be in a relationship, yet you were in one with this girl…London."

He keeps looking into my eyes, really looking at me as he cups my cheek and grazes his thumb across my cheekbone. "Things with London were always intense and easy because we never talked about anything, really. She made me feel free in a strange way, because she never made me feel like I had to give her anything. We just kind of coexisted."

I frown. "It sounds like your dream."

He shakes his head. "I thought so, but I was wrong. I never really knew anything about her. It was easy and fun to be with her, but I think that was because we were high all the time. I think I liked the idea of her, but with you..." He trails off, his eyelids lowering as he chooses his words carefully. "God, half the time you drive me crazy. You challenge my patience. Piss me off. Make me feel things... That's the thing, Lila. You make me feel things for you, even when I'm fighting it. No one has ever done that to me."

"So you want to be with me?" I'm so confused. "Even though we sometimes clash?"

"I told you I did a long time ago," he says, brushing my hair from my eyes.

"When?"

"In the desert. Back when I told you we should go on a road trip together."

"I thought you were kidding about that."

He slowly shakes his head, never taking his eyes off me. "At the time I told myself I was, but deep down I've known for a while that there's no way I could leave you behind." His chest rises and falls as he takes a deep breath. "I... I love you, Lila."

My heart stops in my chest. I've heard the words uttered many times in the heat of the moment, from guy after guy wanting to get into my pants, but never like this. I've never known someone like this before we had sex. I've never been friends first.

Tears start to form in my eyes as the last six years pour through me. All those years of feeling worthless, unloved, unworthy of love. God, it hurt more than I let on. I can still feel the pain inside my body, haunting me, along with every choice I've ever made in life. But the thing is, they're in the past, and moving forward I need to stop being so fixated on the things that have happened and focus on what I want to happen.

"I love you, too," I blurt out, overly excited but not caring. "I really do."

He releases a breath and then smiles. "Jesus, for a second there I thought you were going to reject me or something."

"Never," I say and kiss him softly on the lips, feeling the connection I've never felt with any other guy. "I could never reject you."

I start to move back, but he cups his hand around the back of my head and kisses me forcefully. Our lips melt together as we kiss each other passionately, his hands wandering all over my body, across my bare back, tracing a line down my spine. He tastes me, steals my breath away as I press closer to him, wishing that we could stay this way forever.

My heart knocks in my chest as he slips the straps of my dress down my shoulders. I can feel every single aspect of his touch and I embrace it. All those years I was dead inside, locked in a coffin I built myself, and I'm finally free. The contact of our skin sends a rush through my body and a hunger surges through me. I want to feel what I felt the night we had sex. I need to right now. I pull away and he watches me with confusion as I slip my dress down my body, unable to wait any longer. I need him close to me more than I need air.

After I kick my dress to the floor, I return to his lap and straddle him. Before I reconnect my lips to his, I slip his shirt over his head and he watches me the entire time, his expression unreadable. I throw his shirt onto the floor and then trace my fingers along the lines of his muscles and the tattoos that brand them. Each one I'm sure tells a story and one day in the future—our future—I'll have to get him to tell them to me. I splay my palm flat across his chest, feeling his heart beat against my hand. It thumps hard, erratically, nervously like my own.

"What are you thinking?" I whisper, lifting my gaze from his chest to his eyes.

His tongue slips out as he wets his lips. Then he places his hand over mine and brings it away from his chest and to his lips. "I was thinking about how badly I missed you." He touches the bottom of my wrist with his lips and places a kiss delicately on my skin.

"You already said that."

"I know, but it felt like something that needed to be said twice."

I can't help but smile at the nice, sweet side of Ethan Gregory that I've always loved. I'd tell him, but he'd probably argue, so instead I just kiss him. At first, the kiss starts off sweet, but then suddenly the pace quickens as he undoes the clasp of my bra, tosses it aside, and flips me on my back. I let out a blissful moan as his lips travel from my lips, to my jawline, collarbone, finally resting on my breast. He kisses my nipple, hard, nipping and tugging in a way that almost instantaneously pushes my body to the edge. My back bows up into him and I bite my lip, suppressing a scream as I thread my fingers through his hair, pushing his face closer, wanting more. I'm still not used to it, feeling everything without being medicated. I wish it would always stay this way. I wish we'd want each other as much as we do now. And who knows, maybe we'll turn out to be one of the lucky ones. Either way it's worth the risk.

Ethan is worth the risk.

Ethan

I told her I loved her and she said it back. I'm going against everything I believe in and I don't care. I want her. Want to be with her. Want to do everything with her and the feeling is strange, crazy, unnatural to me, yet it makes me content.

As my fingers wander all over her body, the contentment shifts to passion. I'm trying to take it slow, not wanting her to think that sex is all I'm after, but the desire to feel her, thrust inside her, press our bodies together becomes too overpowering. I rip off her bra, flip her on her back, and cover her body with mine. I suck on her nipples and she keeps whimpering and tugging at my hair and it only makes me more anxious to be inside her. Finally, I can't take it anymore. I kiss a path down her stomach and spread her legs apart with my hands. She lets out a sequence of moans as I slide my fingers inside her and feel her thoroughly until she screams out my name. When I pull them out, she starts to protest until I bury my face between her legs and slip my tongue inside the spot where my fingers just left.

"Jesus...Ethan..." She groans breathlessly, her hips arching up as she threads her fingers through my hair, tugging at the roots. I kiss her and lick her until she's quivering and my dick feels like it's going to explode. Then I move my lips toward her mouth, but she sits up.

Her blue eyes are glazed over as she reaches for the button of my jeans and she flicks it undone, her fingers shaking as she attempts to remove my pants. I help her out and slip out of the jeans and my boxers and kick them to the side. I reach for her panties and jerk them down her legs, noting that she's quivering. I toss them aside, and then take a condom out of the back pocket of my jeans. I'm about to thrust inside, but pause. She's trembling even more and I'm starting to grow worried.

"Are you okay?" I ask, needing to make sure because I know what she's been through and the last thing I ever want to do is pressure her.

She nods her head up and down, her legs opening up as I kneel between them, her hair spread all over the pillow. "I'm fine."

"You're shaking, though."

"I know...I just want this—I want you. Really, really bad."

Relief washes through me as I lower myself over her, lining our bodies together, and prop an arm on each side of her head. I kiss her tenderly, trying to calm her down, but she continues to shiver and it only amplifies when I slowly slip inside her.

"Oh my God…" she cries out, writhing her hips to meet my movement, nearly pushing me over the edge way too soon. "It feels so good… it does… God, I love you…"

The ecstasy in her eyes makes it hard not to come and the sound of those words leaving her lips makes the sensation even more intense. I thrust inside her, over and over again, thinking only about her, feeling every part of it, our bodies connecting. I'd always believed that love was never worth it. That if I loved someone we'd eventually ruin each other, but this has to be different. What I'm feeling right now has to mean something more. This has to be real love.

"I love you, too," I whisper, sealing our lips together and ultimately our hearts.

Epilogue

Lila

Ella seemed really nervous when we left her at the house to finish getting ready. But I'm sure it's normal, since she's about to commit herself to one person forever. I would have stayed with her, but I wanted to decorate around the cliff area where they are getting married. I picked up some flowers and candles on my way down, hoping to spruce up the dirt area as much as I could. Micha and Ethan helped me out and then we took a cab to the cliff so Ella could have the car. Luckily the wind wasn't blowing, otherwise the flames wouldn't have stayed lit and the flowers would have blown away. Thankfully, for one day, the weather decided to be nearly perfect, the sky almost blue, the waves of the ocean content, and the temperature lukewarm, especially for December.

Ethan and I are standing near the edge of a short cliff, the ocean out before us. The sun shines brightly down onto the sand and glows against my skin. Micha is standing next to the minister, waiting for Ella to get here. It's been amazing to watch the two of them and what they've gone through to get to this place and I find myself wondering if I'll ever get here myself. Maybe. Someday. Hopefully. But right now I'm just focusing on Ethan and the fact that he makes me feel happy, one day at a time. And I mean genuinely, freely, breathtakingly happy.

"You know I hate weddings, right?" Ethan remarks, glancing at me from the corner of his eye. "They're super cheesy."

"I thought you liked cheesy." I nudge him with my elbow a little roughly and he winces.

He rolls his eyes, fidgeting with the collar of his button-down shirt that I made him wear. "Just so you know, I'll have my cheesy and nice moments, but most of the time I'll probably be a douche."

I roll my eyes in response to his eye roll and smooth out the wrinkles of my red dress. "You're such a liar. In fact, there are very few times I've ever thought you were a douche."

He turns his head toward me, slipping his fingers through mine. "Not even when I told you to sell your clothes."

I shake my head, holding his gaze. "I might have when you said it, but now I'm thankful you did... You changed me, Ethan Gregory, and in a good way."

He rolls his eyes, but then leans in and kisses my cheek. "I love you."

I smile. "I love you, too."

"Do you feel like you're about to watch something you

created?" I remark, resting my head on his shoulder as I watch Micha and the minister talking to each other. "I mean, if it wasn't for us encouraging them to be together, they probably wouldn't be here."

He tips his head down and rests his cheek on my head. "I think you're right. We are pretty amazing together."

I shut my eyes, breathing in his words. Together. He's said it so much, yet each time it makes me all warm and fuzzy inside. "We really are."

I'm enjoying the moment, basking in Ethan's scent, the feel of him next to me, and how he makes me feel so complete inside instead of empty. I'm not even that jealous that Ella is going to be getting married in just a few minutes, if she'd just get her damn ass down here. In fact, I'm happy for her.

I'm seriously considering keeping my eyes shut forever and staying in the moment as long as possible, but the sound of Ethan's voice causes me to open my eyes.

"Where are you going, man?" he says as Micha heads off toward the turnout area where the taxi dropped us off.

He shakes his head, holding up his phone. "Ella just called, but the reception here sucks and dropped my call." He doesn't seem worried or anything but all I keep thinking about is how worried Ella looked when I left her at the house.

We wait around for a while, and the minister's starting to look worried, too.

"What if something's wrong?" I ask, glancing back in the direction of where the turnout area is.

"I'm sure it'll be okay," he says with a shrug, but there's a hint of doubt in his tone. We've both seen so much happen between the two of them—and with our own lives—that we know better than to think everything will always work out.

"Hey, quit worrying," Ethan says, hooking his finger underneath my chin and forcing me to look at him. "It'll all work out."

"How do you know that, though? I mean, what if it doesn't?"

"It will," he insists, gazing out at the ocean. "Now would you relax?"

"I'm trying." I sigh, fidgeting with my hair.

The sunlight reflects in his eyes as he contemplates something deeply. "You know what? I have an idea that will get you to calm down." He steps toward the cliff, grabbing my arm and hauling me with him. "I say we jump, like how Ella and Micha did right before she moved the ring."

I blink at him, stunned. "They jumped off a cliff right before they officially got engaged. Who told you that?"

He shrugs. "Micha did."

I sigh, wishing Ella would have told me herself. "Well, there's no way I'm doing it."

Ethan grins at me as he reaches into his pockets, takes out his wallet and cell phone, and tosses it on the ground. "Why not?"

I warily glance over the cliff, watching the waves crash against the rocky shore. "Because it looks dangerous and I could drown."

"I would never let you drown," he says earnestly. "I'd never let anything happen to you."

"I know you wouldn't," I say and I mean it. Whether he'll admit it or not, he saved me, not just from the drugs but from myself. I place my hand in his, trusting him, and we inch toward the edge. "We'll be wet for the wedding," I say. "What if Ella gets mad?"

He rolls his eyes. "I doubt Ella's going to get mad at you for being soaking wet at her wedding. In fact, she'll probably love you for doing something as dangerous as cliff jumping."

He's right. She probably will, so I nod and clutch on to his hand. Neither of us counts off, yet somehow we manage to jump at the same time, like we're in tune with each other's thoughts. When we land, he still has my hand and we swim to the top together. We burst through the surface and I gasp for air, looking back up at the cliff.

"God, I can't believe I just did that," I say, raising my hands above my head, my body dripping with water. I feel so liberated.

"Feels good to be bad." He grins and winks at me. Water drips down his hair and his face, pooling on his eyelashes. He moves his arms, paddling to keep himself afloat as waves lull against the rocks.

"It kind of does." I swim after him, then float just in front of him when he stops moving.

He smiles at me. "So what's next on your bad-girl list? We

have you out of those stuffy clothes, you cut your hair, and we've got you looking for a job."

I consider what he said as the water laps against my body. "How about a road trip?"

His expression is blank as he stares at me, the water hitting against his back. "You think you can handle that?"

I shrug. "If you think you can handle being with me like that."

He's emotionless for only a moment, but then lets a grin emerge from his lips. "I can handle that and more." He grabs my waist and drags me to him, crashing our lips together as powerfully as the waves hitting the sand.

I kiss him back, only pulling away for a moment to whisper, "Okay, then, it's a deal."

I return my lips to his and kiss him while the sun lowers in the sky, casting rays of pink and orange across the sky. The moment is perfect, even to a girl who never really believed in perfection, but who kind of does now. Ethan is perfection in a strange sort of way, if I really look at it, because he's real with me and I love him. He's not artificial and not what I'm supposed to have. In fact, if my mother were here, she'd tell me a thousand reasons why he's wrong for me, from the fact that he has tattoos to the fact that he's poor. He's the opposite of everything I was, but not what I am now, and that's all that matters.

He's what I want. What I need. He's the only guy who's ever made me worthy of love. He changed me in the best way possible and showed me that it was okay to love someone. That not everyone out there will break and crush my heart. And the best part of all, the thing that I will forever love him for, is that he showed me that I was worth loving.

After we finish kissing, we swim to the shore and then hike back up to the path that leads to the cliff area we jumped from. I'm so happy at the moment, I can't stop smiling, until we get up there, then all my happiness diminishes.

The minister is gone and Micha is sitting there by himself on a rock with his phone in his hand. His shoulders are hunched over and his head is hung low.

"What's wrong?" I ask, rushing over to him.

He raises his head up and it looks like he's about to cry. "I can't get ahold of Ella. I don't think she's coming."

"Of course she is," I say, wringing the water out of the bottom of my dress. "She's probably just running late."

He shakes his head. "That still doesn't explain why she won't answer her phone. And she was acting weird this morning, too."

I bite down on my bottom lip because I noticed Ella's weirdness, too. I turn to Ethan and stick out my hand. "Give me your phone."

His forehead creases as he walks backward and scoops up his phone off the ground. "Why? What are you going to do?"

I take the phone from him and smile. "I'm going to get ahold of Ella and get her down there, so these two can finally get where they should have been a long time ago."

He smiles and then leans in to give me a deep, passionate kiss that warms me from head to toe and it fills me with the determination that Ella and Micha are going to work out, just like Ethan and I hopefully will. Because he makes me happy and loves me, like Micha makes Ella happy and loves her, and really when it all comes down to it, happiness and love are what's most important and what makes life worth living.

It will change their lives forever...

Please turn the page for a preview of

The Secret of
Ella and Micha.

Chapter One

Ella

I despise mirrors. Not because I hate my reflection or that I suffer from Eisoptrophobia. Mirrors see straight through my facade. They know who I used to be: a loud spoken, reckless girl who showed what she felt to the world. There were no secrets with me.

But now secrets define me.

If a reflection revealed what was on the outside, I'd be okay. My long auburn hair goes well with my pale complexion. My legs are extensively long and, with heels, I'm taller than most of the guys I know. But I'm comfortable with it. It's what's buried deep inside that frightens me because it's broken, like a shattered mirror.

I tape one of my old sketches over the mirror on the dorm wall. It's almost completely concealed by drawings and obscures all of my reflection except for my green eyes, which are frosted with infinite pain and secrets.

I pull my hair into a messy bun and place my charcoal

pencils into a box on my bed, packing them with my other art supplies.

Lila skips into the room with a cheery smile on her face and a drink in her hand. "Oh my God! Oh my God! I'm so glad it's over."

I pick up a roll of packing tape off the dresser. "Oh my God! Oh my god!" I joke. "What are you drinking?"

She tips the cup at me and winks. "Juice, silly. I'm just really excited to be getting a break. Even if it does mean I have to go home." She tucks strands of her hair behind her ear and tosses a makeup bag into her purse. "Have you seen my perfume?"

I point at the boxes on her bed. "I think you packed them in one of those. Not sure which one, though, since you didn't label them."

She pulls a face at me. "Not all of us can be neat freaks. Honestly, Ella, sometimes I think you have OCD."

I write "Art Supplies" neatly on the box and click the cap back on the Sharpie. "I think you might be on to me," I joke.

"Dang it." She smells herself. "I really need it. All this heat is making me sweat." She rips some photos off her dresser mirror and throws them into an open box. "I swear it's like a hundred and ten outside."

"I think it's actually hotter than that." I set my school work in the trash, all marked with A's. Back in high school, I used to be a C student. I hadn't really planned on going to college, but life changes—people change.

Lila narrows her blue eyes at my mirror. "You do know

that we're not going to have the same dorm when we come back in the fall, so unless you take all your artwork off, it's just going to be thrown out by the next person."

They're just a bunch of doodles: sketches of haunting eyes, black roses entwined by a bed of thorns, my name woven in an intricate pattern. None of them matter except one: a sketch of an old friend, playing his guitar. I peel that one off, careful not to tear the corners.

"I'll leave them for the next person," I say and add a smile. "They'll have a predecorated room."

"I'm sure the next person will actually want to look in the mirror." She folds up a pink shirt. "Although I don't know why you want to cover up the mirror. You're not ugly, El."

"It's not about that." I stare at the drawing that captures the intensity in Micha's eyes.

Lila snatches the drawing from my hands, crinkling the edges a little. "One day you're going to have to tell me who this gorgeous guy is."

"He's just some guy I used to know." I steal the drawing back. "But we don't talk anymore."

"What's his name?" She stacks a box next to the door.

I place the drawing into the box and seal it with a strip of tape. "Why?"

She shrugs. "Just wondering."

"His name is Micha." It's the first time I've said his name aloud since I left home. It hurts, like a rock lodged in my throat. "Micha Scott."

She glances over my shoulder as she piles the rest of her clothes into a box. "There's a lot of passion in that drawing. I just don't see him as being some guy. Is he like an old boyfriend or something?"

I drop my duffel bag, packed with my clothes, next to the door. "No, we never dated."

She eyes me over with doubt. "But you came close to dating? Right?"

"No. I told you we were just friends." But only because I wouldn't let us be anything more. Micha saw too much of me and it scared me too much to let him in all the way.

She twists her strawberry blond hair into a ponytail and fans her face. "Micha is an interesting name. I think a name really says a lot about a person." She taps her manicured finger on her chin, thoughtfully. "I bet he's hot."

"You make that bet on every guy," I tease, piling my makeup into a bag.

She grins, but there's sadness in her eyes. "Yeah, you're probably right." She sighs. "Will I at least get to see this mysterious Micha—whom you've refused to speak about our whole eight months of sharing a dorm together—when I drop you off at your house?"

"I hope not," I mutter and her face sinks. "I'm sorry, but Micha and I...we didn't leave on a good note and I haven't talked to him since I left for school in August." Micha doesn't even know where I am.

She heaves an overly stuffed pink duffel bag over her

shoulder. "That sounds like a perfect story for our twelve-hour road trip back home."

"Back home…" My eyes widen at the empty room that's been my home for the last eight months. I'm not ready to go back home and face everyone I bailed on. Especially Micha. He can see through me better than a mirror.

"Are you okay?" Lila asks with concern.

My lips bend upward into a stiff smile as I stuff my panicked feeling in a box hidden deep inside my heart. "I'm great. Let's go."

We head out the door, with the last of our boxes in our hands. I pat my empty pockets, realizing I forgot my phone.

"Hold on. I think I forgot my phone." Setting my box on the ground, I run back to the room and glance around at the garbage bag, a few empty plastic cups on the bed, and the mirror. "Where is it?" I check under the bed and in the closet.

The soft tune of Pink's "Funhouse" sings underneath the trash bag—my unknown ID ringtone. I pick up the bag and there is my phone with the screen lit up. I scoop it up and my heart stops. It's not an unknown number, just one that was never programmed into my phone when I switched carriers.

"Micha." My hands tremble, unable to answer, yet powerless to silence it.

"Aren't you going to answer that?" Lila enters the room, her face twisted in confusion. "What's up? You look like you just saw a ghost or something."

The phone stops ringing and I tuck it into the back pocket

of my shorts. "We should get going. We have a long trip ahead of us."

Lila salutes me. "Yes, ma'am."

She links arms with me and we head out to the parking lot. When we reach the car, my phone beeps.

Voicemail.

Micha

"Why is Ella Daniels such a common name?" Ethan grunts from the computer chair. His legs are kicked up on the desk as he lazily scrolls the Internet. "The list is freaking endless, man. I can't even see straight anymore." He rubs his eyes. "Can I take a break?"

Shaking my head, I pace my room with the phone to my ear, kicking the clothes and other shit on my floor out of the way. I'm on hold with the main office at Indiana University, waiting for answers that probably aren't there. But I have to try—I've been trying ever since the day Ella vanished from my life. The day I promised myself that I'd find her no matter what.

"Are you sure her dad doesn't know where she is?" Ethan flops his head back against the headrest of the office chair. "I swear that old man knows more than he's letting on."

"If he does, he's not telling me," I say. "Or his trashed mind has misplaced the information."

Ethan swivels the chair around. "Have you ever considered that maybe she doesn't want to be found?"

"Every single day," I mutter. "Which makes me even more determined to find her."

Ethan refocuses his attention to the computer and continues his search through the seemingly endless amount of Ella Danielses in the country. But I'm not even sure if she's still in the country.

The secretary returns to the phone and gives me the answer I was expecting. This isn't the Ella Daniels I'm looking for.

I hang up and throw my phone onto the bed. "God dammit!"

Ethan glances over his shoulder. "No luck?"

I sink down on my bed and let my head fall into my hands. "It was another dead end."

"Look, I know you miss her and everything," he says, typing on the keyboard. "But you need to get your crap together. All this whining is giving me a headache."

He's right. I shake off my pity party, and slip on a black hoodie and a pair of black boots. "I've got to go down to the shop to pick up a part. You staying or going?"

He drops his feet to the floor and gratefully shoves away from the desk. "Yeah, but can we stop by my house? I need to pick up my drums for tonight's practice. Are you going to that or are you still on strike?"

Pulling my hood over my head, I move for the door. "Nah, I got some stuff to do tonight."

"That's bull." He reaches to shut off the computer screen. "Everyone knows the only reason you don't play anymore is because of Ella. But you need to quit being a pussy and get over her."

"I think I'm going to..." I smack his hand away from the off button and squint at a picture of a girl on the screen. She has the same dark green eyes and long auburn hair as Ella. But she's wearing a dress and there isn't any heavy black liner around her eyes. She also looks fake, like she's pretending to be happy. The Ella I knew never pretended.

But it has to be her.

"Dude, what are you doing?" Ethan complains as I snatch my phone off my bed. "I thought we were giving up for the day."

I tap the screen and call information. "Yeah, can I get a number for Ella Daniels in Las Vegas, Nevada?" I wait, worried she's not going to be listed.

"She's been down in *Vegas*?" Ethan peers at the photo on the screen of Ella standing next to a girl with blond hair and blue eyes in front of the UNLV campus. "She looks weird, but kinda hot. So is the girl she's with."

"Yeah, but she's not your type."

"Everyone's my type. Besides, she could be a stripper and that's definitely my type."

The operator comes back on and she gives me a few

numbers listed. One of the numbers belongs to a girl living on the campus. I dial that number and walk out into the hall to get some privacy. It rings and rings and rings and then Ella's voice comes on the voicemail. She still sounds the same, only a little unemotional, like she's pretending to be happy but can't quite get there.

When it beeps, I take a deep breath and pour my heart out to the voicemail.